WARRIORS OF THE LATHAR

VOLUME 1

MINA CARTER

NEW YORK TIMES & USA TODAY BESTSELLING AUTHOR

SIGN UP TO MINA'S NEWSLETTER!
https://minacarter.com/index.php/newsletter/

CONTENTS

ALIEN LORD'S CAPTIVE

WARRIORS OF THE LATHAR: BOOK 1

MINA CARTER

1

Sergeant Cat Moore walked down the corridor toward the bridge after an all important stop by the coffee machine. To say caffeine was required for the second half of her shift at the traffic control desk would be an understatement.

The graveyard shift was always the worst, and this one was shaping up to be the one from hell. They'd already had a near-miss in the fighter bay, and two of the bigger troop transports were sporting brand-new paint jobs after both trying to head out on the same flight vector. She didn't even want to think about the fact an Argos-class destroyer had also been assigned the same one. Forget paintwork. If that had come in at the same time, they'd be looking at a new docking arm and a casualty count that made her break out in a cold sweat just at the "what if?"

Sighing, she lifted her mug and sucked down half the blessed java. The sigh of relief escaped her lungs as the hard-hitting stimulant, a compound-caffeine only served in the highly active areas of the base, hit her bloodstream. They did say things came in threes, so surely they were done for tonight?

Wooogahhh-Ahhh-Wooogaaahhh. Wooogahhh-Ahhh-Wooogaaahhh.

The sound of the sirens filled the corridor, lights flicking from white to red.

"Shit." Red alert. Apparently, they *weren't* done for the night.

Cat threw the half-empty mug at a recycling point, hitting it dead center, and set off at a run. She crashed through the double doors to the bridge and emerged into chaos.

"Multiple ships, port side."

"Shields out, sector Four-B!"

"Launch fighters! Sound all-quarters!" That last was the captain yelling orders. "Send a message to Earth that we're under attack."

Who could possibly be attacking them? As Cat made her way across the bridge to her post, the sound of explosions filled the air, and the deck under her feet lurched, throwing her to the floor. More alarms blared behind her as she scrambled up.

"Massive damage to sectors three, four, and seven. Hull breach in four. Shit...we're being boarded."

"Marshal internal defenses," the captain shouted. "Go into Foothold protocol."

Cat's stomach dropped at the words, as she finally made it to her desk. Her hands shook as she logged into her console. Foothold situation was bad. It meant a superior force was attacking the base and had the numbers to take it. It meant they were in last line of defense mode and all sensitive information needed to be locked down.

She met the quick glance of one of the other traffic control officers. Jessica looked as pale as she felt. They'd all trained for this, but with the only enemy in the area using basic surface to orbit technology, they had never expected to actually use them.

"Who is it?" she mouthed, her hands working on automatic as she cleared all the recent flight logs out of the system. Any ship coming into or leaving the base logged their journey. Since most of them ended up or started from Sentinel Five, that meant any enemy could discover the location of all Terran facilities if they got hold of the database.

"No idea." Jess typed as quickly as she did, clearing records. "They must've been cloaked or something. One minute there was nothing, and then we were surrounded."

"Internal defenses offline in sector four."

"Mass breaches in sectors nine and twelve."

"Foothold defenses in sector four and seven compromised."

"Someone get me marines on the defenses," the captain shouted, his deep voice making both Cat and Jess pause for a moment.

"Too late, Captain. Foothold down. Enemy forces in the central ring."

"Divert all forces to protect primary areas. Get them up here!"

Shiiiit. Whoever they were, they were in the middle parts of the orbital base. Cat blinked and renewed her efforts on the logs. She was two-thirds of the way down, her fingers on fire. It would make it so much easier if there was an auto dump on the system, but protocol insisted on manual deletion in case of data loss.

"Shit, I got a lock," Jess cursed, slamming her fist on the table. She looked up at Cat. "I'm still a quarter live. You?"

"A third." Her screen froze just at that moment, then her deleted records started to reinstate themselves in front of her. Crap. Crap. Crap. That was so not good. "Captain..." she called out in warning. "They're in the system."

"Fuck it!" The bridge paused as Captain Gregson drove his hand into the arm of his chair. "Kallson," he looked at Jess. "Try and lock them out. Moore, get your ass into the mainframe and cut all access to everything but the command consoles."

"On it." Cat was already moving, clapping Jess on the shoulder as she passed.

Adrenalin surging through her system, she yanked open an access panel on the wall behind the captain's chair and climbed through it. There was only one way to get to the mainframe computer, by ladder from the bridge. It was a design feature meant to keep the computer systems protected in the event of an attack. That the computer core was also nestled alongside the main reactor, and that someone was firing at the base, was something she preferred not to think about as she started her descent.

Rather than climbing down, she opted for the quick route. Holding the top of the ladder, she clamped the sides with the insides of her heavy combat boots and slid down it. Her feet hit the mesh plate with a crash, but Cat didn't hang about. Rushing around the semi-circular platform, she grabbed the next ladder to slide down it. Then the next and the next. Four down, six to go.

More explosions rocked the station, a particularly nasty one almost flinging her from into the shaft below. Heart in her throat, she clung to the railing for dear life.

She needed to move faster. Much faster.

"Nearly there," she muttered, her feet hitting the platform. A sign on the wall said, "Nine Below." Decks weren't numbered in the bowels of the station core. They were assigned for their position in relation to the bridge.

Before she could reach the next ladder, there was a crash and boom above her. Instinctively, she looked up to catch the tail end of an explosion. Metal fragments, remnants of bulkheads and ladders tumbled down the shaft, straight toward her.

Her scream was one of fear and self-encouragement as she raced for the ladder. One more flight. The skin on her hands burned as she clamped around the rails and let go. She fell more than slid as the station lurched under her. Hitting the deck, she rolled, the tilt of the flooring allowing her to slide into the doorway recess for the computer core.

Her head hit the bulkhead with a sickening crack and she fought to remain conscious. Her heart almost broke her ribs with its frantic pounding; she slapped at the access plate and fell through. Immediately she dived to the side and scrunched into a little ball. Metal crashed into the floor of the shaft as the doors slid shut, the narrow gap spewing a deadly spray of shrapnel.

The barrier closed, and she was on her feet. Running across the deck was like trying to run on a carnival cakewalk. She slipped as the base rocked with more explosions, fervent prayers falling from her lips that one of those shots wouldn't hit the reactor core above her head. At least if it did, she wouldn't feel a thing. Death would be quick. Instantaneous. No suffering.

She grabbed onto the computer console. For such an impressive system, the main control panel was surprisingly simple. Just three monitors and input panels.

Something hit the other side of the door, hard.

It sounded like claws screamed against the metal—fingernails down a chalkboard. Her blood chilled, but she kept typing, even when the door squealed. Whatever was on the other side was coming through. She drilled down, reaching the star charts and any other information regarding Earth's central system. Metal clicked on metal behind her and her legs began to shake.

What was it? She couldn't look...not yet. A small moan whispered from her lips as, at any moment, she expected a laser bolt in the back. Records collated, she hit delete and cleared the system.

Data-dump complete. No records found.

She almost collapsed on the console with relief. Whatever happened to Sentinel Five, these assholes wouldn't find their way to earth.

The noises behind her stopped. There was no breathing though. Odd.

Slowly, Cat turned.

And looked right at a monster.

A red "eye" in a smooth, flat face studied her. Manlike, it stood on two legs, but there the resemblance ended. It lifted its hand, complete with razor sharp claws and she screamed, the sound of her own terror the last thing she heard as she tumbled into darkness.

"WELL?" War Commander Tarrick K'Vass demanded as his troop leaders surrounded him. The human base had fallen quickly, their defenses no match for Latharian technology. But then, not much was. In their many centuries of roaming the myriad galaxies, there were only a few species that could stand up to the Lathar.

"Little to no resistance," Karryl, one of his senior warriors, complained, his lips compressed into a thin line. "One look at the avatars and half pissed their pants, the rest ran screaming. Did come across some problems with some of their soldiers. One of the females —can you believe they let their females fight?—was rather...determined."

The hint of a smile crossed his face, and Tarrick shook his head. The big warrior loved to fight, always moaning he could never find an enemy worthy of his skills. The fact that he'd thought enough of the human female to mention her meant she was probably an army all on her own.

"Gaarn? Jassyn? Talat?" He turned to his other commanders, ignoring the mass of humans the avatars were crowding into the defeated base's flight deck. Some were bloody and bruised, others unconscious, he noted as an avatar laid a female in the same gray uniform as the rest on the deck. He frowned at the blood on the side of her face. If some fool avie-pilot had injured any of the females without good reason, he would be pissed. With no females of their own, the Lathar prized all females, even...Tarrick shuddered, the Oonat.

Unfortunately, the Oonat, with their flat faces, were one of the few species genetically compatible with the Lathar. He'd never taken one to his bed, but with no offspring, he knew that day would come soon. It would be a one-time stand, though, not even a night. Oonat often fell pregnant immediately. And with multiple births, he would have the sons he needed to continue the Vass line.

He paused for a moment to consider the unconscious female. Even unaware, she had curves that caught his interest and triggered something in his male psyche. He couldn't see her face, but a quick scan of the other females revealed pleasing features, not unlike the Lathar. In fact, apart from their smaller physical size, they could *be* his species. Almost. Their eyes were different. Not the myriad colors of his people's.

"How about the rest of you?" he shot the question at the other senior warriors.

"Same, Commander." Jassen was the first to reply. Quietly spoken, he didn't often speak , but when he did, others listened. "Little to no capable resistance, but a lot of courage. Technological they are eons behind us. The avies seem to terrify them."

Tarrick saw that for himself, watching as the remotely piloted avatar robots moved between the humans. They cowered, scrambling to get away from the machines or curling up on themselves when they couldn't.

"Have you found her?" he demanded, reminding them of their secondary reason for being here.

The first was because the station had females, and the Lathar needed them. The second was because of one female in particular. The one that had sealed the fate of the rest on this little alien base. All his senior warriors had been present when they'd listened to recorded transmissions from this place and he'd heard it. A female's voice, soft and melodious. It had struck a chord deep inside him, flipped a switch and changed him.

"The avies are searching for her," Karryl answered. "Trying to match a voice print, but nothing so far."

"Keep looking," he ordered, planting his feet in a wide stance and folding his arms. "I want her found..."

For some reason, his gaze wandered to the unconscious female again. Would this little creature with her mouth-watering curves be the one with the bewitching voice? If she were, he would even be content with having to bed an Oonat to bear his sons.

Given the Lathar's twisted history and genetics that had seen all their women die out and breeding with other species almost impossible, there was no way they'd be lucky enough for humanity to be compatible. But he could keep a more pleasing countenance in his mind as he rutted, then he could present her with his child to raise as their own.

A smile curved his lips as he walked across the flight deck. A woman at his side and sons to carry on his name, what more could a warrior ask for?

2

"*Cat! Cat!* Oh, god, Cat, wake up."

Cat came to, slowly becoming aware someone was rocking her shoulder. Opening her eyes, she slammed them shut as agony sliced through her brain.

"Ugh..."

Carefully, she tried again to find Jessica sat over her, concern written on her features. A livid bruise covered one side of her face, a haunted expression on her face.

"What happened?" Cat whispered, her voice barely more than a sliver of sound between them. Struggling to sit up, she nodded her thanks when Jess slid an arm around her. Hell, that blow to the head in the core had really knocked her about. Memory returned...the metal monster... and she gasped. "There are—"

"Shhh," Jess's eyes were wide and fixed on something beyond Cat. "They don't like us talking."

"They?"

Thunk-whir-thunk-whir-thunk.

The sound penetrated Cat's consciousness a second before the red-eyed monster from the computer core shoved its face into hers. She gasped, scrambling backward and knocking Jess out from its reach, but it followed her. Dropping to all fours, its metal claws scraped on the deck before its "hand" shot out, grabbing her ankle in a punishing grip.

She screamed as it dragged her beneath it, but her kicks and punches did nothing. It wrapped razor sharp talons around her throat and she went weak with fear.

"*Ohgodohgodohgod*," she whimpered, trying to get her fingers under the metal. If it tightened it's grip, she was a goner.

Its eye focused on her, moving over her face. Perhaps looking for the best target. She didn't know. Finally, it spoke in a metallic voice. "Talk. More...words. Talk more words."

"Get your fucking freaky metal ass *off* me!" she yelled, and on instinct drove her knee up into its groin area. She yelped as agony flared through her leg.

It swiveled its head on its neck to look down. "You damage yourself. Why?"

She lost it, screaming back, trying to pry the fingers from around her throat. It was playing with her, taunting her before it killed her. Fuck. That. She wasn't going down without a fight. Granted, resistance against a creature like this might be akin to an ant arguing with a boot, but she'd sure as hell try.

Whirring and clicking told her more of the creatures had arrived and she screamed at Jess to run. The metallic sounds were joined by heavy boot-steps on the deck plates.

A deep voice growled something that her ears couldn't make sense of and instantly, the metal creature let go of her. Gasping, she scrambled backward, ignoring the complaint of her injured knee in favor of putting distance between her and it.

Her hand met Jess's boot and she all but climbed up her friends leg, trying to push them both away. When Jess wouldn't move, she realized the body she had hold of was way too large to be either her friend or female. A strong arm wrapped around her waist, holding her securely when her legs shook. The silence almost deafened her. She turned her head slowly to meet the eyes of the man who held her.

"Hmm...hi?"

He wasn't human. He looked it. Kind of. Like he was an upgraded, better version of homo sapiens. Taller than any guy she'd ever seen, his shoulders were broad and muscled, and the rest of him was plastered against was equally as hard. Hell, even his muscles had muscles. And that pressure against her stomach...oh shit. She blinked. That couldn't be his cock. No way...no guy had equipment that...that...

He wasn't human.

For all she knew he could have two cocks. Her head swam... his face wavering in and out of focus. What was wrong with her?

He smiled, tiny lines appearing around his eyes and reached up with his free hand to touch her cheek.

"Ve'lani," he murmured and bent down to claim her lips.

Which was when the concussion waiting in the wings decided that she'd been conscious long enough and dropped her back into the darkness.

IT WAS HER. The deliciously curved, little human female was the one they were looking for.

As soon as the signal came through from an avie-pilot that he'd found a voice match, Tarrick had set off at a run across the flight deck. The human females scattered this way and that, but he ignored them. Now the property of the Lathar, they needed to get used to warriors running about, since most would end up claimed by one eventually.

He reached the avatar-bot, and a surge of anger filled him. The pilot had the little female pinned down by her throat. That didn't stop her fighting back though. Amusement rolled through him as she screamed right in the machine's faceplate. She didn't know it, but the high-pitched sound would overload the bot's auditory sensors and give the pilot an earful of static.

The bots weren't sexual in any way, but he still didn't like the sight of her pinned beneath it.

"Let her go, *now*," he ordered and the bot released it's grip. The moment she registered the movement, the female scrambled away. She scuttled across the floor on her ass toward him, hand brushing his boot. She clambered up him, using him for balance as she stood.

His protective instincts surged to the fore and he wrapped an arm around her waist. He hadn't realized when she was lying down but pressed against him, he was aware of how small she really was.

The violent trembles that raked her triggered his primal male need to protect and his hold tightened. She was fixated on the avie-bot, still crouched a few steps from them, the pilot no doubt in a panic that he'd angered Tarrick. His men both respected and feared him in equal measure. He was fair, to a point, but a man's claimed female was an entirely different matter and to lay hands on one without permission...

She looked up at him and all thoughts instantly wiped from his mind. Dark curls surrounded her small, heart-shaped face, falling around her shoulders in glorious disarray. Deep brown, with hints of red and black, it was a color he'd never seen before. But her hair paled in comparison to her eyes, a warm shade that reminded him of the forests near his home. Of the leaves of the Herris blossom tree at the bottom of his father's garden and the smile of his mother, a fading but cherished memory.

Blood still covered her temple and cheek, which worried him, but he couldn't resist reaching out to stroke her soft skin, smiling to ease the fear he saw in her eyes.

"Beautiful," he whispered, wishing he knew enough of her language to reassure her everything would be okay. That she was safe in his arms...in his bed.

Touch led to other needs and his gaze riveted to her mouth. The soft, plump curves. The urge to claim her, even in this small way, overwhelmed him. A willing slave to the impulse, he leaned down and brushed her lips with his. They were soft and warm, and her small intake of breath urged him on.

A groan welled up in his chest as she softened. She welcomed his touch...immediately submissive. Triumph swelled within him and he tugged her closer to deepen the kiss. Then her head fell back, her body heavy in his arms.

She'd slipped into unconsciousness again.

"Fuck," he hissed, gathering her limp form into his arms. "If you've damaged her in any way," he growled at the crouching avatar, knowing the pilot could hear him. "Then you'd better pray to the gods. Hear me?"

The bot tucked its head, movement relayed from its pilot to avoid looking Tarrick in the face. He strode past it, toward the troop carriers. "Alert Healer Laarn that his services are required, and start loading the females. Leave the males, they're worthless."

His warriors scrambled to do his bidding as he ducked his head to step into the carrier, his precious bundle in his arms.

"Back to the *Velu'vias*," he ordered the pilot and settled himself into one of the jump seats behind the cockpit. He didn't bother strapping in, not for the short journey. Not like anyone was going to attack with the might of a Lathrian war group surrounding the base.

He looked at the female he held. She lay curled in his lap. A perfect fit, as though she belonged there, and again, he marveled at how small she was. How perfectly formed. Dark eyelashes fluttered against her cheeks and he could see the steady beat of the pulse in her throat. His panic over her collapse receded a little. Stress perhaps? Latharian females, when still in existence, had been delicate and prized, which explained the highly protective instincts of the male warriors. His little female need not worry ever again, he vowed, holding her carefully. She was his and he would do anything to protect such a precious gift from the Goddesses.

The journey to his flagship, the *Velu'vias*, was brief. The pilot had no sooner engaged the engines before he was throttling back to bring the transporter to a soft landing in the main flight bay. Tarrick gathered his prize securely and stood, nodding to the flight crew as he exited the craft.

His boots rang out on the deck as he headed through the

corridors toward the healing bay. No one mentioned the fact he carried the human female in his arms, and any curiosity was carefully kept under wraps. As a K'Vass and the commander to boot, his actions were beyond question.

Apart from for one person anyway...

He strode through the doors and laid the female on the nearest diagnostic unit before lifting his head to yell. "Laarn! Get your lazy ass out here!"

Like the rest of the ship, the healing bay was devoid of luxuries and decoration. Each bed was set in an alcove created by the internal bulkheads and support structures. Summoned by his shout, a tall figure stepped around the corner at the end of the room.

Broad shouldered with the build of a warrior, he wore a warrior's leathers, but with the teal sash of a healer. Except for the long hair and the fact his eyes were green instead of gold, Tarrick might as well have been looking in a mirror.

"Lazy?" His twin raised an eyebrow as he strolled closer. "Do you have any idea of the delicate experiments your bellow just destroyed?"

"Will you ever learn to respect your Lord, healer?" Tarrick demanded, but his lip was already beginning to quirk up into a smile.

"When you learn to respect your elders, pup," Laarn snorted his standard response. Born a few minutes before Tarrick, he often reminded his brother of the fact. Even as he spoke though, Laarn's attention wasn't on Tarrick, but on the still form of the woman on the bed. "What have you brought me this time? You really should resist picking up every waif and stray you find, you know."

"Asshole healer."

"Dickhead warrior."

The banter trailed off as Laarn stepped forward to the side of the unit. Recognizing the presence of the healer, the diagnostic unit flared to life. A holofield covered the form on the bed in an arc of shimmering blue. Symbols that meant nothing to Tarrick crawled over its translucent surface.

"This is one of the humans?" Laarn asked as a diagram of the woman's skeleton formed on the display. Leaning forward, Laarn tucked a long strand of hair behind his ear as he examined the skull area. Tarrick leaned in and breathed a sigh of relief when there was no apparent damage.

"Yes."

"And you're sure it's fully grown?" Laarn's fingers moved on the input panel and the machine scanned her bodily systems.

"Have you actually *looked* at her? Instead of those dry readouts?" Tarrick raised his eyebrow. "Any idiot can see she's an adult."

Laarn snorted. It was his default expression around his brother. "Yeah. Well, not every species expresses maturity in the same way. For all we know, what we consider a physically mature appearance might be a juvenile for her kind."

No. There was no way she could be anything but an adult. The fates couldn't be so cruel as to present him with a female who finally interested him, tugged at his soul, for her to be a child.

"No...they all looked like this. And some of them were warriors as well, so unless their species sends its children to war, she has to be an adult."

"Hmmm...Yeah, I think you're right." Laarn intently studied a list scrolling over the display. "All the hormones and neurotransmitters are very similar to ours, and would suggest she is mature."

Snapping off the diagnostic unit, Laarn moved around her, running strong hands down her limbs to check for breaks. Tarrick had seen him do this often with other patients. Even though he used the diagnostic beds all the time, Laarn always checked himself, saying no unit was as sensitive as a healer's hands.

Tarrick gritted his teeth as the urge to knock his twin aside and snatch the woman out of his grasp assailed him. He trusted Laarn more than he did any of his sworn warriors, so his jealousy was out of character.

"And what were you doing when she passed out?"

"Err," Tarrick paused for a moment. "Kissing her."

Laarn stopped his examination to look up. "So...her base has been attacked by technologically advanced beings, she's sustained injuries in said attack, then is captured by an avatar-bot...which, in case you failed to realize is probably the stuff of nightmares for her. Then you, an alien, kisses her..." He blew out a breath, blowing the bangs out of his face. "Goddesses, give me strength, were you born an idiot, or are you making a special effort today?"

The machine beeped before Tarrick could reply, and Laarn's brows snapped together when he read the message on the display. "That's odd."

"What is?" Tarrick crowded forward." Is she okay?"

She had to be okay. He needed her to talk to him, needed to try to figure out why her voice called to him so much.

"Get your fat ass out of the cleaner field. You don't know where she's been and I'm not letting her loose until she's clean down to her skin." Laarn waved him back irritably as he studied the machines readouts, and then grunted. "Nope. The machine is wrong. I'll run it through maintenance routines later."

Stepping to the side, he prepped two medi-patches before pushing up one of her sleeves and pressing them in place. Within seconds, the plasti-squares turned translucent and dissolved beneath the skin.

"Standard biotic in case she's brought anything aboard or reacts badly to anything onboard. I've also added a shot of ker'ann; I assume you intend to bed her. She's so small, she'll need a little help if you expect her to take you," Laarn said, his light eyes unreadable. "The second contains a neuro-translator. It'll make its way to the correct area in her cortex and install our common languages. From the scans, we shouldn't have any problems with linguistic compatibility."

"Excellent. My thanks." Tarrick stepped forward, unable to wait to get her into his arms again.

"You're welcome. Are... are there more like her?"

Tarrick stopped, his little human in his arms and halfway off the bed, to look at his twin. "There are. Why?"

Although they were near identical, and Laarn was easily as deadly a warrior as Tarrick himself, he'd never once expressed an interest in females. Oh, he had all the male drives, but Tarrick got the feeling it had always been a physical function for Laarn, rather than a pleasure.

Laarn shrugged, picking at an invisible speck of lint on his sash. "They're different. New. Interesting. I might want one for study."

"*Just* for study?" Tarrick grinned, holding his female closer. "And there are, but you might want to get down to the holding cells quickly. More than one warrior has his eye on claiming a human."

3

Cat hadn't had many concussions in her life, but she knew what they felt like. This, when she awoke on a large, soft bed to see a steel beamed roof above her, was *not* what she expected. The fuzziness and weird feeling was there, but everything else, the pain and nausea, was absent.

That blessing paled into insignificance though as she realized she was being watched.

In a chair opposite sat the largest man she'd ever seen. With a gasp she pushed upright and scuttled backward until she hit the headboard. He studied her, an unreadable expression in his eyes. Hand shaking, she shoved her hair out of her face.

"Who are you? Where am I?"

Keeping him in her line of sight, she risked a quick look around. They were alone in what looked like a bedroom. Memory filtered back and her blood ran cold. The attack on the base, the metal monsters—robots she now realized—and...the alien who had kissed her.

Him.

"Tarrick."

"Say what?" She blinked in surprise, attention all on him again.

He hadn't moved, but only an idiot would think he wasn't a threat. Danger clung to him like a second skin, inherent in every line of his body. With those golden, slitted eyes, so odd in a very human face, he reminded her of a big cat.

Would he eat her all up? Heat hit her cheeks as she pushed the thought away. He was an alien, so who was to say his idea of sex would be the same as hers? For all she knew, she could be the appetizer for his main meal or something.

"Tarrick," he growled the word again, but before she could ask, he spoke again. "It's what I'm called. Yours?"

Name. He wanted her name.

She allowed herself a small sigh of relief. Okay, that boded well. Most people didn't introduce themselves to their meals. Then she blinked as she realized she could understand him. He was speaking perfect English. Fuck, she was so screwed.

"Moore, Cat. Sergeant. Three-seven-five-alpha-four-seven-nine," she replied automatically. She'd slipped up by asking him questions, Terran fleet protocol was to give out only the mandated information.

He shifted, gaze still on her. Was that a hint of a smile she saw on his lips before they compressed?

"Your people use numbers as names, Moore Cat?"

She treated him to the "Moore look," a gift from her grandmother, and lifted a hand to check her temple. She'd fallen, she remembered the feeling of blood running down her cheek. Her fingers came away clean. Okay...

"My healer sorted your injuries, little Moore Cat. Does it still hurt?"

She looked up to see him leaning forward, elbows rested on his knees. The leather top he wore pulled against the heavy muscle of his shoulders and arms, but it was his look that was more intimidating. Utter focus. On her. It was like being viewed under a microscope.

"Moore, Cat. Sergeant. Three-seven-five-alpha-four-seven-nine," she repeated, stubbornly. Alien dude might be the hottest thing she'd ever seen, even with those weird eyes and all muscled, but that didn't mean he was getting any information out of her.

"Really? You think I don't know a standard response when I hear it?" His lips quirked again and he sat back. Amusement danced in his expression. "Little human, I'm not trying to interrogate you. I'll have all the intelligence I want once my AI reconstructs your computer."

"Reconstruct?" She allowed herself a small smile. "Yeah, right. Hard to rebuild data that's no longer there."

"Really? No longer there?" He rubbed his fingers against a jaw with just a bit of a five o'clock shadow. "Now why would that be a problem? Your systems are ridiculously simple, it won't take the AI long to restore the destroyed data from the traces in the system."

Her blood ran cold. If they could get that data back...they could locate the other bases, even find Earth.

"You can't...it's deleted," she whispered. "I wiped it myself. Directly in the computer core."

"You? A female?" He blinked, apparently surprised, then smiled. "Do you take me for a fool? No commander would trust a female with such an important task, they are too delicate."

So sexy alien was a chauvinistic asshole. He lost some sex appeal for that.

"Does it still hurt?" He nodded toward her head, a look of concern on his face.

"No." What could it matter if she admitted that? Not like it was giving away any secrets. "Your healer is excellent at his job. Normally I'd have a headache after a knock like that."

Anger tightened his features, and she was reminded even though this chat was pleasant, he was an alien. And a kind she'd never seen before. She'd been briefed on the more primitive species the fleet had discovered in its travels, but humanity had gotten used to being the top dog in the area.

Until today.

"I regret that you suffered an injury," he said tightly.

She drew back, wariness running down her spine. With the danger that emanated from him, she didn't want to risk his anger turning toward her.

Crap, was there a way out of here? Trying to be inconspicuous, she studied the room. There were doors to the left, but they were narrow and set into the walls. Perhaps closets? There was a larger door, big enough for even his shoulders to fit through, to the right.

"Rest assured, the pilot who caused such pain will be disciplined," he closed his eyes, lifting a hand to run through the close-cropped hair. It was all she needed. Heart pounding in her chest, she leaped off the bed and made a break for the door. A stifled yelp broke from her as she skidded and collided with the doorframe, but her flight was spurred on by the shout and sounds of pursuit behind her.

She found herself in another room with a desk and bigger doors opposite. A cry already forming in the back of her throat, she hit them running and fell into the corridor beyond.

Right into the middle of two of the robots.

"Shit...no!" She twisted, trying to wriggle between them before they could stop her, but they were too quick and blocked her path. Rising to her feet, she retreated slowly, in case any sudden movement would make them attack.

Her back hit something warm and solid. She froze.

"On a scale of one to ten, how dead am I?"

TARRICK WASN'T EASILY SURPRISED, but his little human had managed it. He'd barely closed his eyes before she sprinted from the room with an unexpected turn of speed. Bellowing a warning to the bots on guard, he followed her, but she was fast, damn fast, already through the doors to his office before he was halfway across.

He caught up with her in the corridor. Arms wide, she was backing away from the bots. Neither had touched her, their metallic arms spread wide to stop her escape as he'd ordered.

"Dead?" Her words didn't make sense. "Why would I harm a female?"

"Huh? You don't hurt women?" She turned, a look of surprise on her delicate features. Impatient, he waved the avatars back to their posts. Now she knew she couldn't get away, he doubted she'd try to run again. She was intelligent, unlike other species the Lathar had come across. The Oonat were passive, but not his little human. That pleased him.

He'd seen the flash of anger and other emotions in her eyes as she'd refused to answer him. Oh, undoubtedly her intelligence levels would be well below his, but there was a chance he might have a decent conversation with her. That possibility interested him, and if he was honest, was more than a little arousing.

"No, little Moore Cat." His voice deepened, her presence bringing out the rougher edge, as he reached up to slide his hand into her hair. She flinched, and tried to step away to put distance between them, but he had her. He cupped the back of her neck and he held her still. "Calm yourself. I won't harm you."

"Really..." She held herself rigid, subtle resistance to his touch. He whispered his thumb over her cheek. Laarn had healed her, so she wouldn't faint if he kissed her again.

"Try it, alien, and I'll bite your face off," she hissed, snapping her teeth together.

He couldn't help the soft chuckle that escaped him. Bending his head, he touched his lips to hers. The slide of skin over skin caught him in its seductive coils, teasing his senses. Unable to stop, he tugged her closer.

She put her hands on his chest, trying to push, but it wouldn't work. She was his, by right of conquest. He angled his head and demanded access with a sweep of his tongue.

She held still for a moment, frozen against him. Then her fingers curled into claws, clutching for purchase on his leathers as a delicate shiver raced through her. So his little human wasn't immune to him. Pulling her flush against him, he used his free hand to press her hips to his. The thick bar of his cock pressed against her softer belly and she gasped. He took the opening and deepened the kiss.

Her taste exploded on his tongue, and he groaned, resisting the urge to crush her to him and explore more fully. She tasted of Jenin berries and starla water, tastes of the exotic but so familiar he couldn't remember them ever not being part of his life.

Her tongue brushed his, tentatively, and he paused. Waited. Was it a mistake, or had she meant that? The shy touch came again. He growled, and let the male animal free a little to kiss her again. Deeper. Hotter. Twining his tongue around hers, he stroked and teased, letting her see his passion. A glimpse of what she could expect in his bed.

But this was not the time, or the place. Breaking away, he allowed himself a final taste of her lips before looking down. Her eyes were wide and dark, hazy with desire. Just the sight made his cock pulse savagely.

"Don't look at me that way, Moore Cat, or we'll finish this here and now."

HE'D KISSED her like there was no tomorrow.

"Yeah? Over my dead body." Breathing heavily, Cat pushed away and added a glare for good measure. Where had that come from? As soon as he'd touched her, all common sense left the building.

He folded his arms, looking all intimidating and growly. "You will not refuse me, little Moore Cat."

"Cat. It's Cat," she corrected him. Anything to get him off the subject of where ever *that* had been heading. Stepping back, she nearly collided with one of the robots. With a squeak she jumped forward again. "What the hell *are* those things?"

"The bots? They're avatars."

Reminded of their presence, she drew closer to him. The danger he posed was infinitely different to the metal monsters. At least with him, she wasn't worried he'd rip her limb from limb.

"Like a physical representation of something?"

He nodded, a look of surprise on his face. "Exactly. They're operated via a neural link by specialist pilots."

Pilots. So they weren't mindless killing machines. She turned to study them with interest. That made sense. The one that had pinned her on the flight deck seemed unsure of the language.

"Pilots like you?" She slid him a sideways glance. That he was military was undeniable, she recognized the manner and bearing. "The same species as you, whatever you are."

"We are the Lathar." His voice rang with pride and he extended a hand to indicate she should precede him. She stepped forward quickly, moving past the creepy robots. Down the corridor was not back into the bedroom, which was good... Okay, she had to argue with her ovaries on that one, since all her feminine instincts were clamoring for her to climb tall, alien, and handsome like a frigging tree.

"And no, not exactly," he continued, falling into step beside her. Automatically he measured his steps by her shorter stride, a consideration she hadn't expected. "Pilots are warrior level. I am War Commander. In charge of this ship."

She arched her eyebrow, detecting the note of command in his voice. "Then you're not a warrior?"

He shot her a look, ignoring the two leather-clad men who passed them. They wore sashes as well, but in a different color to Tarrick's. "Not *just* a warrior, no."

"Huh." She fell into silence, wondering where he was taking her. So far, this alien attack wasn't at all what she expected. Her questions were soon answered when they reached the end of the corridor and a set of double doors opened in front of her. She stifled a gasp and spun behind Tarrick.

The room was filled with warriors, all with different colored sashes. Most were congregated on one side, next to floor to ceiling windows that looked out onto something she couldn't see from this angle.

A smaller group of men stood near the glass, and as the door opened, one of them turned. His face split into a smile.

"Tarrick! Come join us, we're studying the humans, deciding which ones we want."

~

THE CHILL EMANATING from his little human warned Tarrick that Karryl's comment was not popular. He watched her in his peripheral vision as they approached the group of senior warriors. Her back was stiff, like she had a support strut for a spine, and her expression so blank and forbidding that if he hadn't seen emotions playing over her face earlier, he'd have suspected humans didn't have them.

He knew the instant she spotted the human females in the holding cells below. With a gasp, she rushed to the window. Below were ten cages, for want of a better word, each containing at least twenty females from the base. Just the youngest and fittest. The older ones would be shipped off and sold as servants throughout the Latharian empire.

"Oh my god, what are you doing to them?" she demanded, her small hands on the glass as she watched a couple of avatars stalk between the cages. The females in the cells shrank back as the bots passed, fear on their faces.

She turned, pinning him with an overbright glare. "Let them out. Now!"

Karryl grunted in surprise but didn't say anything. The rest of the room was likewise silent, a fact she became aware of slowly. She looked around, her gaze darting to some of the warriors before returning to him, and her skin paled.

"Until they have been claimed, they will remain in the cells." His voice was quiet but firm, carrying easily.

"Claimed?" She frowned but didn't relinquish her position by the glass. Her concern for the other females was evident. "What do you mean?"

She knew what he meant, he knew she did. It showed in the looks she shot the warriors around him, incensed and protective at the same time, and in the way she backed against the window. As though putting herself between the warriors and the females below.

"You're not stupid, Moore Cat. Each female below will end up in one of my warrior's beds. Why do you think we took your base?" He folded his arms over his chest. "You have nothing else we want. Your technology is primitive, I'm surprised you got out of your own system, and your military capability is laughable. We didn't need half our combat-bots to break your base wide open."

She shook her head, but he carried on anyway. "Your females, little human. That's what we were after. A prize more precious than jewels or rare minerals and ores."

He stalked toward her, not paying attention to the other warriors in the room. This was between them. She backed, pressed against the glass, but he didn't stop until he could feel the heat of her body against his. Tucking his fingers under her chin, he made her look up.

"You are ours, you all belong to the Lathar. The quicker you accept that, the happier your lives will be."

Her skin was still pale, but her eyelids fluttered down as she dropped her gaze. Approval rolled through him. She knew her place already. This was good, perhaps these humans would integrate quickly and easily into Latharian society. Such a boon he hadn't expected. Most new species had to be broken and retrained.

"Females are prized in our culture. All of you will be treated well."

"Yeah, as long as we fuck on command, right?"

She lifted her head and enmity glittered in her hard gaze. He had less than half a second's warning. Her hand shot out and she slapped him across the cheek, the sharp crack ringing through the room. A gasp followed, several warriors taking a step forward, hands on their weaponry.

He held up a balled fist to stop them, struggling to contain his anger. No one struck a war commander, not if they valued their lives.

"I've been patient with you so far, Cat." Leaning in, he invaded her personal space, voice low and dangerous. "But do not push me. Believe me, you and your females are in a much better position than if another species had found you first. The Krin, for example, view the flesh of other races as somewhat of a delicacy."

He reached out to run a finger down her arm where the fabric of her uniform was torn away. "I can only imagine what they would make of such soft skin. They'd hunt your kind into extinction."

She shivered, biting her lip, her skin even paler than it was before. He knew he was scaring her, but he had no reason to conceal the facts. The truth of the matter was that her species would be safer with the Lathar as their masters. At least then they would survive as a species rather than become a fading memory on an interstellar menu.

Looking up, she met his eyes. "So we prostitute ourselves for protection, is that it?"

Something in her dark gaze struck at his heart, an organ he'd thought shriveled and empty long ago, and he reached out to stroke a thumb over her cheekbone.

"It doesn't have to be that way. Your females will get a choice in the claiming, on one condition."

She frowned, her expression wary. "Define choice, and what condition?"

Tarrick bit back his smile. His little human was shrewd, but he had her right where he wanted her. Her concern for her fellow humans was the web he'd use to trap her.

"By choice, I mean they can accept or refuse a warrior's claim." That much was already written into law, not that she'd know that. "Up to three times. If they refuse a third time, they will be sold to the pleasure houses to prove comfort for many. I would advise any female against that. If they have the choice, being a warrior's female is far preferable." From the shudder that ran through her, she appeared to agree.

"And the condition...you, my little Moore Cat, do not get that luxury." He held her gaze, sliding his hand into the hair at the nape of her neck. Bending his head, he whispered his lips over hers. "You are mine."

4

*C*at had never been so scared in her life. The silence from the other warriors around them told her there was no help from that quarter, and inches of thick glass separated her from the women in the hold.

She was alone, utterly alone, and helpless.

She lifted her chin and met his gaze. No, not helpless. Never that. She was a Moore through and through and her parents hadn't raised a quitter. So what if her current situation sucked donkey balls? She did have one—no two—advantages.

The first, according to Tarrick, was that his species prized women. And secondly, he wanted her enough to make her acceptance of him mandatory. Rather than be pissed that he'd taken away what little choice she had left, she found it flattering. Kind of. He was big, sexy, and obviously the boss. She could work with that.

"I have your word that none of my women will be harmed?" Her voice was low, just between them. Even though she kept a straight face, heat at his closeness surged through her veins and pooled between her legs.

His gaze shifted, searching hers, but then he nodded. "You have my word."

She sighed, closing her eyes, and her next words sealed her fate. "I accept your condition."

He didn't speak. Instead, he captured her wrist in one large hand and pulled. They left the room, the warriors parting before them like water on the prow of a boat. She avoided eye contact, heat rising in her cheeks. After that little altercation, there was no question of what was happening. Where they were going.

Sure enough, within a minute she could see the doors to his quarters, still with the robotic guards in place. He pulled her past them without a word, bundling her through the outer room and into the bedroom. His sharp bark at the door closed it behind them, an extra click telling her it was locked.

She tried to pry her wrist loose, but it was no good. His grip was harder than steel. Her breath coming in short pants, she looked up at him to find his feline eyes fixed on her. The irises were wider, more rounded now, like hers. Desire and need shimmered in their depths.

"You have beautiful eyes. Like a cat's." The words were out before she could stop them.

"Really? What is a cat?" he asked softly as he pulled her closer, fitting her against his large, hard body. He was big, all over. Even... She swallowed, nervousness filling her at the feel of his huge cock pressed close and personal against her belly.

"I-it's a small animal on earth," she managed, her voice stuttering as his hand slid around her waist again. Strong fingers began to pull her uniform shirt from her pants. Hurriedly, she reached behind her to stop him. "Domesticated. We keep them as pets."

His lips curved, amusement coloring the darkness of his eyes for a moment. "Why? Do I look like a pet to you?"

He bent his head to kiss her, but at the last minute she turned her head. She couldn't make this too easy, despite the fact need hummed through her veins in time with her pulse. Not when he and his kind had kidnaped them all to use as damn sex slaves. Her evasion backfired when his lips found the soft skin of her throat, leaving a trail of white-hot kisses.

"Pet?" She bit back her gasp as he escaped her grip. "Yeah, you do a little."

"I'll show you pet." He yanked her shirt from the back of her pants and slid his hand beneath. At the same moment, he claimed her lips and the rush of heat that hit her stole any other thought out of her mind.

She moaned, the sound lost under his lips as he parted them to delve within. The touch of his tongue on hers was electric. He kissed her like a starving man suddenly presented with a banquet, determined to gorge himself before the treat was taken away.

All her protests were scattered as the driving need to get closer to him filled her. A gasp breaking from her lips, she pulled at his sash, seeking the fastenings on his jacket with a desperation she'd never felt before. It was all consuming. She had to touch him, more than she needed to breathe. With a sigh of relief she slid her hands within to find no barrier to his skin. He wore nothing beneath.

He wasn't idle. Breaking the kiss for a second, he yanked her uniform shirt up over her head. Rather than fight him, she helped, watching his expression as he looked down at her.

Awe and reverence tightened his hard, alien features and she could have sworn his golden eyes glowed.

"Perfect," he muttered, taking in the plain cotton bra she wore. It wasn't satin and lace, but it was new, and the pushup design emphasized her cleavage. Reaching out, he snapped the clip between and freed them for his perusal. His thumb whispered over her nipple, which beaded immediately as though begging for his attention. "Just perfect."

She bit her lip as the bra hit the floor, the heat rolling through her becoming harder and more insistent. She needed him, like really needed him. Needed sex more than she'd ever needed it in her life despite the fact she was a prisoner and he was her alien captor.

He caught her gasp and looked up quickly. His hand closed around the back of her neck and he pulled her closer. "Shhh, it'll be okay, little Cat. It's normal, you were always meant to be mine. Your body knows that... And our healer gave you a ker'ann shot. To make you more physically pliable. So you can take me."

Her head shot up, fury battling the arousal running rampant through her veins. "You drugged me?"

He walked her backward toward the huge bed, unbuttoning her pants as they went. She whimpered, trying to fight, but it was no good. No sooner had she told herself she couldn't allow this, now that she knew her responses weren't her own, than she found her own hands pushing his jacket from broad shoulders.

"No. Not really. Didn't need to. This is all you... us..." He kissed her neck again, his stubble scraping along her shoulder in the most delicious way. What would it feel like between her legs? Her knees weakened at the thought.

"It's not me at all," she argued, but she felt the truth of what he said. Down to her bones.

"If you didn't find me attractive, you wouldn't be drawn to me. Wouldn't—" He cut off, sucking in a breath as she cupped him through his pants. "Have my cock in your hand like that."

"Perhaps I plan to rip it off," she panted, wriggling to get closer even as she stroked the thick, hard length under the leather. "You really have no idea how we humans mate, do you? For all you know, human females could eat their mates after sex."

"True." He toppled her backward onto the bed, fumbling with the zipper of her pants. When he couldn't undo the button, he growled and yanked, ripping the fabric in a casual show of strength that stole her breath. He threw the ruined garment behind them. Her panties took even less time to remove. "Do they?"

"Ohhhhh..." He slipped a big hand between her thighs, strong fingers parting her pussy lips and finding the slick wetness there. He stroked, collecting the juices of her arousal and used them to circle her clit.

Then he stopped, braced over her and looked down. "Do they, little human?"

"Huh?" She had to blink and refocus on the question. Her hips ached to move, to rock against his hand and claim the stimulation he'd just denied her. "What?"

"Do human females eat their mates after sex?" he asked again, wickedness dancing in his strange eyes.

"Or am I safe to do this?" He rubbed over her clit, sending sparks through her body. But he stopped after two strokes, leaving her more frustrated than before.

"No... don't stop," she whimpered, arching her back and trying to rub herself against his fingers. She needed him to touch her. Now. Sooner. Her arousal was alive, tearing at the inside of her veins to be free.

"Am I safe?" he insisted, a smile lurking at the corners of his lips. This was a game of control. One she'd started, but knew she would lose. Had already lost.

"Yes..." Her words ended on a moan. She'd give him whatever answer he wanted. "Just please, touch me."

"How? Like this?" He bent his head to watch as he rubbed her clit. She bit her lip, her legs parting wider at his urging, a flush covering her cheeks up to her hairline.

"Perhaps this as well?"

At that, he slid his hand down to push two fingers deep within her. Pumped in and out slowly. The whimper broke free before she could stop it.

"Oh god, yeah. That. More of that."

He gave her more, adding the pad of his thumb over her clit as he worked her body. Drove her arousal higher until she writhed and whimpered in his hold. She couldn't take any more. Needed to...

"Oh, *oh*...I'm coming." She turned her head and buried her face against his shoulder as her orgasm hit. Shattering apart, she came over him as he finger-fucked her, not slowing, but adding pressure against her g-spot that made her eyes cross even as sharp-edged bliss cascaded through her.

"That's it, little Cat, give me your pleasure. Make yourself slick and wet for me," his deep voice murmured in her ear as she rode out the waves.

Then he pulled his hand free to move over her. The sound of leather giving whispered on the air and something hard and hot nudged at the entrance to her pussy. Her eyes snapped open and she looked up to find him watching her.

"Mine." His growl was low and possessive and he pushed forward, bearing down into her. She gasped as his thick cock met resistance. Shit, he was so big. She'd never take him all. Panic hit her and she started to struggle, but he held her still easily.

"Shhh, it's okay. The ker'ann ...it helps. It makes your body more...supple?" he reassured her and smoothed the hair back from her face. Pushing again, he groaned when she parted to accept him, his cock sliding into her half an inch.

"Oh god." It felt good. So good she didn't know what she'd been worrying about. On his next push, she arched up to meet him. Then again, and again, until inch by inch, he'd worked himself all the way inside her.

Hips against hers, he paused, eyes closed and lines of tension etched into his face. Lifting a hand, she stroked his cheek. He shook his head, growling a response. "Hold still, or even the ker'ann won't help you, little human."

Stuff the ker'ann, or whatever it was called, she needed him now. Biting her lip again, she rocked her hips. Her moan echoed his as sensation shot through her. Hard pleasure spiked, rolling through her body like a dozen automated wrecking bots on a frenzy. Unable to stop herself, she did it again, feeling his cock slide within her, feeding all sorts of interesting sensations to nerve endings she didn't know she had.

"Oh yes, more..."

He growled, grabbing her wrists and hauling them over her head. "If it's more you want, little human, more you'll get."

With that, he drew back, his shaft stroking her inner walls as he withdrew and almost making her come there and then. Hard and fast, he impaled her again. He pulled back and thrust in until he'd built up a rhythm that had her gasping and arching against him. "Yes... Oh... Fuck. I'm—"

She shattered apart again, the pleasure intense and blinding. Hard granules of ecstasy, like shards of broken glass, burst through her. For every surface they touched, they splintered again, and again. A never-ending cycle of pleasure.

Through her release, she felt him speed up, heard the growl of need as his thrusts got stronger, faster until...

He surged one last time and stiffened. Throwing back his head, he roared as his cock jerked and pulsed inside her, bathing her inner walls with his white-hot seed.

She'd never felt when any of her previous lovers had come, but she felt his, as though it were another way to remind her that she was his now. Branding her as his property.

He let go of her hands and collapsed over her, not crushing her, but protectively curled around her as their breathing returned to normal. For long moments, she lay there, just listening to him breathe.

"Tarrick?"

He looked up at the sound of his name, golden eyes sated, and his sexy as sin lips curved into a smile. "So, little human, since I'm still alive, I guess this means you don't eat your mates after sex."

"You found me out." She shrugged, walking her fingers over one broad shoulder. "But I have to warn you, we have quite the appetite. You might have bitten off more than you can chew."

He laughed, sliding his hands down to her hips. In a flurry of movement, he turned them both until he was lying on his back and she straddled him. Her groan as he impaled her on his thick cock echoed around the room.

"Really? And I was just getting started as well."

Biting her lip, she closed her eyes and began to ride him.

She'd fucked her very first alien and it wasn't half bad. Okay, scratch that, it was absolutely freaking awesome.

Perhaps being captured by aliens wouldn't work out so badly after all...

5

The alien invasion force had five ships. That wasn't many at all.

Cat stood by a large window in the big room behind the bridge of the alien flagship and studied her captors. She refused to think of them as humanity's masters. They might have won a battle by capturing a remote base and enslaving all its personnel, but the war hadn't even started.

Heaven, or whatever gods they worshiped, help them because they thought by sectioning off human women, it would make them docile.

They would learn.

Hand on the cool metal by the window, she glanced over her shoulder. A group of alien warriors clustered around a large table in the middle of the room. They were all big, with more muscles than any man had a right to, and all as handsome as hell to boot.

It was the stuff of one of her greatest fantasies... ripped, leather-clad aliens were *so* her thing. You'd only have to check her digital-reader to know that. The virtual shelves burst at the seams with alien romance. But that was all it was. A fantasy. The reality of being claimed by an alien warrior... sorry, an alien warrior *lord*... was sexy, but if she had anything to do with it, short-lived.

"So you're saying they should never have left their own system, never mind made it this far?" Tarrick, her captor and would be "Master," asked, his hands resting on the holographic display table in front of him.

She paused for a moment, her attention caught as his muscles pulled at the leather of his jacket. A uniform she knew he wore nothing under. Heat uncoiled to loop through her veins, her intake of breath more a shiver. As a species, the Lathar were big and muscled, but there was that little something extra about Tarrick that hit her on a primitive, female level. If she'd met him in other circumstances, he'd have held her interest for sure.

Down girl, she reminded herself and folded her arms. *We're making plans to bring about their downfall, not to climb their leader like a tree.*

Infiltration, that's what it was all about. And what better place to do that than from their leader's bed? She flitted a little closer, her steps silent in the delicate sandals she wore.

"I'm surprised they even made it out of orbit," another warrior, Jassyn, replied as he looked over the schematics displayed on the table.

They were records from the Sentinel Five computer, the ones she'd deleted before the alien combat-bot had captured her. Wiping the computer was standard operating procedure to ensure all data and star charts didn't fall into enemy hands. But they hadn't counted on facing a technologically superior opponent like the Lathar. From what she'd gathered, they'd ruled the galaxies for generations. One primitive little species like homo sapiens trying to pull a fast one would never work.

Not unless they were very inventive...

"But somehow, they got out of orbit and spread like wildfire." Jassyn's hands moved over the console in front of them, flicking documents out of the way to show star charts called from the reconstructed records. Swift movements of his fingers drew lines over the star maps and highlighted the edges of an area. She drifted closer until she could feel the hum of the holographic field over the table. It was human-held space.

"They have quite a sophisticated network here. From what I can work out, they also have a subspace communications array with relay points here, here, and here."

Crap... how had they figured that out? Far from being the beefcake grunts she'd assumed, Tarrick's warriors were scarily intelligent. *Don't judge a book by its cover.* Her grandmother had been fond of saying that.

Tarrick looked up, his gaze focused on the men around him and not noticing her by the edge of the table. "I thought they just had conventional communications? Subspace is a different matter. Does that mean their central command knows of our presence?"

With any luck, yeah... If Earth knew about the attack, they'd already have mobilized destroyers en-route to the base. Five ships shouldn't stand a chance against the joint might of the Terran fleet.

"No, I don't believe so." Jassyn shook his head, his long hair dancing on his shoulders. This close she could hear the faint creak of leather when he moved. "Our suppression fields knocked out any outgoing messages as we attacked. Overwhelmed the signal, and before it came back online we had control so nothing's gone out. We've been getting regular pings on the relay since though."

He pushed the star charts to one side and brought up what looked like a communications log. The rest leaned forward to study it, cutting off her view of the table.

"They're assuming technological malfunction? And what's this stuff... the dots and dashes?"

"That I don't know yet. It seems to be a layer below the primary communication. Perhaps an echo or some kind of repeater pattern?" Jassyn shrugged, his expression saying he had no clue.

She blinked, hiding her surprise. Morse code. She was stunned aliens with such a high level of technology hadn't worked out the simple system. Why hadn't their super-duper computer picked it up?

Either way, it was an advantage she'd take, even if she didn't know how to use it at the moment.

"They haven't encountered an advanced species yet so they weren't expecting us. So yes, they seemed to assume malfunction so far," Jassyn continued. "But they will want to find out what happened. Given their level of technology, I would expect a ship or two to come and investigate soon. From the records we pulled..." He moved the star chart back to the center of the table. "They have ships here and here. Either of these could make it here within twelve hours."

She smothered her intake of breath. That wasn't a lot of time for her to find a security lapse to exploit. Not when she was with Tarrick or he had those monster remote piloted robots watching her. She flicked a glance sideways to the door. The metallic arms of the two guards outside were clear to see through the glass. They were always on watch.

"Okay, monitor the communication relays for movement from those ships. I want to know the instant anything changes. Even if they go dark... *Especially* if they go dark," Tarrick ordered, flicking a glance at her.

"Moore Cat?" he called out, still mangling her name even though he knew its real format. It seemed to amuse him. *Asshole alien.*

Blanking her expression, she turned toward him. Irritation flashed in his golden eyes and she suppressed her smirk. He didn't like her poker face. Good.

"You belonged to your species military." He motioned her forward so she took another step, her stomach brushing the edge of the table and looked at the documents laid out. "What should we expect, by way of response?"

Her eyebrow lifted into a delicate arch and it was a moment before she spoke. "Well, it's rather hard to say, to be honest. Our great leaders would have to consult the oracles before plotting a course of action."

"I recall no mention of oracles or prophets." Jassyn's brows snapped together and he rifled through the documents again, looking for further evidence. "In fact, humanity doesn't appear to be have a main religion."

"Depends on the situation." She shrugged. "When in doubt, you can always refer to one of our standard religious signals. I'll show you if you like?"

All eyes in the room turned to her as she lifted a hand, fingers curled into a fist facing away from them. Then she extended her middle finger and smiled.

"And that means 'screw you.' You really think I will help you?"

There were two snorts and Tarrick's eyes narrowed. She'd insulted him in front of his senior warriors. That had to bite. No, that had to *burn*.

The healer standing next to Tarrick snorted with amusement and his face split into a broad grin. "Ha! I like her."

"Humans," Tarrick hissed, his hard expression promising retribution. She refused to acknowledge the shiver of need that wormed its way up her spine and smiled back. What would he do if she stuck her tongue out and blew a raspberry at him?

"Tell me about it." The growled complaint came from the big warrior at the end of the table.

The look in his eyes hovered somewhere between anger and frustration. "The males were easy to deal with. We worked over a few, showed the others the error of their ways, and they've been quiet as a *gethal* since. The females... *argh!* Half are refusing to eat, at least five keep trying to escape, and all of them refuse to acknowledge any warrior's existence."

The healer nodded, leaning forward. His smile disappeared, replaced by concern. "He's right. I've had to sedate a couple and I'm a little concerned if the fasting continues. None of them will say why they're not eating, so I'm not sure if it's a cultural thing with them. I'm reluctant to let it continue...so perhaps we should force feed them?"

"You do, and they'll make themselves vomit," Cat broke in.

Tarrick looked up, meeting her eyes. "Oh?"

"It's called a hunger strike." She moved away from the table, her movements graceful. Her own clothing was gone when she woke this morning, replaced instead with a thin dress that looked more like a silk nightie. Far from feeling half-naked though, the inner layer of fabric molded to her figure, revealing nothing as the outer layers swirled around her. The effect made her feel as if she were a fairytale princess and she had to resist the urge to twirl just to swish the skirts.

Small pleasures, she reminded herself, don't fall prey to the bigger concerns. Deal with them, don't panic.

"Humans aren't stupid, and we have a pathological allergy to being enslaved. We'd rather starve to death than be slaves. Force feed them and they'll expel whatever you make them eat."

The warriors exchanged startled looks around the table, but it was the big guy who spoke, his lips curled back to display his disgust. "They'd rather die than accept the shelter we offer. How twisted and barbaric is that?"

"It's called free will and choice." She shrugged again. "And you're a fine lot to talk about barbarism. Not a benevolent superior race, are you? Rather than helping a less able species to defend itself... Rather than guide and aid...you storm in and enslave. Humans, for all our primitive and barbaric ways, outlawed slavery centuries ago."

The warrior snorted and she rounded on him, anger surging through her. "What if it were the other way around and *you* were the slave. Would you find it so acceptable then?"

Fury flashed in his eyes and he stood to his full height, glaring down at her. "You go too far, human!"

"Go on then, hit me." Her lips curled into a snarl, but she refused to back down even though he was larger. Just one punch and that would be it. She didn't care. Let him try, she'd go down fighting. Maybe quickly, but it would still be fighting. "Do whatever you want. I'm a slave, remember? No choice, no opinion. Nothing other than a soft body to fuck. Not like we've got brains to use, now is it?"

"Karryl..." Tarrick's voice snapped out in warning, and the temperature in the room dropped several degrees. Karryl flopped into his seat, his expression unreadable, and Tarrick transferred his attention to Cat. Great, she'd pissed off the big-bad.

"Go to my quarters, wait for me there."

"Yes, my *lord*." She mock-saluted him, spun on her heel with a satisfying swish of her skirts and swept out of the door. Two bots peeled off to escort her, with metallic clicks against the deck plating, as she did her best to storm down the corridor in soft sandals.

Asshole aliens, the lot of them.

LAARN BLEW out a breath after the human woman left the room and broke the silence.

"Anyone else think they're a lot more like us than we bargained for?"

"Seems that way, yes." Tarrick sighed and shook his head. It had been less than a day since they'd taken the base and already he was realizing dealing with humans was fraught with headache. His.

"Okay, Karryl, try and get the females in the cells calm. And leave them in there for now. Until Fenriis arrives with his war group. I don't want the men distracted."

"Huh, just you then?" Laarn, as always, got the jibe in at light speed. "And how did your night with the little human go? I see she's dressed as befits the mate of a war commander. She accepted your claim, I take it?"

Tarrick clenched his fists, resisting the urge to strangle his brother. He had a point though. They'd all been without females for far too long. To have them within reach but not be able to touch them would be utter torture.

"Explain that we have to quarantine them for the moment, to ensure their health and safety." The mere mention of a threat to the females, of any kind, would have his men toeing the line, no matter how eager they were to claim one for themselves. "Laarn, run full level tests on them to make sure they are all fit and well. That should placate the warriors."

"Of course." His twin's eyes gleamed at the prospect of being able to gather more data on the new species. Tarrick shook his head.

Sometimes he didn't think Laarn was male in the traditional sense of the word.

"The rest of you, back to your stations. I want full level readiness drills run in case the humans arrive before Fenriis. Dismissed."

The warriors filed out, but Tarrick remained in place. Dropping his head, he closed his eyes for a second in frustration.

They were ready to move onto the next target. The next base in the chain. All the data showed it was larger than the one they'd already taken. Larger meant more females. More spoils. But they couldn't move yet, not without ships to secure the sector.

But he couldn't hold the entire area with just one war group. It meant bringing in another war commander, his cousin Fenriis, and sharing any spoils the sector might yield, but that was preferable to losing it to another clan. It had happened before, and it would happen again. But not this time. Not on his watch.

But first, he had a different problem.

Pushing off from the table, he left the briefing room and headed toward his quarters. The two bots he'd assigned to Cat stood in the corridor. He nodded to them as he passed, his thoughts filled with the woman within.

His little human. Cat.

As soon as he entered the room, her scent surrounded him. Exotic, erotic, and familiar, all at the same time. She stood by the window again. He drank in the sight of her, all sensual curves and softness. Her uniform was gone, replaced by the traditional robes of a Latharian woman.

Gray silk clung to her body, jeweled straps twinkling on delicate shoulders. The garment dipped low at the back to show the curve of her spine. Clips set with gems held up her hair away from her neck, and bangles glittered on her narrow wrists. Not finery from the K'Vass family vault, just generic ornamentation. It was all he had. He couldn't wait to take her home though, and dress her in the starlight sapphires that had marked his clan for centuries.

Unbidden, the image of his mother's bonding necklace flashed through his mind. The most ornate piece of jewelry a latharian woman owned, bonding necklaces were intricate and detailed. His mother's had been modeled after Herris Blossom's, wrought in tri-pladium and set with sapphires. When she wore it, the jeweled flowers looked alive against her skin. They would look even more beautiful against Cat's skin.

He knew she was aware of his presence from the slight intake of her breath and the stiffness that invaded her limbs. She didn't look at him though, and every line of her slender figure radiated tension.

"What was that about?" Crossing the room, he gripped her arm and turned her around to face him. She yanked herself free, leaving red marks from his fingers.

"What was what about?" Turning with all the grandeur of an Empress, she gave him an innocent, yet haughty expression. "Back there? Just the truth. Sorry if it hurts."

"You're sad." The realization startled him. Reaching out, he tugged a strand of her hair loose and wound it around his finger. He loved her hair. The vibrant color and the feel of it against his skin was like silk. A sensual delight he hadn't expected. "Why are you sad?"

"Oh, for fuck's sake. You can't be that dense, surely?"

She tried to pull the lock of hair back, but he held on. A short tussle ensued, one that ended when he slid his free hand into her hair and tilted her head. The delicate bones of her neck felt so fragile in his large, warriors hand. He gentled his grip and leaned in to kiss her, heat simmering in his veins, but she bared her teeth in warning.

He sighed.

"I thought we were past all this resistance."

"We are?" Her lips pursed into a stubborn little pout. He wanted to lean down and kiss it away. "No, that would have been the fact you drugged me. It's worn off. Otherwise, I'd have been climbing those warriors in your office like a tree."

He closed his eyes for a moment. Damn stubborn humans.

"Ker'ann doesn't work that way, Moore Cat. It eases...the differences between our physical sizes, but it can't create something that's not there." He opened his eyes again. "And this...between us? It is there. Any idiot can see you find me attractive."

"Asshole. I think I like the healer more. He kinda looks like you…"

Anger flared without warning. His hand tightened in her hair. She squeaked, her face paling and he eased his grip again.

"Never look at Laarn again." Jealousy dictated his responses. The thought of her in another man's arms triggered a rage so deep it scared him. "The only man you will notice is *me*."

"Whoa, whoa…calm down," She stroked her hands over his forearms. Her touch was like cool water after the heat of the Arakaas deserts he'd visited as a boy. "I was joking."

"Don't."

The order was short and hard before he pulled her into his embrace. His mouth had barely covered hers before she tore away.

"No!"

Pulling back, he looked down at her. "No? Why no? We are compatible…you accepted my claim over you."

"Not like I had much choice, did I?" Her voice was sharp and her eyes glittered with angry tears. Why did the sight of them make his chest ache?

"You took mine from me to give to them. Not that they have much of one either. Fuck a warrior or become a whore. Did it *ever* occur to you that humanity has been looking for other advanced races? That human women might find you guys attractive and come voluntarily?"

He stilled, his expression setting into unreadable lines. She'd called him out. He hadn't considered that.

Shoving at his shoulder, she demanded. "You didn't, did you? You just barged right in with bigger guns and took what you wanted."

He shrugged. "That is the Lathar way."

"Well, the Lathar are idiots," she huffed. "*You're* an idiot."

He ventured a small smile. "It's been said before. Laarn still maintains I was dropped on my head at birth."

"Huh. Makes sense."

Sensing a thawing in her attitude, he leaned down to brush his lips over hers. She didn't move or respond. He didn't like her lack of response. Humans were far more complicated than he'd thought. Last night had been filled with passion and a responsiveness he'd never imagined and he wanted more. She hadn't pushed him away though, that was something.

Under Latharian law, he was more than within his rights to take her as and how he desired, but he found he didn't to take. He wanted her to open up to him, to give herself to him.

She lifted her chin. As a signal, it was tiny, but he had nothing else to go on, so grasped it like a lifeline.

Instead of pushing, he seduced her with soft touches and kisses. His lips learned the shape of hers, teasing at the corners, all his senses alert for any reaction from her. She relaxed, a slight weight against him and he eased her closer. She fit into his arms so perfectly that it had to be by design. The ancestors had to have designed her just for him. There was no other explanation.

Tilting her head back farther, he teased her full lower lip with his own, adding a small nip. She gasped, her lips parting. *Softly, softly,* he warned himself, not rushing in as he would have before. When she didn't close them all the way, he kissed her again, stroking his tongue against the parted seam in a request for access.

Her response was a small moan and then, finally, she kissed him back. Triumph and relief hit hard and fast. A rumble of need and pleasure in the center of his chest, he deepened the kiss. Tasting her again was as good as his memory, wiping out all other thought. All that mattered was the two of them, her touch, as the rest of the universe whirled around them with a rapid beeping sound.

She pulled away, frowning. "What is that noise? It sounds like an alarm."

He blinked, shook his head and focused.

"Fuck. It's the red alert."

6

Cat had to trot to keep up with Tarrick. The low-level lighting in the corridor flashed red in rhythmic pulses. Warriors scattered as the big alien leader stormed through, parting like the seas before him. She followed in his wake, slipping onto the bridge beside him. Her breath caught in her throat when all the combat bots turned at their entrance, arms spread and talons extended as they focused on the two of them.

Oh shit... Fear crawled down her spine at the memory of their sharp claws. They wouldn't make mincemeat of their own commander...would they? He didn't seem worried. Instead, he paused for half a second before a gleam washed over the surface of the octagonal pendant he wore. Interesting, it seemed their necklaces were less jewelry and more identification. Like a dog tag. She filed that nugget of information away and stayed close as he strode to the center of the bridge.

The central view screen in front of them flickered to life and she sucked in a hard breath. There were more ships now, but these weren't the same design as those belonging to Tarrick's group. Black metal glimmered in the light of this system's sun, and weaponry, or what she assumed were weapon arrays, bristled on all surfaces.

"Shields to full. Are those T'Laat clan ships?" Tarrick's voice was sharp and cut through the noise on the bridge. "Who heads T'Laat now?"

Cat tucked herself in by an empty console just behind Tarrick and kept quiet. So far, her presence had been accepted but she didn't want to call attention to herself and be taken back to Tarrick's quarters. The more she saw, the more information she could gather. Never knew what could come in handy.

Jassyn looked up from his station. From what she could work out, he appeared to be the latharian equivalent of a tactical officer; trained in strategy and tactics.

"Varish T'Laat."

Sudden silence fell over the bridge at the name. Whoever this Varish was, it was obvious no one liked him much.

"*Draanth!*" Tarrick swore, his tone dropping to a growl. "That changes things."

"Incoming call from the T'Laat flagship, the *Jeru'tias*. Looks like they want to talk," another warrior announced, his hands flying over the console in front of him.

Cat eyed hers with interest. She had always been good with computers. Perhaps she could switch hers on and get a peek at their system. Waving a hand over it did nothing, neither did touching it. The surface only lit up when she placed her palm flat. Jumping, she yanked her hand back, but the imprint remained in bright blue. Words scrolled across the screen.

Unknown operator, please present identification...

It flickered once, then her handprint disappeared to be replaced by an octagonal outline. She blinked. Okay, so the pendants could access the computers. Today's little outing was proving more fruitful by the minute.

"Stall the transmission. Use interference from the human systems." Tarrick was still talking, rattling off orders in quickfire sentences. "Someone put out a call to Fenriis. See how far away his war group is. We will need backup here. I don't trust Varish."

"Accessing the human comms relays." A warrior on the other side of the room kept up a running commentary. "Boosting to full power."

"Got it. No, wait..." Jassyn flicked his hair back over his shoulders and frowned at his screen. "Oh for fuck's sake, it's this draanthic repeater pattern again. Can you shut it down, Talat?"

"Yeah, cleaning now. There you go..."

Tarrick prowled the central part of the bridge as his warriors worked, his gaze on the view screen. It was as though she wasn't even there, which suited her fine. She could study him without him being aware.

That he knew what he was doing was obvious. An aura of command surrounded him; unmistakable and sexy. For a moment her lips tingled, reminded of the gentle and oh-so-seductive kiss he'd treated her to before they were interrupted. A kiss she shouldn't have given into. Where had the arrogant alien gone? She could handle him, compartmentalize to complete her mission, but when he acted all nice... fuck. She'd be screwed.

No falling for the alien, she told herself. *He's an asshole and you're his slave. Remember that.*

"Bring group configuration to *hanrat-five-nine,*" Tarrick ordered, hands clasped behind his back in the classic at-ease position. Huh, seemed certain things crossed not only cultures but galaxies and species too. "Are their weapon arrays active?"

His words brought her attention to the nasty looking canons on the other ships. She assumed they were canons anyway. The basic design didn't seem to differ much from human models. Still a barrel to fire whatever nastiness at the enemy.

"Powering up. They outgun us."

Shit, this was serious. Cat's lips moved as she counted the weapons facing them. If Tarrick's ships were of a similar configuration, then yeah, they were outnumbered. And if this lot were worse than Tarrick's group...fuck. Better the devil you knew...

"Use the base's weaponry," she lifted her voice so it carried. Tarrick pivoted to spear her with a hard gaze.

"What?"

She met his look. "Give me access to the Sentinel's mainframe. With the weapon arrays, you'll have a better chance against...those." She waved her hand toward the opposing war group.

"She's right," Jassyn commented, not looking at her, his hands busy on his console. "They're crude but have a decent yield. Our shields took a hammering from them yesterday. Firing systems are... well, unique. We can't figure out how to work them at the moment. If she gives us access, we have the advantage."

"Try nothing," he warned her, striding over and accessing the console with swift gestures.

"Not trying anything other than helping to save your asses. Come on, log me in so I can get you in."

"There, you're in."

Sure enough, the screen flared to life but rather than the alien system, she found herself in the base's familiar mainframe.

She input the access codes for the weaponry and gave the Lathar the keys to the guns.

Ladies, forgive me.

"THANK YOU," Tarrick said, watching his little human out of the corner of his eye. That he was surprised at her offer of help was an understatement, but he would not turn down any advantage against an enemy as dangerous as Varish.

He half expected her to try something, like accessing the weapon arrays and turning them on the K'Vass ships. But she didn't. As soon as she'd granted direct access she stepped away from the console, her hands raised.

"Done, all yours."

"I'm in," Jassyn announced. "Powering up."

"Response from Fenriis," Gaarn called out. "Still over half a pasec away."

Tarrick kept his disappointment to himself. Even at top speed, that meant they couldn't rely on reinforcements.

"Okay, we're doing this solo. Take us to combat status but cut the red alert warnings in this room. Activate all bots for possible boarding parties. If I know Varish, he'll want not only the base but extra ships as spoils."

The Lathar comprised of loosely related war-clans, but there was never any family loyalty lost or mourned. If Varish could defeat them, he would, and claim both the human females and Tarrick's ships once he and all his warriors were dead.

He slid a quick glance at Cat. No emotion showed on her face, her manner calm and serene. His heart twisted at the thought of what would happen to her should Varish prevail. He'd given them a choice but T'Laat wouldn't. They'd be claimed and bedded within hours, willing or not.

Taking a deep breath, he nodded to Jassyn. "Put him on the screen."

The view screen flickered for a moment then shifted from a view of the opposing war group to that of a tall, dark-featured warrior. Like Tarrick, he wore the leather and red sash of a war commander, its edges shot through with gold. Unlike Tarrick, he hadn't cut his warrior's braids, his hair over his shoulders. A new commander, but a dangerous one.

"T'Laat." Tarrick inclined his head, a show of respect between those of equal rank. "To what do we owe the pleasure?"

"Can a warrior not check in with a kinsman now, without his motives being suspect?" Varish smiled. It was the oily, slick smile of a politician and Tarrick didn't trust him as far as he could throw him. How the hell had T'Laat found them? His warriors knew the score. They didn't talk about their missions, not even at the pleasure stops, and there was no way to track the ships.

Out of Varish's line of sight, Jassyn coughed. *"Trall-shit."*

Tarrick kept his expression neutral. Varish could use anything, even a flicker of an eyelid, and he'd be damned if he would give the rival warrior anything to work with.

"Your concern is noted."

Varish's smile widened. "And to offer my help with your current situation."

Tarrick offered a smile just as empty and false as Varish's own. "Thank you, but we have things quite in hand."

"Really? Looks like a big sector here... plenty for everyone." Varish moved to the side, his gaze focusing on Cat behind Tarrick. "You have found females?"

"A handful." Tarrick folded his arms. There was no way the T'Laat scanners could pick up the females in the holding cells, not through the *Velu'vais's* shields. "The species in this sector appear to have the same problem as we have. Few females, even less fertile."

"A few is better than none." Varish leaned back, a smug expression on his face. "Since this sector falls within my established remit, you will cede all captured females. At once."

Tarrick heard the slight intake of breath behind him but couldn't turn to assure Cat that Varish's words held no weight. One did not look away from a snake lest it strike.

"I suggest you double check the records," he advised. "This area falls under K'Vass space."

"Ahh, it *did*," Varish looked so smug Tarrick wanted to reach through the screen and splatter that long nose all over his face. "Before I submitted a requisition with the emperor's recordkeepers. And..." he spread his hands. "I appear to have the advantage of superior numbers here. And don't think for a moment I can't see you've activated the weaponry on that primitive little station there."

Tarrick stared back. "Marginally superior numbers, but it will make no difference. This is K'Vass space and we protect our own. Do you want to start something you can't finish, Varish? Because I assure you we'll send you packing with your tail between your legs."

Varish smiled again. "With those ships and one little base? With the looks of the technology, I'm surprised it's even holding its orbit. I'll tell you what, Tarrick, given our kinship, I will give you an hour to think it through. Then you *will* cede the females or your bloodline will end here."

SHITSHITSHIT.

Only an idiot wouldn't have realized that the situation was serious and Cat was far from a fool. Tension rolled around the bridge during Tarrick's conversation with the other alien lord, the reactions of the warriors too careful and controlled. But it wasn't until he cut the communication she realized just *how* serious it was.

"Lock down all comms channels," he ordered as soon as the screen went blank. "And someone get me a direct line with the emperor. I want this shit sorted out *now!*"

He turned, gaze locking on hers and she swallowed. If she'd thought he looked dangerous before, it was nothing compared to the lethal aura that surrounded him now. He stalked toward her, intent written into every movement and swept her up into his embrace.

She bit her lower lip, allowing him to pull her close. Events were moving so fast her head whirled. This morning it had been so simple. All she'd had to figure out was how to liberate just under a hundred women from the clutches of sex-mad aliens, find a ship, and pilot a course back to the safety of human-held space.

Oh yeah, and warn them that sexy, ripped aliens from the outer reaches of spaces were out there looking for women to capture and bed. Okay, scratch that...If women on Earth saw what the Lathar looked like, they'd leave in droves in anything spaceworthy.

With this though, things changed. Now she had a whole new set of aliens to deal with and if she'd thought Tarrick's lot were assholes, Varish appeared to up the ante to total bastard.

"You won't let him take us?" she asked. Despite herself, her strong woman mask slipped a little and she clung to him. She had to be realistic. He might be her captor, but so far he hadn't lifted a finger against her, even earlier when she'd resisted. Instead, he'd seduced her with soft kisses. Something she doubted the cruel-faced Varish would have done. A shudder rolled down her spine as she recalled the way he'd looked at her like he was mentally undressing her. She felt sick, unclean, at the thought.

"No, my love. I won't." The endearment slipped from his lips and warmed her heart even though she tried to stop it. "You're mine and the K'Vass protect what is theirs."

He bent his head and claimed her mouth in a blazing kiss. She moaned, pressing herself against him, but it was over too soon. Pulling back, he looked down at her, smiled and stroked her cheek. "Karryl will take you down to the others while I'm in council with the emperor. You'll be well protected, I promise."

When Tarrick had said the women would be protected, he'd meant it. Within minutes, Cat was ushered into the main holding area in the bowels of the ship. The force field snapped into place behind her and the robotic guard whirled away to resume its patrol. She turned and was overwhelmed as the women in the cell rushed her.

"Oh my god, are you okay?"

"What happened?"

"Can you tell us what's going on?"

The voices rose in a babble of questions, almost deafening her. She didn't know which to answer first. She was saved as another voice broke through, the tone commanding.

"For heaven's sake, leave the poor girl alone."

Cat breathed a sigh of relief as a familiar figure barged her way through the mass of bodies to stand next to her. Major Jane Allen had been the senior female officer aboard Sentinel Five and a Marine. Now, with the loss of the captain and the other men, she was the senior officer overall.

"Ma'am," Cat muttered by way of thanks. At least now she could ease off for a moment. She wasn't alone, Major Allen had years more experience than she did and tactical training only Marines received. Not just that, but she was the Fleet's poster girl for military service, a legend who looked far younger than she was. Some said living space side did that.

"Glad to have you back, Moore." The major reached out to squeeze Cat's upper arms, bared by the alien outfit, reassuringly. Cat spared a quick glance to look through the faces, trying to spot Jess but couldn't. Damn, she must be in one of the other cells.

Major Allen reclaimed her attention. "What can you tell us?"

"So, they're bigger versions of us?"

Cat, seated in a small circle with the other women in the cell, nodded. "Yes. There doesn't appear to be any physical difference other than the size. I can't tell you about the inner workings of their bodies but on the outside, they look like human men, just bigger."

"Bigger, huh?" One woman the other side of the circle sniggered and Cat flushed.

"Enough of that," Major Allen, Jane, reproached. "Focus on the issue at hand. So, they're larger physically, they appear to have a feudal society that uses energy-based weaponry, and these remote-operated bot creatures. What else?"

"They have no women." At Cat's revelation, all the ladies turned to her. She shrugged. "What did you think when we were separated from the men?"

"Well, sex slaves were an obvious when they started the segregation," Jane commented, her expression grim. "So we have a ship full of horny alien warriors here. I'm surprised they left us alone this long."

Cat looked down at her hands.

Crap, crunch time.

"I made a deal," she said quietly. "They have an honor-based system. They're not after one-night stands. They seem to respect and revere women. With none of their own, they look for women to capture...then claim. One warrior, one woman."

"Just one?" Someone chuckled. "Damn, and there I was looking forward to a hunky alien threesome."

"Yeah, right, Kenna...you'd eat them for breakfast. Hey, perhaps that's it. We send Kenna out there and they'll all run screaming."

The group dissolved into chuckles. Cat smiled, sitting back. It was such a relief to talk, even shooting the shit like this. She wasn't alone anymore, didn't have to make all the big decisions. That no one judged her as she'd worried they would was a weight off her shoulders. But then, with the Sentinel bases being so far out on the frontier, all personnel were military. They knew the score. If the shit hit the fan, the military mindset kicked in.

"On the whole, they're decent people. They have an honor code," she carried on. "I mean, look at us... we did the slavery thing ourselves, and we didn't give them a single choice, never mind three."

"Three choices? Of men?" Jane asked, her brow furrowed.

Cat nodded. "That's right. You don't have to say yes to the first warrior who puts in a claim. You can say no twice."

"What happens if you say no again?"

Cat's expression dropped. "Sent to the brothels. I'd suggest no one get to that point."

From the grim looks around her, they all agreed.

"Sounds like we need to consider this from a tactical viewpoint," Jane said quietly, turning to look at Cat. "But first I want to know about this deal you made."

She shrugged. "It's not a big thing. I didn't agree to anything for anyone else..."

"Cat?" Jane's hand closed over hers, battle-scarred but gentle all the same. "What did you agree to?"

She looked up and met the other woman's eyes. They were odd; one green, one blue. Huh. She'd never noticed that.

"Tarrick...their lord..." She paused, looking down as her words escaped her in a rush. "If I agreed to his claim over me, then the rest of you got the choices."

There was silence.

She risked a look up. Sadness and approval shimmered in Jane's eyes, echoed on the faces of the other women. Jane squeezed her hands.

"Thank you. That was a noble sacrifice. He didn't...he wasn't..."

"No." Cat was quick to shake her head. "No, not at all. I mean... there's something they inject into you—"

"The bastard drugged you?" This time it was Kenna who spoke up, her voice outraged. "When I see him, I'm gutting him. With a fucking blunt spoon."

"It's not like that. It...well, they're bigger than us. *Way* bigger. The stuff makes you dilate...down there. You know. You feel buzzed and all, but it's like two shots of decent vodka."

At the word, there were several moans. Supply runs to the base were comprised of essentials, so alcohol was rationed. Cat had even heard tell someone on one of the lower levels had been trying to distil their own. There hadn't been any cases of blindness yet, so she assumed it was an urban myth or they'd been successful.

"We have other problems though," Cat cut through the groaning to bring the conversation back on course. As she did so, she reached out to touch Jane's arm, her finger tapping. Tap or press in quick succession until Jane looked at her, eyes widening a little as she got the message.

They don't understand morse code.

"There's another group of aliens here, they seem to be in a power struggle with this lot."

"Over?" Jane nodded as she spoke, letting Cat know she understood.

The ident tags...

"Us. Women from this sector. The ones who just arrived are mounting a challenge for this area of space. And believe me..." She shuddered. "The T'Laat don't look like they'll give us any choices."

...access the computers.

"Shit. What do we do?" Kenna, another of the Marines, crowded forward, dividing her attention between Jane and Cat. The muscles in her shoulders bunched as she rolled her neck as though preparing for a fight.

The major looked around, frowning at the sound of a commotion by the door. Before she could answer, energy bolts slammed into the field keeping them in the cell. It fizzled out and disappeared as a bot crashed to the floor in front of them, a smoking hole in the middle of its chest.

"Right now? Run!" Jane bellowed.

The women scattered, streaming out of the holding cells as more robots poured into the room to engage the ones that had been guarding them. The black metal carapaces of the newcomers made them easy to distinguish.

Cat gathered her skirts and ran between the fighting monsters, following Jane's lead. If they could just get into the central section of the vessel, they might make it to the flight deck. Find a ship. Failing that, they could at least access the weapons lockers she'd seen in the corridors.

The black robots had the advantage of numbers though, and before they could escape the room, had all but cut down the others. Cat stifled a scream as a silver-colored robot crashed to its knees in front of her, saved from being crushed when Kenna grabbed her hand and yanked her back.

"To the left," she yelled and a black robot whirled around to fix its single red eye on them. "Go, go, go!"

She pushed Cat ahead of her, both of them slipping on grease that oozed from the fallen robot like blood leaking from ruined veins. Her breath escaped in a squeak, Cat righted herself but felt Kenna yanked from her grasp. She glanced back over her shoulder to see the marine in the clutches of a black robot.

"Run!" Kenna yelled at her, fighting to escape her machine captor. Although its talons dripped with the "blood" of the bots it had destroyed, it had folded the lethal blades away so they didn't cut the struggling woman. The same as Tarrick's bots, it looked like these new ones wouldn't kill them...but Cat wasn't going to hang around. As long as one woman got away, there was hope for the rest.

She spun on her heel and sprinted for the open doors. Metal flashed in her peripheral vision, robots reaching out to grab her. All black now, there were no silver ones left on their feet. Bellowing, she ducked and wove, trying to escape their grasp. Her heart pounded in her chest, powering the muscles of her body in her desperate bid for freedom. Just ahead of her was Jane, the other woman's lithe form and fitness more suited for a pitched battle against alien combat robots. Shit.

It made no difference. Before either of them reached the doors, two heavier-set black robots stepped in the way. Their eyes focused on the women and both skidded to a halt as red dots appeared on their chests. Slowly, they raised their hands in the universal symbol for surrender.

"So much for not killing women," Jane shrugged. "I can't believe I'm saying this... Okay, asshole. Take us to your leader."

*a*s evil alien overlords went, Varish T'Laat ticked all the boxes and then some. He wore the same uniform as Tarrick, right down to the red sash, but the leather was darker and battered. Extra sections of sewn-in armor made him look more sinister and the vicious scar down one side of his face just by his eye didn't help him much in the approachable and cuddly stakes.

The women were herded to stand in front of him in a large room. Long and high-ceilinged, it resembled a throne room. An impression that was aided because Varish sat on a damn throne. He leaned forward, dark hair falling across eyes so cold that Cat shivered.

"Who is in charge here?" His voice was silky smooth. Although they should know better, a few of the women glanced toward Jane near the front of the group.

She lifted her chin and looked him in the eye. "That would be me. Major All—"

In a move like lightning, he pulled a pistol from his thigh and fired. Jane cried out, clutching her leg as she collapsed. Cat gasped, her immediate instinct to go to the fallen woman, but Varish motioned with the weapon in his hand.

"Correction. *I* am in charge." He stood, heavy boots clumping against the steps as he descended the dais. When he reached Jane, he glanced down as she panted in pain, half curled up on the floor. No sympathy showed in his expression. Then he looked at the rest of them.

"You belong to the T'Laat now. And you have two choices."

None of the women responded with so much as a murmur. They were all too wary to risk a response that would get them all shot.

"Good, you're learning already." Varish smiled, walking around the small group with a measured tread and praising them like he would a puppy that had mastered a new trick. "Either you behave or you suffer. Simple as that. I'm not K'Vass... your sole purpose aboard this ship is to offer comfort for my men."

He paused in front of them, caressing the barrel of the pistol in a very unhealthy manner. "Remember that you do not have to look pretty, or even be able to move, for them to use your soft cunts. Do you understand?"

No response. There never would be to a declaration like that.

"Good." He clicked his fingers at Cat. "You...K'Vass's woman. Come here."

A chill swept over her skin, but she took a step forward, then another, forcing her unwilling body to approach him. Every instinct within her urged her to run, to get as far away from him as she could as fast as she could but she knew it wasn't possible. He'd cut her down before she'd taken three steps and would laugh as she died in agony.

She came to a stop in front of him, her eyes on the floor. Not the modesty of a slave faced with her master but pure self-preservation. If he saw her expression, he'd know she wanted to gut him. Slowly.

"I can see why K'Vass chose you. You are lovely." He reached out and ran a hand down the exposed length of her arm, hard fingers shackling her wrist and he pulled her up against him. Revulsion filled her, bile rising in her throat as he held her captive against him. She struggled, beating at his chest. The movement was merely a cover as she snapped the chain from around his neck. Tearing free of his grasp, she stepped backward.

His expression contorted in fury and he lashed out, backhanding her across the face. Pain flared in her cheek and she spun, stumbling as she fell onto Jane on the floor.

"Bitch!" he hissed, standing over her. "Never, *never* say no. Ever!"

"I'm sorry, my Lord," Cat sobbed noisily, keeping her hand concealed beneath her body as she pushed Varish's ident tag into Jane's hands. The other woman, lips still pressed together in pain, gave an almost imperceptible nod and folded it into her palm, out of sight.

"You'd better be," he snarled, leaning down to haul her bodily to her feet. "Get the rest of them prepared for the choosing ceremony," he ordered the guards, as he dragged Cat from the room. "Leave that one there until it dies. As a warning."

He said nothing more. Instead, he stormed away, Cat forced to run to keep up. She didn't try to pry his fingers from her arm, knowing that the reprisal was likely to be deadly.

"Please, my Lord. I'm sorry," she whined, keeping up the pretense of a panicked slave. All the while though, she kept an eye out for something, anything she could use.

Hopefully, the throne room would be cleared and Jane allowed to move freely. If she were able. Cat had been in the computer core, then unconscious for most of the Lathar attack on the base so she had no idea how bad injuries from those pistols could be. The Marine had been conscious, at least. And conscious was good, right? It meant they had a chance.

"You will be," he muttered as they reached the end of a corridor and a door opened in front of them. Unlike Tarrick's, which were neat and military-sparse, Varish's quarters were opulent and decadent.

He shoved her into a large room. She had a fleeting impression of huge couches and sumptuous rugs before he pushed her into a bedroom. Her jaw dropped. It looked as though it had been pulled from a bad romance holo-movie she'd once seen, *the Space Sultan's Harem*.

There was already someone there, a tall, slender woman wearing robes in the corner of the room. Cat sucked in a breath. Was Varish into voyeurism too?

"Out!" He barked.

Cat got a look under her hood as the other woman fled without a word. She had a long face, not human or lathar looking at all but more bovine almost.

He pulled Cat toward the bed and looked down at her. He was as well built as Tarrick was, and he was handsome, even with the scar, but she felt nothing other than a mixture of anger and fear.

"You're a pretty one," he mused, as though he were talking to himself. Like she wasn't present...or didn't matter. Given his words earlier, she was going with *didn't matter*. She tried not to flinch as he reached out and touched her cheek. A gentle touch, for now. She doubted it would stay so.

"I can see what K'Vass saw in you. It will kill him to know I've got you...that it's my cock buried in your silken depths. Plowing you over and over until you scream my name."

"I'll never scream your name," she promised and struck. He was so close he couldn't block and an alien man was still a man. The Lathar kept their balls between their legs, just like humans. Bringing her knee up, she clocked him hard in the groin.

He grunted, folding at the waist. She tried to slide to the side, escape him, but his hand shot out and grabbed her arm in a punishing grip. Screaming, she fought like a wildcat, landing blows wherever she could. It made no difference. Straightening up, he backhanded her again, the power of the blow knocking her backward over the bed. On her in an instant, he pinned her to the soft surface, the bulge in his groin pressing hard against her.

"I didn't say you'd be screaming in pleasure, did I?"

"Thank you, Imperial Majesty," Tarrick murmured, bending into a low bow. Light years away his "body," a non-combat avatar, bowed before the Emperor as he swept from the room, followed by his entourage.

The Latharian Emperor was the greatest warrior in their culture, a male both revered and feared as the physical embodiment of the ancestor gods. He was also Tarrick's uncle, on his mother's side. Family connections didn't mean that Tarrick could duck out of a holo-connection with the male early though, not even with a red alert ringing in his ears.

Straightening, he brought the bot to a stable position and released his hold on it. Instantly, he was back on an uplink couch in the pilots lounge. Tearing his headset off, he looked up. Other recliners surrounded him in rows. They were all occupied, each warrior wearing an identical headset to remotely pilot the avatars.

A yell from the other side of the room made his head snap around. A pilot fell from his couch, tearing his headset off. "Avatar down! There are too many of them."

"What the draanth is going on?" he demanded, levering himself up. Before the impression of his body had smoothed from the padded surface of the couch, another warrior slid onto it, headset already on and visor covering his eyes. A second later, it flashed active, the blue light showing a local link rather than the subspace one Tarrick had used.

"The T'Laat attacked," Jassyn, waiting by the door, informed him. "Hit us hard and fast...took the females. They're fighting a ferocious rear-guard action that's slowing us."

Tarrick froze as fear lanced the center of his chest and his body forgot to breathe. Varish T'Laat had Cat. The thought of his little human in that monster's clutches... He gritted his teeth. Varish's reputation preceded him. Ruthless and determined in battle, he was sadistic and vicious in more intimate pursuits. So much so, most pleasure facilities refused to take his credit. Only those that catered to specific...tastes would allow him and his men entry.

"How long?" he demanded, marching past Jassyn. "They'll have taken them back to the flagship. Do we still have that hunter-seeker program on lockdown from the B'Kaar?"

"Yes, my Lord. Want me to break it out?"

Tarrick nodded. Although most Lathar clans focused on militaristic pursuits, some specialized in different forms of warfare. The B'Kaar took digital and subspace combat to the highest level. The program he'd bought had cost Tarrick a lot of credits, and he'd never had cause to use it. But the prospect of losing Cat meant he was prepared to put all his cards on the table.

"I don't care how you do it, but get me onto that ship. They are not keeping our females."

Jassyn nodded, heading for his console on the bridge as soon as they cleared the doors. All Tarrick's senior warriors were present. Karryl threw a blast rifle his way. He didn't slow his pace, catching it mid-air. "Jassyn, you coordinate from here. Gaarn, power up an assault flyer."

"It's waiting on the flight deck, my lord," the pilot confirmed, falling into step behind Tarrick and Karryl.

He nodded. "Good. Now, let's get our females back."

THE FLIGHT between the two ships was short. No sooner had they left the *Velu'vias* than Gaarn had settled the small flyer on the hull of Varish's flagship. The cutter hit metal with a clunk and cut through the tri-plated covering with a squeal. Through the flyer's viewscreen, Tarrick watched other units touchdown, the bigger, hulking forms of the bot transports between them. Impatience made him roll his shoulders and anger tensed his body until his vision faded to red at the edges.

"Easy, boss." Karryl dropped a big hand on his shoulder, his expression both sympathetic and concerned. "We'll get them back, I promise. Just think, they're probably confusing the draanth out of that lot right now."

Unbidden a smile curved Tarrick's lips. "True."

The human females were the most contrary creatures he'd ever come across; fascinating and frustrating by equal terms. But he knew as well as Karryl did that that spirit could be crushed under a Lathar fist. They'd had the females for hours... he bit back a growl. Who knew what the T'Laat had subjected them to.

"We're through." The shout came from the back of the flyer. Like a well-oiled machine, the Lathar warriors formed an attack formation and swarmed through the blown hatchway into an empty corridor. Empty was good, it meant either the ship's internal defenses were offline or engaged elsewhere.

"K'Vass here," Tarrick spoke, triggering his comms. "We are boots on deck. Confirm hunter-seeker program online."

The comm crackled and Jassyn's voice filled his ear. "Active and in their system, sir. Half their bots down. Others on a different codex. Working on them."

Farther down the corridor, more K'Vass poured through similar boarding holes, followed by the metal combat avatars. Tarrick watched as they organized themselves into a slick, well-practiced march of death, and moved deeper into the ship toward their objectives.

"No resistance so far." He kept up a running commentary as he and his men made their way down the empty corridors. Varish would be on the bridge, or he'd be in his quarters.

With Cat.

At the thought of his little female in the vile warrior's arms, fury threatened to rise and overwhelm him again. He fought it, his eyes narrowing as they approached the central hall of the ship and heard the sounds of combat from around the next corner.

"Jass...do we have units this far in?" he asked, his blast rifle tucked into his shoulder, ready to fire. They were the only group on this boarding vector and their time had been fast. It was unlikely another team had gotten ahead of them.

"No. All other units are at least a kilisec behind you."

"Okay..." Tarrick lifted his hand from the trigger grip and gave rapid-fire combat signals, rearranging his men to turn the corner. A female yell made him pause and blink. There were no female lathar...

"Move!" He gave the order, and the warriors swarmed around the corner to find a scene they hadn't expected in a million years. A small group of human females held the corridor, bottlenecking the T'Laat combat bots and warriors. Somehow they'd broken into a weapons cache, and were wielding the big assault rifles with an ability and violence that took his breath away.

"Target the joints," a woman near the front bellowed as she stepped out of cover behind a support strut, favoring a leg and took aim. She fired in short, controlled bursts at a bot trying to break through their line, and shattered its knee.

"They've taken the thermal safeties offline." Surprise rang in Karryl's voice. It was the only way the big weapons would fire that fast. "They'll kill themselves."

It might be dangerous, but it was damn effective. As was the strange manner they fired in, using short bursts rather than precision single shots. The Lathar warriors ran up behind the females, settling into positions beside them.

"About time you boys showed up," the woman controlling the action threw at them as Tarrick and Karryl slid into place next to her. She didn't take her eyes off the corridor ahead of them, continuing to fire until the rifle she held whined.

Tarrick's heart pounded, recognising the sound of imminent overload. Both he and Karryl reached out to snatch the weapon from her hands, but she stood and threw it down the corridor.

"Fire in the hole!"

As one, the human females turned away, shielding their heads and faces as the whine grew to ear-splitting proportions. Tarrick and his men barely had time to throw themselves into cover before it exploded, rendering the approaching avatar bots twisted hunks of metal and leaving the warriors behind either dead or mortally wounded.

"Holy fuck," Karryl breathed the words, but they were the ones every K'Vass was thinking. "You're...scary."

"He gave us two choices. Slavery or suffering. So we made them suffer." The woman turned and smiled. Tarrick recognized her as the human soldier who had impressed Karryl. He could see why.

Her gaze flicked over them and he realized she was wounded, a large dressing on her thigh. Reaching around her neck, she unlooped something and held it out to him.

It was an ident tag. Now he knew how they'd gotten into the weapons cache. What scared him more was how quickly they'd worked out how to get to weaponry.

"He has Cat. Go get her."

He took the tag and nodded, a mark of respect from one warrior to another.

"Thank you."

Taking off down the corridor with the chain wrapped around his fist, he activated his comm. "Jassyn, locate Varish."

Less than three kilisecs later Tarrick crashed through the outer door into Varish's quarters. An Oonat huddled in the corner, her large, doe-like eyes wide with fear.

"Where?" he demanded, knowing he was scaring the creature but not able to do anything about it at the moment.

She shrieked and pointed toward the bedroom. Tarrick's head whipped around. Varish had Cat in his sleeping chamber.

The inner door was no match for his boot as he kicked it in. What was it with T'Laat and this archaic décor? They might have been desert nomads way back when but they didn't need to live like it now.

"You fucking bitch, you *will* submit." The snarl was punctuated by the sound of a fist hitting soft skin. Varish knelt on the bed, a smaller figure pinned beneath him. The spill of gray silk and human-dark hair were all Tarrick saw before fury overwhelmed him and he launched himself toward them with a roar.

8

Cat's world had reduced to two things: pain and ensuring her tormentor didn't take her quickly. He wouldn't kill her, not with women in such short supply, but she made sure he wanted to. Death would be a release. The final escape from a situation in which she saw no other way out. And if she were lucky, she could remove this asshole's ability to procreate so he'd never rape another woman.

He roared as he hit her, landing hits when she couldn't block fast enough, but she fought anyway. And when she couldn't fight anymore, when her arms were too heavy to hold him off, he still bellowed.

But the blows stopped.

Blessed unconsciousness beckoned and she welcomed it. She hoped she wouldn't wake, but even if she did, she'd find another way to make sure she escaped him. Permanently.

A different roar filled the room, followed by more and she struggled to open her eyes. What was it? Did the asshole get off on howling like an animal? Large bodies danced in front of her and she squinted to bring them into focus. They stumbled toward her and she gasped, rolling to push herself off the soft surface. She landed on the floor with a thud and cried out in pain as they fell on the bed where she'd just been.

"I'll kill you for touching her." The snarl was low and almost unrecognizable, but she focused enough to spot Tarrick, his hands around Varish's throat as he throttled him. He'd come for her. Warmth spread through her chest, relief, and something deeper filtering through her bruised body.

She stayed awake as he twisted and dragged Varish off the bed to kneel before him. His eyes met hers as he wrapped a thick arm around her tormentor's neck and squeezed.

Her eyelids drooped down, only to snap up again when there was commotion at the door. More warriors burst in and fear lanced her gut, but then she relaxed as she focused enough to recognize Tarrick's senior officers.

"Shit...he's got T'Laat."

"Secure the room."

"Where's the woman?"

"Over here...got her."

She shuffled upright against the wall as the warriors swarmed in, but her attention was all on Tarrick. His lips curled in a snarl, he throttled the life out of Varish. The other warrior was purple, hands scrabbling at Tarrick's arms, trying to get him to let go. But Tarrick held firm. Varish's eyes turned back in his head and he jerked, then went limp. Shifting his hold, Tarrick snarled and twisted, snapping the unconscious man's neck with a sharp crack. The body dropped to his feet in a heap.

She shivered, not able to muster an ounce of sorrow in her heart for the dead alien.

"Well, haven't you gotten yourself into a spot of bother," a voice murmured softly, gentle hands smoothing down her limbs. She turned her head to see Laarn leaning over her, his face, so like her Tarrick's, lined with concern.

"Iz nothi'," she slurred and tried to swallow. Crap, her throat hurt like hell. "A mere flesh woun'."

She laughed, amused she was quoting old movies in a situation as dire as this. Laarn shook his head and pressed something against her neck. Coolness ran through her veins, stealing away her pain.

"Are the others okay?" They had to be if Tarrick and his men were there.

"They're fine... You worry about yourself." Laarn gave her a small smile. "I'll give you this, you humans are damn tough."

"They are," Tarrick knelt on her other side, reaching out to stroke a gentle finger down her cheek. "And this one's the toughest of them all. But what did you expect from a lord's chosen?"

"Careful," Laarn warned as Tarrick slid his arms under her shoulders and knees. "She's badly bruised. A few cracked ribs, but thankfully humans are easy to mend."

She sighed, feeling no pain thanks to the medication as he gathered her against his chest and stood. Just being held by him again was more than she'd hoped for and to her embarrassment, tears leaked onto her cheeks.

"Shhhh, it's over, little one," he murmured, pressing his forehead against hers. For a moment, they just stood there, and she clung to his shoulders as though she could absorb his strength through touch alone.

"I thought I'd lost you. Never do that again, Moore Cat."

"Yeah, I'll pass on the getting kidnaped by aliens thing for a while. Once is fine." She chuckled, wincing a little at the movement. It didn't help that he began to walk, but she didn't argue. The quicker they got off this damn ship, the better.

"I hope not. Since I plan to kidnap you right now."

"You can't kidnap the willing. Don't you know that?" She smiled, closing her eyes and resting her head on his shoulder. He was here, she was safe, and she allowed herself to relax, letting the medication Laarn had given her do its job.

Soon after, she came to and found him carrying her down the corridors of his ship. The sight of the K'Vass avatar bots almost made her cry with relief.

"Never thought I'd be pleased to see those things," she said, glancing over his shoulder as he carried her into his quarters. Looking up at his tight face, she felt awkward and nervous.

"Tarrick?"

He didn't carry her to the bedroom. Instead, he put her on the couch in the main room and knelt before her.

"Moore Cat..." His big hands enveloped hers and when he looked up, the expression in his eyes made her heart stutter. "When we attacked your base, we didn't know about humans. We...you have astonished me. How you work together to defeat the T'Laat. Amazing. Particularly for mere females."

She pressed her lips into a thin line, brow arched. "You were doing so well there for a moment. *Mere* females?"

He hissed in frustration, shaking his head. "Old warriors struggle with change. We have no women, we're not used to females with intelligence. The nearest thing we have are the Oonat, and they're more animal-like. Grazers."

Her eyes widened. "Varish had a woman in his rooms. Her face was longer, more like a cow...that's an Earth animal. Also a grazer."

"She was an Oonat." Tarrick nodded, stroking his thumb over the inside of her wrist in a way that made her skin tingle. "They're not very intelligent. Don't even mount a defense when we raid their homeworlds for new females. They are nothing like you."

Lifting his hand, he cupped her cheek. It was no longer sore, but even with the best medicine in the universe, she knew she looked terrible. The swelling in her body was gone, but her skin was still bruised dark purple so she had no reason to believe her face had faired any better.

"You are remarkable," his voice lowered at the same time his gaze dropped to her mouth. He was about to kiss her, she realized, a second before he leaned forward to press a soft kiss against her lips. She murmured, lips clinging to his before he pulled back. "And have made me reassess my opinions on humanity. I have confirmation of the K'Vass clan's claim to this sector of space."

"And? Does that mean you'll be raiding to collect more women?"

she asked, tilting her head. "Or have you realized we're more trouble than we're worth?"

His lips quirked. "Sassy creature. You are a lot of trouble."

He looked at her and his expression dropped serious. Her heart fell. They would continue raiding...

"I won't let you go. I *can't* let you go."

The raw admission surprised her, almost as much as his fast move when he swept her into his arms and sat with her in his lap. His lips claimed hers in a rush, his tongue prying them apart to delve within. Heat hit, making her catch her breath and forcing her heart to beat at a rapid pace. His fingers drove into her hair, holding her still as he plundered her mouth with a desperation she'd never sensed in him.

Pressed against him, his bodyheat inflamed her, matched by the inferno that infiltrated her veins. An ache speared her, centered in her pussy as the need to have him touch her, fill her, wiped out her ability to think of anything beyond his next kiss. She'd survived, and that was all that mattered. She needed this, needed the balm of his caresses, needed him.

He broke the kiss, resting his forehead against hers again, his breathing ragged. "I'll let the men go, send out a diplomatic party to your people, but I won't release you, Moore Cat. Never."

She pulled away to look at him in surprise. "So you'll free some of us?"

He nodded. "Just the men. Not the females. My men would lynch me."

"What about the women who don't want to be here? Did you forget the whole kidnap thing? We don't like that, remember? Or would you like to talk to the T'Laat to refresh your memory?"

He groaned, the sound turning into a soft chuckle. When he looked at her, his gaze was level. "Work with me, Cat. I'm changing centuries of tradition here to give you a choice, okay?"

Slowly, she nodded. He was, she appreciated that. But still... Sliding her hands up his muscled forearms, she played with the short hairs at the base of his neck. "Okay, but I have conditions."

He arched an eyebrow, watching her. His hand swept up her waist to settle on her ribcage and his thumb stroked the under curve of her bust. It was distracting, and from the slight quirk of his lips, he knew it too.

"No drugs. Never again. For any of us."

He froze for a second, then sighed. "It doesn't work that way, but if it makes you happy, I'll tell Laarn it's not to be used except by the female's request. Happy?"

A smile teased at the edges of her lips and she nodded. He was serious about this whole changing thing. "And if they refuse three times...You send them home. Agreed?"

His eyes widened. "But—"

"A-a-a!" She put her finger up to hush him. "Work with me, or I won't be a happy little Moore Cat. And you want a happy one, don't you? Or at least one that isn't in your computer system, screwing about with your bots."

As she spoke, she opened her hand, revealing that she'd palmed his ident tag and dangled it in front of him. He swore, reaching for his neck, then smiled. The expression flashed with frustration and fire.

"Damned if I do, and damned if I don't." He sighed. "Okay, three choices, then the ones who are married to human men can return. The others, they must stay and support the claimed females... help us learn about your culture and how to appeal to your females. Do all humans drive such hard bargains?" he grumbled, tilting her head forward to drop a kiss into her hair.

"Harder," she confirmed, shifting her position to straddle him. Her breath escaped in a hiss as she settled and the thick length of his cock pressed right where she needed it. "But if it's harder you want..."

His growl was less frustration and more need as his hands closed over her hips. "Damn humans...I'll give you harder."

"Oh, I hope so."

He had her flipped onto her back in a heartbeat, stretching his big, hard warriors body over her. She was still black and blue from her ordeal on Varish's ship and wore her torn robes, but the look on his face said she was the most beautiful thing he'd ever seen.

"When I think of you in danger..." His eyes were so haunted she reached up to cup his cheek as she kissed him. "He didn't—"

"Shhh, it's over. No, he didn't. I'm safe. I'm here, with you." She punctuated each word with a soft kiss. "Please, Tarrick, help me forget. Touch me."

With a growl, he did as asked, sliding his hands up her legs under the gray silks. His mouth covered hers again and the kiss swept her away.

There was no exploration this time, just heat. She didn't care. After defying death or worse, she wanted to feel alive. And she'd never felt more alive as when she was in his arms. Her hands roved over his shoulders and down his biceps before she pulled at his jacket. She needed to touch him. Now.

His tongue brushed against hers in a hot, slick dance. The fastenings resisted her and she growled, drawing a soft chuckle from him. He broke away for a moment to draw the zipper down, murmuring against her lips. "Ferocious little Cat."

"Rawr," she replied, and sliding her hands under the leather, dragged her nails up his back.

He gasped, spine arching and his eyes flared gold with heat. Need so intense she felt the burn.

"Mine," he whispered, thumb under her chin forcing her head up so he could kiss her neck. She shivered, loving the feel of his mouth on her. "All mine."

His free hand shoved her gown up past her waist at the same time he slid a knee between her legs. He was still clothed and she was naked beneath the robes, but she didn't care, her hands dropping to the fastenings at his crotch. She needed him with impatience and desperation that bordered on painful.

"Now, please," she demanded, her voice a breathy, erotic whisper in the silence of the room, and yanked at the ties. He reached down to tear them loose, freeing his cock. It slapped against her stomach, hot and hard, leaving a wet smear of pre-cum.

"Are you sure?" he stopped to look down at her even as he altered his position to fit the broad head against the entrance to her pussy.

Desire gripped her and she nodded. He was big, but not big enough she couldn't take him.

"Please. I need you..." She turned to kiss the inside of his wrist where he was braced over her. "Now."

His answer was to push into her, parting her to slide in half an inch. She sucked a breath in as a burning sensation sliced through her, followed by pleasure. It hurt, but it was a good pain, one replaced with beautiful pleasure.

"Harder." She gave voice to what they both wanted. He pushed again, and again, sliding deeper into her depths. Each time he did, she gripped him, as though her body was unwilling to let him go even to pull out of her long enough to slide back in.

"Fuck, you're tight." He collapsed onto his elbows over her, not crushing her but gathering her leg up over his hip. She helped by lifting the other and locking her ankles behind him. The change in position slid him deeper. They both groaned. "How can you be this tight? How can you...I..."

She blinked as he cut himself off, sure he'd been about to say something else, but he fell silent. His features tightened as he pulled back and powered into her again. Hard and fast, his rhythm set the couch beneath them to rocking as he took her, both still nearly fully dressed.

It was a wild ride, leaving her no options but to cling to him. He used every muscle in his body to taking her, bringing her pleasure until she was sure she couldn't take any more.

He'd been holding out, and on the next stroke, rocked his hips. His pelvis pressed to hers, trapping her clit between them and she cried out. It felt so good... mind-numbingly, gotta-have-more kind of good.

"That," she panted. "Again."

He did, adding a roll at the end of every thrust, sending her need and arousal higher. Not for long though, within a few thrusts she teetered on the edge of the abyss, tendrils of pleasure reaching up to pull her into the depths.

"Come for me," he growled, slamming into her hard. "I want to hear you scream your pleasure. Want everyone to hear and know you're mine."

His. She was his.

With a cry, she gave in and screamed for her alien lord.

HOURS LATER TARRICK WOKE, wrapped around his little human. She murmured in her sleep and made herself more comfortable on his bare chest. They'd moved during the night to the bed. Mindful that she wasn't as hardy as he was, he pulled the covers up to keep her warm.

He laid back, contentment washing over him. Humans. They'd been a total surprise. Tenacious, resourceful, and brave. Like smaller versions of the Lathar. Perhaps he should get Laarn to run tests to see if they were genetically related.

"Tarrick? You awake, you lazy ass?"

Speak of the devil and he will appear. Tarrick smiled as he reached over to tap the comms unit and froze. Black marks wrapped around his wrist like creeper vines.

Familiar marks.

Marks that shouldn't be possible.

Couldn't be possible.

Eyes wide, he hit the comms button and brought his wrist closer. "I'm awake, but we have a problem."

Laarn snorted. *"Tell me about it. The humans? They're—"*

"Genetically compatible," Tarrick finished for him. "I know."

"How the hell did you know that? The tests just came back."

Tarrick smiled and reached for his little human. This would change the face of his world, of Lathar culture, but he didn't care.

"I know because I'm looking at a set of mating marks on my wrist."

Cat was his destined mate, and he would never let her go.

Ever.

9

*A*liens were as weird as humanity. Just when Cat thought she'd gotten the Latharian warriors worked out, they went and surprised her.

She lay on a diagnostic bed in the Healer's bay aboard the Velu'vias, the flagship captained by Tarrick K'Vass, War Commander of the Latharian Empire and all-round badass. *Her* badass, sexy alien warrior.

He'd claimed her as his when he and his men had captured Earth's frontier base, Sentinel Five, where she'd been stationed. She'd forgiven him for that, mostly. There were worse things than being the woman of a high-ranking alien hottie. There were also... advantages.

Like being able to help form policy on how the Lathar dealt with their human captives, now that they'd realized humans weren't like any other species they'd enslaved. For one, they fought back, even when captured. Hunger strikes and passive resistance had confused Tarrick and his men. However, that was nothing compared to the escape and guerrilla warfare battle when a second, nastier group of aliens decided to steal the women Tarrick's group had captured.

They'd quickly found out that pissed-off human women with military training were more trouble than they were worth. *Way* more trouble. Right now, enemy warriors who survived the combined K'Vass attack/human resistance were cooling their heels in Tarrick's holding cells. They were currently leaderless and broken after Tarrick killed their leader for daring to lay a hand on Cat.

It had been more than a hand, but she shoved the unpleasant memories aside to focus on the here and now. She'd woken this morning to find Tarrick sitting by the bed, fully clothed, rather than naked and in it with her. Instantly, she'd known from his expression something was wrong. Rather than answer her, he'd made her dress and brought them both here.

She watched the holo-field arc over her body shift and change. Latharian technology was massively more advanced than humanity's, but the holo-scanner reminded her of an MRI machine, even if it did seem to do...well, just about everything.

The symbols over her head moved down her body and she glanced at Tarrick on another scanner bed next to her. Because of the size difference between their species, she lay in the middle of the bed, but Tarrick, with his massive shoulders and hard, warrior's physique, dwarfed his.

Laarn, the lead healer aboard the ship, and as she'd learned Tarrick's twin brother, moved between the beds, studying both fields intensely. Like Tarrick and every other Lathar warrior she'd seen, he was tall and heavily muscled. That he was a doctor, as well, surprised her. Wearing the same leather uniform as the rest, although with a teal sash across his wide chest, he was more ready to go to war than into surgery.

He grunted at whatever the symbols said on the arc above her and turned to Tarrick. The field above her snapped off and she sat up to watch. Tarrick was stripped to the waist and she spent a pleasurable moment checking out her alien's ripped body. Where the hell had she gotten so lucky? Tarrick had the kind of build she'd only seen on holo-actors and porn-vid stars, and he was all hers to touch, and explore, and lick...

Snapping herself back to reality, she noticed Laarn focused his study on Tarrick's wrist. Black marks covered the skin, wrapping around his wrist a couple of times. They appeared odd, almost organic, as though vines were buried under the surface.

"What's that? Did you get a tattoo?" she asked, scooting to the edge of the bed. The designs hadn't been there last night. She slept like the dead though, so perhaps he'd nipped out to get it done while she'd been asleep.

Both men turned to her, identical frowns on their faces. Even if she hadn't known they were related, that expression right there would have clued her in.

"A tat-Oo?" Laarn asked, mangling the word. "What's that?"

Cat blinked as surprise rolled through her and thought back. She hadn't seen ink on any of the Lathar.

"Uhm, it's a body modification common among humans. Ink driven under the top layer of skin with needles to create a pattern or design." She leaned closer. The skin around the marks was red and raised, just like a new tattoo. "The skin heals to leave the design permanently in place."

"Needles? And humans do that voluntarily?" Tarrick wrinkled his nose in disgust. "How barbaric."

She chuckled. "Humans have some weird kinks. Tattoos are tame compared to some of the stuff out there."

Laarn studied her with an intent gaze, as though she'd just revealed something fascinating. Being the center of his attention was a little unsettling. Unlike Tarrick, no emotion softened his expression. It was like being studied under a microscope. "Do you have any?"

She shook her head. "Nope. But many people on the base have them if you wanted to take a closer look. My friend Jess has a large design on her back."

"Jess?" The big healer tapped out an enquiry on the console at the other side of Tarrick's bed.

"Jessica Kallson. She's a traffic control officer, like I am." A growl rumbled in Tarrick's throat. She sighed. "Okay, fine. Like I *was*."

"This her?" Laarn turned the screen to reveal an image of a young woman.

Cat nodded. "Yes. That's Jess. She was on the flight deck the same time as I was. I haven't seen her since."

Guilt washed over her. She'd asked Tarrick to make sure her friend was okay, but hadn't seen her since the attack a few days ago.

"She's in stateroom three. One of the quiet ones, doesn't seem to be causing any trouble..." Laarn paused to read. "The preliminary medical scan came back okay. She's in good health and sustained no injuries in the attack."

Although she knew from Tarrick that Jess was okay, hearing the healer confirm it made her sigh in relief.

"I'll bring her in though, do a full check?" Laarn glanced over his shoulder, eyebrow arched.

"Thank you." She smiled her thanks. He seemed to have accepted her relationship with his brother without a qualm, and the fact that the link was important enough for him to check on her friend made her feel all kinds of warm and fuzzy inside. "So... if you guys don't have tattoos, what is that?"

They exchanged looks, and once again, she got the feeling there was more going on than they were admitting. Worry hit her, making her stomach churn and she slid off the bed to stand next to Tarrick. He kept trying to sit up, but Laarn reached out and shoved him down, none too gently.

After the third time, Tarrick blew out a breath. "You're enjoying this, aren't you? He rarely gets to shove me around anymore," he commented to Cat.

"Yeah, right. Just every time we spar. For a war commander, you're like a lumbering *Karatan*." Laarn snorted, his green eyes sparkling with humor. "What my baby brother isn't telling you is that if I hadn't taken my healer's sash, I'd be the one running the ship, not him."

"Really? Is that how it works with you guys?" She smiled encouragingly, hoping they'd keep talking. Although they were over the first hurdle and the Lathar warriors were considering human women as more than mere possessions, the more she knew about their culture the better. No unpleasant surprises that way.

This time Tarrick spoke, laying still as Laarn scanned his wrist.

"It's based on skill and ability. Laarn and I have been training since we could walk and because we're *Litaan* as well as siblings—"

"Litaan? That's your word for twins?"

He nodded. "Same height, same build, same abilities. It's down to performance on the day. And it *doesn't* mean Laarn would be running the ship. He decided to welch on facing me and wimped out to take his healer's trials."

"Trials? What...like exams?"

Laarn frowned, leaning forward to study the symbols on the holo-field as he answered. "Physical ones, yes."

"Ahh, yes. Our medical students have to do similar exams before they qualify. Simulations of operations and procedures, right?"

Laarn's hair danced on his leather-covered shoulders as he shook his head. His voice was flat and unemotional without the snarky tone she was used to hearing. "Not quite, no. All healers must experience every ailment and injury. The pain, the sensation, everything. Depending on how much they can handle...that will be the level of healer they become, then they're trained to that level."

"What?" Her jaw dropped in surprise. "But...that's...They do... They hurt you? So you can become a healer? Fuck no, *that's* barbaric!"

Tarrick chuckled and motioned at the bed around him. "The trials are simulated. Fool the brain the injuries are real."

"Oh, I see." She went quiet, feeling a little foolish.

Of course, they wouldn't intentionally injure their own people just to see what kind of doctors they'd make. Then Laarn lifted his head and she caught a glimpse of his unguarded expression before the mask slid back into place, and her heart lurched. Pain lurked in the back of his eyes and she knew at that moment the suffering he'd gone through to become a healer was beyond most people's understanding.

"But Laarn made it through." Tarrick's voice rang with pride. "He's not only a healer, but the highest qualified healer in the Empire. He *should* be Lord Healer and control the Healer's Hall, but he opted to travel for a quadrasec instead. He's an asshole."

"Better than being a dickhead warrior."

Cat sighed and shook her head as the brothers' conversation devolved into insults and name-calling. Men, the same no matter what galaxy, obviously.

"Okay, so these marks..." She drew their attention back to the matter at hand. "Just so you know, all base staff are routinely checked for STDs, so if he's got something nasty, it didn't come from me." She shrugged when they both looked at her in surprise. "Just putting it out there."

"No. Not that." Laarn frowned. "Your people get infections from sex? That's..."

"Barbaric?" she guessed. It seemed to be Laarn's favorite word when it came to humans.

"No. It's a simple genetic fix though. So simple even a child could do it."

She raised an eyebrow. "Speaking as one of the 'children' present, we have a saying. If it ain't broke, don't fix it. Our doctors don't mess at the genetic level in case they make things worse."

"Huh. Interesting." Finally, Laarn snapped off the holo-field over Tarrick and leaned against the empty bed behind him, folding his arms over his chest.

His expression was neutral. That special blank expression doctors got when they were about to say something awful. Another similarity with humans. Ironic. Humanity had spent so long being scared of the possibility of little green men. Who would have guessed the aliens would be so similar on so many levels?

"I have good news and bad news."

Uh-oh, here it came. Mentally, she braced herself. At the same time, she employed logic. Surely with their massively more advanced technology, the Lathar could fix most things, right?

"The good news is these are exactly what I thought." He pointed to the marks wrapped around Tarrick's wrist. "Somehow, unbelievably, humans are genetically compatible with the Lathar. Not only that, but I think they might be an offshoot. I'd need to run tests at the Healer's Hall to be sure."

Her world lurched sideways and Cat gaped at the healer. "We're Lathar? Not human?"

His shoulder lifted in a shrug. "Honestly, I can't tell at the moment, but it's a good possibility. There are too many similarities to be naturally occurring. To be sure I need to run deep level genetic scans and check all the markers."

He flicked a glance down at her stomach. "A quicker way to tell would be if you'd already fallen pregnant, but I checked and you haven't."

Huh. She hadn't even considered a baby, not with what Tarrick told her about his species' reproduction problems. "That could happen?"

"Possibly, yes."

Shit.

"And the bad news?"

Laarn smiled. "They're mating marks, so you're stuck with my idiot brother. You're...what do you humans call it? Married."

TARRICK HATED WAITING. For anything. He particularly hated waiting on the Emperor while stuck in a non-combat bot. Actually, he just hated the non-combat bots. A little under his natural height, with none of the on-board weaponry or improvements of his own custom-built combat machine, it was restrictive and cramped.

Worse yet, he was surrounded by courtiers as they all waited for the Emperor to emerge from his bed-chamber. They reclined on low padded couches, talking in soft voices. Tarrick used the machine's central eye to study them without them being aware, not that they'd bothered much with the bot anyway. He'd deliberately picked up a standard palace model rather than one which would show his family affiliation and rank, so their sycophantic tendencies hadn't been triggered. If they knew who he was in the metal shell, they'd have been all over him like a bad rash. The sister-son of the Emperor, he was considered part of the Imperial family. One reason he preferred to be incognito here.

Tarrick sighed, his bot body clicking as it inflated its mechanical chest in an approximation of the movement. Most wouldn't have been able to trigger the machine to make the movement, but Tarrick was an extremely experienced pilot. His control of the neural connection needed to operate the avatars was an almost perfect mesh of the biological and technological.

He'd even qualified on the bigger *Drakeen* bots. Heavily armed and armored, they could take on hordes of combat bots by themselves, but were hellishly difficult to pilot. There were only a handful of *Drakeen*-qualified pilots across the entire empire. He was one, as was the Emperor.

The chatter in the room stopped when the big double doors to the Emperor's bed-chamber opened. His Imperial Majesty Daaynal K'Saan strode into the room, resplendent in his warrior's leathers complete with his imperial sash—a dark, regal purple—across his chest. He was a born emperor, rather than one who had gained his position through conquest, so his sash was single color and unadorned. Warrior's braids peeked through the mass of black hair that cascaded over his shoulders.

Tarrick straightened, catching the Emperor's eye as he strode past courtiers scrambling to free themselves from the low couches. Daaynal stopped, looked Tarrick's bot up and down, then snapped an order over his shoulder. "Leave us."

There was a mass exodus. Courtiers raced to be the first to do the Emperor's bidding, resulting in a pile up by the door. The servos in the bot's neck whirred as he watched the stampede. "I have no idea why you put up with them, your majesty."

The last courtier got his cloak stuck in the door trying to get through. Frantically trying to free the heavily tasseled and ornate garment, he glanced up, realized they were both watching him and squeaked. A yank and the sound of tearing fabric later, he disappeared through the door like a *gethal* down its burrow.

Daaynal's lips quirked. "Entertainment value?"

He turned back to Tarrick and grabbed the bot by its metallic shoulders, looking at the avatar with fond affection, as though Tarrick were there in the flesh. "So, my sister-son, tell me how things have developed with your humans?"

The words, and the warm tone of voice they were uttered in warmed Tarrick's heart. Twins didn't run in the K'Vass family. Rather, they ran in the imperial line. His mother, Miisan, had been Daaynal's *Litaan,* his twin. Every time he looked at his uncle, he saw his mother's eyes. That Daaynal insisted on preserving the special relationship that existed between a man and his nephew's past childhood was something neither Tarrick nor Laarn had expected.

"Things go well, which is the reason I'm here to speak to you." He turned as Daaynal looped a massive arm over 'his' shoulders and turned toward the large windows at the end of the chamber. "They are technologically inferior, but in attitude and ferocity, they easily match us."

"Really?" Daaynal's eyebrow winged up as he leaned one massive shoulder against the window frame and gazed out on the gardens below. The Herris blossom, the symbol of the Imperial family, was in full bloom. The sight of them, his mother's favorite flower, never failed to ease Tarrick's heart. "The males are much smaller than us though, correct?"

Tarrick didn't bother to hide his smile. Daaynal couldn't see it on the unemotional face of the bot, but he wouldn't have hidden his amusement anyway.

"They are, but I wasn't talking about the males."

Confusion flittered over Daaynal's face for a second before a sound by the door made them turn. An Oonat, graceful in her hooded robes, slipped from the Emperor's bed-chamber. No prizes for guessing why. Daaynal needed an heir, even an oonat-born one.

Latharian DNA was dominant, so no child born of such a union would be a half-breed. Such children were always male, completely Lathar. His cousin Fenriis, for example, was oonat-born, and he was more Lathar in his upbringing and mannerisms than either Tarrick or his brother.

And no one was more eager for Daaynal to beget an heir than Tarrick. His brother wouldn't be able to avoid the Lord Healer's position for much longer, and his calling there surpassed even that of the imperial throne. Which meant Tarrick himself was next in line. That didn't mean it would be all plain sailing though. Because his claim was through a maternal line, there were at least four other warriors with claims they'd fight to the death for. He'd avoid a power struggle for the throne. He was happy being a War Commander, with his lovely little Cat by his side. Although...she *would* make a beautiful empress.

"Then who were you speaking about?"

"The females. It seems humans don't have the same issues we do with numbers. Their gender numbers are equal. So much so, the base we attacked had female military personnel."

Daaynal stilled, his focus solely on Tarrick. "They don't protect their females? What kind of species are they? Like the Oonat?"

Tarrick laughed. "*Draanth,* no. They mounted a robust defense to our attack on their base but eventually lost to superior technology. Not for want of trying though. We secured their base and separated the males from the females as usual. That's when we ran into problems. These females are not civilians. They're as highly trained in weapons and tactics as the men. We couldn't get any information out of them on questioning, and they were offering passive resistance until the T'Laat arrived."

The Emperor's expression tightened for a second before his face cleared. It didn't last more than a blink of the eye, but Tarrick spotted the brief flare of dislike and anger. Daaynal didn't like the T'Laat, everyone knew that, but as emperor, he couldn't play favorites.

"And then?" he asked.

"The T'Laat made the mistake of kidnapping the females."

"I'm assuming since you're talking to me now and you're only just mentioning it, that you have the situation sorted? How many females did you lose?" Daaynal grimaced and reached a hand up to run through his long hair. "Fuck, I didn't want the T'Laat in that sector.

Now they know there are females there. They'll be impossible to get rid—"

"None," Tarrick interrupted, "We didn't lose any females. They'd already figured out our ident tags were the key to accessing ship systems. They stole one from Varish, used it to open a weapons cache. By the time we boarded the ship with combat teams, they'd freed themselves, bottlenecked the T'Laat forces and were blowing the *draanth* out of them."

This time Daaynal's eyes did widen in surprise. Then he laughed. "By the ancestors, they sound perfect. Almost as bad as we are."

"Yeah, that. You might want to take a look at this." Using the same subspace link he used to control the bot, Tarrick quickly sent the images of his wrist and medical data Laarn supplied, showing them on the chest-mounted screen on the bot.

"*Draanth* ..." If he'd ever wanted to see Daaynal surprised, he was seeing it now. The bigger man's expression was one of utter shock. "If there is even the *chance* they are what Laarn thinks, I want to see. I want to meet some. Bring them here."

10

"The Emperor wants to see us? Really?"

Cat followed in Tarrick's wake like a little lost puppy following its master. The impression wasn't helped by the fact she had to trot to keep up. Every long stride of his needed at least two of hers, maybe even three. It was demeaning, but at the moment she didn't care. She was more interested in what he had to say than any blow to her pride.

"He does. He was most interested when I told him about your species and in particular this." He twisted his wrist in a telling gesture. The marks were covered by the long sleeves of his jacket, and a wrist bracer for good measure.

She appreciated the foresight. If every Latharian warrior realized that, unlike the oonat, humans could trigger their long-dormant mating marks, it would be open season. Competition for a human woman, any human woman, could cause chaos and dissent in the ranks, potentially shattering war clans.

The soldier in her wanted to insist that wouldn't be a bad thing. A fractured enemy was easier to combat, but she had to be sensible about this. Under the control of a sympathetic war commander, the Lathar could negotiate with humanity, sign treaties, and build alliances. But scattered lone-wolf groups of warriors would just invade and take what they wanted when they wanted, and humanity could do little about it. And not all Lathar were as honorable as the K'Vass.

Cat shuddered, remembering Varish T'Laat. The last thing any human woman needed was to be at the mercy of such a monster. No, the best way forward was to put their lot in with the K'Vass and hope the Latharian emperor was as "easy" to deal with.

Besides, she'd always wanted to see new planets and civilizations. It had been the main reason she'd signed up for the Sentinel program; to explore, to be out there on the frontier in a way humanity never had been before. So the chance to see the Lathar homeworld was an opportunity the explorer in her couldn't pass up.

"What's he like?" she asked as they entered the flight bay. She'd gotten used to the fact everything to do with the Lathar was just, well, bigger. Their ship, their furniture, their clothing...their men. Hell, were their men build bigger. *All* over. She dragged her mind away from the gutter quickly and looked around. After a while, she'd gotten used to the larger proportions. It took something like the flight deck—easily big enough to fit a couple of terran destroyers in—to make her appreciate the size difference.

They strode past row on row of fighters. Like the combat avatars present as guards throughout the ship and the main force which attacked her base, they were remote controlled. The pilots' lounge was one place Tarrick refused to allow her. Said something about human women were dangerous enough with the knowledge they'd gathered already; he wasn't handing over any more of the Lathar's secrets on a plate. She'd smirked at that. From assuming humans were simple and easily cowed, the Lathar learnt they might be smaller, but a force to be reckoned with. Especially when they got hold of energy weapons.

"Daaynal? He's a K'Saan. Think Laarn but bigger, same eyes."

She hurried to pull even with him, reaching out a hand to his arm as they turned a corner. A quick glance took in the small group waiting at the end of the row, but she ignored them in favor of curiosity, looking at Tarrick.

"Same eyes? Why would he have the same eyes as your brother?"

Tarrick gave her a sexy little side-glance through the corner of his eye. "Because Laarn has our mother's eyes, and Daaynal was our mother's *Litaan.*"

She paused, her steps faltering as the words sunk in. Holy crap...

"You mean you're a prince? You're a freaking alien prince and you never told me?" She ran to catch up, swinging around to stand in front of him, her tone accusing. "Why didn't you say you were royalty?"

He stopped finally and looked down at her, his golden eyes narrowed. "Would it have made any difference to how you viewed me? That some accident of my birth was more important than the skills and status I have gained on my own?"

Shit. Put like that it sounded bad. "No, of course not. But your culture fascinates me... probably fascinates all of us. Like your clans, your names...the relationships between you."

She'd quickly come to realize the Lathar in a war clan were usually related in some way. Cousins at least. None seemed to be as closely related as Tarrick and Laarn though.

He sighed, but she caught the softer expression in his eyes before it disappeared. It pleased him, her interest in his family. "Yes, I'm technically what your people would call a prince, as is Laarn. And although Karryl shares our father's blood, he is a J'Vass. The clan only gained the right to use the K' signifier when my mother took my father as bond-mate. The K' indicates a line descended from Imperial blood."

She nodded, soaking up as much information as she could while they walked. She'd thought the different names were, while pretty, just that. She hadn't realized they meant something. "Karryl is related to you as well?"

He nodded. "The son of my father's younger brother."

They'd almost reached the small group waiting for them near a docked ship larger than most of the flyers on the deck. If Cat had to guess, she'd put it about the same size as the Captain's Yacht on the base. A fast, luxury transporter for a few VIP passengers. Only this wasn't built like any luxury carrier she'd ever seen. It had far too much armor and weaponry. But then again, that was in line with everything about the Lathar. Their whole culture was based on warfare.

The group contained tall, leather-clad warriors and a small group of women dressed much like she was, in long robes and warm capes. Oddly, for an advanced culture, Latharian fashion tended toward the medieval. Along with the clothing change from their dirty uniforms, she'd noticed a distinct thawing in the attitude of the women to their Latharian "captors."

Her gaze flicked over the women, then shot back to one familiar figure.

"Jess!" she squealed, launching herself across the space between them to hug her friend.

Okay, so it was a bear hug around the neck and caused the taller woman to stagger back a bit but Cat didn't care. She just hugged her friend harder.

"Might want to let her breathe a little?" Laarn, behind them, pointed out.

"Yeah...breathing would be good," Jess gasped, although her hold on Cat was just as tight.

Reluctantly, she eased her grip and studied her friend. Apart from the tiredness around her eyes, Jess appeared in good health.

"I'm so glad you're here. Things have been..." She paused, words drying up as she tried to verbalize the events of the last few days. Jess smiled and grabbed her hands to squeeze them. "I know, don't worry, I know. Just...I'm here, you're here. Let's work from that, eh?"

"Yeah..." Cat's breath shuddered from her lungs and she looked up to find Laarn watching them. His gaze was locked onto Jess, his expression possessive until he noticed her watching him. Instantly his face blanked and he gave her a smooth smile. So, the aloof healer did have a weakness after all. She smiled at him, mouthing "*thank you*," sure Laarn was the reason Jess had been included on this trip.

He didn't reply, looking away without acknowledging her thanks. She didn't argue because a commotion behind them caught their attention. The group turned to find Jane Allen stalking toward them with Karryl dogging her steps.

"You were injured, female. You should be resting, not running around the ship risking further injury." Frustration obvious in his voice, the big warrior danced around Jane, trying to get her to stop so he could lift her in his arms. His strange half-scuttle and scoop with his arms spread wide made Cat chuckle, a sound she quickly smothered as the soap opera in front of them unfolded.

"I'm all right," Jane hissed, her gaze focused on the group by the transport as though Karryl were nothing to do with her. "How am I going to come to harm on a ship this well armed?"

Somehow, she'd managed to avoid the robes and cape combo the rest of them had and wore leather pants a la Latharian warrior and a singlet vest. Her dog tags bounced against her chest as she walked. She'd even managed to keep her boots, which somehow fit with her mishmash ensemble. All in all, the Marine looked badass. A fact that didn't escape the attention of the two other warriors with the group, who sucked quick breaths in at the sight of the human woman.

She, however, wasn't paying any attention to their little group, mainly because at that moment Karryl had decided enough was enough and tried to scoop her up over his shoulder. The women, knowing what was coming, winced.

He'd no sooner got his hands around Jane's trim waist when she turned the tables on him. Grabbing his arm, she twisted and turned in a quick movement that dumped the big warrior on the floor. To add insult to injury, she dropped and pinned one arm with a knee, jamming her other booted foot right in his throat.

"Don't you ever try that again, sunshine," she warned, her voice cold and level. "You lot might have all these young women atwitter with the muscles and the charm... But I'm older, wiser and with a shitload more experience under my belt of dealing with pretty boy soldiers like you."

Cat leaned in to whisper in Tarrick's ear. "She likes him."

His eyes widened. "She does? How can you tell?"

She hid her smile. "She hasn't killed him yet."

Jane rolled away, and Karryl scrambled to his feet. Glaring around, he spotted Laarn. "Healer, do something about this defective female! Make her understand what an honor it is to be chosen by a warrior of my standing."

Jane snorted, boot stomping on the deck she joined them. "Stow it, big boy. Humans don't consider it an 'honor' when a guy wants to stick his dick in her. You've got a hand, I suggest you put it to use if that's all you're interested in."

The women dissolved into giggles quickly smothered when Karryl glared at them.

Tarrick sighed. "Children! If you're finished, the Emperor awaits."

As CAT EXPECTED, the yacht was utilitarian, set up more for combat than luxury. The metal of the bulkheads in the corridors they passed was unadorned, and at no point on their journey through the ship did she see carpeting covering the deck plates. The design was simple, with barracks and other rooms off the central corridor. At one end was the "bridge," little more than a fancy cockpit, and at the other was a large common room.

All the rooms had their own facilities, though, for which she was thankful. She didn't fancy wandering the central corridor at night trying to find a toilet. Not that she thought any of the warriors aboard would even look at her sideways, but a girl liked her privacy, especially when bed head was an option.

Voices rose in the corridor behind them as Laarn assigned rooms. None of the warriors were bunked with a human woman, a fact Karryl argued intensely about. From what Cat could gather, Karryl thought his claim over Jane was a done deal, and her consent a mere formality. Meanwhile, Jane was simply ignoring the big warrior. Tarrick led Cat up a flight of stairs tucked in a corner. Cat hid her smirk and followed Tarrick.

The flight of stairs led to a secondary deck. Smaller than the main one, it was one room, with a large bed set in the middle of the wall under a sloping picture window. Clearly designed so the occupant could gaze at the stars. There were two doors in the wall opposite. She raised her eyebrow at Tarrick in question.

"Washroom and storage," he replied quickly. Absently.

His attention was all on her, steady gold gaze unwavering. It was impossible to look away, and her heart rate increased as the gold became darker, more heated.

She knew that expression. Her body knew it well.

"Tarrick, we don't have time."

"Nonsense. There's plenty of time... Or did you forget, I give the orders around here."

She backed as he stalked her, somehow managing to get himself between the door to the stairs and her. Not that it mattered, if she ran it wouldn't be very far. He'd catch her in the corridor below, where she knew he'd take her anyway, regardless of whom watched.

"Around here... Yes. But have you forgotten about the Emperor?"

He shrugged and continued to stalk her. "Laarn will get us underway."

There was no arguing with that, so she didn't bother, her lips curving into a smile as he reached her. Snagging a hand around her waist, he pulled her against his hard, muscled body and claimed her lips.

She melted, her knees weak as he swept his tongue past her lips to plunder her mouth. His tongue found hers, sliding against it in sensual strokes that took her breath away. The small whimper in the back of her throat was purely instinctive and she drove her hands into his short hair to hold him to her.

His kiss turned hard, frenzied, and she broke away to gasp. That didn't stop him, his lips blazing a trail down the length of her throat. Held in his iron embrace, she couldn't escape. Didn't want to escape. Ever.

Strong fingers shoved the cape from her shoulders, the fabric pooling at her feet. She shivered as the cooler air of the room hit her bare shoulders. The dichotomy of the chill and the heat from his body drove her crazy. She moved closer, her hips urgent against his as the fever in her blood grew. Need became all encompassing and she tore at the zipper at the front of his uniform. Anything to get to the smooth, silken skin over his hard, muscled chest. A chest and a body she would never tire of exploring.

"Fuck...you're hot. So sexy," he muttered and claimed her lips with open-mouthed, hard kisses. His hands tangled in the straps of her dress, yanking them down with a twist that unraveled the alien design of the garment. It slithered down her body, leaving her naked apart from the heeled sandals he'd had her wear this morning.

He gripped her shoulders, putting some space between them. His eyes burned with passion. He didn't speak. Instead, his face tightened, hardened until his features became almost cruel.

She squeaked as he spun her around with a quick movement and pushed her toward the bed. The push and the unaccustomed heels made her stumble, and she half fell across the soft surface. As she got to her knees, he wrapped his sash around her wrists with a lightning fast movement. Securing them to the bedpost at the foot of the bed, he pulled the fabric tight until she bent at the waist. Hard fingers dug into the sides of her hips, pulling her ass up even as a large, booted foot kicked her feet apart.

"Tarrick! Slow down!" Her exclamation devolved into a small moan when he swept a finger through her already wet folds. Shit, that felt too good.

"As you pointed out, the Emperor is waiting," he rumbled, rough voice carrying a trace of amusement as she lifted her ass for more of his attentions. Bastard. He knew he only had to touch her for her to go up in flames. "So, this'll have to be quick."

The broad tip of his finger collected the slick juice of her arousal and rubbed it over her clit. She whimpered, biting her lower lip to stop from crying out as he worked her body. Rubbed over and around the little nubbin of flesh, then, when she was least expecting it, gave her a little spank. There. Right there. On her clit.

"Yeoooohhh!" she moaned, the soft tap intensifying her pleasure in a way she hadn't expected. No time to reflect though, because he started to rub again. Teasing and caressing her clit, adding the short little taps that didn't hurt, exactly, but soon had her arching back against him. She needed him to fill her... cock, fingers, anything. Just now. Sooner.

He didn't. Instead, he drove her to the edges of her endurance, rubbing and teasing until her hips rocked and the moans that rolled from her lips merged into one soft sound of need. It didn't take long, her orgasm rushing up faster than it ever had and then she was there, balanced on the precipice.

And he moved his hands.

"No!" She couldn't help the moan that escaped her. So close. She needed him to touch her, stroke more. Take her over the edge and into the rolling abyss of pleasure that awaited when she fell.

He grunted, moving behind her, and then her attention was all on the broad head of his cock where it pressed against her. Not for long. Adjusting himself, he pushed his long, thick length into her in a single, hard stroke.

"Fuck!" she gasped, fingers curled into claws with pleasure. He was big, so big, but she loved the feeling of being stretched. The throb of her pussy around his cock. The friction the tight fit afforded. Even the burning pleasure-pain when he first entered her.

"That was the idea. Or did you have something else in mind?" As he spoke, he pulled back and thrust again, drawing out the tight, burning ecstasy of his initial penetration. She was back to biting her lip, trying to contain her sounds of pleasure.

With her bent over in front of him, he set up a hard and fast pace, slamming into her over and over. She couldn't move, but she didn't care. Her body was a mass of hypersensitive nerve endings all attuned to his every movement. Tightness coiled within her, drawing into a tight knot in her core.

Reaching around her, one large hand covered her left breast, tweaking and pinching the nipple. A line of fire arrowed down to her clit, making it throb, as though it and her nipple were connected. She panted, shoving her ass back against him with each thrust. That was it. Wouldn't take her much longer. Just a little more.

He reached around with the other hand, sliding it between her thighs and tweaked her clit.

It was all she needed.

She shattered, screaming his name as she came.

11

*W*hen Cat and Tarrick rejoined the rest aboard the vessel, they were well underway and everyone was gathered in the common area at the back of the ship. All eyes turned toward them as the door opened, and Cat ducked her head, cheeks flaming at the knowing looks the women shot them. The warriors were either clueless or far too worried about Tarrick's reaction to bat an eyelid.

They wore leather uniforms, but with the jackets unzipped to show their hard, sculptured chests. When they'd left their quarters, she'd thought Tarrick was just lazy. Now though, she realized it was more than that. The half-undressed deal seemed to be more akin to casual dress for them.

"Ey, ey...the lovebirds return," Kenna smirked as Cat slid into the seat next to Jess, which earned her a play cuff around the ear from Jane behind her. She ducked, laughed, and stuck her tongue in her cheek while hollowing the other in the universal gesture for a blowjob.

"There's always one." Cat sighed, shaking her head at the woman's antics and took the glass Jess held out to her. "What's this?"

"Tastes like lemonade," Jane answered, lifting her glass in salute.

"Just be careful and go slow. It's got quite the kick, as you can see."
She nodded toward Kenna, who bristled with indignation. "I am not
drunk!"

Her denial fell on deaf ears because right at that moment Laarn
chose to remove his jacket. Instantly he had the attention of every
woman in the room. Like Tarrick, he was tall, broad-shouldered and
heavily-muscled. Unlike Tarrick, he had shoulder length dark hair
that brushed his shoulders.

And scars.

Everywhere.

They crisscrossed his pecs and over his arms. Fine scars like lace
over his skin, old and faded, but that still looked painful. Farther
down, deeper marks highlighted his rib cage, also healed and old. A
single, thick scar ran down the center of his chest, reminiscent of old
style open-heart surgery back on earth. It trailed down, disappearing
under the low cut pants.

"Fucking *hell*..." Kenna murmured what they were all thinking.
How much had he suffered? And why?

Unable to tear her eyes away as Laarn folded his jacket and
turned to a kitchenette in the corner of the room, Cat leaned toward
Tarrick, seated next to her. "What happened to him?"

Tarrick leaned against the padded back of the seat, arm spread
behind her. "All healers have them. From their trials."

She looked at him, not bothering to hide her shock. "I thought
you said it was holo-stuff...simulation? That he wasn't actually hurt?"

"No, he wasn't. But the injuries were real to the mind, which
caused a reaction in the body." Tarrick's expression was neutral. "It's
why we never use lifelike avatars. It's the same technology. If we used
something that felt too right, too similar to our real bodies and the
machine 'dies' we'd die too."

The shudder rolled from her toes, raced up her spine, and
crawled over her scalp. "So becoming a healer could have killed
him?"

Tarrick's expression was blank and polite, but Cat was quickly
coming to realize the Lathar put up a mask when they wanted to hide

something, much like humans. She stayed silent and kept eye contact, a trick she'd learned years before. Most people felt uncomfortable and automatically filled the silence. A quick flare of lighter gold in his eyes told her that he knew what she was doing, but finally he gave a small nod of his head.

Not to be outdone by Laarn, Karryl started to strip his own jacket. Like the rest of the Lathar, he was tall and heavily muscled but... bigger. He made Laarn and Tarrick seem like greyhounds in comparison. Kenna, well through her glass of the alien lemonade, wolf-whistled in approval as the warrior strutted his stuff, eyes on Jane.

"See, female? Your companions find me appealing," he said, puffing his chest out.

Kenna muttered something, catching an elbow from Jess for it and toppled over backward off the bench.

Jane shook her head. "She's drunk. She'd find anything with a dick appealing."

"Hey!" Kenna complained from the floor. "I resemble that remark!"

"Karryl, if you're finished trying to show off?" Laarn's voice cut through the banter like a heated knife through butter. "I'm trying to show the females what food they're likely to be offered at the Emperor's court."

At the word *food*, the women in the room were all ears, even Cat. So far she'd eaten what Tarrick ate, which was some field ration slop that tasted a bit like porridge. After a couple of days on the stuff, she'd kill for something with a little more flavor and texture.

"Okay, these are all typical dishes at court," Laarn said as he started to place bowls on the counter between them. He moved quickly, with a quiet efficiency that was mesmerizing. With a quick glance up, he offered a small smile. "Come on, they won't bite."

Chairs scraped, glasses forgotten in the stampede for the counter. Even tipsy, Kenna managed to get herself off the floor and fought for a place near the food. The kitchenette counter was small, with a hot plate on one side and the bowls on the other. Laarn had put a pot on the hot plate and poured something gloopy and brown into it to heat before he turned back to them.

"This is *kervaas*." He pointed to the first bowl. The contents were gray, slimy, and wriggling.

"Ugh. Worms?" Jess wrinkled her nose in disgust.

"If that's what you call them." Laarn shrugged. "They grow on certain grasses and are highly nutritious. Gather enough and it'll keep a warrior going for a day."

"What's this?" Cat leaned forward to peer into the next bowl. It contained what looked like flat strips of dried meat, like jerky.

"*Veritan*," Tarrick answered for him, reaching over to snag a piece. He turned Cat toward him, offering it to her lips. "Try it, it's good."

She smiled and took a little bite. The taste of spice and sweetness exploded onto her tongue and she groaned. "Oh my god, that is *so* good. Guys, you have to try some of this."

The rest dived in, plucking strips of the meat from the bowl. Moans of appreciation filled the room. Laarn looked up and grinned at Karryl. "See, warrior? I can do with my cooking what you couldn't with all your posturing."

Karryl snarled, snapping something Cat couldn't pick up.

They went through several other bowls, with different forms of meat and some with salad and vegetables. Finally, Laarn set a plate on the table and reached for the pan he'd been heating. With careful movements, he ran a knife around the brown mass in the pan, then flipped it over and out onto the plate.

"*Cake!*"

"*Oh my god, is that chocolate cake?*"

"*Laarn, I think I love you.*"

The healer grinned, actually grinned, as he cut the cake and handed each of the women a piece. Cat cradled hers carefully. It was still warm, but not too hot to eat. Tentatively she broke off a corner and popped it into her mouth.

Heaven melted onto her tongue. Hot, delicious, sweet heaven. It was like the best, expensive chocolate cake she'd ever tasted that faded into a mousse when she chewed.

"Blow me, that is *the* best chocolate cake I've ever had!" Once again Kenna was the one to say what they all felt, with moans of accompaniment from the rest of them. Halfway through the cake, though, the Marine paused, then wrinkled her nose.

"How fattening is this?" she demanded suddenly, her focus intent on Laarn who was cutting more cake. "You guys are not like feeding us up or something are you?"

Laarn paused, surprise washing over his features. "Why would we want you as anything other than how you are?"

"I've seen it in the holos." Once on a topic, Kenna was difficult to dissuade. "Men who like bigger women. Feed them up and all that. Because I'll tell you something, I worked my *ass* off for an ass like this. Squats man, you have *no* idea how many squats. And I'm not having it all ruined because of your wicked chocolate cake."

Laarn looked confused.

"You mean will it make you gain weight? Highly unlikely, the active ingredient raises metabolism. It's why we don't cook it when operational. Our nutritional needs would go through the roof."

Cat blinked a couple of times as she mentally translated healer 'speak.' "You mean it's good chocolate cake? It makes you burn the calories you eat?"

Laarn tilted his head to the side as though he were working out her words. Then he nodded. "Yes. It will do that. Makes your body more efficient."

The women all gaped at him.

"Screw hot as hell aliens," Kenna said, taking another slice. "Man, you got every earth woman's dream right here... Chocolate cake that doesn't make you fat."

THEY HADN'T BEEN BACK to Lathar Prime, physically, for far too long.

Two days later, Tarrick and his warriors stood in the tiny airlock of the commander's transport. The human females were tucked into the middle of the crowded space as they waited for the door in front of them to cycle and open. There was far too much male in such an enclosed area. He could feel the same eagerness radiating from them that coiled within him.

The door clunked and he looked down at Cat standing next to him. A wash of pleasure and love rolled through him. He still couldn't believe how lucky he was. Couldn't believe he'd found the one woman in the galaxy who had been able to pull the mating marks to life within his skin. All he'd had to do was cross the galaxy and search a backwater system for her.

She smiled up at him, her eyes alight with intelligence and humor. With her traditional robes and cape, and her hair piled up to bare her slender neck, she looked so lovely, she took his breath away. Heat exploded through him like an energy blast and he had to fight the urge to drag her up to his cabin and have his way with her.

Again.

Before he could move though, the door clicked a final time and rolled open. His desire was overruled by his need to see how Cat reacted to his home planet. What would she think? Would she like it? Could she see herself living here?

"Oh my, it's beautiful." Hand raised to her lips, his little Cat moved forward to the edge of the airlock and peered out. She was quickly joined by the other females and Tarrick had to smile. They looked for all the worlds like *Deearin* kits about to escape their mother's den and venture into the world for the first time.

He hadn't let any of them see out any of the viewports as they'd landed. Instead, he'd kept the blast shields up so they'd get the full effect of seeing the Emperor's court for the first time. It appeared to have worked.

"It's like ancient Greece or something."

"Awesome columns. How high do you think they are?"

Tarrick half listened to the females chatter as he signaled his men to move. Absently, he wondered if all earth females talked so much. It was enough to give any warrior a damn headache. A constant stream of verbal...noise. But despite the fact they didn't seem able to keep silent, he was very aware they were moving as a military unit.

The one they called Jane had taken point, her odd-eyed gaze sharp and assessing as she looked around. Of them all, she was the least talkative. Tarrick flicked a glance to Karryl, who was paying more attention to the lithe human than on his surroundings. Perhaps that was a blessing. Karryl, while he had a heart of *siivas,* was famous for his short-temper.

In the middle were his own Cat and her friend, Jess, flanked on the other side by his brother. At the back, with Gaarn and Talat behind her, was the sassy-mouthed Kenna. He glanced over his shoulder to see her half turn, her keen gaze scanning the rear. She caught him watching her when she turned back and winked at him. Plainly she knew he knew what she was doing and didn't care.

Shaking his head at the odd behavior of human females, he turned and concentrated on getting them to the court and to the Emperor. Like the rest of his warriors, he bristled with weaponry. Court dress for a Lathar consisted of attitude, armor, and as many weapons as a male could carry. Although elegant, the Emperor's palace was a dangerous place. All warriors were armed—regardless of rank or status¬—and challenges were common. Extremely common.

Which meant no one was surprised when their path was blocked by a small group of warriors. R'Zaa. Their facial features were distinct. The warrior at the front Tarrick recognized. J'aett, the son of the clan leader.

"I heard you'd found females," he commented, his gaze assessing the humans. They stood still, not an ounce of subservience in their manners as they glared back at him. Not one of them gasped or backed up, making him proud. They didn't behave like the weak species the Lathar had originally taken them for.

Still didn't stop him wanting to spread J'aett's nose all over his face. Especially when he gave Cat the once over. But it was Jane, at the front of the group with her arms folded and a "fuck you" expression that caught his attention the most. Unlike the rest, she wore a strange combination of lathar and terran clothing and her bearing marked her as exactly what she was: a soldier.

The R'Zaa warrior stepped forward, reaching out to grab Jane. "I claim this one."

Karryl moved faster than Tarrick had ever seen him move, shoving between J'aett and his prey to knock the other warrior's hand aside.

"Too late, *draanthic*," he snarled. "She's already claimed."

The other warriors closed ranks around the rest of the females, and Tarrick shot a look at Jane, shaking his head to warn her not to argue Karryl's claim over her. Not here. Not now. The R'Zaa had almost as bad a reputation as the T'Laat. No human woman wanted to find herself at their mercy, not as a slave.

He didn't want any human woman being claimed outside the K'Vass until he'd had a chance to petition the Emperor to have their status as a lost offshoot of the Lathar confirmed. Once that happened then all Lathar would have to honor them, and to injure one would be punishable by death. A death he'd be happy to mete out personally, he realized. Somewhere along the way he'd become protective of the humans.

"Yeah?" J'aett wasn't put off that easily. He backed up a few steps, the warriors behind him scattering, and motioned to Karryl. "Then I guess I'll have to challenge you for her. Unless you don't think you're up to it..."

Karryl snarled and launched himself forward, blade in hand, accepting the challenge through action rather than words. J'aett met him mid-attack, twin blades flashing in the air as battle was joined. Karryl was bigger, but J'aett was lighter and faster. Tarrick held his position, hand itching to go for his own blades as the two fought, dancing around each other, but held off. All Karryl needed was one blow, a knockout, and it would be over.

But it didn't look good, not with the R'Zaa warrior dancing rings around him. Jane tried to leap forward to help, only Laarn's arm around her waist stopping her. Her features were wreathed in worry and fear. Not for herself, but for the big warrior being cut to ribbons by his smaller opponent. Tarrick blanked his smile. So, despite her protests, the human did have feelings for his warrior.

"Please," Cat tugged on his arm. "Aren't you going to help him?"

Tarrick shook his head. "Challenge fight. If we intervene, Karryl will be pissed. It will be like us saying he can't handle it. That he's not man enough."

"He's bleeding!" she protested, her stubborn lips setting in a line. "How can you stand there and not help him?"

"Seriously, Moore Cat," he allowed her a small smile, "he can take it. Believe me."

J'aett leapt, spinning in the air to land a hard kick across Karryl's jaw and for a moment, Tarrick thought that was it, the R'Zaa had actually gotten the better of the big warrior. Karryl grunted and fell to his knees.

"*NO!*" Jane bellowed, fighting Laarn's hold.

"You'll be mine, little one." J'aett took his eyes off the fallen warrior to leer at Jane.

Which was the moment Karryl made his move. Flicking his dark hair out of his eyes, he dropped to the floor and spun on his hands, twisting his body and scissoring his legs to tangle in J'aett's. The R'Zaa tumbled to the ground, Karryl over him in a heartbeat. Pinning J'aett's arms to the ground, he raised his fist. Before he could deliver the knockout blow though, one of J'aett's warriors pulled an energy pistol and aimed it at the side of Karryl's head. "Not so fast."

Tarrick and his men froze. This was not how challenge fights went. Karryl had won, all the rules stated as such, and for the R'Zaa to pull weapons was a clear violation of protocol. On an ordinary day, Tarrick and his men would happily take on the other clan, and anyone else who wanted to pile in, but now they had the females to protect... That changed things. He couldn't allow any of them to be hurt.

A flash of fabric fluttered in the corner of Tarrick's eye. Kenna stepped behind the R'Zaa warrior and pressed the muzzle of a pulse pistol firmly against the back of his skull.

Oh. Shit. Tarrick's eyes widened. This was not going to end well.

"I've never trained with these weapons, just on our type. At this range I figure it'll probably make a mess of whatever, if anything, you got in that pretty little head of yours." All traces of the joking woman Tarrick had seen before were gone. Her hand was unwavering and her voice cold as she spoke. "Now how about you let my friend's man go and I won't redecorate with your brains. How about that?"

Before anyone could react to Kenna's bold move, a cold voice cut through the tension.

"Would someone like to explain why this...woman is threatening to redecorate my outer courtyard?"

Tarrick closed his eyes.

The Emperor had found them.

Draanth.

$\mathcal{E}$veryone froze in place, like a holovid on pause. Kenna had her arm outstretched, the alien weapon looking heavy and clunky in her grip, its muzzle pressed against the skull of the alien who was about to shoot Karryl. Who had yet another alien warrior pinned beneath him. All in all, it looked like a scene from a space action-adventure movie.

Cat's gaze sought the owner of the voice. At the head of a crowd, he walked down the steps like he owned the place. Which he probably did, she thought as she realized he looked like Laarn. A *lot* like Laarn. But without the scars, a little bit older, and a helluva lot bigger. What was it with these damn aliens? Why couldn't they come in normal-sized, rather than big or freaking massive? Sheesh. And Laarn thought humans were a version of the Lathar? She didn't think so. She'd never seen any human guy as big as even the smallest Lathar. Ever.

The Emperor—because everyone bowed as he passed, not to mention Tarrick's description of his uncle, it had to be the Emperor—was stripped to the waist. A light sheen of sweat that said he'd been working out covered his skin.

"Kenna. Might want to put it away," Cat said carefully, watching the Emperor as he stalked towards their little group. The guy looked scary impressive. His handsome face, so like Tarrick's and Laarn's, was set in hard lines and his body coiled with power and aggression.

She risked a glance at the other woman to find Kenna hadn't moved. Where she'd gotten the pistol, Cat had no idea. The robes they wore were great for concealment so she could have lifted from one of the warriors at any point.

"Kenna?"

The Marine shook her head, not looking away from her target even though the curiosity had to be killing her. "No can do. He puts up first, or I swear to God, I'll ventilate his skull."

At a nod from the Emperor, another warrior peeled off from the group behind him. Like the big man himself, this one was also sweaty and stripped to the waist, but that wasn't what made the human women gawk.

He was blond.

The Lathar were almost universally dark-haired so to see one with what looked like peroxide blond short hair was startling to say the least. He moved with a dangerous grace, his heavily muscled body covered in tattoo-like designs. He wasn't young, his face lined with experience and a large scar carved a line over one cheek.

Reaching Kenna, he put a big hand on the pistol and pushed the muzzle aside. "No one will hurt the K'Vass warrior, little..." He looked down at her, then further down, taking in every aspect of her appearance. "You are one of the humans?"

Kenna refused to let go of the pistol, and a short struggle ensued, but the light-haired warrior won in the end and simply held the weapon out of reach.

"They are indeed," the Emperor strode forward, arms outstretched, "and they are welcome in my court."

He paused to cast a quick glance at the fallen warrior Karryl had pinned. With a curl of his lip that showed his disgust, he motioned for the warrior to rise. He did, slithering from Karryl's grip.

"You are a disgrace, J'aett R'Zaa. Using your warriors to end a challenge match in such a manner," he sneered. "Begone from my sight until you can conduct yourself with honor and be thankful I have not taken up the challenge on behalf of my kinsman."

The quick breath Tarrick sucked in told Cat those words were important. Leaning slightly to the side, she whispered, "I thought you said Karryl was related to you on your dad's side?"

Tarrick nodded. "He is, but by claiming kinship, Daaynal has raised our entire clan above the others, which includes Karryl."

Cat watched in carefully hidden amusement as the R'Zaa warriors scattered like fall leaves on the wind. They were obviously scared of the Emperor's wrath, and by the looks on their faces, terrified of the thought of ending up in a challenge match with him. She didn't blame them, danger and lethality oozed from the man's pores. Both he and his blond shadow were scary SOBs.

Daaynal turned to their small group and smiled as he spread his arms wide.

"Welcome to our lovely planet, Terran visitors. I apologize for not being here to greet you, but your arrival was a little sooner than expected." He shot a small, annoyed look at Tarrick, but it was more frustrated affection than the cold fury he'd treated the R'Zaa with.

Cat breathed a small sigh of relief. She had the feeling Daaynal was not a man to piss off.

"We made excellent time, Your Imperial Majesty," Tarrick replied. "And I assumed you would want to meet the human females as soon as possible."

"Yes, indeed. Come. Come." Daaynal shepherded them up the steps and through the now open double doors. Gone was the ice-cold warrior, his eagerness to get them inside giving him the look of an enthusiastic puppy.

They followed obediently, and Cat's eyes widened at the sheer luxury that met her gaze everywhere she turned. A far cry from the stripped down practicality of their ships, the palace was like something pulled from a dream.

Cool marble, or whatever the alien equivalent was, as far as the eye could see, with high ceilings and murals on the wall to rival any of the old Terran masters. Heavy drapes of gold and silver surrounded doorways and even the guards' uniforms while the same basic design as Tarrick and his men's, had embroidered panels, sashes, and braiding. Far from appearing the poor cousins though, Cat caught the guards eyeing the battle-scarred leather with envy.

"Ahh, here we are. Come in, please!" Daaynal shoved open a set of double doors at the end of a long hallway and led them into a large room. High vaulted ceilings met tall windows open to the outside air, drapes fluttering in the pleasant breeze.

The room was occupied, around twenty people lounging on low couches, talking softly. One off to the side was playing what looked like a harp. They were mostly male, but there were a few of the oonat females Cat had seen before.

"Crap, we've walked into a *TQ* photo shoot or something," Kenna, near the back of the group exclaimed, naming a popular fashion magazine. Cat had to agree. The men were gorgeous with the lean, lithe build of models paired with the natural good looks of the Lathar.

And they left her flat. Utterly devoid of emotion. They were all pretty, but their muscles, while toned, didn't have the battle-hardened appearance of the warriors. They seemed... soft in comparison.

"Out! The lot of you...freaking useless bunch of ingrates," Daaynal snarled, and the room cleared in seconds.

Cat watched them go, fascinated. For a culture that revered warriors, finding non-warriors was...strange. Particularly in the heart of the court.

"Who were they?" she whispered to Tarrick, but it was Daaynal who answered, turning to fix her with a direct look.

"Bloody useless. The sons of clan lords and others who owe me fealty. They're here to ensure their clan's...behavior, shall we say? Most of them have been at court since they were children."

She blinked. Now it all made sense. Warriors were dangerous, so if they hostages to ensure compliance, then Daaynal wouldn't want them trained in warfare.

"It seems..." She paused, looking for the right words, aware the

Emperor watched her with interest. "I feel sorry for them. Your culture revers warriors and they aren't allowed to aspire to that."

Surprise flickered in Daaynal's eyes for a moment, then he smiled, looking at Tarrick. "Perceptive. Is this your female?"

"She is, yes. Your Majesty, may I present Sergeant Cat Moore of the Terran base, Sentinel Five."

Unsure of the protocol, Cat took the hand Daaynal offered and attempted a small curtsy. She wobbled as she stood, catching a little smile on the Emperor's lips for a moment, but she refused to be embarrassed. How the hell should she know how to greet an emperor, especially an alien one? It wasn't like the Sentinel program ran "Alien Etiquette 101" or "Family faux pas: what to do when you meet your alien lover's royal uncle" now, was it?

"A pleasure to meet you, Sergeant Moore." Surprisingly, Daaynal didn't have any problems with deciphering human ranks and names. "Do you mind? I've never seen a human so close. Are you all this small?"

Stepping closer, he gripped her chin with strong fingers and tilted her head. Despite his size, his touch was gentle, but she did feel a little like livestock being examined. She held still, even though she wanted to squirm. Thankfully though, Daaynal's touch was impassive, not sexual, which helped her stay in place as he examined her face from all angles. Amusement filled her as she considered asking him if he wanted to check her teeth as well.

"I'm a little shorter than average for a woman," she replied, noticing he seemed just as fascinated with her hair as Tarrick had been. Perhaps it ran in the family. "But yes, we are representative of female heights. Men tend to be a little taller. Not as tall as the Lathar, though."

Daaynal nodded, his expression preoccupied.

"And they are completely compatible?" he asked Laarn, standing nearby.

"Totally."

She could feel the slight tension in Tarrick's body next to her, as though he didn't like the other male touching her. Lathar were highly possessive of their women it seemed.

"Good. Good." Daaynal nodded, his long hair dancing on his shoulders. "Nothing...strange going on down there?"

Her cheeks burned at the question as Daaynal waved at her genital region. He noticed, his gaze snapping back to her and he winked. "I don't suppose you'd like to strip so I can see for myself?"

"I'd rather not, Your Majesty."

She shook her head, her cheeks flaming. She had to be beet-red by now. The only person she planned on stripping for was Tarrick. In private though, rather than flashing her pink parts to anyone in the court who wanted to know the differences between Lathar boys and human girls.

"Perfectly understandable," he said with an easy smile. Charm and looks...add an emperor's, what, crown...throne...and that was a lethal combination.

"Totally compatible, even with their smaller size," Tarrick said, sliding an arm around Cat's waist and pulling her against him now that Daaynal appeared to have finished his inspection.

"*Especially* with their smaller size." Karryl coughed behind them, smothering his words.

Cat kept her smile in place, ignoring the comment. She enjoyed that size difference, thank you very much, but she wasn't about to tell everyone that.

Daaynal turned to Tarrick. "Show me."

It was an order, no more, no less. Letting go of Cat, Tarrick pulled back his sleeve and removed the bracer on his wrist. The marks were there, darker than they had been. Gasps echoed around the room.

"Fuck me," Karryl muttered aloud. "Are those what I think they are?"

Laarn stepped up on Tarrick's other size as the Emperor grabbed his brother's wrist. "I would need access to the main diagnostic suites in the Healer's Hall to confirm, but my suspicion is humans are a lost branch of the Lathar. Records indicate that millennia ago, several expeditions were sent out to seed far-flung areas of the universe.

Most we kept contact with, but at least three were never heard from again. My theory is humans are descendants of one of these expeditions, genetically adapted to be smaller in stature."

Daaynal shook his head, his expression one of wonder as he examined the marks on Tarrick's wrist from all angles. "Of course, whatever you need."

He lifted his head to look at Cat and once again she was struck by how much he looked like Laarn. With a better sense of humor. "Do you realize what this means?"

She shrugged, shaking her head. "All our bits fit together nicely?"

Daaynal chuckled, the tiny lines at the corner of his eyes crinkling. "No, my dear. It means you and your friends might well be the saviors of our race."

"You're getting married? Why didn't you say so?"

"I *thought* these dresses were way too fancy for a simple ball."

"Kenna...what would you know about balls? You bitched for a week straight before the last regimental ball, then got yourself thrown in the brig so you didn't have to go. Three hours of paperwork you cost me. *Three hours!* I should've just left your ass in there."

Cat stood by the window in the guest suite of the palace and let her friends' chatter fade into the background as they put the finishing touches to their outfits.

It was strange to think that a week ago she hadn't known either Jane or Kenna that well—just to nod and say hi in passing—but now she counted them among her closest friends. After all they'd been through together, she'd walk through hell and back for any of them and she knew they'd do the same for her.

They'd spent the morning being poked and prodded, then scanned and tested by Laarn in the Healer's Hall, so they had been thankful to escape to their suite for a light lunch.

When they'd arrived, they'd discovered a message from the Emperor that they were all cordially invited to escort Cat to a blessing of her union with Tarrick that afternoon. At the mention of the word 'wedding,' even the hardened Marines softened, Kenna diving into the garment bags that had been delivered with a squeal of delight.

"Ha!" Kenna threw back. "Well, look at who's all dolled up in a dress! Looking to catch some handsome warrior's eye, are we, *Major?*"

"Screw you, brat. If anyone's after catching a warrior's eye, it's you. What about that blond hottie? Xaandril or something? He seemed mighty taken with you when we arrived."

The conversation behind her devolved into good-natured insults and name-calling between the two Marines, who from what Cat could work out, had been friends for years.

The door opened and she turned in a swish of silken skirts as Tarrick's warriors filed into the room: Karryl, Gaarn, and the quieter Talat. She hid her smile as their steps faltered when presented with the vision of loveliness her friends presented. Because the way they looked now was a far cry from the bedraggled bunch they'd been after the attack on the base.

Military uniform wasn't the most glamorous at the best of times, but throw in an alien attack, panic, and a stay in holding cells, no one would ever look their best.

Now though, with all the preening and pampering of the styling team the Emperor had arranged—comprised of vaguely insectoid looking creatures who talked, *constantly*—they'd morphed from not-quite ugly ducklings into beautiful swans.

Like Cat, they wore Latharian gowns, but where hers was the deepest sapphire, theirs were an iridescent platinum. Far from washing out their complexions, as Jane had feared the moment she'd seen them. The shifting color suited all three. Although one size, the dresses were cut cleverly and didn't overpower. Somehow they managed to give the lithe Jane curves (And boobs. Something she'd remarked on at least twice, to Cat's surprise. It seemed even uber fit Marines had hang-ups about their bodies. Go figure.) and made the fuller-figured Jess gasp in delight and scurry between mirrors checking herself out. Kenna's sole worry had been where to stash her purloined pistol. Somehow she'd managed to keep hold of it after the altercation in the courtyard.

"You look…"

For once Karryl seemed lost for words as he approached Jane. Gone was the curt, overbearing manner, and the look of frustration he seemed to have permanently around her was replaced with one of awe.

"You can say it. She looks hot. If I were into women, I'd do her," Kenna broke in, grabbing Talat's arm as Gaarn extended his for Jess. Cat noticed Jess's hopeful glance toward the door. Perhaps looking for a particular healer?

"My lady," Karryl offered his arm. "Would you do me the honor of accepting my escort to the blessing?"

"I'd be delighted." Jane smiled and inclined her head graciously. The light caught the tiny silver flowers and leaves the stylists wound through her short hair.

With all the women partnered, Karryl turned to Cat.

"Your bond-mate awaits, my lady," he said with a small bow that surprised her. He'd never bowed to her before, or called her that. Did her marriage to Tarrick confer status within Latharian society on her or something?

With an out swept arm, the big warrior signalled she should precede him.

"A lady always walks alone to meet her mate, as an indication she has chosen him of her own free will."

Huh. Interesting, and different from the human custom of giving the bride away.

"And the honor guard?" She pointed out the three warriors.

"To ensure no one interferes with your decision," he replied, then his lips quirked. "Not even your mate."

That was a new one. Cat blinked. So they'd gone from slaves and having no choice, to a situation where she seemed to have all the power. All because of a few marks on Tarrick's wrist.

"And if I decided not to go through with it?"

"Then our duty as your guard is to take you away from the hall, by force if necessary." Karryl's smile grew broader, his relish at the idea of a fight clear, but it quickly disappeared. "Although I don't want to fight Tarrick and Laarn, so please don't do that."

Cat shifted her grip on the bouquet in her hands and shook her head.

"Don't worry. I have no intention of backing out now. A gorgeous guy who actually wants to get married and have kids... do you have any idea how rare that is on Earth? Most men run a mile at the mere thought of commitment."

All three warriors glowered, their opinion of Earth men obviously not high.

"Earth men are idiots," Talat rumbled, which earned him a chuckle from Kenna, who patted his arm.

"That they are, handsome. But don't worry, there are plenty of human women who will take one look at you and beg you to give them babies."

A distant sound, like a clarion call, stopped the conversation and Karryl urged them all toward the door. "Time to go. We do not want to be late, not with the Emperor doing this blessing."

"Good luck, Cat!" Jess called, ushered into line by Gaarn as they formed up behind Cat.

"Yeah, break a leg!" Kenna offered with a broad grin.

Jane rolled her eyes. "She's getting married, you idiot, not acting in a play!"

The doors opened and Cat stepped out. A sapphire carpet snaked in front of her so she followed it, her steps in the delicate sandals soundless on the plush surface. Guards resplendent in palace uniform lined the route to the throne room where the ceremony was to be held. They looked ahead, expressions and stances like stone, but she caught a few peeking sideways as they passed. Every now and then, one of the doors along the corridors cracked open and she spotted long-faced oonat servants peering through. Several gasped in delight when they saw her and she smiled, feeling like a real bride.

And she was.

The dress might have been sapphire rather than white or cream, but it fit her like a silken glove, the skirts swishing around her ankles before flowing into a train behind her. Her hair was gathered on top of her head in an elaborate updo, complete with a delicate tiara she'd been told came from Tarrick's family vault and she carried a bouquet in her hands. The tiny flowers looked like a cross between orchids and cherry blossoms—her two favorites. They were called Herris blossom and were apparently the symbol of the Imperial family. Only royal brides were allowed to carry them.

Huh. Her. A royal bride. Just three weeks ago she'd been convinced that the dire state of her love life meant she was destined to end up a crazy cat lady (substituting real cats with fluffy toy ones, because real cats on a station? Recipe for disaster.). Instead though, she'd hooked herself a hot, alien groom. But Karryl's words about this being her decision struck deep. Was she ready for this? Did they *need* to get married formally? Couldn't they just consider the marks on his wrist an engagement ring and date for a while?

Her heart twisted, rejecting all those ideas, and in one perfect moment of clarity, she realized why.

He'd kidnapped her, wanted her so much, he twisted the truth to get her, then saved her from one of his biggest enemies.

He'd killed that enemy for daring to lay a hand on her...

A wash of emotion filled her chest, the warm feeling filtering out to fill the rest of her body.

She loved him.

She was head over heels, hopelessly and totally in love with her alien lord.

Tears gathered at the corners of her eyes and she blinked rapidly to clear them. Alien makeup was probably waterproof, but she didn't want to take the risk and look anything other than perfect when Tarrick saw her in her finery for the first time.

Nerves assaulted her as the carpet led to a large set of double doors. The throne room. Tarrick waited for her on the other side.

Before they reached the doors, two guards either side moved forward to open them.

Shit. This was really happening. Cat trembled, forcing to hold tightly to her flowers in case she dropped them, she shook so much. She would walk through those doors and the Emperor would bless her union with Tarrick. From what she'd been told, the marks on his wrist meant they were already married, but apparently a blessing from his Imperialness himself conferred more status on their union. Made it *special*.

Personally, she thought their relationship was already pretty damn special. Tarrick's mating marks were the first since the last fertile Lathar female died decades ago. Ergo, special. No matter what anyone else thought.

The doors opened and a wash of noise hit her. What sounded like hundreds of people chattering, suddenly stopped to look toward the doors. Expectation filled the air, so thick she found it difficult to breathe.

They were all waiting to see her. Their first glimpse of a human woman.

"The Lady Cat Moore, of planet Earth," a loud voice announced and she walked through the door, her head held high.

Murmurs and gasps rolled through the masses either side of the aisle. Her heart tried to climb into her throat at being the center of so much attention. She focused on Tarrick's broad shoulders by the throne and started to walk. She could do this. Totally do this. Hopefully without tripping on her own skirts or otherwise making a damn fool of herself.

Her groom didn't turn, a Lathar tradition she'd been warned about, but Laarn did. His eyes widened and he leaned in to whisper something in his brother's ear.

Finally, she reached Tarrick's side and he turned his head. Emotion and reverence washed over his hard features.

"You look beautiful, Moore Cat," he whispered, reaching for her hand, his words unheard by anyone else as at that moment Daaynal stood.

13

"Warriors, welcome!" His voice carried the length of the hall. "Today we gather to celebrate a momentous event and one I didn't think we would ever see again. A true bonding."

Shock resounded through the hall in a wave of utter silence. A bonding hadn't occurred for decades. It required more than genetic compatibility, otherwise half the men in the room would have bonded to their Oonat broodmares.

Tarrick shuddered at the thought. To be bonded to a creature of such limited intelligence for the rest of his life...it didn't bear thinking about.

"Impossible!"

"How can that be?"

"She is no Lathar!"

"No marks, no bond!"

"This is an outrage!!"

Within seconds the assembled warriors had gotten over their shock and the protests came thick and fast. Tarrick closed his eyes. He recognized the loudest voice among them. Maal J'nuut was a purist, one who regularly petitioned the Emperor about the preservation of Lathar genetics. He and his clan of fanatics believed breeding with other races should be banned and the Lathar should only reproduce through cloning. As they did. It was widely known that the J'nuut eschewed the use of the Oonat, to avoid diluting their "pure" bloodline. The rumors even said Maal refused to allow his warriors Oonat for companionship and sexual relief.

Daaynal lifted his hand and all noise in the hall ceased. "As many of you are now aware, the K'Vass recently ventured into a backwater system and discovered a previously unknown to us species. One with a pleasing appearance and many females. As soon as contact was made, the healer with the K'Vass suspected that humanity—"

"Ha! *Humanity?* What kind of name is that?"

Daaynal, interrupted, glared at the commenter with an expression that would have frozen the fire-moons of *Dranratt.*

"As I was saying. Lord Healer Laarn K'Vass suspected humanity was genetically compatible with us."

Daaynal cast a glance down at Cat and smiled. "I am glad to say his suspicions are correct and Lord Tarrick bears evidence of this."

Stepping down from the dais, his uncle grasped Tarrick's arm and lifted it. His sleeve fell back, baring the marks on his skin. Murmurs of shock rippled through the crowds.

"A true bonding has occurred. Furthermore," Daaynal's voice turned to ice, "the entire human species is now under my protection. No clan is to invade their space, or raid any of their planets or installations. Punishment for such a transgression will be death. No challenge. No appeal, just execution. *Do I make myself clear?*"

There was no reply to the Emperor's announcement, not that Tarrick expected there to be. No one argued with such a direct proclamation, not from a man like Daaynal. Ever. He breathed a sigh of relief. With a few short sentences, Daaynal had secured the safety of the human race until proper alliances could be put into place.

"Right. Now to the matter in hand."

Daaynal stood before Cat and Tarrick and held out his hands. "Your hands please."

Without hesitation, Tarrick reached out, pleased to see Cat did the same. Her beauty always stunned him, but seeing her in the traditional robes of a Latharian bride took his breath away.

"Blood calls to blood and soul to soul," Daaynal intoned, his deep voice low and charismatic. "Soul calls to skin, woman to man, binding the halves of a whole together for all eternity. Lady Cat, do you take this warrior who bears your marks on his skin to bond-mate? To support and honor him for the rest of his life?"

She nodded, the light twinkling off the jewels in her hair. "I do."

Daaynal looked at Tarrick, his expression grave. "Lord Tarrick, do you take this woman who has called marks in your skin to bond-mate? To protect her and honor her for the rest of your life?"

"I do."

There was no other answer, he realized, standing there as Daaynal transferred their hands to one of his, binding them with a sapphire sash. Bonding them in the eyes of the ancestors.

"Then...as Emperor of the Lathar, I bless your bonding. May it bring much solace and be fruitful."

Tarrick leaned in to brush his lips over Cat's. Screw the warriors who watched, he had to touch her. She moved closer, her tiny body nestled against his and lifted her lips to his.

Before he'd registered the taste of her though, shots rang out in the hall. Energy blasts sizzled through the air, closely followed by grunts of pain and bellows of anger as warriors drew weaponry and fired back.

Tarrick whirled, shoving Cat behind him, out of danger. Fear for her pumped through his veins and in that moment he realized he would do anything, even sacrifice his own life, for her. She was his bond-mate, her life was his to protect...but it was more than that.

He loved her.

From the moment he'd laid eyes on her, he'd loved her. He hadn't realized it at the time, telling himself all sorts of lies to cover what his heart had always known. Had known from the first moment he'd heard her voice. She was the other half of his soul.

"What the hells is going on?" Daaynal demanded, his champion already at his side. Both warriors had weapons drawn, a pistol in one hand and a blade in the other.

"We will not stand for this insult!" a warrior screamed across the hall, voice raised over the sound of energy bolts. The J'nuut were gathered in a knot at the side of the room, firing wildly around them with their leader, Maal, yelling purist rants from atop a table. His face was purple, twisted with hatred as he glared across the throne room.

"*He* wishes to dilute our blood!" Maal screamed, pointing at Daaynal. "To have us consort with sub-Lathar creatures and create... abominations! Destroy what we are! He is not fit to be emperor! *Kill him! Kill them all!*"

"Well, he's a sandwich short of a picnic," Cat commented, peering around Tarrick's shoulder even as he tried to push her to safety with the other females. However, trying to keep the human females behind the relative safety of the throne was like trying to herd *viisnaas*. They'd formed themselves into a tight group, eyes bright and focused as the battle raged around them. Both Jane and Kenna somehow managed to acquire pistols, and were using the throne for cover as they fired into the J'Nuut. Each time they did, warriors fell.

"Damn good shots," Xaandril grunted, a rare show of approval from a warrior who hated pretty much everything.

"Down, stay safe, little Cat," Tarrick ordered, shoving Cat behind the throne. When she tried to follow him, he pulled her up for a brief, hard kiss. "Please, let me protect you."

"YEAH, HE'S A KEEPER," Jess commented as the two women crouched behind the throne as the battle raged in the hall. Concern threaded through Cat's veins as she peeked out from cover. Damn Lathar and their warlike nature, not even a wedding was sacrosanct.

She picked out Tarrick and his brother, just steps from the dais, fighting off what looked like a horde of the enemy all by themselves. They moved in perfect tandem, ducking and weaving around each other. Cat gasped as Tarrick turned his back on an opponent even as the warrior lifted a blade to drive it through his chest. Without missing a beat, Laarn twisted and blocked the blow, his return swing taking the other warrior's head off at the neck. The corpse had barely hit the floor before both brothers turned and fired, dropping two more warriors about to charge them.

But it wasn't all going their way. The Emperor and his men fought on the dais, but were being picked off by snipers from the other side of the room. A warrior to their left was hit, staggering backward against the wall, then slowly slid down. His eyes were wide and lifeless before he reached the floor.

Cat scuttled over and grabbed his weaponry, ducking her head as energy bolts slammed into the wall behind her. She threw the blade to Jess and checked the charge on the pistol. Nearly full. Good. They could at least defend themselves.

"They've bottlenecked reinforcements," Xaandril yelled across at Daaynal, the two big men protecting the area at the front of the throne. "And looks like the R'Zaa have allied with the purists."

"Excellent!" Daaynal grinned as he swung the massive blade he held and lopped the arm off a warrior trying to sneak up on him. "Some real opposition then!"

Neither looked worried, in fact, both looked like they were intensely enjoying themselves. Cat shook her head. Bloody Lathar.

"Contact at twelve o'clock," Jane yelled, as another wave of purists surged through the main doors at the end of the hall. Cat ducked out of cover, picked her target and fired. A purist fell, clutching his throat. She had to admit, as well trained as the Emperor's men were, the numbers were against them.

The situation looked dire. The end was nigh, and all that.

Then she spotted him. A single warrior, one of the R'Zaa she'd seen earlier, the ones disgraced by the Emperor, crept through the melee in the middle of the room. His attention was on Tarrick, his grip firm on the blade in his hand.

Her heart stalled. Neither Tarrick nor Laarn had seen him. A few more steps and he'd be in range. Yanking off her shoes, she darted out from behind the throne, yelling over her shoulder. "Cover me!"

They must have heard her, because energy bolts peppered the air around her as she darted through the seething mass, dropping any enemy warrior who got near her. She paid them no mind, her focus on the warrior who crept up on Tarrick, blade raised to plunge it into his unsuspecting back.

"Hey, asshole!" she called out and he whirled, eyes narrowing with malice when he spotted her. Cat's universe narrowed down to the alien pistol in her hand, hidden by her skirts, and her finger on the trigger.

She heard Tarrick's bellow, but not what he said. She was aware of the battle pausing around them as the R'Zaa bore down on her with death in his eyes.

"Say hello to your ancestors, human bitch!" he snarled, and charged.

In one smooth move, she lifted the pistol, aimed, and fired. Once, twice, three times. The first bolt hit the center of his chest, the second his throat, while the third created a starburst pattern in the middle of his forehead before the bolt shattered the back of his skull and gave him a red halo.

He staggered two more steps, then dropped like a stone at her feet. She looked down, feeling nothing at the sight of the body. He'd been about to kill her husband, on her wedding day.

Not. Happening.

"How about you say hi for me, asshole." She looked up and around. The battle had stopped, all the warriors looking at her in horrified fascination.

She smiled. "He wasn't on the guest list. Anyone else?"

The silence in the hall broke when Tarrick closed the distance between them and grabbed her upper arms, shaking her. "Cat! What the hell were you thinking? You could have been killed!"

His expression was furious, and his grip hard. She winced, trying to get free.

"In case it escaped your notice, saving your damn fool life!"

Their near shouting match was interrupted as combat bots crashed through the doors and windows, landing neatly to train weaponry on the remaining purists. There was a short fight in the corner which no one took any notice of, all eyes on the two of them in the middle of the room.

"Or would you rather I have let you be killed?" she challenged, knowing she was pushing it, but dammit, a girl had to lay down some laws. What better day to do it than on her wedding day. Besides, she hadn't promised to obey him, had she?

"Damn annoying humans." His expression shifted, his lips threatening to quirk into a smile and before she realized what he was about, he bent and threw her over his shoulder.

"Tarrick, you asshole! Put me down this instant!" she demanded, beating his broad back with her fists. Not that she thought it would make any difference.

"Problem with your bond-mate?" Daaynal inquired, his deep voice projecting amusement. Cat twisted in Tarrick's grip, trying to look at the Emperor.

"Make him put me down. Now!"

"I'm sorry, my lady, but as the lord's bond-mate, it is up to him to... errr, discipline you for any transgression of our laws."

Crap. What law had she broken now?

Tarrick bowed and she squeaked, clutching at his waist so she didn't fall. His arm was firmly over the back of her legs though, so she remained securely in place.

"Thank you, Your Majesty. If I may take my leave with my... wife?"

"Oh, *now* I'm your wife, am I? I was just damn annoying when I was saving your life!"

Daaynal answered as though she hadn't spoken. "Of course. Enjoy the rest of your bonding day."

"Thank you, we will." With that Tarrick turned and strode from the hall. Cat managed to wave at her friends, all clustered by the throne with weapons in their hands. Jess waved back just as the doors closed cutting off Cat's view of them.

"Hey! Put me down!"

Her demands were met with silence as Tarrick strode through the palace corridors. Combat bots lined them now, as well as more guards, no doubt as a result of the purist attack.

It didn't take them long to get wherever they were going, Tarrick shouldering open a door and barking an order at the bots outside.

"Now, my little mate..." He slid her down the front of his body, slowly, making sure she felt every hard muscle of his big frame. His eyes sparkled with amusement and something darker. More heated. More volatile. "How should I punish you for putting yourself in danger?"

Despite his teasing words, his hand shook when he lifted it to stroke her cheek. Stark fear eclipsed the desire in his eyes for a moment.

"Please, Cat. Never do that again. If anything were to happen to you...it would kill me. I..." He swallowed and gathered himself, looking her in the eye as serious as though he were about to go into battle.

"I love you, little Moore Cat, and without you I am nothing. I could not go on. I need you."

Tears of emotion welled in her eyes, making her vision waver.

"I'm sorry...say that again?"

He loved her? She knew he cared for her, that he couldn't get enough of her, but...loved her? She hadn't seen that coming. She didn't think the Lathar even had a word for it.

"I need you."

Stubborn man.

"No, no. Not that part. Well, I like that part, but say the bit before it again?"

"If anything were to happen to you, it would kill me?" His lips began to curve, amusement heating his alien gold gaze again. Bloody man was teasing her.

"Yes...go on."

He smiled, bent at the waist to scoop her up into his arms and carried her toward the big, circular bed in the middle of the room. "Cat Moore, lady of my heart, I love you. I've loved you since the moment I first saw you, and I will continue to love you until the end of my days. How's that?"

She sighed, reaching up to turn his face toward her as he stopped next to the bed. "Perfect. Now, Mr. Moore Cat...how about you kiss your wife?"

And he did, sealing their bonding with a kiss as he laid her on the bed. Following her down, his lips didn't leave hers. Heat enveloped them, their hands everywhere, peeling clothing away to reveal skin until they were both naked on the bed.

Cat gasped as he parted her legs with a knee, sliding between them to shelter in the cradle of her thighs. Big hands swept the hair away from her face, each touch a promise, each kiss along her throat an oath.

Reaching between them to grasp his freed cock, he rubbed the broad head between her pussy lips. She was already slick, wet for him, and the sensation of sensitive flesh sliding against sensitive flesh made them both gasp.

"Please, now..." she begged, her arms around him to hold him close. "Make me yours."

He pulled back to look her in the eye, his expression open and loving as he looked down at her.

"Mine," he murmured as he pushed forward and claimed her in one slow slide of pleasure.

"Now and forever more. Mine."

"Yours," she agreed, closing her eyes and wrapping her legs around his hips.

From her greatest fantasy and worst nightmare, she'd found the best thing any woman could wish for...

Her soul mate.

∼

CLAIMING HER ALIEN WARRIOR

WARRIORS OF THE LATHAR: BOOK 2

MINA CARTER

1

*L*ittle green men weren't so little.

Or green.

A member of the Terran Military Defense Force all her life, Major Jane Allen had expected to be involved in a first contact situation at some point. She hadn't, however, expected the Lathar. Somehow, she doubted that *anyone* expected the Lathar.

They were less little green men and more large, ripped, scarily-attractive alpha male warriors hot enough to make any red-blooded woman weak at the knees. Even one mid-divorcee, who sworn off men, of any species, for life, like her. She had to admit, they were nice to look at. Considering she was a guest on the Latharian home world, it was a good thing she found them appealing.

"No, Your Majesty. *One,* two, three...*one,* two, three...that's it. Perfect."

Jane looked across the room. Kenna, formerly a Marine under her command, and now one of the four women visiting the Latharian home world, was teaching the emperor, Daaynal, how to waltz. Jane's lips twisted into a small smile.

Like most of the Lathar, Daaynal wore leather armor and heavy combat boots. With the warrior's braids in his long hair, and a face that could have coined the phrase "wickedly handsome" he made an odd sight with Kenna in his arms. Especially as she wore the flowing skirts traditional for Latharian women but with a blaster strapped to her waist.

She and Kenna were living proof you could take the girl out of the Marines, but never the marine out of the girl.

Daaynal was a quick study, his hold and steps perfect within minutes to spin and twirl Kenna around the room. A large room, it was part of the emperor's personal chambers and grandly decorated. Jane lay on a luxurious couch, full after the excellent food at lunch and watched the dance lesson.

Daaynal, she'd decided within minutes of meeting him, was a delight. Handsome, charming...and ruthless. No one kept such a high position in a warrior society where assassination was a viable promotional tactic unless they would do whatever it took to stay there.

He might have Kenna and Cat enthralled, but Jane had seen enough of his type during her long career to have her head turned by a pretty face and hot body. As if to prove her point, Daaynal caught her looking at him as they turned in front of her couch and winked.

She grinned and winked back. He knew what she knew about him and didn't care. He also thought he had her worked out.

Oh no, handsome. We're just getting started.

Talking of good-looking faces, it was almost time for her comm call with her liaison at Terran Command. The highlight of her day. Not. Myles Fuller was not her favorite person. He was too cookie-cutter career track officer for her liking. One who had his eye on a political career and using military service to pad his resume. A service record always looked good on the campaign trail. Plus he had a father with enough brass on his collar to make sure little Myles was in no danger of ever setting foot on a battlefield.

Good. Because he was the sort of rich, entitled asshole playing soldiers she fucking hated. The sort who'd hole up safe in their offices during the colony wars while real soldiers did the dying. Soldiers like her brother, who'd never returned.

Sighing, she levered herself off the couch.

"With your permission, Your Majesty, I have a prior appointment to attend to."

"Of course, of course!" Daaynal replied as he and Kenna breezed past. "I look forward to the pleasure of your company at the banquet this evening."

Ugh, more food. She doubted she'd be able to eat another thing this week, but she bowed anyway and backed out the door.

Her boots rang out against the polished floor of the corridor as she headed toward her quarters. As honored guests, the human women had suites near the emperor's rooms. Security into the wing was high, as it should be after the purist attack at Cat and Tarrick's wedding. No one knew when and where they'd strike again, but Daaynal was taking no chances with the human women. Jane approved. One thing she'd learned about fanatics during her long career was they were unbalanced as hell and never, ever, gave up.

She sighed and ran a hand through her hair. A close-cropped blond pixie cut, it fascinated the servants. She'd stopped them putting flowers and jewels in it. They'd finally realized she took them out within minutes anyway.

The palace reminded her of old movies about ancient Rome. It was all white columns and gauze drapes. She half expected a bunch of giggling handmaidens in togas to walk by. Instead, a broad-shouldered figure in leather armor rounded the corner.

Recognition hit. Karryl K'Vass.

Suppressing the quiver of awareness deep in her stomach, she kept walking. Karryl was one of the warriors who'd attacked and boarded the base she'd been stationed at, Sentinel Five. Even though she and the rest of the personnel aboard had put up a good fight, superior weaponry had won the day and the Lathar had taken them all prisoner. Not before she'd given them a damn good run for their money though. She and her unit had holed up in the central section of the base and made a right nuisance of themselves to the invaders.

Then... Karryl had happened.

She studied the warrior walking toward them. Taller than most Lathar, he was well-muscled with inky-black hair she itched to run her hands through. He had beautiful turquoise and violet eyes that should have looked out of place on such a strong face, but suited him to perfection. His battered leather armor fit him like a second skin, its only ornamentation the broad dull-gold sash across his chest. It marked him as something similar to a security officer.

A security officer with a face like thunder.

Uh oh.

He marched up to her, stopping barely a foot from her to loom dangerously. The moment they'd met, the big Lathar had tried to lay claim to her. Tried and failed. Since then he'd tipped between charming in an effort to get her to accept his claim, and frustration when she wouldn't. From his dark expression, looked like today was the latter.

"Why didn't you tell me you had a mate?"

MAJOR JANE ALLEN, warrioress from Earth, was the bane of Karryl's life.

Slender and lithe, she had cropped light hair an almost white color he'd never seen before but it was her eyes that mesmerized and frustrated him in equal measures. Different colors, one blue and one green, they met his gaze head on with a firm expression and steely disposition he'd struggle to find in many warriors.

He waited for a second and there it was, the slight uplift of her left eyebrow that either showed curiosity, or she thought he was a freaking idiot. He had no idea half the time which it was. Probably both.

"Why didn't I tell you I had a mate?" Her voice was low and melodious, with a pleasing timbre that stroked along his senses like a caress. "Perhaps because I don't?"

He bit back a sigh of frustration.

"Your base records say otherwise. They say you are mated to an Admiral Scott Johnson."

He almost snarled the words. Fury surged through him at the thought of the slender female in another man's arms. *His* woman. He'd wanted her from the moment he'd seen her, crouched behind a makeshift barricade on the base, bellowing orders as she and her men fought the Lathar boarding parties.

Not expecting women on the human base at first, he'd thought the higher-voiced, slender-figured warrior was a youth. Her face shielded by a cap, her body armor had hidden any hint of her female figure. The battle had raged back and forth. He'd been impressed with the youth's training and command over his men. It wasn't until she'd removed the cap he realized his opponent was female. Their gazes met across the battlefield and he'd known. This woman was his, sent by the ancestor gods to be the other half of his soul.

His own little warrioress.

He fought the urge to shake his head. That any society with fertile females would send them into battle was incomprehensible to him. Females were to be pampered and protected, cosseted and looked after... Not allowed to put themselves in harm's way.

But as much as he tried, Jane resisted all his attempts to pamper or protect her. She seemed to delight in thwarting his efforts to claim her, as though she found them, and him, amusing.

"They do, do they?" She folded her arms over her chest and the movement pulled the fabric of her tunic tight across her breasts.

He tried to ignore it, really he did, keeping his eyes level on hers, but the effort cost him. Unlike the other human women, Jane had not adopted the flowing robes of a latharian woman. Instead, she wore an earth top that bared her arms, tucked into a pair of reenaas combat pants, the hardy material conforming to her curves in a way that made his mouth water. Combat boots and a heavy blaster pistol on her hip completed the picture.

His jaw ached and he half lifted a hand to rub at it as he remembered just how fast she could move, and what one of those boots felt like jammed under his chin.

"Yes, they do."

He folded his arms to match her posture. She was shorter than he was so he had to look down at her to glare, but he wasn't under any illusion he had the upper hand. Sure, he was bigger and stronger, but she was fast and mean as a liras snake. If she'd been male, she'd have made the perfect warrior.

Humans didn't call themselves warriors. They used words like *soldier* and *marine* instead. It all amounted to the same. From what he could work out, Jane was a famous warrior on her home planet. The standard to which all female warriors aspired to, probably half the men as well.

"Well, I guess we still are then." She shrugged. "At least until I sign the divorce papers. I was going to, but then these asshole aliens blew holes in my base."

Her words rocked Karryl. He'd been expecting a denial, some story about records error... that she had never accepted this Admiral Johnson's claim over her... Not a calm confirmation she was, in fact, mated. Which meant, under the terms of the fledgling agreements between their peoples, she could leave Lathar and return to Earth any time she chose.

Unlike an unmated woman, she didn't have to consider any warrior's claim. Even his.

For a week she'd dodged his attempts to claim her. He'd made no pretense of his interest. He'd played nice, been polite, tried to understand her culture was different from his... All the time she'd known she could just laugh and walk away.

"No," he snarled as rage clouded his mind. "Not his. Mine."

Reaching out a hand, he cupped the back of her neck and hauled her up against him. She hit his chest with a gasp, her eyes wide. Good. Finally, he'd surprised her.

"Karr—"

He didn't let her finish, crushing her mouth beneath his. The first taste of her lips almost unmanned him. She might have been forged in the fires of combat, her body all lean lines and toned muscles, but her lips were a different story.

Soft under his, they were as delicate as a *quuarrian* fruit. She'd frozen, hands on his broad chest and he braced himself for a hard knee to the groin. She was not a woman to let an assault on her person go unpunished.

Determined to experience as much as he could before she pushed him away, he moved his lips over hers. Tasting, exploring... needing. Desperate. He needed to remember this. Imprint what it felt like to hold her in his arms, to feel her soft lips under his. Because she would push him away, he knew she would. If she found him suitable as a mate, then she'd have already accepted his claim.

Her lips parted on a soft moan and offered him a glimpse of the seven heavens. Stunned for a second, he didn't move, then all his male instincts roared into life. With a growl, he tilted his head and plundered her lips. The warmth and sweetness of her mouth almost brought him to his knees.

Sliding his tongue against hers, he sought her flavors. The sweet fruits and wine they'd dined on for lunch combined with something else...something haunting and unique. Within a heartbeat he knew one kiss would never be enough. He could kiss her for this lifetime and the next, but it still wouldn't suffice. With one kiss, she'd made him an addict, seeking that next hit until the day he died.

"No..." She snatched her lips from his with a gasp, looking up at him with wide, dark eyes. For a moment, he saw desire and need before her expression shuttered again. "No. We can't."

"What?" His demand was barked as he gripped her upper arms. She'd surrendered to him, he'd felt it, but now she was saying no?

She looked away, trying to wriggle free of his hold and her cheeks turned bright pink. Since he'd met her, she'd been captured, held prisoner, fought her way out of an enemy ship and almost killed by purists and never once had he seen her bat an eyelid. But now she looked rattled. By him. By what they'd shared.

"You prefer women."

It was the only explanation that made sense. Her brow furrowed as her gaze snapped to his. "What? Don't be ridiculous. I was married to a man. I like men plenty enough."

"Then what?" he demanded, shaking her a little by her upper arms as his anger got the better of him.

Her eyes shimmered with something, but the expression disappeared before he could analyze it. "Have you ever thought I might not be into *you?*"

～

OH CRAP, she shouldn't have said that.

Jane leaned against the door inside her quarters and took a fortifying breath. The stunned, then hurt, then furious look on Karryl's face when she'd lied and told him she didn't like him had cut her to the quick. She *did* like him, way too much for comfort. That was the problem.

Well, no, that wasn't the real problem. The real issue was she had morals. And she was a spy. She wouldn't, *couldn't*, use Karryl's feelings against him like that.

The soft *ping-ping-ping* of the comm center in the corner of the room called for her attention. She sighed. Time for her scheduled call with Terran Command. She had to report in every day to let them know more about the alien culture she was immersed in.

What they really wanted to know was how to defeat the Lathar.

Heart heavy, she walked across the room and slid into the seat in front of the console. A touch on the screen activated it. Myles smiling face filled the screen. She smiled a false smile. If the guy were in the room, she'd break his fucking nose.

"Greetings, Major Allen. How are we today?" he asked, rubbing his ear. "I hope you and your lovely companions are having a pleasant break on Lathar Prime."

His words were in code, a predefined speech pattern and set of phrases all high-level command officers knew by heart for just such instances as these. *Translation: Sit-rep.*

"Doing well, thank you, Colonel. And yourself? How's your lovely wife?" Her words followed the same protocol as she flicked her gaze to the top right corner of the screen. *No change. Nothing to report.*

She didn't have anything past the information she had already given them. As charming as the Lathar were, they were careful to keep guests out of sensitive areas. So far, she hadn't been able to gather any information on military numbers or weapons capability.

Myles's expression darkened for a second. "Oh, I'm afraid she's not been well..." *Information required urgently.* Yes, asshole, she knew that. "So she's taken a short break to my uncle's cabin near the lake." *Defense perimeter on high alert.* "If she doesn't get better soon though, I'm insisting she go to St. Michaels."

Shit. Ever the professional, she kept a straight face at the last line. The Terran defense perimeter, comprised of bases and automated defense satellites, worked on a series of named levels. On a normal day the alert was low, at level George, but it went up through Jeremy, Roxanne (she'd love to know who got that one in) and up to Michael. If the defense net was that high, it meant the president had authorized nukes.

"Are you sure that's a good idea?" she frowned. *Stand down, I got this.* "I've always found Dr. Roxanne at All Angels to be an excellent doctor."

Myles rubbed at his chin. "You think? We'll see how she rallies in the next few days. If she doesn't come through then, I'm going to take her to St. Michaels."

She nodded. "Understood. Please pass on my regards to her."

They weren't going to let this go, so the clock ticked. Find out something they could use, or they were arming nukes. And if they fired nukes at the Lathar, long-lost genetic relations or not, humanity was fucking toast.

"Of course, Terran Command out."

She sat for a moment and closed her eyes as tiredness washed over her. President Halland had always been an asshole, but she couldn't believe he'd be stupid enough to arm the nukes. It shouldn't have surprised her. Once a person gained enough power, they seemed to stop listening to common sense and believed whatever their yes-men told them. After his mismanagement of colony farming resources, Halland would never be re-elected so a war was his best bet for retaining power.

With a sigh, she stood and brushed nonexistent lint from her pants and headed for the door. Damned if she did, damned if she didn't, but to prevent an all-out war, she needed to find something to give to Myles.

2

The emperor had summoned him. A private audience.

Pride filled Karryl's chest as he strode along the corridor heading for the Imperial War room. He'd never been summoned personally. He'd only seen the emperor as part of a group under Tarrick's command. He'd be surprised if Daaynal had even known his name before the fight in the courtyard with the R'Zaa, so it was a sign of his growing standing in the court. First Daaynal had publicly declared him a kinsman and now this?

He entered the war room to find it empty. Face set in implacable lines, he scanned the large room, taking in the massive holo-table and the arching windows that gave a view of blue skies overhead. They didn't show the real sky. Buried beneath the palace, the war room was an impenetrable bunker the emperor could direct his armies from. The windows gave the place a little light, and as the holo display from the table could be extended; they served a functional purpose as well. With one command, the emperor could see the view from any Lathar ship or installation.

A warrior at the far end of the room stepped forward from a shadowed alcove and cleared this throat. Karryl's attention snapped to him. Unlike the other guards in the palace, he wore the insignia of the emperor's own guard.

"This way, *deshenal*," he said with a small bow, pointing to the door behind him. "His Majesty is waiting for you in his inner office."

Deshenal. Honored warrior. It was an old term, not used lightly or without the emperor's command. Karryl couldn't help his chest puffing out with yet more pride as he walked across the room toward the door. He was a male on the up and up, with a good reputation and the favor of the emperor himself.

Anger and frustration rolled through him in equal measure, tightening the muscles in his shoulders and neck as he clenched his hands into fists. Why couldn't Jane see he'd make a good mate? That he had the standing and power to protect and nurture her?

"Have you ever thought I might not be into you?"

The words slammed through his memory, cutting him to the soul. His boots stomped onto the carpet in the short corridor behind the war room as though they were waging war on the plush pile. Perhaps he should look at other earth women... Palace gossip had it that Daaynal planned to send a diplomatic mission to the human's home planet. There were plenty of women there, and from what the most talkative of the human women, Kenna, had said, many human women would jump at the chance to be a warrior's mate.

The door at the end of the corridor opened. He walked through, a little surprised there was no guard. As soon as he entered the small room he understood why.

Daaynal was not alone. The Emperor's Champion, Xaandril, leaned in front of a console, his big, scarred hands against the smooth surface as he glared at the screen in front of him. A tall, powerfully-built warrior, he was both Daaynal's champion and the man's shadow. Where the emperor went, so did Xaandril.

"It has to be a code," his voice was deep and full of gravel. He flicked a glance up and speared Karryl with a direct look that made him shiver. "Welcome, K'Vass. Come in, don't lurk in the shadows."

Karryl stepped forward, not wanting to be seen as lurking like a coward or to anger Xaandril. When he was a kid, he'd been brought up on stories of the great war hero, Xaandril. He was a war General. A hero of the Battle of the Nine Wastes, where the Lathar defeated the *Ovverta,* a barbaric race who slaughtered other races for fun.

They'd been the biggest threat the Lathar had ever faced. Now they were all but extinct thanks to Xaandril. Since the man had lost his mate and young daughter to an *Ovverta* attack, Karryl didn't blame the man for his bloodthirstiness where the vile creatures were concerned.

"Thank you, my lord." Karryl inclined his head to Xaandril, then turned his attention to Daaynal and added a small bow. "You wished for my presence, Your Majesty?"

"Indeed." Unlike earlier in the day when he'd hosted a lunch for their human guests, Daaynal was not smiling. He pointed to the screens the two senior Lathar were looking at. "Watch. This may be of interest to you."

Xaandril turned the screens so they could all see, and Karryl stilled. An image of Jane was frozen on the screen, her face set in what he could tell was a false smile. A flick of Xaandril's fingers and the holo-screen expanded to show a human male in a uniform. It was different than the one Jane or the men on the base had worn, with more fancy bits. It had to be a dress uniform since it would be useless in battle for anything other than making its wearer a prime target.

"The human woman, Jane Allen's, call back home," Daaynal said.

"You're spying on her?" Karryl hid his surprise behind a bland expression. They had to have hidden cameras in her quarters. He knew enough about her to know that if she'd found them, she'd be as mad as a *draanth* and have destroyed them already.

Daaynal inclined his head. "Indeed. It seems our beautiful little human warrior is keeping secrets."

Anger burst through him with the force of an energy blast. *His* warrior, not Daaynals, not anyone else's. His alone. He fought the blaze of fury and the need to introduce Daaynal's face to the console several times. He was a good warrior, fast and merciless in battle, but he was under no illusions. A physical attack on the emperor would end with him getting his ass handed to him on a plate and a prolonged stay in the med bay before his execution. If Daaynal was feeling charitable. If he weren't, then Karryl would die right here in this room. Slowly and painfully.

It answered a question though. The reaction to the thought of someone else claiming Jane as theirs meant he wouldn't be looking for another female on earth. He didn't want another female. He wanted this one. Her.

He looked at the screen again, studying the male. His rage simmered within. Was this her mate? Was that who she called when she excused herself to "report to Terran Command"? The male was smooth-skinned and plastic-looking, smaller in stature than any Lathar. He didn't look like he'd ever seen a battlefield in his life. She preferred that?

"Who is he?" He kept his voice level with supreme effort. All he wanted to do was reach through the screen and smack the ever-loving *draanth* out of the guy.

"A Commodore Myles Fuller."

Karryl let go a sigh of relief. Not Admiral Scott Johnson then. This wasn't her old mate. Good, he wouldn't have to track this one down and remove his spinal column from his body.

"See here and here?" Xaandril activated the recording, pointing out two time stamps. They stood in silence listening to the two humans talking. It seemed to be a harmless conversation about Fuller's wife.

"She sounds normal, other than a little stilted. Have you considered she might not like this Fuller?"

Xaandril shook his head. "It's more than that. I ran their conversation through several algorithms against the databases your war group recovered from their base and two words stand out: Roxanne and Michael."

Karryl shrugged. "What do they mean?"

Daaynal folded his arms, feet spread in a classic at ease posture. "They're names, but they're also part of the human defense system. The names of alert levels. From what we can work out, the humans have armed their crude nuclear capabilities. Which, as I'm sure you're aware, is considered an act of war by intergalactic convention."

"Shit."

Everything within Karryl went stone cold. If that's what the humans had done, then they were fucked. By all the laws of the combined species within the galaxies, just arming "dirty" ordnance like nuclear weaponry was cause to wipe a planet out. They didn't even need to get close to do it. A terraforming warhead from deep space would destroy anything on the planet's surface, wiping the slate clean, then forces could swoop in and pick off any colonies or space stations.

"She appears to be arguing against it," Xaandril mused, rubbing his chin. "So perhaps her punishment should be less severe..."

Daaynal nodded. "Agreed, maybe five lashes of the energy whip instead—"

"Wait, what?" The words escaped Karryl's lips before he could stop them. "We're considering punishing a *female*? A fertile female from a genetically compatible species? For what? For arguing against her superior officer arming nuclear weaponry?"

Both warriors looked at him. It was like being stared at by two *keelaas* snakes. Large enough to swallow a man whole, and with a necrotic bite, they were as scary as hell.

"He seems to want something from her. The only thing she can give them is information. On us. She's spying for them." Daaynal's voice was level, but Karryl got the feeling this was a test. That his reactions now would change things.

"Then we feed her misinformation."

Crap that sounded like he was giving the emperor himself orders. It was too late to back out now. He had to follow through. "We create a situation with the promise of what she needs, then feed her *draanth* shit."

Daaynal's face split into a broad smile and he looked at Xaandril in triumph. "You owe me ten *lindari*, old man. I told you he'd protect his woman *and* have a sensible idea."

Xaandril grumbled and dug in his pocket for a credit slip. He slapped it into Daaynal's hand. Karryl blinked in surprise. He didn't know what shocked him more; the fact the two most senior warriors in the empire were betting for small change, or that the emperor had bet on *him.*

"Okay, down to business." Daaynal flicked out a chair and shoved it on its rollers toward Karryl. "We need to work out how to tempt your little human warrior."

THE LATHAR WERE A CONTRARY RACE. All war-like one moment, then the next they took a pleasant afternoon ride into the countryside like they were in some Regency novel.

"This is lovely, isn't it? I love the colors of the flowers they have here," Cat commented. The four women were safely tucked into a carriage rather than given mounts. Kenna had argued, as usual, saying she was a more than competent equestrian back on earth and that the horses had six legs rather than four was no problem.

Jane hadn't argued. She'd never been the horsey type anyway, and the fact the monsters the Lathar rode had teeth like vampires' and claws to boot, meant she wasn't likely to change her mind soon. At all. Ever.

The trouble was, how the hell was she going to get any intel from a carriage?

"The flowers are pretty," she replied, sitting up in her seat to look ahead. They were traveling faster than she'd thought possible and the horse-creatures' six-legged gait was almost beautiful. She'd had to look down to make sure they didn't have wings on their feet or something as strange, but no, they ran just like earth horses, only a lot faster.

"Looks like we're slowing down."

The warriors around them tightened their reins, pulling their steeds to a trot then a walk at the top of a rise. Jane looked around and couldn't help sucking in a breath as the carriage pulled to a stop. The alien countryside lay beneath them, a jade and turquoise masterpiece. A swathe of golden-leaved trees cut an arc across the landscape with the white splendor of the distant palace like the jewel in a crown.

"It's beautiful," she breathed, her mission forgotten for the moment. How many humans had seen something like this... The sheer beauty of an alien planet. She'd been on other planets before, but the colonies weren't anything like this. They were dull, drab places full of broken-down people desperate for a better life than being crammed into slums back on earth. Only the wealthy got to live in places like this with open skies and vegetation.

"I'm glad you approve of my home."

A deep voice beside her made her turn in surprise to find Karryl at the side of the carriage. He extended a hand to help her down and the side stair slid down to allow her to step out. Putting her hand in his larger one, she suppressed her shiver at the latent strength she felt.

He was a large man, strong and so gentle at the same time that she didn't know how to react to him most of the time. But something was different, his easy smile the same, but the expression in his eyes guarded and shuttered.

Shit. She'd hurt him when she'd said she wasn't into him.

Pausing on a step, she looked him in the eye. "Karryl, I apologize for what I said earlier. I didn't mean the insult or to be cruel."

He shrugged. "Think nothing of it. Can I persuade you to accept my company for the afternoon?"

"Of course, I'd be delighted."

Taking the rest of the steps more delicately than her heavy boots and combat pants would suggest, she smiled up at him. "Your planet is lovely. Did you grow up here?"

"I did. On a small estate to the north. It's a lot colder than it is here but with mountains so high you can't see the tops."

The other warriors and their mounts milled around them. Taking her arm, he used his body to shield her from the snorting, stamping creatures, and led her onto the grass where blankets had been laid.

"Really?" she smiled, glad to have found common ground. He

ushered her to one of the blankets to take a seat. A quick glance behind her confirmed the other women were well looked after. "I love the mountains at home. My father used to take us rock climbing in the summer. Do you have any pictures?"

He shook his head, his inky-black hair dancing on his shoulders. "Not with me. I have one in my qua—" A strange expression crossed his face. "I'll find it and bring it to the banquet tonight for you."

She sat back, her arms wrapped around her knees. Karryl stretched out next to her, leaning on one elbow, more relaxed than she'd ever seen him. For a moment, like almost every conversation they'd had, she'd been sure he would try and get her into his rooms. He hadn't. Proof of just how much she'd damaged things between them with her words.

She needed him. Guilt made her stomach churn. Crap. She'd never thought she would be this kind of person. A user. Even though she knew how he felt about her, that he wanted to claim her as his mate... He was her best hope of getting the information she needed.

"Okay, I'd like that." Not wanting to overplay her hand, she slid him a sideways smile and concentrated on the scenery. Silence fell between them and she kicked herself. Oh great, what the hell did she say now? Looking around her, she tried to find inspiration. There was always the weather, but she was so not going there. She couldn't be *that* bad at conversation...surely?

Three painful, silent minutes later, she had to admit she was. And it was no surprise. She'd been in the military since eighteen, so dates had been few and far between. Quick shags when off-duty? Sure, she'd had plenty. They hadn't needed much in the way of flirtation and talking. Then she'd met Scott. Three months later they were married, again with the minimum of talking or flirtation.

She wrinkled her nose as she thought back. They'd had, what... six in-depth conversations in their entire marriage? During the time they'd been "together" anyway. They separated after a year but remained married for...well, until now. She still had to sign the papers...the only reason that Karryl hadn't pressed his claim against her.

"Do you think it would be possible to get my personal belongings sent from the base?" she asked.

He turned his head to look at her and she was caught by his unusual gaze. She'd never tire of looking at his eyes. They were jewel-like with multiple colors and slitted.

"Your eyes are similar to a cat's I once had." Great, now she was babbling. "His pupils went round like that. Usually when indoors. Why do yours?"

He lifted one eyebrow, and then his lips quirked. An actual expression rather than the polite mask he had been giving her. "You mean pupil dilation? What does it mean for humans?"

"Hmm..." She nibbled her lower lip. "Either being in a darkened environment so the eye can gather more light. We don't see well in the dark, though, something about the way our eyes are constructed."

"Or?"

She frowned. "Or what?"

He watched her. "You said 'either' but gave one choice. What is the second?"

"Oh." She couldn't do anything about the blush that hit her cheeks at light speed. "It means attraction. Sexual attraction and to attract a member of the opposite gender."

His smile widened a little. "There you go then."

She blinked. "It means the same for Lathar? Well, the eye rounding thing?"

His nod was distracted by a commotion on the other side of the group. Several warriors sprang to their feet, weapons appearing from nowhere.

"Is there a problem?" the emperor called out, levering himself to his feet from the rug he'd been sitting on near Tarrick and Cat. His face was wreathed in frowns.

"A rider, Your Majesty," a guard replied, binoculars to look through. "Approaching at speed. He's... yes, he's wearing imperial colors. One of your personal guard."

"Interesting." Daaynal stood to the side of the guard and held out his hand for the binoculars.

Jane, sensing the tension in the group, rose when Karryl did. His expression was implacable, but she could feel the coiled strength in his body. Ready for action at a moment's notice. His hand hovered over the blaster at his hip and she envied him being armed. This was a bad location for cover. An air strike would take them all out in one go.

"Ahh, it's Caayan. I know him." The tension in the air disappeared at the words. "It has to be something important if he's ridden out. Let him through."

The rider, Caayan, reached them within minutes and the outer circle of warriors parted to let him ride right in. He brought the snarling, stamping creature to a stop just before Daaynal. The beast snarled at him, but the emperor smiled and rubbed the animal's nose.

"Caayan, you bring news?" he asked as the rider jumped to the ground and bowed low.

"Indeed, Your Majesty." The warrior's expression was careful, but even Jane could see the concern lurking behind the polite mask. "We've received word the facility at *L'Raanis Three* has been compromised. There's been no communication since early this morning and the drone we sent on a flyby was rendered inoperative by unknown forces."

Jane's ears picked up. Caayan had kept his voice down, but she had excellent hearing. What facility was *L'Raanis Three*? As far as she'd been able to work out, the Lathar infrastructure was comprised of the war group ships. She hadn't been able to find any information on orbital or deep space communications arrays anywhere, but they had to have them. This sounded like it could be it.

Daaynal sighed, shaking his head. "If L-three goes down, then we'll lose contact with the war groups in the *Rivaas* Sector. We can't afford that."

Yes! Jane almost punched the air. She'd been right, it *was* a communications array. And she'd found that out without using Karryl.

The emperor looked up and around, spotting the two of them. He motioned Karryl over. "Karryl, my kinsman. Attend me."

"Stay here," he murmured, sliding his hand down her arm in a brief, and unexpected caress. Surprised, she did as ordered, watching him cross to Daaynal. She realized her mouth was open like a damn guppy, so she snapped it shut as the small group of Lathar huddled and spoke in lowered voices she couldn't hear.

It didn't matter. If Karryl was going to this L-three facility, then so was she. Whatever it took.

3

"I'm thinking a purist attack." Daaynal kept his voice low, so the group around them didn't hear.

Karryl didn't blame him, a hill in the middle of the countryside was not the best place to be discussing a potential threat to the empire, but he wasn't going to argue. This was the second time the emperor had called on him, and the second time Daaynal had called him kinsman. Always before, he would have been one of the warriors guarding the perimeter, not one of the chosen few. But that didn't mean he was going to keep his mouth shut and play the yes-man. It just wasn't in his nature.

"Divide and conquer?" He folded his arms and considered other warriors. Tarrick had joined them, his mate Cat gathering the human women and keeping them safely within the center of the ring of guards.

Daaynal nodded. "The war groups currently in that sector have known purist leanings. Isolation would leave them ripe for infiltration."

Shit. Yeah, it would. He'd been thinking more outright attack, but warriors without a clan often attached themselves to others. A sharp charlatan could have some of the less intelligent males dancing to their tune quickly. From there it was a quick hop to a coup and taking over the clan. If that happened with enough war groups... It would be a disaster. All-out war in the empire.

"That's..." Tarrick curled his lip, "dishonorable."

Daaynal shrugged. "We're not dealing with men who have honor. I want intel and fast, and the group of warriors I trust is small and select. I do not want anything to threaten this alliance with the humans."

Unless the humans threatened it themselves, of course. Karryl kept his thoughts and their previous conversation to himself, not sure if Daaynal had confided in Tarrick or not. He probably had. It was no secret at court that Daaynal wouldn't allow his nephews to roam the galaxy forever. Take Laarn, for example, any moment now the court expected an announcement that he had been confirmed as Lord Healer. Tarrick would suffer a similar "fate." Karryl's money was on Imperial Viceroy, so much so he had a book running with the other warriors in the war group.

One thing none of them would bet on was who would take over the K'Vass on Tarrick's promotion. Karryl and Jassyn were of equal rank and status, it could be either... Karryl intended it to be him.

Daaynal carried on talking. "Okay, Tarrick. You will return to Earth space and strengthen our position there. I assume Fenriis has now arrived, that will give you two full war groups to hold the sector. You will need to handle negotiations in my name, which will be good practice."

Karryl hid his smile as Tarrick blinked in shock. "Good practice for what?"

Daaynal merely waved his hand, apparently not in the mood to answer, and speared Karryl with a look.

"Karryl, you will take one of my combat flyers and investigate the situation at *L'Raanis Three.*"

"Of course, Your Majesty." He inclined his head in respect, then looked up. "Regards to my ...previous task?"

The emperor shrugged. "Inconsequential for now; this takes

precedence. You'll leave as soon as possible after we return to the palace."

Turning, he raised his voice. "Change of plans. Playtime is over, pack up everything."

It took mere minutes for the blankets to be packed and the group on their way back. Deliberately, Karryl didn't look at Jane as they set out. She called his name when he'd mounted his *kervasi* but he picked a position at the front of the group instead.

"Trouble in paradise?" Tarrick asked, drawing his mount level.

Karryl lifted an eyebrow. "Another Earth phrase, my lord? You'll be totally converted soon."

"You *draanthic!*" Tarrick chuckled, shaking his head, but despite his amusement, Karryl knew he wasn't going to get away without answering the question. Tarrick had *that* look in his eye, one all his warriors knew. And sure enough, his next question was straight to the point. "So...you've decided to give up pursuit of the lovely earth major?"

He reined in a little, knowing the carriage was coming up behind them. Open-topped, it would be easy for the occupants to hear everything he and Tarrick said. Good. Payback time.

"A warrior can only beat his head against a bulkhead so long before brain damage occurs." He shrugged. "The hopes that I harbored my claim would be welcomed have been relegated to daydream and fantasy. Perhaps another human female will find my advances acceptable, should I get the chance to return to that area of space."

Tarrick's expression shifted, and he nodded. The barest flicker of his gaze toward the carriage told Karryl he read between the lines.

"Perhaps that is the wisest course. These earth women are unpredictable and prone to decisions that make no sense to us. Perhaps the differences in our cultures are a little too wide."

"Indeed, indeed. At present, though, I don't have the time to study another culture to make myself more amenable to a mate. I have duties to fulfill."

"Of course. Totally understandable."

They topped a rise to find the palace laid out below them and came to a stop as the carriage got a wheel stuck in a rut. Karryl took a moment to gaze on the palace. He couldn't help a small sigh of contentment. He'd always loved the place. Its peace and tranquility, its sense of history and grandeur. It reminded him of an old Imperial lady, content in the sunset of her life.

"In case I don't see you before you leave on your new mission..." Tarrick reached out an arm, palm up. A warrior's handshake, between equals. "Go with honor. Do the K'Vass proud."

It was an honor Karryl hadn't expected, the third in a day of complete surprises. It seemed his misfortune in love became fortune to the rest of his life.

He grasped Tarrick's arm with a broad smile. "I intend to, my lord. I intend to."

～

"KARRYL! KARRYL, WAIT!" Jane called out after the swiftly disappearing figure of the Latharian warrior.

She'd jumped out of the carriage almost before it had stopped, almost trampling Kenna in the process. Throwing a quick apology over her shoulder, she set off after her quarry. For a big man, he moved fast, those long, leather-clad legs eating the distance. By the time she reached the door he'd disappeared into from the stable courtyard, he was halfway down the corridor within.

"Karryl, please...would you bloody well hold on!"

He paused near the next corner and looked over his shoulder. Trotting down the deserted corridor, she reached his side.

"You're leaving?"

No sense in pretending she hadn't heard the conversation that had resulted in them all coming back to the palace, or the exchange with Tarrick. The one that had confirmed her suspicion that her hasty words had ruined things between them.

He inclined his head in reply, a formal gesture that reminded her of an old world vampire from the retro films she'd loved to watch years ago. He'd make an excellent vampire, she realized, with his jewel-like eyes and black hair.

"I am."

"Don't."

The word was out before she could stop it, a plea direct from her soul. She didn't want him to go. Didn't want this whole charade anymore. She wanted things to be simple. To, heaven help her, to have been captured by bloody aliens and not have to play spy for her home world.

"Don't what?" He frowned, turning to her.

Arms folded across his chest, he looked down at her. His lips were a thin line, his expression forbidding, but all she could think about was how his lips felt on hers... about his strong arms around her. Stood as they were, the difference in their sizes, male and female, lathar and human, was more noticeable. And it thrilled her.

"Don't go."

She was committed now, she might as well go whole hog.

His eyebrow winged up. "Don't go? Did you forget the part about me being a warrior? I go where I am ordered. I would have thought you, of all the earth women, would understand that."

She glared up at him. "Of course, I do, but that's not what I meant."

"Then what did you mean?" he asked, voice a velvet temptation. She caught the little glimmer in his eyes. The bastard was enjoying this.

"Why can't another warrior go? I thought you were assigned to us humans."

He shrugged, a bland expression in place. If he'd have yawned next, it wouldn't have surprised her. Anger surged and she had to resist the temptation to kick him in the shins.

"There are plenty of warriors here to protect you."

A growl of frustration fought to break free of her throat. He *knew* exactly what she was talking about. He was just being difficult. Fucking men.

"You're an asshole."

"*I'm* the asshole?" he barked out a laugh. All amusement dropped from his expression in a nano-second. He moved in a flash. Hard hands closed around her arms and he yanked her against his solid body.

"Have a care, little human, that you don't push me too far." His lips hovered mere-millimeters from hers. His eyes glittered with anger. "I've been willing to look past your ignorance of our culture. I've tried to court you, have let you humiliate me in front of my peers, but never forget I am a man, and a warrior."

Her ability to breathe seemed to have disappeared, her breasts crushed against his broad chest.

"Now, I have a mission. A dangerous one. If you are here when I return, then we will discuss this further."

She started to nod but then found her voice. "Let me come with you."

He shook his head. "It's too dangerous for a female."

His hold relaxed minutely, enough that she could breathe easier, and he slid a hand up to cup the back of her neck. His gaze softened as it moved down to latch onto her lips. Unbidden, they parted in invitation and his eyes darkened in response.

He bent his head and his lips covered hers in a soft kiss that disarmed her. She'd expected him to be rough with anger and demanding, but he wasn't. Instead, he seduced her with soft brushes of his lips against hers, clinging and exploring. She relaxed against him, curling her fingers into the lapels of his uniform jacket.

It was over too soon though, and she murmured in disappointment. Opening her eyes, she found him looking down at her with a small smile on his lips. He reached up and swept a gentle thumb over her lower lip.

"Until I return."

Releasing her, he turned and walked away, not looking back. She wrapped her arms around herself and watched him go.

"Sorry, sweetheart. I'm not prepared to wait that long."

FINDING out which ship Karryl was taking had been child's play. All Jane had to do was follow him when he left his quarters an hour after he'd left her in the corridor. Dressed in the long hooded robes of one of the Oonat servants, she barely warranted a glance from the lathar she passed in the halls as she tailed her mark.

He'd headed for the landing pads visible from the windows of her suite, tucked just behind the emperor's wing of the palace. As a human, she'd never been able to get near the place, but with her face covered and pretending to be one of the Oonat, it was surprisingly easy.

Walking through the last door, she ducked quickly to the side and scooted behind crates rather than walking across the courtyard and through the other archway that led to parts unknown. She hadn't managed to explore this far into the restricted area before.

Karryl's boots rang against the concrete-like surface of the landing pad across from her. Three sleek surface to space shuttles sat in a row on the pad. The boarding hatch was open on the rightmost one, a short flight of steps leading up to it. The big warrior disappeared inside for a moment. When he re-emerged, the large pack over his back was absent. Stowing his gear.

Movements as silent as she could make them, she crept forward. She needed to get inside that shuttle. But how? Despite the fact that it was easily as large as a twenty man troop carrier, she could only see one entrance hatch. Right next to where Karryl stood, a panel on the ship slid back to expose what looked like pipes. Perhaps he was checking the engine or something... she hadn't been able to work out exactly how the Lathar ships were powered. Not conventionally, that was for sure.

Fate played into her hands. With a shake of his head and a frown, he slid the panel back into place and stomped to the back of the ship. Heart in her throat, she took the chance and darted forward. Her boots made no sound on the concrete as she ran across. Every second she expected him to walk back around the ship and spot her, or for someone to enter the courtyard behind her and raise the alarm.

There were no shouts though, and Karryl didn't reappear. She reached the steps without incident and raced up them. Her robes almost caught in the doorway, but she felt the tug and yanked them clear before they tore.

The inside of the craft was more spacious than she'd expected. There were two seats in the cockpit, more like recliners than the upright seats she was used to seeing in human crafts. The rest of the interior was open, an empty space she assumed was multi-functional. Recessed handles in the walls and floor would indicate where furniture unfolded and slid out. Which was all fine and dandy but gave her very few options for concealment.

Hearing heavy boots outside, she bit back her gasp and ran to the back of the cabin. There were three doors in the back wall. On instinct, she opened the smallest one built into the curve of the wall.

Storage boxes and crates met her questing gaze. Bingo. She squeezed into the space and closed the door behind her. Holding her breath, she pressed her ear to the door. Footsteps clunked against the steps. Crap, that had been close. A moment later and he'd have spotted her.

Relief rolling through her, she worked her way to the back of the compartment and wriggled behind a large crate. Unless he actually got in here on his hands and knees, there was no way Karryl would find out she was here.

It was cold, though, and she quickly discovered when the light by the door snapped off, dark. Huddling into a small ball to keep warm, she listened to the noises of the ship around her. There was the *slam-clunk-click* of the outer door as it shut, then a strange whirring which could only be the engines. Frowning, she reached out a hand to the surface beside her to find it vibrating.

The ship lurched and she gasped, reaching out to grab onto the crate but in the next second she was slammed back against the floor and wall. Gritting her teeth, she tried to lift her head but was pinned into place. They were taking off.

She closed her eyes and tried not to think. Unfortunately, her brain hadn't gotten the hint and a small part started to wonder how much more G-force the average lathar could take compared to the more delicate human frame.

Shit, she was about to become space-jam.

4

*K*arryl was an experienced pilot, but he'd never flown anything quite as luxurious as the personal transport the emperor loaned him. The engines were state-of-the-art, the latest development in hyper-threaded, quad-core faster than light technology. It showed. He barely felt lift off from the planet, the power only detectable when the engines kicked in to slingshot the sleek ship into the planet's outer atmosphere.

Pinned back into the low, padded couch, he kept an eye on the readouts. Well, that's what he told himself. All the screens were within normal parameters, which was good since he wasn't paying attention to them. Thoughts of Jane swirled through his mind, preoccupying his thought processes. He tried to shut them down, put thoughts of the tempting little human out of his head to concentrate on his mission, but the memory of her face when they'd said goodbye kept sneaking in. The image of her eyes, wide and dark, over lips plump from his kisses, tormented him and he groaned.

He didn't have time for this shit. He had a mission. An important one. One that would prove to the emperor he was ready to take on the role of War Commander. He couldn't afford to fuck it up because his brains had been addled by his prick.

The G-forces let up as they reached higher orbit and with a skill belied by the size of his warrior hands, he nudged them around the orbital defenses and into space. A quick course correction later and he engaged the FTL. There was a slight lurch, barely noticeable, and the stars in the view screen became streaks of white.

With a sigh, he released the four-point harness and rolled to a standing position. For a moment, he stood by the pilot's couch, thoughts of Jane filling his head. She hadn't seemed to want him to go. Of course, she was a spy. He'd expressed an interest in her, so he was the soft touch, the one most likely to be open to emotional manipulation. If she thought that, she hadn't learned anything about the Lathar, or him.

The thought of her spying didn't sit well with him. He knew her better than that. She wasn't a spy. She was too open, too honest, a warrior through and through as he was. They'd both been forged on a battlefield, not in the shadows.

With a sigh, he ran a hand through his hair. He didn't want her to be a spy, that was the problem. While he knew she wasn't innocent, he wanted to think of her as honorable.

The same kind of honor that stopped him pressing his claim over her when he really, *really* wanted to. If she turned out to be an underhanded, deceitful *shylakster,* though...he didn't know how he'd react. Severely probably.

Stomping to the middle of the central cabin, he lifted and twisted three catches high on the port side wall, grabbed the handle that protruded from the sleek metal and pulled down the bed. Since this was the emperor's own craft, it wasn't the hard, narrow cot Karryl was used to. Instead, it was a wide, well-padded haven of luxury, complete with cozy *eedireen* blankets.

Not wanting to get such expensive bedding dirty, he sat on the edge of the bed and pulled off his boots. They hit the deck plating with dull thuds. He lay back with a small groan. It felt good to stretch out on a bed where his feet didn't hang over the end. Even for a Lathar, Karryl was tall, almost as tall as Daaynal himself, and most warrior accommodations were built for men at least half a foot smaller.

Closing his eyes, he tried to summon sleep. He should rest. The journey was long and he had no idea what he would find at the other end. If it was worse than he expected or he needed to gather intel, then he may need to stay on his feet for hours...days even, so best to rest now.

As soon as he shut his eyes though, all he saw was his little human warrior. Images of her as she'd fought back when they'd attacked the base, the defiant tilt of her head when they'd finally captured her and her team. Her hard expression on the T'Laat ship when she faced down rival enemy warriors to keep her women safe. Her evasion of each move he made on her until...finally, the memory of her soft lips parted in surrender beneath him.

With a groan, he rolled over and punched the pillow. If he carried on like this, he'd get no sleep. At least, he wouldn't until he took matters in hand... but the last thing he wanted was to have to explain to Daaynal why there was a mess on his beautiful, expensive bedding, so he thought of something safe. Like *draakis* kits, or Xaandril in his underwear. *Eww,* Kaaryl wrinkled his nose. Okay, that was enough to put anyone off.

Closing his eyes again, he let his body relax, deliberately keeping his mind clear so he could drift off. The ship was on autopilot and he was using remote space lanes so there should be no issues between him and his destination. If there were, the computer would wake him. The sheets rustled around him as his limbs went lax and he started to drift into sleep.

Seconds later, the smallest sound from the back of the ship made his eyes snap open. He was alone in the cabin, but his gaze fixed on the small storage door tucked between the wash facilities and the side of the ship. Something moved in there. It couldn't be the cargo settling since it was all crated with mag-grav fastenings. No, it had sounded more like the slide of fabric when someone scooted across the floor on their backside.

Silent and focused, he slid off the bed and padded toward the door. A flick of his wrist dropped a blade into his hand from the sheath on his inner forearm. Light from the strip lights along the top sides of the cabin glittered off the lethal edge. If he had a stowaway, the stupid *draanthic* would regret the day he'd been born. Karryl was in no mood to play nice guy or even semi-not-violent guy.

His lips curled back into a grim snarl as he yanked the door open, reached a hand in and pulled the intruder out. With a spin and a hard shove, he pinned his captive's front side against the door with his bigger body, the knife kissing the skin of her throat.

Wait, what... *Her* throat?

His intruder was small and curvy, wearing the silver-gray robes of an Oonat. His body took that moment to remind him that thanks to his pursuit of Jane, he hadn't been with a female for far too long. After having spent more than five minutes in the company of the human females, the animal-like docility of the oonat disgusted him. His lip curling, he made to push the creature away when her hood slipped to reveal a short crop of silver-blond hair.

"Jane?" Snatching the blade away from her throat, he spun her around so her back hit the wall. "What the hell are you doing here? I almost killed you!"

OH, shit. Jane met Karryl's angry gaze and tried not to shiver. The big warrior had a face like thunder as he looked down at her and the blade he'd held at her throat had been all business.

"Hmm, I got lost?" she tried, watching as he let her go and backed up, crossing his arms over his massive chest. Somehow, here in this enclosed space, he seemed even bigger and she struggled to draw breath.

"Try again, little human," he rumbled, his expression unchanged. "Wearing an oonat robe, I'd say getting lost was the last thing on your mind."

The silence stretched between them; a hard, uncompromising silence and this time she did shiver, rubbing her hands up and down her arms. She hadn't had a plan beyond getting aboard, which she now realized was the dumbest thing ever. For all she knew that storage compartment might have been vented to space during take-off.

Crap, she just wasn't cut out for this espionage lifestyle. Give her an assault rifle and a battle plan any day.

"I wanted to know what had you disappearing off. I honestly didn't expect to get this far," she admitted. "I expected to get caught before I reached the shuttle. You really do need to review your security procedures. As myself, I couldn't get anywhere near the restricted sections but put on one of these?" She plucked at the robe. "And I walked right in."

"Right."

His expression grew darker, more forbidding, as though she said something wrong. Which didn't make sense. She'd told the truth, what more did he want?

"So you admit you've been spying for your people?"

For a moment she just looked at him. Then she laughed. "Of *course,* I'm damn well spying. I'm a soldier. I'm going to gather whatever intel I can. What else did you expect?"

He moved faster than she expected, grabbing her by her upper arms with a growl. "You stupid female, do you know the punishment for spying in the empire?"

She opened her mouth to answer, shaking her head, but he didn't let her get a word out.

"Flogging, with an energy whip. Fifteen lashes." Each word was punctuated with a little shake, his fingers digging hard enough into her arms to make her wince. "Most warriors don't make ten. A human? A female? *Draanth,* it would kill you."

He pushed her away to pace the cabin, shoving a shaking hand through his long hair. "Gods, I didn't want to believe them when they told me you were passing messages to that soft-bellied male. I didn't think you were so..." He looked her up and down and the expression in his eyes made her cheeks burn. "Dishonorable. I thought you were a real warrior."

She gathered her stolen robes, mangling them with her hands as she looked at him. All of a sudden, it mattered what he thought of her. Something inside her died when he looked at her that way like she was something that had crawled out from under a rock. Her throat tightened, but she ignored it and lifted her head.

"Are you going to turn me in?"

He paused his pacing to glare at her. A muscle in the corner of his jaw jumped as he looked at her. Finally, he sighed and shook his head.

"No. I don't have the time. *But,*" he barked, cutting off her sigh of relief, "you're not out of the woods yet, little human. When we get back, they're going to question you. And you're going to tell them that you stowed away because you couldn't bear to be parted from me."

Jane froze, and lifted her gaze to his hard, multi-colored one. "You're going to use this to force your claim on me?"

Her words were hard, but inside she trembled. Wasn't this what she wanted, the decisions removed from her? Faced with the possibility they might be, she suddenly realized that yes, having the decision meant a great deal to her indeed.

His jaw worked, lips compressing. "No. I do not need to force any female, much less a short, stubborn, pain in the ass human female with no concept of honor. You merely need to tell them you pursued me to get me to claim you, but I declined."

"Oh great, so I'm a bunny-boiler now, am I?"

"I do not understand this phrase 'bunny-broiler.'"

He'd moved closer, one eyebrow raised and she was suddenly reminded that however much the Lathar looked like humanity, they were very different. More graceful, faster, stronger. If the two species were related, then humanity had definitely gotten the shitty end of the stick.

"Boiler," she corrected automatically. "It means an older woman who is emotionally unstable and possibly dangerous when it comes to relationships."

"You're not old." His expression was hard to read, but she thought she caught a glimmer of amusement. "I can't say anything about unstable, and we both know you're dangerous."

She just looked at him. It couldn't have escaped the Lathar's notice that she was at least fifteen years older than the other women they'd captured. In fact, a few eyebrows had raised when she requested assignment to Sentinel Five, along with a few muttered comments about her being "past it."

"I'm forty-three years old," she said flatly. "Welcome to bunny-boiler territory, and according to some of the base staff talk, practically in my dotage."

After having given her age in such a matter-of-fact manner, the last thing she expected was for him to burst into laughter.

"Really? Forty-three? Hells, you're practically a baby." He grinned, shoving his hair back with a large hand. She caught her breath, arousal surging through her as he looked up, the smile transforming his cruelly-handsome face to something more boyish. "I'm sixty-seven next month."

"SERIOUSLY, SIXTY-SEVEN?" Hours later, Jane still couldn't believe how old Karryl was. "I wouldn't have said more than what... thirty-five, at the most."

The big Latharian warrior sat in the opposite recliner at the front of the cockpit, his gaze focused on the holographic screens in front of him. She had to admit, seeing him stretched out like that, with his attention elsewhere was more than handy. She could look her fill without him noticing.

"Yes, sixty-seven. Do human women ever stop talking?" he grumbled, throwing a scowl her way, which she ignored.

"Be thankful I'm not Kenna. That woman can talk the hind legs off a donkey. Creatures like your *kervasi,* but smaller, and more beasts of burden rather than to ride elegantly."

He did look at her that time, his expression quizzical. "Their legs detach? That seems a strange evolutionary feature. Is that common on your planet?"

"No, they don't really come off. It's just an expression," she chuckled, rocking back on the comfortable recliner and hugging her knees. The co-pilot's couch was just as big as the pilot's and built for the Lathar, so it was almost the size of a bed. "It means she talks a lot. Nothing to do with animals at all. I actually don't know where that phrase comes from. One of my old combat sergeants used to say it."

His hands moved over the display in front of him. They'd dropped out of FTL a while back and were approaching L-three with Karryl piloting, but she knew his attention was on her.

"You've been a warrior a long time?"

"Since I was eighteen."

She glanced out the view screen. This area of space was beautiful. Big gas giants with more rings than she'd ever seen cosied up to huge white-violet nebulae. Most of that was secondary, though, to the vast asteroid field they currently picked their delicate way through. Well, rather, *he* was now picking a way through. She had no idea how to pilot the alien craft and, to be honest, her one and only flying lesson in a beat-up troop carrier had ended badly. Her instructor leaped from the ship as soon as they'd touched down, swearing never to get into anything she was piloting. Ever again.

"Joined up the day I left school. A city kid, from one of the less salubrious areas. Money and food were tight. Joining meant I got three squares a day and could send money back to feed my siblings."

He glanced across at her. "Did your parents not have sons to send instead? Why send a female?"

Her hard look went unnoticed as the consoles bleeped and claimed his attention again.

"My brother at that time was four. A little young to be sent to basic training." She sighed, and rubbed her hand down her calf. "He became a soldier in the end. He'd have been twenty-nine now."

"Been?" Karryl asked as he neatly maneuvered them around a large asteroid. They were almost at the end of the rocky field and a large satellite rotated slowly in the clear space ahead of them.

"Yeah, lost him in the colony wars," she replied briefly, sliding forward to the edge of her couch as the satellite got larger. "Is that it?"

Even with her limited knowledge of Latharian technology, it looked wrong. The sleek metal looked misshapen. Not burnt and destroyed but more like it had been melted. "That doesn't look good at all."

"No. I'm pinging it, but it's totally non-responsive. Scanning now..." His lips compressed into a thin line. His hands moved over the holo display, tapping on the thin lines in mid-air. The engines kicked in, slowing the shuttle in front of the satellite. "There's nothing left—Oh, fuck!"

Swearing in Lathar too quickly for her to understand, his hands flew over the controls. The engines roared to life, the ship lurching as they raced away from the satellite. The sudden movement dumped her into the foot well in front of the co-pilot's couch with a yelp.

She clambered onto the couch and strapped herself in, just in case Karryl felt the need to hit the gas again. "What's going on?"

"It's emitting high levels of *keraton* radiation." His face was pale as the lights in the cabin turned orange, blinking from the cockpit to the rear. "Running a de-com routine now. The shuttle is shielded but I don't want to take any chances—"

With her. She finished his sentence silently, realizing that he wasn't worried about himself, but about the effect of radiation on her. His concern was touching. Actually, rather unexpected.

"Is it dangerous?" Keeping her voice light, she pretended to double-check her harness. "We weren't in range long enough for it to have an effect, surely?"

"No." The little muscle at the side of his jaw worked again as he shook his head. "We weren't, thankfully. It's not overly dangerous to a male my size, especially with the shielding on this thing, but I don't wish to risk a female."

"You're a big softy really, aren't you?" She teased him to lighten the mood. "So boss, the thing's toast. What's the next move?"

"Well, there are only a few species that have *keraton* technology, and given the damage, they couldn't have gotten far. There's a trading outpost not far from here. We might be able to pick up some gossip on who's been in the area, then get back within range of long distance comms to report back to the palace."

The engines rose in pitch as Karryl turned the shuttle and laid in a new course. There was a slight lurch as the FTL drives kicked in and then she found herself looking at streaks of light as the stars raced past.

"So," she grinned, relieved that they weren't going back to the palace, and the probability she'd have to face the music, "we get a road trip."

ot far from here turned out to be a two-hour journey. Lulled by the soothing hum of the engines and the lure of the comfortable recliner, years of military training to rest when she could, ensured that Jane slipped into a light doze.

A change in the sound of the engines as they dropped out of FTL woke her and she sat up, blinking and ruffling her hair so it wasn't flat. Pure feminine vanity. She'd lived in trenches and barracks for months at a time and never bothered about her appearance. For some reason with Karryl it was an entirely different matter.

"Coming up on the outpost now," the big warrior announced, his voice low and gruff. He hadn't slept but didn't appear fatigued at all. A comment Daaynal had made a few days ago came to mind. The Lathar were experts at tinkering with genetic code, much like humans would alter and enhance vehicles, they did to themselves. They'd increased their strength, endurance, and cognitive abilities to make them better warriors.

Diseases though had proven more difficult. Curing one had changed something else and caused a worse mutation, one of which had wiped out their women. Proof positive in her mind that trying to play God bit you in the ass eventually.

But they'd created humanity. She still struggled to get her head around that revelation. That she was from the same genetic stock as Karryl, albeit it a Lathar mission a millennia ago that had been genetically engineered for different conditions. Not conditions on earth, but another planet. Something had gone wrong and they'd lost contact with the mission. It had been assumed they'd all died. Not found a new planet and survived, the memory of where they had come from lost over time and new legends and stories growing up to explain that ever-present existential question.

"It's..." Jane paused for a moment as she considered the best way to describe the outpost. A hulking mass, it was comprised of what looked like old earth storage shipping containers, hexagonal in shape, clustered around a central tube-like core. Other constructions rose from the center, tethered by metal stalks that themselves had extra structures bolted to them. Nothing matched. It looked like it had been salvaged from some intergalactic junkyard and bolted together.

A bulge at the top had to contain the docking bays by the look of the large doors on the side. Karryl turned the small shuttle toward it, then flicked her a quick glance. "Be quiet. I want them to think I'm alone."

She nodded, trying to maintain a professional expression when inside she was ready to squeal like a big kid. She was going to see aliens. Real aliens on a real alien space station. Wild west in space kind of stuff. Of course, the Lathar were aliens, but they were so human-like at times...and now it had been discovered that they and humanity were related, could they actually be called aliens?

Perhaps the real little green men were on this space station. She couldn't wait to find out.

"*Pernassis*, this is shuttle *Lei'anna* requesting permission to dock." Karryl's voice had changed from the one he usually used when speaking to her, and was firm, deep and brooked no argument. Once again she was reminded he was far more dangerous than she took him for at times.

"*Lei'anna*, this is *Pernassis*," the reply came in a female voice that dripped sex. "We have you with a Latharian palace tag, are you sure you're not lost out here, honey?"

"That is correct, and the Lathar are never lost." Karryl almost barked the reply, obviously in no mood to play games. "I have business on the outpost. Are you going to give me permission to dock, or do I have to come back with a war group?"

There was a small squeak in reply. "No, no, there won't be any need for that. Permission to dock granted, *Lei'anna,* you're allocated to bay seven. Have a pleasant stay on *Pernassis."*

"I sincerely hope so," Karryl left the subtle threat hanging in the air for a moment, then said. *"Lei'anna* out."

As he closed the connection, Jane lifted her eyebrow. "You lathar are bullies, you know that? There was no need to bully that poor woman like that."

"Bully? A Krin?" He chuckled, shaking his head. "Not likely. That *poor woman* is the male of 'her' species, taller than most Lathar, with eight arms and a fondness for the flesh of other species, preferably served raw and screaming."

"Shiiiit." Jane shivered. "She sounded like a phone sex worker."

Karryl nodded, movements sure on the controls as he took them into the docking bay. Obviously he got the reference. "That's how they hunt. Pheromones and sex appeal. Their scent glands fetch a high price for use in the perfumery industry. The trouble is they tend to be rather attached to their body parts, so harvesting them to sell is a high-risk occupation. A well-paying one if you can avoid getting slaughtered and eaten. I do believe some of them prey on their own for that reason."

She blinked in surprise. "What? They kill their own to sell their scent glands?"

He shrugged, turning the shuttle about neatly and easing them into bay seven. At least, she assumed it was bay seven. The painted number on the metal bulkhead in front of them had long since worn off. There was a small bump as they hit the docking clamps, then a whir and clunk as the clamps engaged. A wave of Karryl's hand killed the shuttle's engines.

"It's economical when you think about it. Get paid for the glands, the rest they eat."

She covered her mouth for a moment. "That's just sick."

Karryl unbuckled his harness and levered himself out of the recliner. The holo-consoles snapped off at his movement. "Not every species has humanity's morals. Spend any time out here and you'll learn that. Fast, if you want to survive."

"So I'm finding out."

She unbuckled, and tumbled off the couch, following him to the back of the cabin. Lathar were always armed, but he opened a door on the side of the cabin, the handle recessed like the rest, to reveal a weapons cache. Whistling through her teeth, she looked along the racked weaponry. For a two man shuttle, it sure was well stocked.

Already carrying a heavy pistol holstered on his hip and blades nestled in his boots and wrist sheaths, Karryl picked out a second gun belt. He buckled it about his hips and added not one but two pistols. Huh, double-decker holster, that was neat. She looked for another one but could only see a standard belt with a holster on each hip.

Karryl paused, what looked like a shotgun in his hand, as she picked up the belt. "What do you think you're doing?"

Giving him a "well, duh" look, she buckled the belt. There weren't enough holes so it didn't fit snugly, sliding down to wedge over her hips at a slant. "Arming up. There's no way I'm walking onto an alien space station without a shit-load of weaponry."

He plucked the pistol she'd picked up out of her hands and shoved it back into its slot. His look could have melted perma-steel. "Oh, no, you're not. I am not riski—"

Fury surged. She snatched the gun out and jumped down his throat before he could get another word out. "Because I'm a woman? I'm a goddamn soldier, this is what I do!"

He hissed in anger and frustration, showing his teeth.

"I meant risking the *mission*. These people have never seen a human. You'll stand out like a fucking sore thumb." He plucked the weapon from her fingers and jammed it back, shaking the rack. "Not everything's about you. I need to get information, not announce our fucking presence to all aboard."

Fuck. She hadn't thought about it like that. Silent, she took a step back and nodded. There was no way she wanted to interfere with his mission. She was already on a sticky wicket where the palace was concerned because of her attempts to spy for Terran Command, she didn't need to compound her errors. Her desire to see little green men would just have to wait.

"I apologize, you're perfectly correct. I'll stay here and guard the ship."

He nodded, swinging what looked like the lathar version of a shotgun over his shoulder. Or a grenade launcher, it looked like it could be either or both.

"Ship, activate surveillance perimeter on my bio-signature."

"Affirmative," a disembodied voice made Jane jump and look around.

The holo-consoles in the cockpit reactivated, casting a blue glow over the two control couches. There were two images: one showing a corridor with an airlock door, and the other showing the two of them standing in the middle of the shuttle's cabin. At the same moment, the door opened onto the airlock.

"The ship's AI will track me as I move through the station," he explained, taking a step forward to tuck a finger under her chin and lift it so she had to meet his eyes. Her breath caught as he loomed over her. Not through fear. Something else surged through her veins. She preferred him like this, as he really was, rather than trying to be civilized to charm her into his bed.

The ghost of a smile whispered over his lips. "You'll get to see your little green men."

She hadn't told him that. Her eyes narrowed, but he smiled. "You talk in your sleep, little one."

Before she could argue, he bent and kissed her. It was firm, but brief, the contact ended before she'd registered it.

"Stay here, don't touch anything and behave. I don't want to have to explain to Daaynal if something happens to his ship."

With that, he left the shuttle, door closing behind him.

Jane stayed where she was for a moment, lifting her hand to her lips. They tingled from his kiss, every time he touched her. Frustration surged through her. She liked him, a lot, and she knew he wanted her.

If he was human, she'd have jumped him in a hot minute and enjoyed every inch of that lean, hard warrior's body. Then, when whatever they had worked itself out, they could have parted amicably, as friends. But he was lathar so it wasn't that simple. If she shared his bed, accepted his claim, that was it...they were joined for a lifetime. And that scared the living crap out of her.

But he wasn't pushing his claim anymore, which confused her. The man was a born predator so she knew he hadn't given up, doubted he even knew the meaning of the concept. No, he was playing another game, one she hadn't figured out yet, and her blood thrilled at the thought.

Sighing, she ran a hand through her hair and headed for the cockpit with its twin displays. No time to figure out what he was up to now; she'd have to bide her time.

The pilot's couch was just as comfortable as the co-pilot's, but her attention was less on the padding beneath her posterior, and all on the big man displayed on the screens in front of her. For a moment, he dominated both as he stepped out of the airlock and walked down the corridor away from the ship. The image on the right shifted to another camera and she could see Karryl walking toward her, his expression grim and forbidding, while the picture on the left showed the empty corridor outside the airlock door.

The images changed as he moved through the ship, the AI moving from one camera to another to keep him in view. As he entered the main area of the outpost, which looked like a mall back home, Jane got her first view of aliens in the "wild." There were two levels to the main promenade, the upper with wraparound balconies that looked down on the lower. A line of dried out fountains in the center of the ground level gave hints toward more auspicious times, long since passed.

Both levels were packed with creatures of all shapes and sizes. Tall, yeti-like creatures walked next to what looked like a blob of pink slime. She recognized one of the more insectoid creatures as the same species from the Latharian palace, and there were many oonat, mostly on leashes. The poor creatures appeared to be everyone's whipping boy.

One thing she didn't miss was that Karryl was the only Lathar aboard, and everyone was quick to scuttle out of his way. She didn't blame them. There was an aura of lethality around the big warrior that no one in their right mind wanted to mess with.

"Stop," she said suddenly, catching something in the corner of the screen. "Can you roll that back a little, or expand the view?"

"Affirmative," the AI replied smoothly and the screen on the right grew in size, moving the airlock corridor one up above, as the camera panned out.

"There and there," Jane pointed to two dark-clothed figures in the crowds behind Karryl. "I've seen them too much. Are they following him?"

"Assessing..."

The AI split the screen again so there were now three views. The corridor above, Karryl moving through the crowds on the left while on the right, the AI flicked rapidly through different images from the outpost camera feeds. Each image concentrated on one of the men she'd pointed out.

"There is a 97.375 percent probability the subjects are following Warrior Karryl," the AI said, its voice unemotional. "Analysis of physical movements suggests subjects are likely to be *Krynassis* mercenaries."

"What the hell are they?"

Jane's heart rate picked up as the two closed in on the unaware Karryl. He'd entered a bar on the second level and appeared to be in conversation with an insectoid. His back was to the entrance of the bar, which made all her soldier instincts scream. He was an open target.

"Regardless of their physical location, the Krynassis are a highly dangerous reptilian-derived lifeform with similar physical capabilities to the Lathar."

Helpfully, the AI changed the image on the right side of the screen and a new face appeared. It was male, with close-cropped short hair and at first glance could have been mistaken for human or lathar. Then she noticed the shimmer of scales over the high cheekbones, and as the man in the image smiled, the sharp fangs. Still, he wouldn't have looked out of place as a male centerfold. For ladies into scales...

"Shit, why are all aliens freaking hot?"

"The Krynassis are cold-blooded," the AI interjected. "Pack hunters, they are considered extremely dangerous in hand-to-hand combat."

Karryl was on his own and unaware he was being stalked.

"What are Karryl's chances on his own?" she asked bluntly. Sliding off the seat, she strode across the cabin and yanked the weapons cache open. Her hands were steady as she armed up. There was no way she was allowing those lizard men to take him down. Not without going through her first.

The ship's voice continued. "Poor. Alone, he is likely to sustain life-threating injuries. However," she heard the disapproval in the computer's voice, "his chances will not be improved by the addition of an inferior being to protect."

Jane paused, pistol in hand and looked at the consoles. She isolated the AI's location at the front of the craft, given away by a small blinking blue light whenever it "spoke."

"You want to run that by me again?" she asked, eyebrow raised. "Inferior being? And before you answer, I would invite you to consider that this *inferior being* has an energy weapon and a direct line of sight to your processor housing."

The AI was silent for a few seconds, then the lights flickered again. "Point taken. May I suggest some...enhancements?"

There was a click and a door to the left of the weapons cache slid to the side. A rack smoothly extended from the dark space within and Jane sucked in a breath. Body armor, but not like she'd ever see. This stuff was bad-ass and made of the same metal as the combat bots the K'Vass used to attack Sentinel Five. Pity the shuttle was too small to carry any of them.

"Armor?" she asked, already unbuckling her gun belts to put on the stuff.

The lower half hit the floor with a clunk and she turned so that she could step back into it. The small of her back hit the belt and the whole thing moved, adjusting to her more diminutive stature as harnesses snapped around her legs and tightened. She lifted a leg experimentally. Despite the metal and straps, she didn't feel any different.

"Combat exoskeleton," the AI replied. "Designed to enhance a warrior's performance on the battlefield. It should overcome your natural...limitations."

Its speech pattern had changed, becoming more fluid and... human. It was mimicking her, Jane realized.

"You learn fast. I'll give you that."

Jane grinned as she lifted the breastplate over her head and settled it on her shoulders. Like the lower half, as soon as it sensed it was in the right place it started to adjust. Straps shot from the sides and wrapped around her torso, hooking into loops on the leg portion and pulled tight. A flap on the shoulders flipped down and with a *click-click-click* a row of plates not unlike scales covered her arms.

"So I should," the AI sounded huffy, as though she'd insulted its intelligence. "My brain patterns were modeled after one of the greatest mathematical engineers in Latharian history, Miisan K'Vass."

"Tarrick's mother?" She'd heard Cat mention the name.

The AI made a small noise. "And sister to the emperor. She was beloved by all and a genius. A lot of the technology currently used by the Lathar was developed from her work. Mathematics was a great passion amongst women of her class before the plague took them from us."

Great. She'd always had the impression Latharian women were delicate, frail creatures who needed looking after, not freaking geniuses. Mathematics was not her strong point, unless they were talking enemy numbers and how much ammunition she had left. Anything past the mundane and she was lost. The fact that the women Karryl had grown up with were highly intelligent made her feel even more like the dumb grunt she was.

"A helmet too?" She cleared her throat, covering her discomfort and reached for it.

"Indeed. It should conceal your gender although there is nothing we can do about your physical size. Since no one will expect you to be female, most will assume you are a younger warrior."

"Good."

At least her hair would be covered. In the palace, nearly everyone seemed fascinated by the short, platinum locks. Blond was an uncommon color amongst the Lathar. The only one she'd seen so far was the emperor's champion, Xaandril.

Helmet in place, she blinked as the screen showing Karryl in the bar appeared at the bottom right of her field of vision. It alternated with the view outside the bar where the mercenaries were gathering. She needed to move. Now.

"Seal the airlock behind me," she ordered, grabbing her weaponry. The exosuit moved, providing holsters so she loaded up. Never could have too many guns. Not when going into a hot situation that involved lizard men. Perhaps she should take a mouse or two as a distraction. "Don't open the doors for anyone but me and Karryl."

"Understood. And Jane?"

She stopped halfway out of the door and looked back. The cockpit screens had changed to show the face of a Latharian woman. Tall, she was ethereally beautiful and Jane knew she was looking at a facsimile of Miisan K'Vass.

"Yes?"

The AI woman smiled. "Good luck."

6

Karryl had been in many low down, disgusting dives in his adult life, but *Pernassis* beat them all, hands down. He shouldn't have expected anything else though. This area of space was a no man's land between sectors, well off the main space lanes. An area of lawlessness and chaos most people avoided.

A small smile curved his lips at the thought of the stubborn, beautiful little human woman. Well, little next to him anyway...she was the tallest amongst the earth women he'd seen so far.

"So, have you seen my cousin, or not?" he demanded, glaring down at the *Kalaxian* bartender on the other side of the counter.

Small, overweight, and universally bald, there was no way of knowing whether the creature was male or female. Even other Kalaxians had trouble working that out.

Whatever gender it was, there were two constants about Kalaxians. Thanks to a near religious knowledge of alcoholic drinks they were usually employed as bartenders, and they loved to gossip. A perfect combination. If anyone wanted to know anything, all they had to do was head to the nearest bar and hit up a purple-skin for information.

"Your cousin, you say?"

This particular purple-skin was shrewd, beady little eyes far too perceptive as they wandered over him, lingering over his chest and trailing down his abdomen to his groin. *Draanth,* he hoped this one wasn't female. They weren't particular about the species of their sexual partners if they were in heat or much concerned with consent. Just breathing the same air could be considered a yes.

"Cousin. Twice removed." He kept his voice firm, altering his posture to loom a little. "Took off in a flyer a week ago. It was an expensive bit of kit, we'd like it back. Him as well, if he hasn't managed to kill himself."

"Well..." The bartender edged forward, a primary hand swiping a dirty cloth over the counter at the same time one of the secondary arms just beneath shoved a proto-paw out in an unspoken demand. "There may been some warriors through here recently. But they looked more J'nuut than K'Vass. You *are* K'Vass, aren't you?"

Karryl narrowed his eyes. Like any warrior on a hush-hush mission, he'd been careful to remove all identifying markers from his leathers before he'd left. The braids in his hair marked him as a senior warrior, but the fact that the Kalaxian identified his family affiliation so easily rang alarm bells. Unlike most of his clan, Karryl didn't bear the traditional K'Vass features.

"I could be, depends on who wants to know." He changed tactics, relaxing his body language to lean on the bar and press a credit chip into the creature's paw. His lips curved into a small smile designed to charm and beguile. "Why do you ask?"

The creature's purple skin flushed yellow, not a pleasant combination, and the fluttering of its eyelashes confirmed his suspicions that it was female. Great, he could charm the pants off a four armed purple-skinned blob, but not the woman who sat safely in his shuttle.

His life sucked.

The Kalaxian pulled a glass from under the bar, filled it with something from one of the taps that looked more like black sludge than anything remotely palatable.

"Certain friends have asked to be informed of your arrival," she said, her voice low as she tapped the front of the glass with a horn-like fingernail.

He flicked a glance down. The black sludge had turned the simple glass into a highly reflective surface. One good enough for him to spot the three dark figures sneaking up from behind.

Draanth. Hand closing around the glass, he turned and threw it at the nearest of his opponents. A glimpse of scales and a hiss as the man ducked, the black sludge cascading over his hooded head and shoulders told Karryl they were Krynassis mercs. Crap, lizard men were pricey and there were three on his tail, which meant someone out there really didn't want anyone asking questions.

The other two rushed him at the same time, their mouths wide to reveal vicious fangs. Dropping to the ground, he swept a hard leg out to drop one and shoved the bar stool into the path of the other. The first went down hard, rolling away just as Karryl stamped hard where his face had been a moment before.

He didn't waste time, spinning around and bringing his guard up just in time to stop a scaly fist slamming into the side of his head. Twisting his wrist, he grabbed the lizard man's hand, trapping him with his arm extended. A practiced flick dropped a blade into his hand and he sliced at the guy's rib cage.

The krynassis grunted. Wet heat cascading over Karryl's hand told him his blade had struck true. Snarling, he planted a booted foot in the center of the creature's chest and kicked him away. The merc went down, sliding in his own blood to curl up under the nearest table.

One down, two to... The door banged again and three more lizards stalked through, their yellow gaze fixed on him.

Just fucking great. More lizard men to the party. And they ran in packs, so if there were a few, there were definitely more around. He pulled his blaster and pulled the trigger. Nothing. Just a flat *ppphsttt*. Shit, they had a mobile suppression field.

"Oh, so this is how it is?" He backed up, making sure they couldn't get behind him. With a pack, he couldn't hope to hold them off indefinitely. Which meant this was going to hurt. A lot. "Okay, who wants to dance first? I warn you, I don't intend to make this easy."

"Good." The nearest added a hiss to the end of the word. "We prefer the prey fights back. And it's been a long time since any of us tasted Lathar blood."

Karryl curled his lips back, showing his teeth. "Come and get it then, if you think you're tough enough."

Hisses filled the bar, the rest of the patrons having wisely cleared out, and the five mercenaries rushed him at once. Within seconds, he was fighting for his life. His existence narrowed down to each kick and slash, to the physical exertion required to block each punch thrown his way.

His senses expanded, hyper-alert to every movement from the men around him. He didn't bother with any of the flourishes or showing off that he might have done against a lesser enemy, or back in the court to impress the woman he yearned to claim as his own.

Jane, the thought filled his head as he fought and he bellowed in rage. If he fell here, she would be alone, on an alien outpost. That was not happening.

One jumped on his back, fangs perilously close to his neck and he fell backward, landing heavily on it. There was a crunch and a scream, but the move left him on his back, his belly exposed to the others. A hard, scaly arm wrapped around his neck. He struggled like a wild *deearin,* trying to get loose, but they fell on him as a pack. There were more than five now, way more than five.

Fists slammed into his unprotected abdomen, no claws yet, but that would come. It was just a matter of time.

Then one was ripped away from him. Its grunt of surprise changed to a scream of pain as bone crunched and the smell of lizard blood blossomed into the air. He took advantage of the lizards' momentary distraction to heave them all off and flip to his feet. Slamming his fist into the side of a scaled skull, he cast a glance to the side to check who his unexpected savior could be. He hadn't seen anyone on his way here who looked like they would be an ally. A few might consider the Lathar owing them a favor worth the risk of tangling with a pack of Krynassis though.

It wasn't a mercenary. Instead, another Latharian warrior, fully armored, fought beside him with a level of skill that took Karryl's breath away. Lithe and fast, he was too small to be an adult. He could only be a youth, not yet attained his full growth. As he watched, the boy took on two of the krynassis at once, combining punches and kicks in a manner he'd never seen before but lethally effective. One lizard ran at him from behind and Karryl opened his mouth to shout a warning. It wasn't needed.

The youth flicked a glance over his shoulder, and with a hard right hook to the jaw of the one in front of him, he dropped to his knees to slam a foot backward. There was a crunch as the mercenary's knee went the wrong way. He fell and the young warrior followed him, grabbing an arm as he went. With a roll and tuck, he wrapped his legs around the lizard man's torso, holding his arms out of the way. Gloved hands gripped the creature's skull and without a moment's pause, he wrenched it sharply, snapping the neck. Shoving the body away, he rolled back to his feet again, facing off against another opponent.

Young he might be, but he was a true warrior.

The fight took Karryl's attention again, and he put his back to the younger warrior, confident they could take on any number of krynassis that turned up. With a bellow, he dodged and weaved, looking for gaps in their defence and hitting hard. Ribs, noses, joints...they all cracked beneath his fists. Grunts of pain and the occasional scream filled the air, all from the lizard men. Eventually, the few who were left backed off, then ran for the door, scrambling over each other to get away from the two lathar.

They both stood for a moment, breathing heavily. Leaning forward, Karryl rested his hands on his thighs to ease his bruised abdomen. Looking up, he nodded to his new companion.

"Well met, friend. My thanks for your assistance. Without it, the outcome here would not have been as good."

Carefully, he avoided mention of his ship and the fact he had a female companion. Most Lathar knew of the existence of the human race now, and that they had women. As young a male as this one appeared to be, Karryl didn't fancy ending up in a challenge fight with him. Even though he wore body armor, honor dictated the enhancement levels were set to minimal, so he'd be just as lethal out of it.

Straightening, he offered his arm, palm up, for a warrior's handclasp.

The youth didn't move. His faceplate completely concealed his expression but for a moment Karryl could have sworn he was surprised. Perhaps not a stretch of the imagination. If he was not yet a warrior and this was his proving mission, he wouldn't have expected to be treated as a full-fledged warrior.

"For your assistance, I'll happily vouch for your first warrior's braid." Karryl smiled, hand still out.

His smile remained in place as the kid bent his head and lifted his hands to remove the helmet. He waited for a look at the youth's face. Most Lathar clans bore a distinct family resemblance and fought in similar styles, but he couldn't identify the style this one had used. So which clan had he come from? Certainly not one of the bigger ones. Perhaps a back-system clan? Instantly, he dismissed the thought. The armor looked to be top of the range, a type Karryl had never seen before. But then, the K'Vass preferred not to use armor at all...

His hair was blond, nearly white and cropped short. Karryl frowned. There weren't many light-haired Lathar and a warrior in training should have long hair, not shor—

The breath hissed out of his lungs as his companion lifted her head.

"Jane."

Surprise held him captive for a moment, as he tried to make his brain absorb everything. The lethal young warrior he'd mentally been congratulating a moment ago was a female. *His* female.

His female had just taken on a horde of Krynassis mercenaries and kicked their asses.

"What the fuck did you think you were doing, woman? You could have been killed!" Her mouth dropped open in shock as he grabbed her helmet and jammed it back on her head. "Put that back on, before someone sees you."

Fury and fear rolled through him in equal amounts. She shouldn't be here. Not out in the open like this. If other races knew there was a human out here, female or not, there would be a bloodbath. They'd band together, kill him, and sell her on the auction block to the highest bidder. Fuck, there was a Krin on board... that fucker would bankrupt its entire pod for a new species to "sample."

His body shook with suppressed rage and the fear of what could have happened. Hand hard on her arm, he frog marched her from the bar and through the crowded promenade.

"What the fuck, Karryl!" she hissed, trying to get free but he didn't let go. If anything, his grip tightened.

The crowds scattered before them, but he didn't care. All that mattered was getting her back to the ship. To make sure she was safe. The need to protect her, even though she'd shown herself more than capable, was like the need to breathe. He didn't have a choice.

"Let me go, you idiot!" She didn't give up, struggling all the way back to the docking ring and the corridor outside their airlock. "I saved your life!"

"By putting yourself in danger," he snarled, shoving her through the airlock door as soon as it opened. They'd barely cleared the first door than the second was already opening, so he pushed her through that as well.

She stumbled into the main cabin, tearing the helmet from her head as soon as the door was shut to glare at him. If looks could kill, he'd be colder than stone.

"What the hell are you playing at? Is this the thanks I get for saving your life?"

"At the risk to your own!" Now they were alone, he didn't bother to regulate his tone.

His bellow made her wince but not back down. Anger flared in her eyes.

"Risk? What risk? I can take care of myself!"

"Really?"

He stilled, all the heat of his anger draining into something else. Something far more dangerous. For her. Taking a step forward, he crowded her against the wall. Deliberately invaded her space to threaten her. His lip curled back a little.

"Prove it, little female."

Without giving her further warning, he attacked. Her gasp of surprise was audible, but she got a block up in time, stopping his blow to her ribs just in time. She was armored, so he didn't bother pulling his punches. The exo-suit would take the brunt of the blows.

The fight was fast and furious, ranging through the tiny cabin and around the extended bed. She was quick, blocking his blows with a speed and strength that surprised him. Some of it was the suit, but not all. He'd always known she was a good soldier, lethal with a rifle, but she was also formidable in hand-to-hand combat.

Even with the suit to help her, he was bigger, faster, stronger, and better. He pressed his advantage ruthlessly, blocking each try she made to get away from him and out of the corner he'd penned her into. The only advantage he let her have was that he couldn't bring himself to hit her in the face. Just the areas he knew would be shielded by the armor.

She fought silently, her expression a blank mask even though he knew some of his blows had to hurt. That she shielded her pain made him proud; that he'd been the one to cause it made him ashamed.

He'd never lifted a hand to a female in his life...

He spotted the opening before it happened, reading the movement of her body to gauge the exact moment she dropped her guard a little on the left and struck. The solid blow to her solar plexus made her reel back, her face suddenly pale and tight with pain. Not giving her chance to recover, he moved in, wrapping up her arms and falling backward with her onto the extended bed.

Within a heartbeat, he'd twisted and had her pinned beneath him. Hissing, she tried to buck him off, but her struggles were weaker than a day old *deearin*. She tried to punch him so he captured her hands, pinning one above her head and the other against her body.

"Ready to give in?" he asked softly, riding out her bucking and thrashing until she quietened. Her gaze latched onto his, both colors cold and jewel-like.

"Lesson delivered and assimilated." Her voice was clipped, angry. "Thank you for the life re-adjustment."

Her anger didn't put him off. Rather it clashed with his own and fed it, then fed an entirely different type of rage. He shouldn't, he knew he shouldn't, but the urge to taste her again consumed him. Dipping his head, his mouth crashed down on hers in a hard kiss fueled by the fear and rage that coursed through his blood.

He expected her to stiffen. Expected her to freeze him out and lie stiff beneath him, but she didn't. Instead, she kissed him back, meeting his anger with a fury of her own. Matched him, challenged him, and when he paused, nipped his lower lip.

Lust shot through him. His gasp was lost beneath their kiss as he moved. Sliding one leg between both of hers, he tore at the breastplate of the armor, desperate to get it off her and feel her soft curves beneath. How he could have thought her a male he had no idea. His cock certainly knew the difference. It was as stiff as a support strut and throbbed against the constraint of his leathers.

The straps retracted and she raised her shoulders, toned stomach crunched to allow him to lift the armor clear. He discarded it on the floor, the lower section following a moment later. Passion shrouded his vision and his common sense. It didn't matter to him that she wouldn't accept his claim, he had to touch her, had to taste her and prove to himself that she was safe. Protected in his arm. *His.*

Her hands moved over his chest. Reaching up, he yanked the zipper free, desperate to feel her caress. The knowledge that she found him attractive... that she wanted to touch him made him swell all the more.

Despite all his instincts roaring at him to push her back and take her, make her accept his claim, he held still to let her explore. His brain blanked, short-circuited by the movement of her lips beneath his, the passion as she stroked her tongue against his. He'd expected her to fight, and to put him off as she had so many times before.

She wasn't saying no anymore.

He gasped as she slid her hand under his leathers to cup him boldly.

Shit, she *really* wasn't saying no anymore.

"You like that, huh?" she broke away to whisper against his lips and he nodded. The hunter had become the prey. He wasn't sure how she'd turned the tables on him so easily, but he wasn't going to argue. His entire existence narrowed to the two of them on the bed, and her hand on his cock. She stroked him with feather light touches, then firmer ones, both designed to drive him crazy.

"Yeah," he admitted throatily. "I like that."

He held the dominant position, braced on his hands as she lay in the cage of his arms, but she was in charge. No doubt about that at all. And he was a willing participant in his own submission. Her lips whispered over his. Kissing him lightly, almost innocently, her hand carrying out more carnal deeds. Blood surged, heat cascading through his veins until his body shook with the effort to keep still. Then he'd had enough. Sliding one arm under her neck and the other around her waist, he rolled until she was on top of him.

Cupping her delicate face in his hands, he threw caution to the wind and deepened the kiss, sweeping into the softer recess of her mouth with a hard tongue. She moaned in pleasure and gripped him tighter, both a boon to the ego damaged by her constant rejections.

"Undress me," he ordered, his voice thick with passion. "I want to feel your hands on me. All of me."

She nodded, eyes wide and dark and let go of his cock. He bit back a moan of disappointment, lying back to watch her as she undid his leathers. Her movements were quick and efficient. Shook with the need he saw reflected in her eyes.

Triumph wrapped around the desire surging through him. His little human wasn't as uninterested in him as she'd made out. She wanted this as much as he did. Now that he knew, he'd never let her get away with such a charade again.

The fastenings on his leathers gave and his cock sprang free to arch in a proud curve toward his stomach. So close to her, he caught the small intake of breath and the way her eyes widened suddenly. Shit, he'd known Lathar men were bigger than human, but he hadn't thought it was that much of a difference. Obviously, it was.

"Hey, shhh..." he caught her to him, reaching up to kiss her again. Long, drugging kisses to bind her to him and calm her. "I'll be gentle. Slow. I promise."

How he was going to keep that promise when her smallest touch set his entire body on fire, he didn't know, but somehow he would manage.

She nodded, her trust in him humbling. Sweeping his thumb over her delicate cheekbone, he pulled her closer. Held her as he began to undress her. So close...

"I appreciate that you're busy," the AI spoke abruptly. "But I thought you'd like to know there are twenty Krynassis in the corridor. With a cutter."

7

Jane froze, her gaze locked with Karryl's for a split second as the reality of their situation sank in. She saw the instant he collected himself, his gaze sharpening as he pushed her off him and leaped off the bed.

"*Draanth*, twenty?" he demanded, tucking himself in as he strode across the cabin. Jane followed, all desire quashed at the thought of those creatures getting in here. The thought of what they'd been about to do...she pushed that to the back of her mind to deal with later. *Much* later.

The AI already had a view of the corridor outside the ship on the holo display and as Jane watched, more lizard men piled in behind the three carrying what she assumed was the cutter.

"At a low estimate, yes," the AI replied dryly. "There's probably more. Records indicate there are seven Krynassis ships docked at present."

"Great, just fucking great." He dropped into the pilot's couch, hands moving in mid-air to access the pilot's controls. "Bring the engines online."

"Online and powering up."

"How many per ship? On average?" Jane asked as she slid into the co-pilot's couch and buckled herself in. The shuttle began to vibrate as the engines came up to power.

"Three clutches per ship, twenty in a clutch give or take." The AI's voice betrayed a hint of worry. "We have another issue. The docking bay doors are closing. I'm trying to countermand, but they've input an override code. Without being physically in the control room, I can't block it."

"Got it," Karryl hooked his arms under the harness on his couch and looked across at Jane. He nodded in approval when he saw she was already clipped in. "Hold on, this is going to be a bumpy ride."

She nodded, not bothering to answer and distract him. The ship surged forward, banking sharply at the same time before Karryl opened the engines to full. They hurtled toward the bay doors closing and blocking their view of the stars beyond.

"We're not going to make it," she yelled over the sound of the engines, loud in the confines of the bay. "Does this thing have weapons?"

Before she'd finished her sentence, a holo console flickered to life in front of her. She stared at it, worried that the alien technology would be beyond her. However, a target was a target, and a trigger was a trigger whatever culture a person came from, and thankfully, Latharian technology was intuitive.

With a grin, she put her hands on the screen. It was a tactile display, the light bending under her hands and forming constructs she could feel and manipulate. Focusing her gaze up, she brought both crosshairs on the screen to bear on the bay doors. They went yellow, then red, which she sure as hell hoped indicated the guns were locked on. She squeezed the triggers.

Rat-rat-rat-rat-rat-rat-rat-rat-rat-rat.

Laser bolts spat from the front of the shuttle, chewing into the metal of the bay doors as though they were soft as cheese. With a yell, she carved out a hole in the doors big enough for the shuttle to pass, removing the last hunk of metal barring their escape as they moved through.

"Nice shooting," Karryl commented, his voice tight and his focus on the screens in front of him as they roared from the outpost.

"Krynassis in pursuit," the AI informed them. "And two more incoming, bearing three-seven-alpha-five."

"Reinforcements," he commented grimly, canting the shuttle to the side as space in front of them shimmered like the haze over asphalt on a hot summer's day. One moment there was nothing there and the next two ships blinked into existence. Big, with overlapping armor plates, they looked reptilian to match their owners.

So that was what ships looked like when they came out of faster-than-light. Jane filed the information away as she aimed again.

"Take out their shield generators," Karryl ordered, swinging the ship around. "How long before we can hit FTL?"

The view through the port in front of her changed to clear space, but her screens continued to show the Krynassis ships. It was easy to identify the guns, they were the bits spitting laser fire at them, but the generators were a little more difficult. Suddenly she spotted smaller structures set way back from the gun turrets and focused on them.

Rat-rat-rat-rat-rat-rat.

Her volley took one out, the explosion causing a shimmer over the section of the hull nearest to it. Jane grinned. Bingo.

"Thirty seconds before FTL drive fully operational."

"We can't last that long." Karryl's voice was the sort of controlled shout she knew all too well. The sound of a commanding officer who was rapidly running out of choices.

"Jump as soon as possible to the nearest suitable coordinates."

The AI was silent for a second, then said, "Affirmative. Ready to jump in five."

"Keep them off us," he ordered, pushing the engines until they screamed.

"Trying to." Her lips compressed into a thin line as she kept aiming and firing, trying to open a section on the nearest ship's shields over the engines. If she could hit an engine, then perhaps she could take both of the bigger ones out.

Space around them was live with laser bolts, each one that hit them rattling the smaller ship until she was sure the next hit would be their last.

"Jumping in four…"

Rat-rat-rat-rat-rat-rat.

"Three…"

Two more sections out. She grinned nastily and aimed for what looked like exhaust vents.

"Two…"

The crosshairs converged, laying over each other and she pulled the triggers, emptying both barrels into her target. Laser bolts slammed into it, peeling away the metal. Blue flame blossomed into space, quickly enveloping the Krynassis ship before it exploded in a beautiful and deadly display.

"One…jumping to FTL."

The shockwave from the Krynassis ships rolled toward them. Jane held her breath, praying they'd jump before it hit. She'd never seen an alien ship explode but in her experience, explosions in space where there wasn't anything to slow the shrapnel was never good.

The now familiar lurch of an FTL jump grabbed the ship. Rather than the stars around them turning to streaks of light as they sped past, they winked out of existence only to reappear almost instantaneously. The view screen was filled with a bright blue planet looming ominously in front of them. Before she could stay anything, something hit them hard from behind, sending them hurtling into the upper atmosphere.

"*Draanth,* the shockwave from the explosion," Karryl yelled over the din as the ship screamed under the stresses and red alarms blared. "Boost power to the engines, we need to pull out of the atmosphere before we're too far in."

"Engines at maximum." Even the AI shouted. Jane gripped the edges of her couch as the nose of the shuttle began to glow. Shit. Shouldn't it take longer than this for them to start to burn up. "Engaging maneuvering thrusters to try and break away."

"It's no good." Karryl's face was tight, knuckles white as he tried to hold the shuttle steady. "Use them to keep us level and divert all available power to shields."

"Diverting." The lights in the cabin went out, leaving only the blue haze from the pilot's console and the red glow from outside for illumination. "Shields maxed out. At current rate, they will burn out in forty-five seconds."

"It'll have to be enough." Karryl nodded, lips compressed into a thin line. He flicked a glance to her and she read the concern in his eyes. "Hold on," he ordered. "It's going to be a rough ride."

And rough it was. The ship bucked and screamed in distress, shields white hot as they burned through the atmosphere. She squeezed her eyes shut, concentrating on controlling her breathing to ignore the panic that wanted to surge through her system. They seemed to be plummeting like a stone. Faster than she'd thought and at the same time not fast enough.

"Almost through, just a little more." Karryl's deep voice reached her, the familiar tones comforting. Despite the danger they were in, she felt safe. He wouldn't let anything happen to her. If he drew breath, he'd make sure she was safe. She knew that as sure as she knew she would take her next breath.

"Coming through now, we're saf—" His triumphant announcement was cut off as they dropped through the cloud cover only to find a cliff face looming right in front of them. The high-pitched scream as Karryl barrel-rolled the shuttle couldn't be hers, surely? She was sure it was though as they dropped like a stone.

"Brace!" Was all the warning she got as they hit the snow-covered vista below the cliff. Then they tumbled, rolling over and over. Metal screeched and her couch came free of its fixings. The view screen shattered at the same moment, dumping tons of cold snow into the cabin. Darkness and cold slammed into her, and she slipped into nothingness.

"Hhhhuhhnnnn!"

Karryl snapped back to consciousness with a sharp groan. Every part of his body hurt like he'd been on the battlefield for a week or more. For a moment, he lay where he was, doing a mental once over. Everything ached, but no one part gave the sort of deeper pain that would indicate something more serious. Cuts and bruises. And he was cold. Damn cold.

Since he'd just crashed the ship into the side of a mountain that was a pretty good outcome.

Jane.

His eyes snapped open, giving him a slanted view of the side of the cabin. His couch had come loose in the crash and flipped on its side. He was still in it though, covered with a thin layer of snow, held in place by the harness straps over his shoulders. But the space next to him, where the co-pilots couch should have been, was empty. Ragged holes in the deck showed where it had torn loose. Fear and panic forced his heart into a rapid beat. Where was she?

"*Draanth, draanth, draanth,*" he muttered, tearing at his harness and dropping to the floor.

Instantly he was on his knees, craning his neck to look around the cabin. A biting wind whipped through the shattered view screen, bringing more snow to join the rest already crammed into the small space. From the way it settled, he'd been out for a while. Humans were more susceptible to the cold than Lathar. She could have died from hypothermia while he was unconscious. A small moan forced its way past his lips.

No, she couldn't have died. He wouldn't allow it. Ever.

Scrambling across the cabin, he plunged into the snow, hands cast wide to sweep through it and discover what lay beneath. The bed was still in place, beyond it a large lump of something. The other couch upended with its broken deck brackets uppermost.

Whispering the closest thing he'd ever come to a prayer, he grabbed at it. The metal groaned, snow whipping at his face, as he managed to move it half an inch. His hands slipped, pain lancing his palm as sharp edges sliced deeply. He ignored it, pain was inconsequential when he had a mate to save.

Setting his feet more steadily, he found a better grip on the brackets and heaved again.

"Aaaarrggh!" he bellowed, putting everything he had into the movement. His arms pulled, shoulders tight as the powerful muscles in his thighs pushed to maximum. Body tensed into an arch, he held tight, waiting for that slight give from his burden.

With a crack, it moved, faster than he'd expected. With a yell of triumph, he turned it over, desperate to check on its precious cargo. It thumped to the floor, upright, with Jane fully clipped in her harness. She lay still, too still, her face turned from him. Blood covered the side he could see, crusted at her temple, and his heart skipped a beat.

"Please no..." Hands shaking, he reached out to press two fingers against her neck.

And found a steady heartbeat.

"*Draanth.*" The breath left his lungs in a rush and for a moment he felt physically weak. She was alive. Hurt, but alive.

"Come on, little human," he murmured as he pulled her free from the wreckage of the couch and into his arms. "Let's get you out of there."

Dropping back to the bed on his ass, he cradled her close and closed his eyes. They were on a remote planet, with a crashed ship, without food or water, but he didn't care. All that mattered was the small woman in his arms still drew breath.

Leaning forward, he placed a gentle kiss atop her hair, remaining there for a moment to breathe in her smell. He'd always wondered what her hair smelled like, how it felt, but she'd never let him get close enough before.

It held hints of herris blossoms... he smiled. The flowers were tiny and delicate, so feminine that he was surprised his warrior-like mate had chosen their scent. But it suited her. Despite the fragile appearance of their flowers, herris trees were strong and steadfast, capable of weathering any storm or drought. Just like his Jane.

She murmured and he eased up his grip, letting her head roll back against his arm so he could see her face. Her eyes fluttered open, unfocused and dark at first, then latched onto him with effort. Awake, but groggy, he realized.

"Hey, beautiful." He smiled. "About time you woke up."

"Hi," she said, her voice so low he wasn't sure he'd heard it. She swallowed, and winced. "How long was I asleep?"

"Only a little while." He shrugged one shoulder, careful not to jostle her, and reached up to smooth a lock of her cropped hair back. It wasn't out of place, but he needed to touch her. "You bumped your head and needed the rest."

Her speech seemed fine, and her pupils were the same size, not showing any signs of cerebral damage. She hadn't moved other than to burrow closer to him, as though desperate for his body heat. The small shiver she gave assured him he was right. She was cold.

Reaching around, he grabbed for the bedcovers. They were *eedireen* so the temperature would need to be colder than deep space for them to freeze.

"That makes sense. Is that why I can't remember my name?"

He froze, arm half twisted around behind him. "What did you say?"

Her gaze was level on his when he looked back at her. But despite her calm exterior, he could see a hint of panic and vulnerability in her eyes.

"I can't remember who I am." She bit her lip, searching his face as though looking for the answers she needed.

"Do you remember me?" His voice was careful. Pulling the blanket around with one hand, he shook the snow free and wrapped it around her.

"No..." she admitted softly, eyelids fluttering closed for a moment as she nestled into the new warmth of the blanket. "But for some reason I trust you, and something tells me I don't trust many people."

He almost smiled at that. Even without her memory she was a strong woman, and intelligent. She knew things about herself, about her personality, even if she couldn't remember why. Perhaps because of the military training she'd had.

But one thing was evident. The harder mask had been stripped away to reveal the woman she'd been concealing within. One he'd only caught glimpses of and very much wanted to get to know more without her shields set at maximum.

"No, you don't trust many." He paused for a moment, trying to fight temptation, but lost. "You do trust me. My name is Karryl; I'm your mate."

Surprise flowed across her face for a second. "Mate? Like...married?"

Karryl nodded, pulling her closer. "Yes, little mate. Married. We're married and it's my job to look after you. Protect you."

He sighed when she murmured happily and settled closer to him.

It wasn't a lie. Not really, she'd have accepted his claim...eventually.

He'd just hastened things along a little.

JANE. Her name was Jane.

The blanket wrapped around her shoulders, she huddled by a small fire in front of the crashed shuttle. The name meant as much to her as the word tree or mountain. She couldn't make it connect in the blank fog that was her memory. But she remembered other things. Like the sound of rain on the windows, and the unbearable heat of late summer in the city. She remembered playing as a child on a crowded sidewalk beside towering apartment buildings and looking at the sky, wondering what was out there. And she remembered the utter silence of space as she'd looked on her home planet from orbit for the first time. She knew that while this wasn't earth, she was human.

And the man who sat on the other side of the fire wasn't.

Tall, broad shouldered and clad entirely in leather, he was hot whatever species he was. With a capital H-O-T. Long dark hair cascaded over his shoulders as he concentrated on the device he was trying to fix, his unusual, cat-slitted eyes narrowed. Even without access to her memories, she knew he was the sexiest man she'd ever slapped eyes on. She watched him boldly, not bothering to conceal her curiosity.

My name is Karryl, I'm your mate.

Mr. Hotty was her husband. Holy hell, how had she gotten so lucky? He was obviously strong and capable, clearing the snow from inside the shuttle and covering the broken view screen so the interior was weatherproof. The fire was likewise his handiwork, and now he was fiddling with the electronics in the box on his lap with an expertise that spoke of intelligence.

As though he sensed her attention, he looked up and smiled. The expression took his cruelly handsome features into panty-wetting gorgeous, those turquoise and violet eyes twinkling. She blushed and looked down, only to glance up again a moment later to check him out. He still watched her, but the smile had gone, replaced by a raw hunger that took her breath away.

He held her gaze for a moment, then looked down, his lips quirking as a braid of his hair fell forward.

All that heat directed at her... she swallowed, barely containing the little moan that wanted to escape her lips. They were married. That meant they'd had sex. Hell, if he looked at her like that a lot, like he wanted to eat her alive, she'd be surprised if they were ever out of bed.

Clearing her throat, she asked. "How long have we been..."

He flicked a glance up, spearing her with a direct look. "Mated?"

"Yeah. Married, mated, whatever you want to call it."

Mated sounded weird but struck a chord deep within her. It felt right, the idea that they were a couple. Like they'd been made for each other. Figured, her perfect man would be alien. Probably all the years in the...she almost caught it, but the thought slithered away like an eel. Dammit.

"Not long. Only a couple weeks."

He pushed some loose wires back into place and put the cover on the box he'd been working on and screwed it down. Some kind of rescue beacon, apparently. His lips curved into a little smile, a dimple playing peekaboo in one cheek. "We would have been mated sooner, but you made me chase you."

"Really?" She couldn't keep the surprise out of her voice. "What, with the way you I—"

Crap. She cut the sentence off before she embarrassed herself further, heat crawling over her cheeks.

"No, no. What were you going to say?" he asked, elbows resting on his knees and the beacon held loosely in large hands. She'd always loved men's hands and his were beautiful. Strong and well formed. "The way I what?"

"You're fishing for compliments. I'm surprised I led you on a chase with the way...well, look at you." She waved her hand in his general direction. "You're drop-dead gorgeous, ripped as hell and intelligent to boot. What's not for any woman to like?"

He looked stunned for a moment, then a shit-eating grin worthy of any smug testosterone-fueled grunt spread over his face. "You think I'm gorgeous?"

"Oh, get over yourself. I married you, didn't I?" She chuckled and snuggled into the warmth of her blankets. "I really should be helping you with all this. I'm not helpless, it was only a little bump on the head."

"Not a chance, little human," he shot back, expression firm. "That little bump, as you call it, has caused enough problems already. You're not making it worse by overexerting yourself. You need to rest."

He stood, flipping a switch on the beacon. It chirped, green lights flickering to life on the front panel.

"Success?" she asked, sitting up a little.

The movement of the blankets caused a gap around her neck, and the cold was quick to reach icy fingers within. With the shuttle behind them trashed beyond repair, the beacon was their only way off this ice-ridden planet.

"Indeed," he smiled over his shoulder as he turned to fit the beacon into a bracket attached to a tripod, its feet buried beneath the compacted snow. The muscles in his back and shoulders worked as he winched it higher. Jane's attention wandered down, admiring the width of his shoulders, the lean waist, and trim hip. And his ass...

"Like what you see?"

His amused comment made her snap her gaze up. He wasn't even looking at her, his back still turned. She frowned.

"What makes you think I'm looking at you?"

He chuckled, the deep rich sound stroking along her senses, like he'd touched her himself. "Little human, I can always tell when you're looking at me. It pleases me that you like my body."

Liked his body? Hell yeah, she liked it. More than liked it, but she didn't say that, shaking her head instead. "Yeah, well, get over yourself. Once you've seen one guy with his kit off, you've seen them all."

He dropped in front of her, faster than anyone had a right to move, and she squeaked. His strange eyes flashed with fire. "You won't be seeing any other males without their clothes, ever again. You're mine, Jane, now and forever."

8

Jane had always been beautiful, but every time Karryl had seen her, she'd been guarded. A whirlwind of driven purpose and energy with her shields set so high, no man could hope to breach them. No doubt a result of all her years as a soldier and he could see her aboard one of the Earth vessels, bellowing orders.

He'd seen her in action a few times. A deadly beauty with an assault rifle and an aim that put half his men to shame; she was all hard edges and lethality. A package designed to make even a holy man give up his vows on the spot. Whatever else Karryl was, he sure as hell wasn't a holy man.

He'd always wondered what lay beyond the hardness. Her circumstances and life had shaped her into a warrior, but he wanted the woman. He'd seen the occasional glimpse, like when she'd dropped her guard with her friends and forgot to be the hard-ass soldier, but the walls went back up before he could see more. But those glimpses made him ache to discover more. He wondered what she looked like when she relaxed totally. When she didn't think anyone was watching her, when she forgot to be the "Marine major" her people spoke about with such awe and was just...Jane.

Now he knew. Without her memory, the harder edges had fallen away. She was still confident, self-assured, and had retained the sharp wit that delighted him, but she was softer. Her movements were more feminine and graceful. As though in an attempt to fit into a man's world, she'd suppressed some of what made her a woman and now she didn't have to.

It was fascinating, and alluring at the same time. Especially the way she kept flicking him little glances from under her lashes as she moved around the now dry and warm interior of the shuttle. He'd cleared it out and secured the broken screen, so even though a snowstorm raged outside, they were safe within.

Though the engines were trashed and power in the shuttle was offline, he'd managed to string power cells together into a makeshift heating unit and had melted snow for them to wash in. She'd taken hers into the little washroom at the back of the cabin for privacy but since the door was broken off, used in the view screen repair, he'd snuck a look anyway. Even though his back was supposed to be turned.

Naked to the waist, he stretched out on the bed, putting his hands behind his head. When he spotted her watching, he clenched his abdomen. Showing off maybe, but he liked the look in her eyes when she looked at him.

She liked to watch, he'd discovered, and those little glances, full of heat and need, set his blood on fire. Already painfully hard, his cock strained against his leathers. Watching her watching him just made it worse.

She was a funny little thing, full of idiosyncrasies he hadn't realized. Like her habit of humming softly under her breath as she moved. Little tunes without words that soothed something feral within him. She was shy around him. Not skittish, she was too confident in herself for that, but the high flush on her cheeks as she disrobed to sleep suited her. Made him ache to wrap her in his arms and protect her.

"Come to bed, little human," he urged, patting the soft surface beside him.

Her gaze flicked to the bed, and he held his breath, waiting for her to come to him. She did, sitting on the side of the sleeping mat then swinging her legs up to lie down. Avoiding his eyes, she wriggled a little closer. He hid his smile and pulled her in, settling her against him with a contented sigh. So many nights he'd dreamed of her lying next to him, sleeping safely wrapped in his arms. If he was honest, although his body burned for hers, it was the closeness, having a mate of his own, that his soul craved.

He planted a soft kiss on the top of her head and relaxed, closing his eyes. His cock throbbed in frustration, but he ignored it. Now was not the time and place. Jane was injured, and he wouldn't risk his little mate, not even to ease his frustrated passions.

They were safe, for now, and warm. The emergency beacon was transmitting on a frequency only the Lathar were aware of, so rescue should be on its way. They couldn't be far off the main space lanes, so it shouldn't take long. Hopefully a couple of days, long enough for him to seduce his way far enough into Jane's heart that when she recovered her memory, she couldn't reject him.

Her hand whispered over his chest, the movement more than accidental. He looked down to find her looking up at him.

"My love?" The endearment was startled from him, but at the sudden warm look in her eyes, he refused to take it back.

"So, we're married..." She trailed her fingertips in little patterns over the width of his chest. Never had he been so aware of the skin there as she brushed it gently with soft fingers. Unbidden his arm tightened around her waist.

"Yes, we are." His answer was automatic, all his senses focused on her. A herd of *kervasi* could have rampaged through the cabin and he wouldn't have paid any attention.

"I can't..." she paused, as though searching for the words, and her indecision, the little wrinkle of her nose, made him want to kiss her all the more.

"I can't remember us...being together." Her eyes, wide and dark, lifted to his in entreaty. "Help me remember?"

Fuck. The breath punched from Karryl's lungs as he realized what she was asking, what she wanted. She wanted them to... His body reacted instantly, back to painfully hard from the half state of arousal he always found himself in around her.

"Are you sure, little human?"

He heard himself say the words as he shifted on the bed, taking her with him so he leaned over her, protective and possessive. The memory of their brief encounter on the outpost, on this same bed, surged to the front. Inflamed his arousal. She was so tiny compared to him, and that fired his blood even more.

"You are injured, it might—" he ducked his head, hardly believing what he was saying. Looked up at her through the veil of his hair. "I would never forgive myself if my taking you caused you pain."

Her lips curved into a soft smile and she reached up to thread her fingers through the fall of his hair, smoothing it back in a loving gesture that hit him right in the middle of his chest.

"I might not be able to remember much about my past, just fragments here and there, but I sure I'm not the sort of woman to cry over a broken fingernail. Correct?"

His chuckle was soft, rueful, and he nodded. "Yes, my love. You're a strong woman. Independent and capable. It's what drew me to you."

Her fingers were still tangled in his hair, curling around the nape of his neck to pull his head down. Her words were soft puffs of air over his lips. "I won't break, I promise. Help me remember us...me and you. Love me."

He closed his eyes for a moment, trying to find the strength to refuse. The pull to take what she offered beat at him, but she didn't remember...yet how could he refuse such a gently-worded plea?

Her mouth over his ended his mental debate. She kissed him softly, hands in his hair as she pulled him to her. It would be okay, they were headed here anyway, he told himself, they would have mated back on the outpost had the Krynassis not interrupted them.

With a groan, he gave into her invitation and wrapped her up in his arms. His tongue sweeping the closed seam of her mouth, he demanded entry and growled softly when she granted it with a soft moan.

She was pliant and willing, and nothing would stop him making her his.

HEAVENS, Karryl kissed like a sex god. No wonder she'd married him.

Jane moaned as he slid one arm beneath her neck, the other around her waist as he pushed a leather-clad leg between hers. He surrounded her, above and around her as his tongue invaded her mouth. Slid and stroked hers in demand and temptation. The need that had been simmering all day flared into life. His kiss was full of wicked mischief and pure alpha dominance, a contradiction that confused her and kept her coming back for more.

Her moans were lost under kiss after kiss. He alternated open-mouthed, hot as hell kisses with long, drugging ones that left her breathing ragged and her heart racing. She squirmed against him, riding his thigh. Heat flooded her cheeks when she realized she was practically dry-humping his leg.

Hands splayed out over his broad chest, she reveled in the hard muscles and satin skin. She brushed her fingertips over his nipple and he jerked. A low hiss escaped his lips as she kissed along his jaw at the same time her hands smoothed down his body.

She teased along his waistband, dipping beneath the leather to stroke the satin skin. Each time she did, his stomach tensed and clenched to drive his hips against her. She reached for his belt buckle, but before she could undo it, his hand covered hers.

"No," his lips quirked into a wicked grin. "My turn."

Within a half second, she found both her hands pinned above her head by one of his. He moved over her, kissing the side of her neck as his free hand yanked her top loose of her pants. A whimper slid from her as his big, rough hand smoothed over her skin, moving upward to cover her breast.

He paused, breath hot on her throat as he encountered no barriers. She wore nothing beneath, soft skin and sensitive nipples open to his touch. A deep groan whispered against her skin. He dipped his tongue into the gap at the base of her throat between her collarbones, rolling her nipple between his thumb and forefinger. Sharp pleasure arrowed through her and she arched her back, offering more of herself to him.

A deep ache filled her. An ache for him and only him. For him to touch her, stroke her, tease her, and then bring her the kinds of pleasure she'd only dreamed of. She knew he could, the knowledge was there every time he looked at her. In every touch, every little look. The heat that flared every time he looked at her. There was a fire in her blood with only one remedy: his cock buried so deeply inside her she didn't know where he ended and she began.

"Please..." she begged, moving restlessly against him.

"Soon, my love." His words were a caress against her skin. He pushed her top up, letting go of her hands to pull the garment clear. She tried to touch him, but he stopped her, pushing her hands up and placing them against the wall.

"Don't move them," he ordered, eyes blazing with command. She swallowed, a thrill shooting through her. Hunched over her as he was, he looked dark and dangerous, a feral god about to consume the offering laid out for him.

Her.

Her clit throbbed in agreement with that plan. She bit her lip, leaving her hands where he'd placed them as he moved down over her body. His breath curled around her nipple a second before the wet rasp of his tongue flicked over it. The peak beaded into a hard point as if begging for more, a message he read easily. His tongue laved over her and around the sensitive nipple. His big hand cupped and caressed her, plumping and molding the slight mound and holding her in place for his mouth. She held her breath as he hovered over the peak.

Closing his lips around her, he pulled her into the wet heat of his mouth and sucked. Her low moan was liquid with pleasure as sensation shot through her, her clit aching in response. She couldn't help moving restlessly against him. She needed more, of everything. Of his touch. His kiss. Everything. Her hands moved on the metal of the bulkhead, one losing contact and almost reaching down for him.

His hand shot out, slamming hers back into place and covering it. "I told you not to move, little human. Do as you're told or suffer the consequences."

His rough tone made her whimper, but not as much as when he moved farther down. His lips flirted with the soft curves of her stomach. He kissed the soft skin, hands urgent on her pants. Any finesse was gone now as he tore at the fastenings. She lifted her hips to help him slide them and her panties over her hips. In an instant, they were gone and she was naked before him.

Chills chased over her skin as he sat back on his heels, eyes dark as he swept his gaze over her body. A flush spread over her cheeks as he looked his fill, as though he'd never seen a woman before. Never seen her before. But that was madness. They were married so he'd seen her naked before. He'd seen everything about her...had to have.

"You're beautiful," he said roughly, reaching out to wrap a big hand around her ankle. "So beautiful you take my breath away every time I look at you."

Emotion filled her and she made to move, but the warning flash in his eyes made her put her hands back. His dominance frustrated and thrilled her. She wanted to disobey, just to see what he'd do, but something about him warned her against it. Like he needed her this way at the moment, needed to look and touch without her touching him.

Slowly, he pulled her legs apart, gaze devouring the sight of her body opening for him. She kept silent, watched his face tighten in need as her pussy was revealed. He crawled forward, the power and strength in his body evident. Heavily carved muscles moved smoothly as he shouldered her legs apart and settled between them.

She had to close her eyes, the erotic sight of him between her spread thighs, too much for her. He'd seemed big before, clad in his warrior's leathers, but now...

He blew a soft breath over her and her clit throbbed in response. All thought processes scrambled as he leaned forward to run his tongue over her pussy lips. The warm, wet brush made her jump, then melt. With a small grunt of approval, he wrapped big hands around her hips, holding her still for him as he found her clit and latched onto it.

He sucked and she was lost. Soft moans and whimpers filled the air around them, her body arching and writhing at his sensual attack. He gave no quarter, driving her higher and higher without mercy. Just when she thought she couldn't take any more, he pulled back. She sagged against the sheets, but he wasn't done with her yet. Two strong fingers teased the entrance to her core. She tensed, all attention on him. She felt his smile against her lower lips and the tiny flicker of his tongue, then he thrust the digits deep into her needy pussy.

The scream escaped her before she could stop it, her release crashing down over her without warning. Her hips rocked, riding his hand and mouth as he guided her pleasure and drew out her release, each wave stealing her ability to form a coherent thought.

Finally, they died away a little and he released her, stripping his clothes and crawling over her with predatory intent written into every line of his body. His face was tight, handsome and cruel at the same time. The banked fire she'd seen in his eyes earlier was in full flame now and the intensity of it scorching. She caught her breath, knowing that no matter how many times they'd been together in the past, *this* was the one that mattered. This time would brand him on her very soul.

"Mine," he murmured, gripping her behind the knee and holding her leg high against his hip. The thick head of his cock nudged at her entrance and she swallowed. He was huge. Enormous. But they'd done this before, she reminded herself, so it had to work. Really had to work.

She brushed her fingers along his jaw and smiled. Tried to smile. Her breathing caught halfway when he pushed forward and her smile became a gasp.

Holding himself above her, he watched her expression as he pressed in. His cock split her, her pussy parting around him, stretching to accommodate his girth. Forgetting his instruction to keep her hands on the wall, she clutched at his muscled upper arms. Bracing and holding herself still as his cock slid deeper.

Her lips parted into a small O. His possession was pleasure and almost-pain, her body burning even as it accepted him. Stopping the forward motion, he pulled back, giving her a moment's reprieve, then pushed in again. Each back and forward motion was easier, until finally, he was in her to the hilt.

He gripped the back of her neck, holding her still so he could look into her eyes. His expression was full of fire and concern. For her. The little pause melted her heart even more. No words passed between them; none needed. The fire in her pussy eased, leaving her with a sense of anticipation, and she nodded.

The muscles in his forearm bunched as he moved. He held her close, pulling back to drive back into her. The first hard thrust, eased by the juices of her own arousal, stole her breath. The second scattered her ability to think. By the third, she was screaming his name, her nails digging into his shoulders as he took her over and over again. She locked her gaze with his, unable to look away. Each drive, each time his hips met hers, felt like he was claiming her.

"Mine, always mine," he said, his grip tightening on the back of her neck. Not tight enough to hurt, but firm. "Say it, Jane. Say you're mine."

"Yours, always yours," she whispered and shattered again, her body convulsing around his cock buried deeply within. His expression tightened and then it was as if her release opened the floodgates to his.

With a growl, he pulled her to him, his thrusts harder and faster as she came. Within a few thrusts he stiffened, throwing his head back to roar his release as he spilled his seed within her silken walls.

9

The planet they'd crashed on was beautiful.

Early the next morning, Jane stood outside the shuttle, bucket in hand, and stood to take in the view. Mountains rose on either side, majestic peaks covered with glittering white snow. High cliffs decorated the pale vista with slices of lavender blue. The sky was cerulean, without a cloud in sight, and the heat of the twin suns overhead made even the icy temperatures feel bearable.

With a contented sigh, she trudged through the snow. The leather pants and boots she wore, similar to Karryl's, shrugged off the icy white particles trying to cling to her. Just a little way up the rise, she decided, and there would be enough clean, fresh snow for her to melt over the fire for coffee.

"Don't go too far. There are predators on this planet." Karryl's voice sounded behind her, the familiar, deep tones sparking a rush of emotion within her.

With a smile, she turned and looked over her shoulder. "Oh, I'm aware of that. I'm looking at the biggest one out there."

"Then you need to be doubly careful, don't you?" His answering grin set a fire burning within her veins again.

Falling asleep just before the dual sunrise, they'd slept in late after a night of passion that would be etched in her memory forever. He had been insatiable, letting her rest only for a little while before waking her again in a variety of sensual and erotic ways to take her again. If this was married life, then why the hell had she waited so long to get married?

"A delectable little morsel like you could get snapped up, just like that." He moved quicker than any man that big should, powerful thighs driving him through the snow as he launched himself towards her.

With a delighted squeal, she dropped the bucket and ran. She didn't have his power, though, and the knee-high snow hampered her progress. Her heart pounded in her chest, thrills running through her as he closed in. She dodged and weaved, but it was no good. Within seconds his arms wrapped around her, spinning her around, hauling her into his embrace.

"Look what I've caught," his lips, surprisingly full in such a masculine face, curved into a wicked little smile. She wrapped her fingers in the lapels of his jacket as he bent his head. His lips grazed hers, and she parted them in anticipation...

Ssssww whoooosssshhhh...

The loud sound overhead had them both looking up. A streak of blue-white fire across the sky announced the arrival of another shuttle.

"The beacon worked! They've found us!" She gasped, hugging him in delight.

Karryl didn't seem as impressed or happy about the imminent rescue as she was. His body tight with tension, his expression was set as he watched the shuttle execute a lazy loop to head back to them.

"Go back to the shuttle," he ordered. "Put the gray robes on, and pull the hood up. Don't come out unless I tell you to."

She opened her mouth to argue, but paused and frowned. A chill of unease crept along her spine. With or without her memories, he didn't strike her as the panicking type. If he was worried, then there was something to be worried about.

"Go. Now. Run, before they see you." He gave a little push in the direction of the shuttle. It didn't take her long to reach it, lifting her knees high to clear the snow as she ran. Reaching the shuttle door, she dove inside, casting a prayer of thanks to the woman she had been. She might not be curvy, or appear particularly feminine, but she was obviously serious about fitness.

Once inside she grabbed the gray robes and hauled them on. Pulling the hood up to conceal her face, she peeked out the door.

The shuttle had landed, door on the side open, and three warriors stood in front of Karryl. Even from this distance, it was obvious he was bigger and more heavily muscled than any of them. They wore leather as he did, and sashes across their chests. One red, two gold. A memory surfaced of Karryl wearing a similar gold sash, his expression heated and frustrated...full of anger as he looked down at her. Deliberately, she didn't try to hold onto it, knowing it would slip away as soon as she did, and the scene filled out.

They were in a corridor. He was angry with her. She didn't want him to leave...

The three warriors from the shuttle moved, looking past Karryl as he motioned at the shuttle. She shrank back into the shadows. He'd said to stay hidden, and since he knew more about this world at the moment than she did, she had to trust his judgement. She couldn't stay hidden forever though. Since the point of rescue was to get them both off the planet, they'd have to come clean about the fact there were two of them. Not just one.

After a few minutes conversation, Karryl turned and motioned her forward with a wave. Hesitantly, she stepped out of cover. Making sure her hood and robes secure about her, she picked her way to the group of warriors.

Karryl held his arm out for her as she reached them. She slid beneath it, her hands against his chest and side as he pulled her close. The embrace was both protective and possessive and he turned back to the others.

"This is my mate, Jane Allen of Earth."

Surprise flowed over the three men's faces. The one in the middle, who she assumed to be the leader, started a little before looking her up and down. "Really? I had not thought to be fortunate enough to meet any of the Terran women."

He smiled and offered his hand. "I am Ishaan F'Naar, my lady. A pleasure to make your acquaintance."

Something about him rose the hackles on the back of her neck. There was no way she was taking his hand. He was handsome and polite, but she didn't trust him. The idea of touching even the smallest part of him made her skin crawl. He reminded her of someone, but like all the others, she couldn't place the memory.

"You will have to excuse my mate." Karryl's arm tightened around her, his voice low with overtones of *fuck off and die*. "She is from a culture which frowns on casual touching. They keep their touch for their mates alone."

She kept her expression neutral, just in case they could see under the hood. She was pretty sure her culture wasn't like that, but if it meant she didn't have to touch Mr. Snake in the Grass, then it worked for her.

"Of course. I do apologize, I did not mean to cause offense." Ishaan inclined his head. Looking at Karryl once more, he stepped back and motioned toward the shuttle behind him. "If you and your mate are ready to leave, my ship is at your disposal."

RESCUE OR NOT, Karryl wanted to punch Ishaan F'Naar in the face. Repeatedly. With the butt of a laser rifle.

Sitting on one side of the shuttle, Jane tucked into his side, he feigned the worn-out rescuee and studied Ishaan and his men from under lowered lashes. No one would be fooled that he was resting. His body was coiled tightly, ready to retaliate should any of them make a move.

He didn't trust the F'Naar. Never had. They claimed loyalty to Daaynal, but he'd long since had his doubts about them. Neither large nor particularly skillful like the K'Vass, nor with any particular advantageous bloodlines, they were the kind of war clan who kept their cards close to their chest and played the odds.

He hadn't been inclined to trust them before. The hairs on the back of his neck had risen as soon as he'd recognized the clan insignia on the shuttle, and the speed they'd responded to the distress call bothered him. They'd gotten here too fast, which meant they'd been in the area. An area of space no Lathar were supposed to be. An area of space where Latharian technology had been attacked with *keraton* weaponry... which the F'Naar had dabbled with in the past.

Arm around Jane, he tucked her closer to his side. *Draanth*, he really did not like her in this situation. For a moment, he wished she had all her memories. Having another experienced battle-hardened warrior at his side would be an advantage. Well, right up to the point she handed his ass to him on a plate for lying to her about them being mated.

He didn't regret that. There was no way in this lifetime he'd ever regret their night together. Taking her, feeling her delicate, strong body moving beneath his had been an experience he'd never thought he would be blessed with. She'd been soft, and sweet, clinging to him in passion in a way that fed into his male ego. Soothed and baited the primal animal within. She'd felt so right in his arms, he knew he'd never look at another female, of any species, ever again.

She was it for him.

Their joining had been... he'd never known sex could be so mind-blowing. Not just physical but spiritual as well. When they'd joined, shared release together, he felt her soul mesh to his.

At least he hoped so, because if they had bonded, the presence of mating marks on his wrist might stop her from killing him when she recovered her memory. He hadn't forgotten how lethal she was.

Amusement quirked his lips. Stars, wouldn't that confuse the F'Naar? Having their first experience of humans being a hard as nails female warrior brave enough to face down a horde of Krynassis and beat them into submission? He almost felt sorry for them. It was so

far out of their realm of experience, they wouldn't know what to do
with her.

It had taken him long enough to get his head around it. At first
he'd bemoaned the fact she wasn't sweet and compliant like Tarrick's
little Cat. He seemed to have little difficulty getting the Earth beauty
into bed, whereas Karryl had to fight tooth and claw to get so much as
a kiss. But now he wouldn't have her any other way. She was perfect.

Shifting position on the bench, he ran a finger beneath his wrist
bracer as if to scratch an itch. Without being obvious, he lifted the
edge to check underneath, hoping beyond hope that there would be
black marks on the skin.

Nothing. The skin was unmarked and pale. Not surprising. It had
taken almost a week before the marks had shown up on Tarrick's
skin, not less than the twelve hours it had been since he'd made Jane
his. Not that mating marks would stop Ishaan and his men from
trying to kill him if the F'Naar wanted to claim Jane.

This time his grin broke free. Poor bastard, Karryl didn't pity him
if he tried to force the fierce little human female. He knew her,
probably as well as she knew herself. She was a warrior through and
through. Forced into such a situation, she'd pretend compliance, then
as soon as her enemy's guard was down, she'd rip his guts out with
whatever she had at hand. Slowly.

"Almost there," Ishaan leaned forward as the shuttle slowed to
maneuver into the shuttle bay. A slight bump indicated touchdown.

"Zaanar here will show you to our guest quarters so you and your
mate can refresh yourselves. May I assume the pleasure of your
company tonight? We have an *Esatliine* chef on board. His dishes..."
He closed his eyes in pleasure. "Exquisite."

Karryl's gaze flicked to the indicated warrior for a moment. "My
thanks, you honor us. Now, if you don't mind, I'd like to get my mate
rested."

Ishaan and the remaining warrior stepped back with a half bow,
allowing Karryl and Jane to follow Zaanar out the now opened
shuttle door. Tension crawled up Karryl's spine as they walked. He
didn't like having his back to heavily-armed warriors not of his clan.

He'd do anything to have some of his brothers in arms around him. Hell, he'd even hug that asshole healer Laarn if he showed up.

Their footsteps, two heavy male treads and the lighter steps belonging to the woman at his side, rang in the corridor as Zaanar led them through the ship. Tall, broad-shouldered, and heavily muscled, he had dark hair shaved to the scalp at the sides, numerous warrior braids decorating the top section, pulled tightly and secured at the back. A lot of braids for such a young warrior, almost as many as Karryl himself wore. He seemed familiar for some reason, but Karryl couldn't place him. He shook off the feeling. He'd probably seen Zaanar the few occasions the F'Naar had put in at Lathar Prime.

Finally, he paused in front of a door. His hand shot out, stopping Karryl as he turned to enter the rooms.

"A warning to the wise," his voice was deeper than Karryl had expected, with a gravelly quality that pulled at his memory. "Have a care with what belongs to you." His gaze flicked to Jane as she moved silently past them and through the open door. "Some aboard this ship have eyes for what is not theirs. And to say they are not bedfellows with honor would be an understatement."

Karryl nodded, placing his hand over the other warriors. "Understood. My thanks."

Turning, he walked through the door and paused for a moment as it slid shut behind him. No way to lock it from this side, and no access panel he could hack into to secure it. *Draanth.* Not good.

A familiar female voice made him snap his head up, eyes narrowed. That sounded like Cat, Tarrick's mate... His eyes widened as he saw Jane sitting on the bed, her gaze riveted on a console in front of her. Cat Moore's face filled the screen and his heart sank.

Slowly, Jane turned around, tension in every line of her body. Her eyes lifted to meet his, the mismatched orbs cold and angry, and he knew.

Her memory was back.

∾

JANE HAD TRIED NOT to gawk on their walk through the alien vessel. Everything seemed so big, larger-than-life, and looking at the warriors that surrounded them she could understand why. Every time she looked at Karryl, his size took her breath away. From the few memories she did have, she realized the Lathar were far bigger than humans. But she kept her thoughts to herself, walking silently at Karryl's side as they were shown to their quarters. With a sigh of relief she slid past him into the room, eager to get rid of the concealing robe. She understood why he'd wanted her to wear it. There was just something about that Ishaan F'Naar she didn't trust. Something about him that tugged at her memory, and she had a feeling that wasn't a good thing.

Leaving Karryl talking to the warrior at the door, she advanced farther into the room. It was bigger than the shuttle had been, with the same kind of molded to the floor and walls furniture. One thing she had to say for the Lathar, their technology was both functional and beautiful. She hadn't expected any kind of beauty from a race so warlike.

As though triggered by movement in the room, a screen on the wall opposite the bed flickered to life. A woman's face filled it, expression filled with concern. Jane froze, stopped in place as though she'd been poleaxed. She knew that face...

"Jane? It's Cat. If you get this, we just wanted you to know we're worried about you... That we're all worried about you," the woman leaned forward, eyes intent. "Even the emperor, Daaynal, is concerned. There have been... developments at home. No one will talk to me, Commodore Fuller just keeps asking for you. Apparently, I don't have the correct *clearances*. Please, wherever you are... You need to get in contact with us. Sergeant Cat Moore, over and out."

Jane closed her eyes as memory hit. It returned hard and fast, slamming into her like a barrage of hollow point bullets. Cat. Earth. Fuller... *Oh shit.*

Her eyes snapped open. That asshole Fuller demanded information from her or he was arming the nukes. There was still so much they didn't understand about the Lathar, but she couldn't imagine that would be good. Just like she couldn't imagine they wouldn't know. Their technology was so much more advanced than humanity's, there was no way they would miss a little thing like nukes being armed. No way in hell. She dreaded to think what their likely reaction would be.

More memories crowded in, one after the other until she thought her head would explode. The attack on the base, her trying to hold the central section, the big warrior and his men who'd attacked them. Her gasp echoed the sliding of the door as it closed, and slowly she turned to look at the man standing framed in front of it.

Karryl K'Vass. One of the aliens who had captured the base, kidnapped her and the rest of the women aboard. The alien warrior who'd been trying to claim her as his mate since. The sexy alien she hadn't been able to get out of her mind from the moment she'd seen him. The man she'd almost given herself to on the outpost, ready to agree to whatever he wanted just so he'd carry on kissing her. The man she'd trusted on the planet, when she couldn't remember anything.

He'd told her they were married...

"You fucking asshole." Rage burned within her as she rose slowly to her feet, body tight, ready to attack. She didn't give a damn about the beauty of the room anymore, or the fact her home planet might have made a decision that would get it blown out of space. Her attention was solely focused on the man in front of her. "You fucking lied to me. Why?"

He stepped forward, hands out in the universal gesture of surrender. "Jane, please..."

"Don't you fucking please me, you—"

"Yeah, lying asshole, I get it. You're mad at me."

For a scary as hell alien warrior, Karryl did a damn good impression of a penitent man. The trouble was, she wasn't impressed, and right at that moment, didn't believe a word that came out of the man's mouth. Her brain chose that moment to remind her just how talented he was with his mouth, and his lips...and his tongue. Heat simmered through her, a shiver washing over her skin as he stalked closer.

He must have caught the little movement because his expression changed between one heartbeat and the next. She wanted to hit him and kiss him at the same time. What the fuck was wrong with her?

"Mad?" She barked out a laugh. "You lie to me, use memory loss to get me into your bed...what do you fucking think?"

He stopped within a step of her. She refused to back down, her head tilted to glare up at him. Awareness shot through her, holding her as the tension built between them. His expression was hard, features drawn tightly as he looked down at her. Her pussy clenched, liquid heat slipping from her to dampen her panties.

His nostrils flared and her cheeks burned. Shit, could he smell her excitement? She hoped not. Sure, his hard-edged warrior thing might make her hot, but he was still a fucking asshole and she didn't want to jump his bones. Not really. Well, maybe a little...but sex wouldn't solve the issues between them.

"What do I think?" He moved without warning, hard hand wrapping around the back of her neck. She gasped at the contact, the sound cut off when he hauled her up against him. "I think you needed an excuse to admit you wanted me."

"What!? Of all the egotistical, misogynistic fucking twaddle!"

Fury overwhelmed her arousal. Winding her arm back, she punched him in the shoulder. Hard. The blow rocked him on his feet for a moment, but he held fast. Lips compressing, he grabbed for her wrist and they wrestled for a moment. It didn't last long, his strength far superior to hers. Within seconds, he captured her hand, twisting it up her back. Not hard enough to hurt but enough to immobilize.

"Last night you came to me, little human. Begged me to take you..."

Shit. She had. Her cheeks went from warm to supernova in a nano-second. "Because you lied, remember?"

She hit him with her free hand, the blow glancing off his other shoulder. A warning. She couldn't get enough room for a proper blow to the face. At least that's what she told herself. "Let me go, asshole."

He increased pressure on her pinned wrist, making her gasp. His lips hovered tantalizingly above hers, mere millimeters away. "I will, on one condition."

She paused as everything within her went still. What game was he playing now? "What?"

"Prove you don't want me. Kiss me."

10

Jane snarled, fighting Karryl's hold, but it was no good. He held her easily, absorbing her struggles with his larger body. His larger, very hard, very...aroused body. The thick bar of his cock pressed into her stomach, making her knees weak and her resolve waver.

Oh, screw him. He wanted a kiss, so she'd give him a damn kiss. Then she'd walk away, feathers totally unruffled and show him just who had control of this situation.

Rising on her toes as much as his grip would allow, she pressed her lips to his and kissed him hard, taking no prisoners. There, she could do this... She could so do this. Who did he think he was messing with? Some wet-behind-the-ears young girl with a crush? Hell no, she was a battle-hardened marine, a mature woman who knew exactly what she wanted, when she wanted it, and how she wanted it.

Then his lips softened under hers and she felt the world tilt on its access. With a groan, she couldn't resist the urge to feather the tip of her tongue over that parting. Then within. As soon as her tongue tangled with his, she was lost. A bolt of white-hot desire raced through her, making her body sing as she crowded closer. She needed to touch him. Feel his body against hers again. His skin sliding over hers as he drove deep within...

"Bastard," she broke the kiss to pant.

Her free hand drove into his hair to pull him down for another almost punishingly hard kiss. This time, when they came up for air, their breathing was ragged and the fire in her blood demanded more. Screw it, they'd already done it so what was one more time. Just one. Then she'd tell him it was over. For good. Done and dusted. But just one more time wouldn't hurt, right?

"How about we get naked and you show me a good time, soldier?"

He pulled back a little, his expression quizzical, but the heat in his eyes and the surge of his hips against hers left no doubt as to how he felt. "I'm a warrior, not a soldier."

She shrugged. "Tomatoes, tomartoes. You want to argue semantics or do you want to screw?"

His eyes flashed and he grabbed her knee, hauling her leg up to press the hard cock still constrained by his pants against her pussy. "What do you think, little human?"

His lips crashed down over hers, tongue thrusting within as he rocked against her. The pressure right where she needed it and the darkly sensual invasion left her lightheaded. By the time he lifted his head, she'd forgotten where she was and whimpered in need at the loss of his touch. "Like that? You think you can take on this warrior?"

Oh god, yes. All night, for a week. She'd never felt so horny, like she hadn't had sex for years, never mind only last night. Sliding her hands down his body, she gave him a sultry look from under her lashes. "I'll eat you for breakfast, handsome. Bring it on."

His lips quirked, dark amusement flashing in his eyes for a moment before swallowed by heat. Without speaking, he lifted her, strong hands on the backs of her thighs. Her legs automatically wrapped around his waist as he walked her backward.

This time when he kissed her, he took charge. He didn't just kiss, he stormed in and claimed ownership, branding her with his touch. Her back hit the wall, her little gasp lost as he made love to her with his mouth, demanding her response. Every wicked thought and erotic need was written in the touch of his lips on hers, sweeping away all her resistance.

He dropped her legs abruptly. There was nothing gentle about him as he placed a hand in the center of her stomach to hold her in place as he tore at the fastenings on her pants.

"Off," he growled in warning. "Now. Or I'll rip them off."

Aching with need, she shoved her pants over her hips and dropped them to the floor. He unfastened his leather bindings to free himself, barely giving her time to pull off her boots before he crowded her against the wall. A hard grip behind her knee pulled her leg up his hip again.

She lost her balance, clutching at his shoulders for support. The broad head of his cock pressed against the entrance to her body and she moaned. Her pussy clenched, clit aching as she bathed him in a rush of liquid heat that dragged a deep groan from his throat.

"*Draanth*, you're already wet for me." He pushed in as he spoke, driving the steel-like thickness of his cock deep into her needy pussy. "You like this, little human, admit it."

She couldn't speak, her hands spread wide on his chest. Held off balance, with his cock pulsing deeply inside her; she was completely at his mercy. And he knew it. His lips quirked into a dark smile. "You might hate me, but you like my cock buried in your cunt, don't you?"

She couldn't answer, all her cognitive processes taken up by processing the sensations coursing through her body. He pulled out and thrust in again. Hard. Fast. Ruthless. There was no softness in the way he took her, fucking her like he hated her. Like she hated him. Raw power bent to one purpose. Pleasure or punishment, she wasn't sure which.

They moved together, straining against each other. The sounds of sex filled the room; the slap of skin on skin, wet sounds as her body clenched around his invading cock... She bit her lip, trying to keep silent, but he saw.

"No. I want to hear," he ordered on a hard thrust, pausing with his cock balls deeply inside her. "Those moans belong to me, and I'll fuck them out of you if I have to."

At the end of the thrust, he rocked, trapping her clit between them. Pleasure exploded through her and she whimpered. He did it again, then again, until she was panting with need, shaking with holding the sounds of her pleasure within. A battle of wills she was determined to win.

He moved to kiss her but she turned her head. She couldn't, not with him buried inside. The way he kissed, if he got his tongue inside her as well, she'd lose focus. Lose the battle. His lips landed on her neck and she realized her mistake. With a soft sound of pleasure, he nuzzled the soft spot beneath her ear. The one that made her weak and prepared to do anything he wanted.

"Bastard," she gasped, losing the battle against herself, temptation, and him.

"Always, just for you, and you like it, don't you?" He nipped her earlobe and she groaned, turning toward him.

Their kiss was open-mouthed and hot. Each slide of his tongue was accompanied by a hard jerk of his hips, a two-punch combination cracked her defenses. A small moan escaped, quickly stifled.

"No. More," he ordered his voice a dark temptation. "Surrender. Give yourself to me, you know you want to."

She whimpered as he pinned her hands above her head with one of his. Stretched her out as he used his body to pleasure her. Her defenses against him, already broken, started to crumble and fall. He surged forward, upward. His arm was hard around the back of her waist as he held them away from the wall. He thrust his tongue deeply. Made sweet love to her mouth even as he ravaged her body.

Her sigh of surrender was lost, but she knew he heard it. A growl of triumph rolled from deep in his chest and he renewed his efforts. With each slide of his cock within her, pleasure grew and coiled on itself until she didn't know which way was up. Giving herself over to him, she became a creature of reaction. Rode his cock as he impaled her over and over and until...

Time paused. The moment between one second and the next stretching out until it seemed infinite. Pleasure and anticipation coursed through her as she gazed into the face of the abyss and saw ecstasy staring back.

He thrust and the moment broke. Pleasure exploded through her with the force of a nuclear blast. She screamed. Something. His name. She didn't know. All she knew was she never wanted the feeling to stop.

He increased speed, hips slamming into hers as he chased his own release. Rough. Powerful. But she didn't care. Each movement stroked nerve endings she didn't know existed and spiraled her pleasure out of control.

Finally, he stiffened, throwing his head back and the cords standing out in his neck as he reached release. His groan of pleasure was music to her ears and she wrapped her now free arms around his shoulders, stroking the back of his neck as they both came down from the heights of pleasure.

He was a damn liar, but hell did he fuck like a god. Perhaps this thing would work after all...

∼

"REMEMBER, keep the hood up and make sure the robe stays closed."

Karryl's voice was firm as he fussed about her, pulling the silver-gray robe this way and that until he was satisfied no part of her could be seen. He was the most worried she'd ever seen him, the raw and primal lover giving way to the professional soldier...warrior, whatever he wanted to call himself.

"Honestly, I can handle this." She took a step back and rolled her shoulders, easing the stiffness across the base of her neck. An old injury from the colony wars, it flared up from time to time but wasn't anything she couldn't handle.

Her words didn't seem to reassure Karryl, the big warrior checking his weaponry again. He was less armed than when they'd arrived, two of his knives and a pulse blaster now concealed under Jane's voluminous robes.

"*Draanth!*" He ran a shaking hand through his hair, his agitation clear to see. "These males...they're not honorable. I don't like this at all."

"Worry wart," she teased him with a small smile. Then her expression dropped serious as she looked directly at him. "Karryl, I survived a decade in one of the most vicious wars my kind has ever known. This isn't my first rodeo, and it won't be my last."

He paused, eyes narrowed and then shook his head at her words. "Half the time I have no clue what you're talking about."

She chuckled. "Rodeo? It's a terran thing with horses. What I mean is this is not the first time I've walked into a dangerous situation with no backup. You know what humans say about the female of the species?"

His eyebrow raised a fraction. "No. What?"

She winked and pulled up the hood as the door chimes announced their escort. "We're more deadly than the male."

There was no more time for talking. Karryl strode to the door and opened it to reveal Zaanar and two other warriors waiting on the other side. She paused a moment as she looked at the F'Naar warrior. She had the strangest feeling that she'd seen him somewhere before.

"Lord Ishaan awaits the pleasure of your company," he announced with a bow and she couldn't shake a nagging sense of familiarity. It wasn't so much the way he looked, but something about the way he moved that struck a chord within her.

Odd. She shook off the feeling to move silently to Karryl's side. Her combat boots were well worn and she'd long since developed the ability to walk quietly when needed—¬an essential survival skill for any soldier whatever the species.

"Thank you," Kaaryl turned and extended his arm to her. "Come along, my love."

She reached out to take his arm, sliding her hand onto the leather in a gentle touch. Zaanar's gaze flicked to her and for a moment she saw a flicker of curiosity. That was to be expected. Most of these men hadn't seen a female of their own species since childhood, and by now, the rumors had to have circulated that humanity was a smaller version of the Lathar. She was going to feel like a goldfish all night.

They were led in silence through the corridors of the ship. From within the all-concealing hood, Jane missed nothing. Mentally, she noted the layout of the vessel. It was a lot smaller than the K'Vass flagship, or even the T'Laat battle-cruiser. Perhaps an indication of the F'Naar war clan standing in the Latharian hierarchy.

Fortunately for humanity, the K'Vass were about as large and powerful as Lathar clans got. They also had royal links up the wazoo and a sense of honor that appeared to be absent in some of the others. She dreaded to think what would have happened had the T'Laat discovered them first. It wouldn't have been pleasant.

They passed several corridor intersections. She studied and noted each. One seemed to lead to personal quarters, the second to what looked like engineering sections, but it was the third that interested Jane the most. She recognized a discolored patch of metal on one of the bulkheads that she'd marked on the way in. That way led to the shuttle bay, and there was a weapons locker nearby. Nice to know.

"Lord Ishaan is looking forward to hearing about Earth, Lady Jane," Zaanar commented, motioning them ahead of him as they neared the end of the corridor. The double doors in front of them slid open at their approach. "He's been intrigued about your planet since we heard of your discovery."

She bet he was. He and every other horny warrior out there. Her lips compressed under the hood. They heard about a new planet and all they thought about was the possibility of getting their rocks off.

"Come in, come in. Welcome!" Ishaan rose as they entered the room, his leathers replaced by a loose silk suit that reminded her of old style martial arts uniforms in the dojos she'd hung around as a teenager. His dark hair was cropped short and his odd colored eyes, a muddy orange and green, glowed with anticipation. "Sit, please..."

"Thank you," Karryl murmured, seating her at the large circular table in the center of the room. It was loaded with covered dishes and platters of food. Most of them she recognized from the court. Looked like someone was out to impress. "Quite the spread, F'Naar hospitality is indeed as generous as the stories say."

"I would like to think so. Please, dig in." Ishaan's smile was broad as he took a seat opposite but didn't reassure Jane one little bit. They might look good, and be utterly charming at times, but she wasn't fooled. All Lathar were dangerous as fuck. "So, Lady Jane. Where did you say you were from on Earth?"

I didn't. She suppressed her initial reaction. It was an interesting and not unexpected question. She doubted any of the Lathar were familiar with earth geography, but there was no reason to lie. "I was born just outside New London, in a secondary level complex."

"Ahhh. Sounds very pleasant." Ishaan nodded as though he had a clue where she meant.

"Indeed, but it pales in comparison to Lathar Prime," she replied, keeping her voice soft and sweet in her best impression of the perfectly submissive Latharian bond-mate.

Ishaan cut a glance at Karryl, then smiled. "I must say, brother, I am very impressed. I'd heard that earth females were difficult to manage and aggressive but you seemed to have trained your mate well in our ways. She seems as obedient as an Oonat."

At her side, she felt Karryl jerk slightly. His leg shook where it was pressed against hers, as though he was having trouble holding in his amusement. They both knew she was in no way, shape, or form subservient.

"I have been fortunate." Karryl reached for the goblet in front of him, turning the ornate vessel in one large hand. Ishaan's gaze flicked to it for an instant before returning to Jane.

"Some of the terran women are... well, let's just say they're more like men. Aggressive, warlike...deadly warriors who refuse to bow to any man." He leaned forward conspiratorially. "If you ask me, it's why their society is in such a shambles. Allowing their women such control..." He shrugged. "They need to feel the proper control of a man."

She was going to kill him. Like, *proper control* dead on the floor, kill him.

Karryl sat back, sliding her a little side look as he did with a little gleam in his eye. The bastard was baiting her on purpose. "I am, of course, lucky. Some human females are not like that. They know their place," he said and took a drink.

Ishaan nodded, triumph flaring in his eyes. "Then I am doubly fortunate. One, that you have such a well-trained mate and two, that you're stupid enough to drink from an unshared vessel."

Poison. Fear stalled Jane's heart as Karryl dropped the goblet. It bounced off the table, the contents spilling across the surface.

"No! Karryl!" She leaped to her feet, trying to get to him as he sat, his expression frozen. Hard arms wrapped around her from behind, Ishaan hauling her up against him to chuckle.

"Come now, my little terran beauty. Did you really think I'd let him keep you?" He pulled her hood clear, breath warm on the side of her neck. "You were mine the moment we rescued you on that planet. You just didn't know it yet."

"You make me sick," she hissed as Zanaar and another warrior yanked the immobile Karryl by his armpits out of the chair. "There is no honor in using poison."

"Honor?" Ishaan barked out a laugh. "Who cares about honor? I care about results. Take him below and space him," he ordered Zanaar.

"No! Leave him alone," Jane cried out, struggling against Ishaan but not too much. She had one shot at this, and she damn well better make sure she pulled it off, or they were both dead. "Karryl, help!"

"Shhh, shhh." Ishaan released his grip with one hand to soothe her. "Your warrior can't save you, beautiful."

She went still, not sagging against him but centering herself. "You know something?"

"What?" he asked, sick eagerness in his voice as he crowded his front side to her back, hands starting to move over her body.

"I don't need any man to save me."

Lifting her knee, she stamped on his foot, then shoved her ass back hard into his groin. He grunted with pain, forced to bend at the waist to keep his hold on her. She slammed her head back and savored the crunch as the blow spread his nose over his face.

"You little *draanthic!*" he hissed, backing as she spun around, and wound his fist back to hit her.

She didn't give him the chance. Bursting into movement, she landed two solid jabs into his face, right into his broken nose. He howled in pain, stumbling away from her but there was no chance she was letting him go.

He swung wildly, but she ducked under the punch. Her movements explosive, she hammered a body shot into his ribcage, then followed it up by slamming her elbow into the side of his face. Stumbling, he tried to get a decent block into place but she was on a roll. Kicking out, she drove her foot into the side of his knee. He swore as the limb gave under him, sprawling to the ground.

Flipping faster than she'd expected, he pulled a knife from the sheath on his wrist. Adrenalin coursed through her, making everything brighter and louder. She kicked the blade away and pulled the blaster from her hip holster. This asshole had poisoned her man, so he was going to pay.

Ishaan froze, his gaze flicking from her to the muzzle of the blaster and back again. "You wouldn't... women don't have the—"

She pulled the trigger. The bolt slammed into his forehead, right between the eyes. Eyes that retained their look of surprise even as the light faded from them.

"Women don't have the balls?" she asked the body before her, eyebrow raised. "Mate, mine are cast fucking iron.

11

-----

uck. Karryl swore mentally to himself as the two warriors carried him out of the room. Poison. Of all the low down, dishonorable... He should have expected something like this from Ishaan F'Naar. The man was no warrior, he was a *keelaas* snake.

"Goddess, he weighs a ton," one of the warriors carrying him complained, grunting with effort. No surprise there. Karryl wasn't the smallest of men, his body packed with muscle from years of combat. A body now rigid from the effects of the poison, and unwieldy to carry.

Travenis Root. He knew immediately what Ishaan had used. It was the only thing that would render a warrior incapable within seconds. Although a small dose wouldn't kill a man as large as him; the cold embrace of space would end his life just as sure as a larger dose would.

He had to get out of this, but how? He was on an enemy vessel, poisoned, and with no way out. The only advantage he had was that they didn't know Jane wasn't the meekly submissive woman they thought her to be. Or that she was armed.

His only regret was that he wouldn't be there to see their reaction.

Help, when it came, was from an unexpected quarter. The

complainer grunted again, his grip slipping. Karryl snorted in his head. The male needed to spend more time in the training rooms if he couldn't carry an inert body.

"Let's get this piece of *draanth* to the airlock. Maybe when Ish is done boning the earth woman, he'll put in at *Zentan Four* and we can get some action. There's an oonat female in one of the brothels just begging for my dick."

The warrior on the other side let go suddenly. Karryl held his breath as he canted sideways, recognizing the unmistakable sound of a blaster gun sliding from its leather holster. His view changed to a pair of heavy combat boots.

"Not happening." The growled voice of the second guard was deep and familiar—Zaanar's. The sound of a blaster shot was followed by the dull thud of a body hitting the deck.

"Asshole," Zaanar muttered, crouching next to Karryl. He pulled a med patch from his pocket, and ripping it open with his teeth, slapped it on the side of Karryl's neck.

The antidote surged instantly through his system and he took a ragged breath. Lurching to a sitting position he coughed violently, trying to expel the drug as quickly as possible.

"Sorry about that, friend," Zaanar murmured, clapping him on the back. "I didn't expect that piece of *draanth* to stoop to poison."

Karryl nodded, waving him away as he clambered to his feet. The fact this other man carried antidote patches sang volumes. That was the least of his worries. His body ached like he'd played chicken with a sub-light shuttle but he had more important things to think about than why the other warrior had helped him.

"Jane!" Tearing himself away, he raced back into the room, fear surging through him at what he'd find and stopped dead in the doorway.

The scene was not exactly as he'd expected. Jane stood over Ishaan's body, a pistol pointed at his head, and her robes open and billowing to reveal she wore a warrior's combat leathers. The pool of blood under Ishaan's head said she'd shot him point blank. The hard look on her face as she turned around said it was without mercy.

"*Goddess,*" Zaanar murmured behind him. "She's..."

"Mine," Karryl growled, striding forward to haul her into his arms. She didn't argue, embracing him fiercely.

"Shit, I thought you were dead," she murmured, face tucked against his neck. Pulling back, she looked him in the eye. "I was going to take this fucking place apart."

"So I see. I gather he upset you. Didn't like his submissive comment, eh?" Karryl looked over her shoulder at the dead warrior. The sight inspired no pity. He'd never liked the F'Naar and so far they'd proven his suspicion correct.

Her lips quirked. "Something like that, yes."

She stepped away, looking with interest at Zaanar. The warrior hadn't taken his eyes off her, utter reverence on his face. Karryl hid his smile. The earth females were beguiling, none more so than his Jane.

"And who's your little friend? I'm assuming he's the reason you didn't end up sucking cold space?"

"A very good question." He hadn't expected much in the way of hearts and flowers from his mate, but her pragmatism and the speed she reverted to warrior impressed even him. Turning, he studied Zaanar with a hard look. Sure, the male might have saved his life, but no Lathar did anything without an angle.

"Who are you? Because you're sure as *draanth* no F'Naar."

Zaanar opened his mouth to speak but Jane cut in, her eyes narrowing. "You're Xaandril's son, aren't you?"

The younger warrior gasped. "How the fuck did you know?"

Karryl swore as recognition hit. It was all there, all the clues. The hair that was slightly lighter at the sides where dye couldn't get a hold, the voice...hells, even the way he moved. He was the Champion's issue through and through.

Jane arched her eyebrow. "A child could see through your disguise. Looks like your lot could take lessons from humans on spying. We've been doing it to each other for millennia, with great success."

"Oh?" Zaanar seemed eager for any tidbit of information. "You are a spy?"

She laughed, checking her blaster before re-holstering it.

"Hell no, I'm a professional soldier, son. Live hard, die young, take out as many of the bastards as you can. Death or glory." She winked. "What's your name?"

"Xaandrynn..." He stood, feet shoulder width apart as he studied them carefully. Only an idiot would not have realized they were far more dangerous as a team than apart and that he was outgunned. "My friends call me Rynn."

The sound of booted feet and shouts in the corridor outside drew all their attention. Karryl snatched his blaster, palming a blade at the same time. The F'Naar were going to be pissed that their leader was dead, and just as determined to take a female as a prize for whichever warrior emerged triumphant as their new leader.

"Well, Rynn. Looks like we need a ride for three off this ship," he growled, moving to the side of the door, ready for action. "Shall we take a stroll down to the shuttle bay?"

THE FIGHT through the F'Naar ship was fast and furious. At first the two warriors tried to put themselves between Jane and the enemy but thanks to the sheer numbers they faced, that didn't last long.

Her world became a maelstrom of laser bolts and hand-to-hand combat as they ripped through the opposition like a ball of razor wire. Blaster in hand, she used it with surgical precision to cut a swathe through the F'Naar. They fell before her, and those who didn't, fell prey to Karryl's or Rynn's blades.

They reached the shuttle bay, fighting a fierce rear-guard action as another group of F'Naar followed.

"Get the engines started," Karryl bellowed at Rynn as he took up position by the side of the hallway door. "Jane, get this thing closed."

She scooted into cover as a volley of laser blasts peppered the air where she had been. One thing was sure, they might revere women but they sure as hell weren't bothered about killing her now battle was joined. Obviously a case of if they couldn't have her, no one could. Childish assholes.

Yanking the cover off the console, she looked in dismay at the control pad. Unlike the emperor's shuttle with its AI enhanced control panels, this was all lines and squiggles.

"This makes no sense," she yelled, ducking out of cover for a second to fire off a volley down the corridor. "You do it, I'll cover!"

He nodded, and things happened fast, too fast for her to stop them. As he launched himself out of cover to the other side of the door, a warrior ducked around a corner down the corridor with what looked like a grenade launcher on his shoulder.

"*Kaaaaarrrryyylll!*" she yelled a warning, but it was too late. Time seemed to slow as the energy blast raced toward him. Throwing herself to the side, she tried to knock him out of the way but it was no good. It hit him in the shoulder and spun him. He slammed into the deck and lay motionless.

"*Nononono!*" she cried out, turning and firing at the door control panel. It exploded into a shower of sparks and the door slid shut on the warriors charging up the corridor. It wouldn't hold them long.

Heart racing with fear and adrenaline, she skidded to her knees next to her fallen warrior. Instantly, she knew it wasn't good. He looked terrible, his skin pale and the leather over his shoulder blackened and cracked. Blood and burned flesh visible through the gaps.

"Karryl? Talk to me," she ordered, shoving two fingers into the side of his neck. There was a pulse. Relief left her lightheaded for a second.

He groaned, eyes flickering open. "Jane? Go...you have to go. Get out of here."

"Without you? Not happening, handsome." Standing, she pulled him up. "Come on, soldier. We're hauling ass. We live or die *together*. You got that?"

"Yes, ma'am." He chuckled and clambered unsteadily to his feet, then coughed.

It was weak and blood traced a thin line from the corner of his lips. Shit, that didn't look good. She'd been on enough battlefields to know when a soldier was badly, *badly* injured. Panic hit her, wailing in the corner of her mind she banished it to.

"Good. As long as you realize who's in charge, we'll get along fine." Sliding under his arm, she ignored the muffled blasts and shouting behind the shuttle bay doors and headed toward the ship. It was the longest walk she'd ever taken. She took as much of Karryl's weight as she could, expecting the F'Naar to break through the door and shoot them in the back any second.

They didn't, nor did Karryl collapse as she'd expected. He made it through the door before his legs gave out. They sprawled on the floor.

"We're in, punch it!" she ordered Rynn, but he was way ahead of her. The engines roared, lifting them even as the shuttle door slid shut, sealing them safely inside.

She looked down as Karryl coughed, struggling for breath.

"Don't you dare die on me, asshole. Or I'll bring you back just so I can kill you myself, you hear me?" she promised, but he'd already slipped into unconsciousness.

"Hold on," Rynn yelled over his shoulder. "This is going to be a rough ride."

Unable to do anything else, she covered her fallen man and held on for both of them.

THE JOURNEY back to Lathar Prime seemed like an eternity. Karryl didn't regain consciousness, his skin deadly pale and his pulse growing more sluggish by the hour. Rynn, more familiar with the Latharian medkit and its mobile single-body stasis unit, grew so silent that she had to look at him to reassure herself she wasn't alone.

Through it all, she sat by Karryl's side, stroking his hair back from his face until Rynn finally announced their approach to the Latharian home world. Now, less than an hour later, she felt even more useless as Laarn moved around a big diagnostic bed. Her unconscious warrior lay on it, still out for the count. He'd been stripped, his leather jacket cut from him to leave him naked to the waist, revealing the bloody and blackened mess of his shoulder.

The healer's face was grim as he studied the blue arc over Karryl. It showed a diagram of the warrior's body, red warning lines and lights all over it. A big scarlet area over his shoulder radiated lines outward, all reaching for his heart. More red surged through his veins, lights that represented his circulatory system flashing in warning.

As she watched, more and more alarms sounded. Laarn moved with the speed of a demon, altering settings and administering medication. Her hand stole up to her mouth. She didn't need to be medically trained to know Karryl was barely hanging on. Nor did she need to be psychic to realize that despite the fact they bickered all the time, Laarn really cared for his friend. It showed in his expression, in the tense set of his body as he fought to save Karryl's life.

He had to get better. He *would* get better, she told herself. Latharian technology was much more advanced than humanity's. What would kill a human was little more than a common cold for the Lathar. Surely?

Finally Laarn paused, gaze intent on the readouts as they stabilized. The red warnings had been flickering between red and amber. One by one, each turned to amber and held steady. She wrapped her arms around her waist, trying to hold her hope in check. She'd seen that look on the faces of medical staff before. It often preceded the words "don't get your hopes up."

The healer sighed and stepped back, shoving a loose strand of his hair behind his ear. Unlike most warriors she'd seen, he wore his long hair tied at the nape of his neck. Probably because of his job.

He turned to her, arms folded across his chest, and she swallowed. Laarn had always been the one warrior of the K'Vass she'd never been able to work out but his expression now made her shiver. It was cold. Dead.

"There's a lot of damage. He took a direct hit from a high yield energy weapon, which alone would be bad enough, but his system was also weakened by the Travenis Root..." He shook his head. "The next twelve hours will be critical as we drain the poison. *If* he survives that, we'll know more about what we're dealing with."

Tears welled in her eyes. Not bothering to hide them, she bit her lip. "Can...can I stay with him?"

"You *are* staying with him." Anger flared in Laarn's eyes, taking her by surprise. Grabbing her by the back of the neck, he shoved her toward the bed. "Look at his wrist. *Look* at it!"

She didn't cry out, even though the healer's grip was punishing. Instead, she reached out with shaking hands to remove the brace from Karryl's wrist. When the skin was revealed, she gasped and dropped the cuff.

Black marks wrapped his skin like vines. Mating marks.

"All he ever wanted was a mate. You. He wanted you, waited for years and knew as soon as he saw you on that fucking base. Sure, he's loud and a bit of an idiot, but he is my friend," Laarn hissed in her ear. "And I would die for him, I would take his place on that bed in a fucking heartbeat...so you, faithless female, will stay right here. *If* he wakes up, it will be to see the face of his mate, with his marks on his wrist, as least once before he dies. Do I make myself clear?"

He shoved her forward, letting go and she fell across the bed. She didn't bother standing, the pain rolling through her too intense. Catching her breath, she nodded. "I'll stay. I'll stay as long as it takes. Whatever he needs."

Heavy footsteps behind her announced Laarn's departure. Closing her eyes, she rest her forehead against Karryl's wrist. Her fingers entwined with his and she desperately hoped for him to squeeze back, but they were lax. Unresponsive.

"I'm so sorry, love. I should have been faster, stronger, should have gotten you out of the way of that blast."

Tears fell, hot and stinging, as hope died a painful death.

She loved him. Completely and utterly. The only man in the galaxy who was her perfect match, her perfect Mr. Right...and she'd pushed him away, again and again.

Now he was dying and there was nothing she could do about it.

Death wasn't an enemy she could charge down with a pulse rifle in her hand, or throw a grenade at. It wasn't an opponent she could outwit or out-strategize.

"Please God, or anyone who's listening," she whispered, praying for the first time in her adult life and not caring if Laarn or the whole damn Latharian race could hear her. "I'll do anything, just spare him. Please, I can't live without him."

Turning her head, she placed a gentle kiss on the inside of his wrist. "I love you, Karryl. You hear me? You can, I know you can. I love you, I have since the first moment I saw you...I was just too stubborn to admit it. Please come back to me. Fight and come back to me."

Unable to hold the tears back any longer, she crawled onto the big diagnostic bed and lay next to him. If they only had one more night together, she was going to spend it as close to him as possible.

One night to last a lifetime. She would make it enough.

12

Jane's soft tears tore his heart out.

Medicated and drowsy, Karryl swam up through the layers of unconsciousness to find his little human mate nestled against his side. Nothing hurt, but the fuzziness in his head said he was doped up on painkillers. Not a bad thing. He remembered the F'Naar ship, being poisoned and the fight in the shuttle bay. No one in their right mind would ever forget being hit with an energy blast; the blinding light and all-consuming agony would be etched into his memory as long as he lived. So would the fact his mate fought for him. Had carried him to safety and shielded him with her own body.

But all that paled into insignificance under two facts:

He had his mating marks.

Jane loved him.

Emotion and relief rolled through him. After all they'd been through, she loved him. Finally, everything was going to be okay.

She was nestled under his arm, against his side, her tears hot against his shoulder. Pulling her tighter, he rubbed her back gently. Her soft murmur was muffled against his side and her silent sobs deepened. Misery and pain filled the tiny sounds she made. The grief of such a strong woman brought so low brought him pain.

She shouldn't be crying over him. He needed to make things right, protect her. Make her smile and laugh. Love her as he had from the moment he'd seen her.

"Shhhh, my love," he whispered, pulling out of the sedative enough to lift his other hand and stroke her hair back from her face. "I'm not going anywhere. Not yet anyway."

"Karryl?" she lifted her head to look into his face, hope warring with pain as though she couldn't believe what she was seeing and hoped, but dared not to, at the same time.

"You're awake! Oh my god, how are you feeling?" She scrambled to a sitting position, pushing his hair back from his face.

"Laarn! He's awake! Karryl's awake," she yelled, trying to slide from the bed to get the healer, but Karryl stopped her with a hard grip on her arm.

"No, stay with me. We're bonded, it helps to hold you close."

He flicked a glance down to the dark marks around his wrist, tired triumph filling his body. She was his mate in every way that mattered. The other half of his soul made just for him.

"Laarn will know I'm awake. The diagnostic program will alert him."

And if the pain in the ass healer thought he was moving Jane, then Karryl would just have to hand him his ass on a plate. No one was moving his mate now that he'd gotten her into his arms. No way, no how.

"Are you sure I'm not hurting you?" Concern was written on her face as she lowered herself tentatively into his embrace. He shook his head, closing his eyes for a moment to savor touching her.

"No. I think Laarn hit me up with enough painkillers to drop a *penachia.*" He chuckled, knowing she wouldn't have a clue what one was, and the thought striking him as highly amusing. They were so different—born on different planets, from different races—who knew they'd find perfection in each other? "Not enough to mess with my hearing though...and I recall a certain female telling this male she lo—"

"Loves you," she interrupted, rising on her elbow to look down at him. Her odd-colored eyes were steady and honest as she held his gaze. If he'd thought she'd act coy and verbally dance around the subject, he was wrong. Like the soldier she was, she went right for the bull's eye.

"You heard right. I love you. You're stubborn and a pain in the ass, and luckily damned hard to kill, but I love you." Leaning forward, she brushed her lips over his. "And if you're still serious about your claim over me, then I accept."

Emotion and love exploded through Karryl, warming his body from his chest out, and he slid his hand up her back into her hair. Slowly, he drew her down to kiss her softly, then not so softly.

"I've always been serious about claiming you as mine," he broke the kiss to whisper. "The moment I saw you, that was it. We didn't know humans had women, let alone fierce warrior women. I'd always thought I wanted a meek, biddable little mate to ease my body at the end of a hard day..."

He chuckled as she made a noise and slapped his uninjured shoulder lightly.

"Turned out I didn't want that at all." He massaged the back of her neck lightly, delighting in how delicate, yet strong she was. "Turned out I wanted a stubborn little female who would argue with me at every turn and fight for my life with her own. Even if she did dump me on my ass in front of my brothers. Do you know how much *draanth* I got over that?"

"Hey! You asked for it. Never touch a soldier without her permission."

His thumb paused on the side of her neck and he tilted his head in question. "Do I have permission now?"

Her eyes warmed, still looking suspiciously wet, and she smiled softly. "Always, now and forever."

～

"AREN'T humans supposed to wear white dresses or something to get married?" Laarn asked, standing next to Karryl as they watched the human women crowd around Jane.

It had been a week since he'd left the medbay, fully healed. The only reason they'd waited this long was because Jane insisted the divorce papers from her previous marriage and her resignation from the Terran military were delivered to Earth before they'd married.

Their bonding ceremony had been short and sweet. No grand hall and crowds like Tarrick and Cat's, just a simple exchange of words in the garden of Karryl's home surrounded by their closest friends. The sun was low in the sky, lending a golden glow to the scene as they'd pledged their love beneath a canopy of herris blossom and under the eye of the emperor himself.

A fond smile creased the big warrior's lips as he watched his newly-bonded mate...or bride, as he should call her since she was human. Sliding a sideways glance at the healer, who had surprised him by offering to act as second at the ceremony, he asked. "I believe so, but do *you* want to tell her that?"

Like him, Jane had opted for black leather for the ceremony, although she'd relaxed enough to let the other women thread tiny flowers through her short hair. In her hands, she carried a bouquet of wildflowers, their chaotic beauty a perfect match for his unpredictable mate. He didn't care that the outfit was unconventional, from neither of their cultures. Somehow it combined both and was absolutely, uniquely, Jane.

"Hell no," Laarn snorted, folding his arms, his feet shoulder width apart as he watched the women. His gaze seemed to light on the slender figure of Jess, Cat's quieter friend, rather a lot, but Karryl chose not to mention it. "Do I look suicidal to you?"

"Maybe not. But you are a ruthless bastard." Karryl took a swallow from the tankard in his hand. "Letting Jane think I was at death's door was cruel."

Laarn shrugged, eyes narrowed. His expression, as usual, was difficult to read. Of the two brothers, he was the more inscrutable.

"Maybe. But effective. I figured she was just as pig-headed as you and needed the push. Would you rather I hadn't?"

"Hells, no." His gaze tracked his bride as she spoke with the emperor.

Daaynal, as always, was impressive and charismatic. Like most of the warriors present, he wore combat leathers. A lesser man would have felt inadequate, but Karryl had no fears that even a throne would turn his mate's head.

She was very much her own woman and knew what she wanted. Fortunately, that was him. She lifted her head to catch him watching her and her smile heated his blood from his toes up.

"No, I appreciate all the help I can get. Human females are damn hard to work out at times."

Laarn's gaze cut again to the little human female next to Cat. She was quiet, absently rubbing her stomach as she listened to Tarrick and Rynn talk. A little devil prompted Karryl.

"Looks like Xaandril's son is popular with the Earth women. Who do you think will catch his interest, Kenna or Jess?"

Laarn didn't say anything, his body stiffened for a second before he shrugged nonchalantly. "One or the other. Perhaps Kenna, she seems more talkative."

"Yeah... probably." Kaaryl hid his smile. He had his answer. The healer was sweet on Jess. "So, would you really have taken my place on the bed and died instead of me?"

Laarn arched his eyebrow, accepting a tankard from one of the circulating waitstaff. "And gotten myself a woman? Hell, yes. To save your ugly ass? I'd have to think about th—"

"Heads up!"

Jane's call cut him off mid-sentence and her bouquet sailed through the air, landing smack-bang in the center of Laarn's chest. He caught it neatly with one hand, confusion written over his features. A second later the two of them were surrounded by laughing women.

"Errr, this is yours?" he held it out to Jane, who shook her head, her eyes alight with mischief.

"Not anymore. They're yours now. Human custom."

Karryl couldn't help a grin at his friend's confusion and reached for his mate. She settled against his side happily, her hand splayed over his chest possessively. "And...according to human custom, catching the bouquet means you'll be married next."

"Not. Happening." Laarn's expression darkened and he held the flowers at arm's length as though they were dangerous.

"Here," he shoved the bouquet at Jess, to the delight of the other women. She blushed, trying to refuse them. "You have them. I give them to you. You can get married next, not me."

"I don't think it works like that, brother." Karryl bent and scooped Jane into his arms, hefting her easily despite her squeal of protest. "Now, if you'll excuse us, I have a mate to claim."

THEY WERE MARRIED. Finally. And it was all without the pomp and ceremony of a typical human ceremony. Just two people promising to spend the rest of their lives together. Nestled comfortably in her new husband's arms, Jane smiled as he strode through the corridors of his childhood home.

Single story, its low ceilings and white plasterwork were rustic and a world away from the elegance of the palace but she didn't care. It was a family home and she could almost hear the echoes of a child's laughter. From the past or the future, she wasn't sure, but she could imagine the former and hope for the latter. Later though. Right now all her focus was on the man who carried her in his arms as though she weighed nothing.

"You planning on carrying me over the threshold?" she asked, winding her fingers through his hair, playing with the tiny braids. It was the threshold of his bedroom, but that counted, right?

He caught her gaze, his own darkening in a way that made her blood race. "I'm carrying you to bed, little female, where I plan to do wickedly delicious things to your body."

She grinned. "I like the sound of that. As long as I get to do the same to you."

He shouldered open the door to the master bedroom and ducked inside. The room was dominated by a large bed, covered with blankets and furs. Candles were already lit, casting a soft glow around them.

Two steps took them to the edge of the bed and he stopped, looking directly into her eyes. His were clear and honest, so honest that she could see down to his soul. "You can do whatever you like, my love. But first, I'm going to prove to you which male you belong to...which male you'll always belong to."

"Oh yeah?" she arched her eyebrow as he slid her down the front of his body. Her breath caught. She felt every inch of his heavily carved muscles against her, the latent strength in his body as he held her, the power coiled within. "Do I know this male?"

He growled, crashed his lips over hers and kissed her like there was no tomorrow. Like this moment here and now was all they had, and all they'd ever have. He kissed her like he needed to commit every detail about her to memory. Heat and need crashed into her, over her, and consumed her. By the time he let her up for air, she was moaning and clutching at the front of his jacket.

"You might know him," he muttered, reaching for the zip down the front of her jacket and sliding it down. "He's the male whose heart you own. I love you, Jane. Don't you ever forget that."

"I won't. I love you, too," her admission was softly spoken but secure in the knowledge of his love for her.

He moved to shuck the jacket off her shoulders and she bit back her smile. She might have eschewed the traditional wedding dress in favor of black leather, but she hadn't forgone lingerie. No bride passed up the power of lingerie, even her. Especially delivered from earth, the silk and lace bra barely contained what little she had in the way of a bust, giving her a cleavage for once in her life.

"What sorcery is this?" he murmured, his expression reverent, one hand splayed around her waist as though he dare not touch.

"Well... I *am* female. Occasionally we like to wear lovely things."

His gaze collided with hers, the heat there enough to flay flesh from bones. She loved that look on his face. Loved knowing she'd put it there. That she could bring this powerful man to the edges of his control. "Things...implies plural. There's more?"

She barely finished her nod before he tumbled her to the bed behind them. Within seconds, her pants and boots were gone, leaving her clad only in the tiny thong. And a garter.

"What is this?" he asked, sliding the tip of his forefinger under the elastic.

"It's a garter. Human wedding tradition." Her explanation was breathy, catching with each brush of his fingers. She'd laughed when Cat had given it to her, but worn it as a bit of silliness. Right now, seeing the effect it had on him, she was glad she had. "You're supposed to remove it with your teeth."

"Really?" His face tightened and he slid down her body. "Who am I to deny tradition?"

Big hands smoothed up her thighs, holding her still as he bent his head. He ignored the garter in favor of placing gentle kisses on her thigh.

A murmur in the back of her throat, she let her legs fall apart, a blatant invitation for whatever he wanted. His sigh of pleasure whispered across her skin and he gripped the garter gently, dragging it down. Lifting her leg, she helped, a soft giggle escaping her throat. One that became a moan when he slid a big hand up the inside of her thigh.

"Any more human traditions I should know about?" he asked lightly, deceptively.

She shook her head. "None I can think of unless you count the—" She gasped as he pushed her thong to the side and stroked his fingers through her folds. "Ohmygod, yes that..."

"Good, because now I have a few traditions to follow." His grin was wickedness personified as he moved closer to claim her lips, his fingers stroking a sensual pattern over her needy clit. Within seconds, he growled at the barrier of her panties and tore them from her. The bra followed, thrown heedlessly to land somewhere on the floor behind them.

Her moan was visceral and lost under his lips. She eagerly took everything he had to give and more. Not a shred of embarrassment rolled through her as she rode his hand. Her hips rocked, urging him on. A message he obviously got loud and clear because he slid two fingers deep. Pumped them in the silken grip of her pussy to make her ready for him.

She whimpered, their kisses hot and open-mouthed. Drugging and addictive. He was a fire in her blood. A need she didn't want to be cured of. It didn't matter how many times they did this, it was always as explosive as the first time. More so. Like their need and passion for each other increased each and every time.

Reaching down, she grabbed his wrist. "Now, please. No teasing. I need you."

He pulled back and searched her eyes. The tightness of the control he exerted over himself was written on his face.

"Are you sure? I don't want to hurt you..."

"You won't. Do it. Now."

He nodded, his hair falling forward to frame his face. His knee thrust between hers and he moved over her. Settling himself between her thighs, she sighed with pleasure as the head of his cock brushed against her. Hot, hard, slick with precum, she parted her legs wider in invitation.

He dipped his hips, gripping his cock to fit the head against her properly. He bit his lower lip, the look on his face so sexy, she caught her breath, and surged forward. Claiming her and mating them one in a single, smooth thrust.

"Ohhhhh..." she moaned as he filled her. Her body tensed, pussy throbbing and pulsing around his invasion. "That feels so good."

"Yeah?" He slid his arm under her shoulders, his hand cupping the back of her neck to hold her still, altering her position to where he wanted her. "Then you'd better hold on, little human, because it's about to feel a hell of a lot better."

And he set about proving his statement, for the rest of the night and a promise for the rest of their lives. Claiming her, just as she'd claimed him, her alien warrior.

***

PREGNANT BY THE ALIEN HEALER

WARRIORS OF THE LATHAR: BOOK 3

MINA CARTER

1

"*S*o, they're *both* princes?"

Jessica Kallson, Jess to her friends, sipped her drink and watched the small group of men on the other side of the room.

Unlike Jess and the two women standing next to her, they weren't human. Standing well over six feet apiece, with more muscles than she'd ever seen on a man, they were Lathar, the warrior race who had attacked and captured the frontier defense base she'd been stationed on.

Since then, relations had warmed somewhat. Not quite captives anymore, Jess and the other women who'd been brought to the Imperial Court on Lathar Prime were now treated as honored guests of the emperor.

The emperor with the *very* nice ass in his tight warrior's leathers she was ogling as he greeted the two men in front of him—both his nephews. But her attention didn't remain on Daaynal, the emperor, for long. Instead it was hijacked by one of the other men.

Laarn K'Vass was identical to his brother, the husband of Jess' best friend Cat, but where Tarrick's hair was cut short, Laarn's was long. Where Tarrick wore the red sash of a war commander, Laarn's was the teal that denoted he was a healer. There were other differences as well. His eyes were green, not gold like Tarrick's, and the body under the jacket Laarn wore buttoned to his neck was badly scarred. The scars were from his profession. She'd only seen them once, brutal marks that decorated his lean, hard body like artwork.

"Hmmm... say what?" She blinked as Cat, standing next to her, clicked her fingers in front of Jess' face.

"If you can tear your eyes away from my brother-in-law for a moment," Cat chuckled, amusement on her face. "I said that yes, they're both technically princes. Their mother was Daaynal's *litaan,* his twin."

"Huh," Jess started a little in surprise. "I didn't realize they had male-female twin sets."

"Yeah. At least, they used to." Cat sighed. "But with girl babies dying in the womb... there haven't been any born for a long time."

Jess nodded, silent at the reminder that for all their military might, the Lathar were facing doomsday as a species. She swirled the drink in her glass and continued watching the three men. Well, she continued watching Laarn as he stepped aside from his brother and uncle, leaving them to talk. She'd noticed that about him.

Although he was as big-built and muscular as his brother, he often stepped back out of the way when Tarrick was talking, as though not wanting to take the attention. He wasn't shy, though. She'd seen him training and interacting with the other warriors, and he had an easy aura of command they all obeyed. He was quieter, but no less alpha for it. It was more a quiet power, as he watched all around him with a critical eye, and it sent shivers down her spine.

"He's going to see you looking soon, you know?" Cat commented, her eyes alight with amusement as she looked over the rim of her glass.

Like Jess' it was filled with a Champagne-type drink, but lilac in color. And, unlike Champagne, she'd found it didn't give her a hellish hangover in the morning. That wasn't to say it wasn't strong. Already she felt a little merry, so she always made sure only to drink one or two glasses. While they were "honored guests" of the court, there were more than enough dangers to watch out for...

Unbidden, her gaze slid to the other side of the room where a large group of warriors had congregated. Most of them were drinking and laughing amongst themselves, and... yes, there was a fight going on in the far corner. Nothing serious by the looks of it, just a friendly bout between two warriors. In the middle, though, one warrior stood steadfast and silent, his light gaze fixed on her. Saal.

Quickly Jess looked away, not making eye contact. Saal had been pursuing her since they'd arrived on Lathar Prime, the fact that he'd happily claim her for his own clear. But, handsome as the guy was, Jess' attentions lay elsewhere. With a tall, handsome healer...

Her gaze returned to Laarn, who also had a drink in his large hand. But he wasn't drinking it. Instead, all his attention was on the pad in his hand. A sheet of flexible plastic, it was the Lathar equivalent of a computer and cell phone all rolled into one, but it could be folded up and slipped into a pocket.

"I doubt he'll even notice, or care much." She buried her nose into her glass and took another drink, hating the hurt little sound in her voice.

Laarn was a healer and dedicated to his work. He probably hadn't noticed her, or the fact she was a woman. His entire interest in her was solely based on the fact she was Terran.

She'd tried to chat with him when she'd been in the medbay, offering to spend countless hours in the high-tech hologram bed thing in there as he scanned her DNA over and over, but he'd only ever talked about medical issues. What was her medical history, had she had any diseases in her lifetime, had anyone in her family had anything unusual?

He'd been fascinated when she'd told him about cancer, even though it had all but been eradicated, and about childhood diseases. As soon as she tried to get something personal out of him though, he clammed up, declared they were done for the day and left medical.

She'd soon learned not to ask him anything personal, in the hope of spending more time with him. Perhaps if he saw her often enough, he might start seeing her as a woman.

So far, though, no such luck.

"Hmmm... yeah, he's very focused on his work," Cat admitted, a frown between her brows. The frown was noticed as they were joined by a third woman, her fingers laced through that of a tall, heavily built warrior. Jane Allen had been the Marine commander on the base but was now happily married to one of their former captors, Karryl.

"Who is? What did I miss?" Jane asked, her gaze following the direction they were both suddenly not looking in. She sighed. "Laarn? Is he *still* being obtuse?"

"Obtuse? What is this word?" Karryl looked around the small group, his expression curious as, obviously not satisfied with just holding Jane's hand, he wrapped his arm around her waist and pulled her into his side.

"It means he's being dense," Jane explained, her hand on the broad chest of her man. Jess all but sighed at the loved-up look the two exchanged. She wanted that, the all-consuming love and passion she saw between Cat and Tarrick and now Jane and Karryl. "It means he's not seeing what's standing right there in front of him. In this case, Jess."

Karryl blinked, the surprise evident. "But she isn't standing in front of him. She's standing right here."

"No, that's not what I me—" Jane paused as she clocked the tiny curve at the corner of his lips. "Asshole. You know what I mean."

He grinned. "I do. But why do you think he doesn't see her? Laarn's a healer, but he's as male as the rest of us. I think you'll find he's probably *very* aware of Jess."

"He is?" Cat and Jess asked at the same time. Then Cat gestured toward where the big healer stood, his attention still riveted on the pad in his hand. "How does that equate to being aware of Jess?"

Karryl's expression went blank for the moment in a neutral expression Jess had noticed a lot of the warriors used, usually when they didn't want to talk. He shrugged. "A man is a man, whatever else he does."

～

LAARN HATED SOCIAL FUNCTIONS. They were pointless. A waste of time that could be better spent elsewhere, doing something productive or in the training arena.

He sighed as he looked up at the sounds of a fight. Seemed like some warriors had decided to bring the training arena here. A small group hovered around a pair who were going at it hammer and tongs. The betting had already started. By the looks of the combatants though, and the quick glances they kept shooting across the other side of the room, they were less interested in the winner's cut and more interested in catching the eye of one of the human women.

Bloody show offs, Laarn snorted to himself, but he couldn't resist a quick look that way himself. There were nearly twenty of them at court now, and all delightfully feminine in a way the Lathar, without women of their own, hadn't seen in decades. The fact that they were the descendants of a Lathar colony team only added to their allure.

Even he could see the appeal. They were tiny but intelligent, and some were as fierce as any warrior. Not that all males found that kind of fierceness attractive. Some did. His gaze fell on the tall figure of his lifelong friend, Karryl.

From the same clan, they shared blood on their father's side and had grown up together. The big warrior had his arm wrapped around the slender waist of his new mate, the human warrioress, Jane Allan. Laarn had seen her in battle, and she was as ruthless as any Lathar. He'd heard tale that she'd shot the warrior who'd poisoned Karryl and tried to claim her point blank between the eyes, not a shred of mercy in her body. Karryl beamed with pride as he looked down at his mate, obviously head over heels in love, with his wrists bare to show off his mating marks.

But, for all that he'd been brought up a warrior before going down the path of healer, Laarn didn't want such a warrior woman for himself. His gaze slid to the side a little, to a slender woman standing between Karryl's mate and his brother's mate, Cat.

Jessica Kallson.

For a moment, he was frozen in place, watching in fascination as she turned to place her empty glass on the tray of an *oonat*, a waitress.

The light conspired and highlighted the slender curve of her neck and jaw, his gaze riveting to the luscious line of her lips as she smiled at something Karryl had said.

Jealousy ripped through him in an instant, his fists clenched at his side as he glared across the room. The only man she should be looking at, smiling at, was *him.*

"She's a pretty little thing. Isn't she?"

Laarn turned slightly to find Daaynal standing next to him. Slightly taller and heavier than Laarn himself, he had the same green eyes Laarn saw in the mirror each morning.

"She appears to be attractive for her species, yes."

He returned his attention to Jess, immediately tapping down his reaction to the little human female. Daaynal might appear to most to be a big, dumb warrior, but Laarn knew better. His uncle was as ruthless as the day was long and far cannier than he appeared. He'd survived countless assassination attempts since he'd been on the Imperial throne, and many before that, when he'd been a crown prince. There were even rumors that he'd killed his first assassin before he was ten cycles old, saving both himself and his sister, Laarn's mother, in the process.

"Attractive for her species?" Daaynal snorted, burying his nose in his tankard and taking a deep swallow. "Have you heard yourself? *Attractive?* She's beautiful. They all are..." He lifted his head to look across the room at the group of women, warm appreciation in his eyes.

When he looked back, his gaze was sharp. He looked over Laarn's shoulder for a moment, pointedly, and then back again.

"Careful that the prize you want isn't stolen out from under your nose while you're not looking, sister-son," he advised in a low voice. "Now, tell me of your research."

Laarn groaned inwardly. He'd hoped Daaynal wouldn't ask, but he kept his expression neutral.

"So far the genetic material confirms that the Terrans are descendants of the lost exploratory mission. There is some deviation, but after so long that's to be expected."

"They're still close enough genetically to us though?" Daaynal asked.

Laarn nodded. "Yes, they are. Procreation between human and Lathar is more than possible, expected even. In fact," he mused, looking across the room to where the two human-Lathar couples were standing, "since the bonded males can't keep their hands off their mates, I'm surprised we haven't seen a pregnancy yet."

He managed to keep the frustration out of his voice. Just. As the premier healer in the Latharian empire, he was leading the research project into the condition that caused all female young to die in the womb. Because without women of their own, they were doomed as a race. Even with the influx of human women, there was always the possibility that the same thing could happen to any human-Lathar children. If it did, gaining human mates for their warriors was at best simply a stay of execution. In less than a generation, they would be facing the same problem.

And that wasn't the worst of it. He'd been tracking the problem with their DNA for years, and it was speeding up. If his suspicions were correct, before too long it wouldn't just be the female fetuses that were affected. It would be any viable fetus. And shortly after, the ability of any warrior to get his woman pregnant would be eradicated.

"I just don't get it," he added. "It's not progressing like any disease I've ever seen before. If I had to guess from the raw data, I'd say we were looking at more of a bio-genetic agent at work, but on a massive scale with no clue as to the method of infection."

He sighed, running his hand through his hair in a rare display of agitation. He was a good healer, a damn good one. Probably the best in the empire and, some said, better than even his grandfather, the last, near-legendary lord healer. Some said, but not all. More said he wasn't as good as his grandfather, that the K'Vass line was muddied by the fact the lord healer had married a commoner. Never where any K'Vass warrior could hear, of course—no Lathar was *that* suicidal —but he knew what they said.

He couldn't heal them.

"You'll find something," Daaynal said, belief in his voice.

"Although, wouldn't it be easier if you had a mate of your own... for close observational purposes, of course. You'd be able to monitor any possible pregnancy in real-time, wouldn't you?"

Oh, his uncle was good. Laarn almost found himself nodding in agreement before he stopped dead. Even the flicker of an eyelid might be taken by Daaynal to mean he agreed, and thus seal his... and Jess'... fate. He allowed his gaze to flick over to her. She was so tiny and delicate compared to him. When he was around her, he ached to claim her. But he couldn't. And he couldn't allow Daaynal to remove her choices either and make her mate him.

He'd seen the looks on the human women's faces when he'd removed his jacket during the journey to court. The shock and then the careful looks away. Or if any of them had to look at him, they ensured they looked him directly in the eye, no quick glances down to his body.

For the first time in his life, he'd been concerned about how others viewed him. How *Jess* viewed him. Did she see the strength it had taken to endure the marks he carried? Or did she see him as a scarred monster?

His jaw tightened. From the way the humans acted around him, it had to be the latter. He was under no illusions. He wasn't pretty to look at. And, if their species treasured physical appearance so much, why would she want him when there were better looking warriors around?

"Think about it," Daaynal ordered, clapping him on the back and then moving away to circulate.

Laarn stood where he was a few moments longer and then turned with a sigh. He should make an effort and talk to a few people. Then, at the first opportunity, he would make his escape and return to the lab.

He had work to do if he was going to save them all.

2

*L*aarn had disappeared on her yet again.

Jess sighed in frustration as she slipped from the ballroom unnoticed and made her way toward where she was sure he would be.

His lab. She sighed. Seriously, the guy took workaholic to the next level and then some. Attached to the med-bay, he seemed to spend most of his time in there. So much so, she was sure he either had a pallet set up in his office, or he simply didn't sleep.

If she had to guess, she'd say the latter. Sometimes he looked bone-weary tired. Hot as hell, but tired down to his soul despite the determined aura that surrounded him like a cape.

Biting her lip, she turned the corridor. She just wished he'd turn some of that determination on her, the way Tarrick had with Cat, or Karryl with Jane. With the latter couple, Jane had wanted nothing to do with Karryl, but the big alien warrior had persevered, stuck at it like a terrier with a bone and not given up on getting the woman he wanted.

Now they were happily married... or mated... Whatever you wanted to call it, they were it. All she knew was that Jane had a ring on her finger and Karryl had tattoo-like marks around his wrists all the other warriors looked at with envy. It was a love story from beyond the stars... and her silly romantic heart couldn't help sighing and wanting that herself.

Her slippered footsteps were near silent in the high vaulted corridors. Like the Lathar ships, the Imperial Palace was built on a much bigger scale than anything she was used to, but then, so were they. She was getting used to it though. She'd always been a little bit claustrophobic in space, sometimes feeling the metal walls and bulkheads were pressing in on her, but not on a Lathar ship. Not with all the wide open spaces and high corridors.

Yeah, she could get used to living in a place like this, leaving the dirt and dust of the crowded human colonies behind...

As she looked up a tall, leather-clad figure stepped into the corridor, just before she reached the double doors to the medbay, and blocked her path.

Saal. *Again.*

She came to a stop, the long sweep of her skirts disguising the fact she'd almost skidded to avoid running into him. The Lathar were touchy-feely if they could get away with it, but mostly only if contact was initiated first. Bumping into, brushing up against, stepping close to... all counted as initiation, and she really didn't want to go there with Saal. Like *really* didn't want to go there. The keen look in his eyes and the determination said that would only end one way—with him trying to formally claim her in front of the court.

According to the weird rules the Lathar worked by, she could only refuse a claim three times before it got ugly. Originally, when they'd first been taken, the human women had been warned they'd end up in one of the pleasure houses—prostitutes used over and again by any warrior that walked through the door. Now they were under Daaynal's protection, she doubted it would come to that, but she'd probably be sent home. Away from the alien culture she was starting to love... away from Laarn.

No way. No how.

"Good evening." She inclined her head, trying to imitate the cool elegance she'd noticed Cat use around the Lathar warriors. Her voice came out breathy and cutesy.

Dammit, where was her inner bitch when she needed her? There was no way she could do what Cat did, her graceful manner a far cry from Jess' bumbling ineptitude. They'd been friends for years, but at times she was envious of her beautiful, slender friend for her poise and grace. She loved Cat to bits, but she was so perfect... and Laarn was Tarrick's twin, presumably with a similar upbringing and likely the same tastes. Probably why Laarn didn't see Jess as a woman.

"Good evening? It would be a good evening if you would allow me to spend time with you." Saal smiled as he stepped closer. Jess resisted the temptation to step back. It would be an admission of fear and she knew better than to show fear to a predator. Even one that walked on two legs like a Lathar warrior... *especially* one that walked on two legs like a Lathar warrior.

His gaze flickered over her hair, her face, and downward, over her figure encased in the floating robe-like dress of a Lathar woman. Pleasure flashed over his features. "You are the most beautiful female I have ever seen."

Probably one of the only females he'd seen in recent years, the snarky voice in the back of her head added.

She ignored it, inclining her head in thanks for his compliment. Warlike they might be, but Latharian society did have rules and etiquette, and the human women had discovered the best way to deal with them at times was with politeness and formality.

Saal stepped closer, almost into her personal space, and she froze as he leaned in. "I want you, little human female, and I intend to have you," he murmured in a deep voice, his lips not far from her ear. "You can run as much as you like, but you will be mine."

The shiver rolled down her spine and she'd taken a step back before she could stop it. The feral smile that curved his lips said he'd seen the small movement. Fuck.

"Not this evening, she won't," a cold voice sounded from behind him.

Saal turned quickly to reveal Laarn standing in the doorway of the medbay, his arms folded over a broad chest. The look on his face was hard as he looked at Saal, but it softened somewhat as his gaze flicked to Jessica.

"Miss Kallson, thank you for coming so promptly. The test we were talking about is now ready." He stepped slightly to the side, sweeping an arm toward the open door behind him. "If you would step this way?"

She could have kissed him out of sheer relief, sweeping past the hulking form of Saal where he almost filled the corridor and into the safety of the medbay behind Laarn. She turned just in time to see the look of fury that crossed the other warrior's face as he squared up to Laarn. The temperature in the corridor dropped a couple of degrees. Although the healer hadn't moved, the set of his body and the sudden tension in his frame said he was more than happy to meet violence with violence should Saal offer it.

Holding her breath, she waited as the two men locked gazes, a tremor running down her spine. She'd seen challenge fights erupt between warriors over the slightest little thing, and they were always brutal. But fights over women seemed to be something else.

She'd only seen one, when they'd first arrived on Lathar Prime and a warrior had taken a liking to Jane. The fight between him and Karryl had been furious and ruthless, and it had nearly claimed Karryl's life when the other guy cheated. Karryl only survived because one of the women, not giving two hoots about the warriors' honor code, pulled a gun on the challenger and threatened to blow his brains out.

But the three of them were the only ones here, and she didn't have a gun. Saal didn't back down, taking a half step toward the big healer. The tension between them was electric. She wouldn't have been surprised to see sparks flying between them as Laarn dropped his hands to his sides.

"You want to do this?" the healer growled, his voice far lower and more dangerous than Jess had ever heard it before. The rough edge and tones shivered over her skin, the sound turning her on. Hell, what was wrong with her? A guy's voice alone shouldn't turn her on this much.

Laarn lifted a hand, and the sound of tearing fabric filled the corridor as he ripped open his jacket, shrugging it off to dump it on the floor at his feet. Jess caught her gasp as his body was revealed, all hard, ripped muscle and scars over every inch of skin. The power there turned her on, even as what he'd been through made her heart ache. The scars were from his healer's trials, where he'd suffered through every disease, ailment and surgery he would treat as a healer. In the Lathar tradition, the more pain a healer could take, the higher their level of training.

Laarn was a lord healer... the highest level of doctor they had. *The highest-ranking healer in the empire.*

Saal's expression shifted as he saw the scars, his eyes widening imperceptibly. His skin paled a little as he inclined his head.

"My apologies, Lord Healer. I meant no offense. I merely wish to protect Lady Jessica."

Laarn clenched his fists, white showing over his knuckles. "That duty is not yours to assume. Lady Jessica and the other Terran women are under the protection of the emperor, and by extension, his family. *Me.* Leave. Now. Before you overstep your bounds, warrior." Laarn practically spat the words.

Saal backed up before he started to step forward, ducking his head. "Of course, Lord Healer. My apologies," he muttered, and turning, disappeared down the corridor.

Jess sagged a little, her hip against the nearest diagnostic bed as relief washed through her hard and fast that it hadn't come to a fight.

"Oh my goodness, thank you." Her voice was soft, heartfelt, as the double doors to the medbay shut at a wave of Laarn's hand. She'd seen the gesture many times before, but not the one that followed it. The door turned red, indicating he'd locked it.

"You shouldn't thank me," Laarn's voice was a growl as he turned and she sucked in a hard breath at the look on his face. "All you've managed to do is shut yourself in with a worse danger. *Me.*"

ANGER ROLLED THROUGH HIM, hard and fast, at the danger Jess had put herself in. Why she'd left the ballroom without an escort he had no idea, but it just proved how *draanthing* clueless she was about their culture.

"You? Dangerous?"

She laughed, but the sound was a little unsure, her eyes wide and wary as she watched his every movement. As expected, there was the little flicker downward of her gaze to his scars for a second, but then she fixed her eyes resolutely on his, as though by ignoring his scars they didn't exist.

"You're not dangerous, to me..." She cleared her throat, a small cough to cover her unease. "Not to any of us. You said it yourself, we're under your protection and that of the emperor..."

Oh goddess, she really was clueless. Laarn bit back a growl as he started to advance. She really needed to be taught a lesson if she thought any Lathar warrior was harmless.

"Not dangerous?" he asked, his voice light as he stalked forward. Her survival instincts must have kicked in because she backed up, keeping the diagnostic bed between them like a shield. "Sure about that?"

"Uh-huh." She nodded, but he could see the tremor that rolled through her tiny frame. Lust flared to life within him, his cock rock hard in an instant and ready to burst through his leathers. It had been a long time since he'd had a woman, a long time since *any* woman had interested him. But *she* did.

All he could think of was pinning her against one of the beds, boosting her up onto its large flat surface, and what she'd look like beneath him, her hair spread out around her head like a dark cloud. The mental image brought a growl to his throat, and he stalked her around the bed.

"Laarn?"

Her voice was breathy. Soft. He could almost imagine what she'd sound like if she moaned. It didn't help the state of his body any and his cock jerked savagely. He was hard enough to punch through steel, never mind through the well-worn warrior's leathers he wore beneath his healer's sash.

She circled the bed again, but he was ready for her. Instead of going around it, he planted a hand in the center and vaulted over to land on her side. Her little gasp fed his arousal further, and she backed up with her hands out as if to ward him off.

"Still think I'm not dangerous?" He couldn't help taunting her, each stalking step forward slow and deliberate. "Think again. *Every* warrior is dangerous. Especially to you. *Every* warrior out there has spent a lifetime without a woman... Only the oonat." He curled his lip in disgust. "*Animals.* Some of us won't touch them... Meaning there are men out there who have spent a lifetime without knowing the soft touch of a woman, having felt delicate skin under a calloused palm, or the scent of her skin wrapping around his will like a siren's call."

Her eyes widened as each of his descriptions matched a further step back until her back hit the wall between two support struts. He reached them, planting his hands either side of her head so she was corralled. Captive. At his mercy.

Just where he wanted her.

"And with men like that around," he continued, knowing he was talking about himself as much as any of them. "Men half-crazy with lust and hunger, you still think it's a good idea to walk around alone? Unprotected? Unguarded?"

He inched forward with each word, until he pressed against her, her breasts flush with his broad chest. This close, he could see the flutter of her pulse at her throat, fast and wild... the shortness of her breath as she struggled to breathe, and the darkening of her eyes as she looked up at him.

He had to be scaring her, but he didn't care. She needed to know this. She needed to be scared, to be wary of any warrior. And who better to give her the lesson than a scarred monstrosity like him. A man she was already terrified of... and couldn't bear to look at. Scaring her sent a lance of pain through his heart, but he steeled himself against it. Better him than another warrior. Any other warrior wouldn't just scare her to make a point, he'd claim her, bind her to him, and then she would have no escape.

Just as he wanted to... He fought that thought down, locking it away in the back of his mind. He wouldn't claim her, couldn't claim her because there was no way she would want him to. So he'd stick to just scaring her into being more sensible. Or, goddess help him, he'd kill any warrior who claimed her when she didn't want them to.

*What happens when she **does** want them to?* The little voice in the back of his head wanted to know. He ignored that as well, not even wanting to think along those lines. He would deal with it when it happened.

"I'm not unguarded. You're here to protect me," she argued, her hands on his broad chest as she tried to push against him.

The warning growl from the back of his throat put a stop to that and she looked up at him with wide eyes. They were the clearest blue, pale and piercing, and haunted his dreams. The round shape, so unlike his own slitted pupils, fascinated him.

"Perhaps I don't want to protect you."

His voice was blunt and rough as he slid a hand into her hair, cupping the back of her neck and hauling her up against him. He expected her to struggle, steeled his hold against it as he covered her lips with his. Hard and ruthless, he swept a tongue against her lips, prying them open to delve inside.

But she didn't struggle. Her lips parted as she melted against him. Her sweet taste exploded on his tongue, the softness he found almost bringing him to his end then and there. Soft hands went from pushing him to clinging, and then one of them slid up into his hair. Another growl broke from the back of his throat as her slender fingers tangled in the long locks, teasing and tempting him.

It was just too much. He'd intended the kiss to be a warning, nothing more, nothing less. But feeling her surrender against him, her mouth soft and pliant under his kiss, as her curvy little body was submissive against his was just too much. Sliding his hands down her sides, he ducked down and hoisted her up to pin her against the wall with his body, wrapping her legs around his hips.

She whimpered under his lips and the tiny noise sent arousal thundering though his veins like a *drakeen* tank-bot on a charge. His kiss turned from hard and brutal to slow and sensual. Expecting her to push him away at any moment, he concentrated on memorizing the taste of her, how she felt under his hands, the feeling of her hands in his hair. If he never had another taste of heaven like this, he wanted to remember every moment.

But she didn't push him away. Instead, her hips rocked against his and he groaned, his cock hard and heavy against the warmth of her covered pussy. His hands tightened on her hips and it was all he could do to keep them there. The long skirts of her robe swirled around them, trapped between them, but they were nothing more than a flimsy barrier. It would be the work of a moment to tear the delicate fabric from her, rip open his leathers and bury himself balls deep in her softness. Claim her as his own.

And she would hate him for it. She couldn't even look at him.

Pulling away, he ignored her little sound of disappointment with iron control and looked down at her with a hard look.

"See how easy it would be for me to take you?" he bit out, hands turning hard on her hips, holding her still before he lost all sense or reason. "I could easily tear this pretty little thing from you and fuck you senseless up against this wall, and there's nothing you could do to stop me. *Nothing,*" he growled, shaking her slightly when she opened her mouth to speak. A roll of his hips had his cock pressing hard against her.

"I could take you, use you any way I wanted to, and there would be nothing, *nothing,* you could do about it. You think all warriors are like Tarrick and Karryl?" He laughed harshly. "We're not. They're the good guys. You get that? They're both honorable and *nice.* I'm not. Not many of us are. You understand me?"

Her eyes widened, fear finally sneaking into the blue, and she nodded. Hating himself for putting it there, he let go of her and set her on her feet. "You're lucky I came along to save you from Saal J'Qess," he rumbled as he stepped away, trying to ignore the fact she was unsteady on her feet as she straightened her dress. "He's an asshole. I've heard him boasting about his exploits. He'd claim you and keep you on your knees, your mouth, pussy or ass filled with cock."

Just the thought of her in the other warrior's bed was enough to send fury ripping through him. Quickly, he turned away so she wouldn't see his expression, the need and lust he knew had to be written on his features. She wasn't for him, no matter what his uncle said, and the quicker he got that through his head the better.

"Right, since you're here," he grumbled. "We might as well make use of the time. I have extra tests I can run, and then I'll take you back to the women's quarters."

*T*hree days later Jess' lips still tingled from Laarn's kiss. He'd barely looked at her as he'd run a barrage of tests, ignoring the few questions she'd gotten up the courage to ask. Her body had been on fire for his touch, but once he'd let her go, it had been as though she hadn't existed as a woman.

Again.

Frustration beat at her as she paced in the central room of the women's quarters, a common feeling where the tall, handsome healer was concerned. Her steps took her across the plush run in the middle of the floor and back again, the soft swish of her skirts against her ankles a calming refrain completely ignored in her agitation.

He'd kissed the daylights out of her, giving her a hint of the kind of passion she'd only dreamed of before he shut her out. Stopping at the window, she looked out over the courtyard below. A number of the K'Vass warriors were training down there and she absently watched them, admiring the strength and speed they moved with and the power in their big, masculine bodies. The fact that they were related to her on a species level still boggled her mind. How had they gotten from the lethal grace and sheer size of the Lathar to humanity?

"They're amazing. Aren't they?" Kenna's voice sounded by her ear as the other woman came to stand beside her. "Utterly amazing in a firefight. Have you seen them training with the combat bots yet?"

Jess shivered, remembering the attack and subsequent capture of the sentinel base where all the women had been captured. They'd used the red-eyed, silver-skinned bots then. Their bladed fingers still gave her nightmares. "No, not yet. I hate those things."

Thankfully, there weren't many of them in the Imperial palace, within the walls anyway. It seemed that for anything other than exterior defense, the Lathar preferred "real" guards. Warriors guarded the corridors and halls in pairs.

"Oh, they're not that bad." Kenna moved forward, cocking up a hip and perching on the edge of the wide windowsill, the better to watch the warriors training below. "You should see the bigger bots, the *drakeen*. They're awesome."

Jess watched the other woman's gaze search through the big fight happening in the middle of the training area. It looked like a bloody and brutal free-for-all, but within a minute, there was a roar and a warrior emerged from the bottom of the pile, shedding the others like a dog shook water off its coat.

Xaandril, the emperor's champion, was instantly recognizable with his short, silver-blond hair and the tattoo-like marks all over his body.

Kenna breathed a sigh of relief and then caught herself, glancing quickly at Jess as if to see if she'd noticed. Jess hid her small smile and kept the neutral look on her face.

"He's a big guy," she commented, noncommittally. "Not sure many warriors could take him on. Good job he's not shown an interest in any of us," she couldn't help adding, just to see if she got a reaction. She did. A flush spread over Kenna's high cheekbones.

"He lost his wife and daughter apparently." The former marine's voice was softer than usual. "I don't think he's interested in trying again."

Jess had been about to answer that she didn't think that was the case when a chirp from the other room drew her attention. The sound announced an incoming communication, and it was coming from her room.

She frowned. The only people who knew where to reach her were Terran Command and her family. Command usually contacted either Jane, since as a major, she was the highest ranking among them, or Cat, who, thanks to her marriage to Tarrick, was technically a Latharian princess now.

"Sorry, I just need to get that," she called over her shoulder as she headed for her room.

All the rooms branched off the central area, and they were all the same. Large with high-vaulted ceilings, they were all decorated in the marble and white color scheme of the rest of the palace with gauzy drapes at the windows. Despite the elegant opulence, the windows were some sort of blast, laser and bullet-proof glass to match the heavy-duty defense shutters that could be rolled down over the doors at the touch of a button—all for the protection of the human women within.

Some among the Lathar hadn't rejoiced at the discovery of what at first had been hailed as a genetically compatible species, dismissing them as sub-Lathar in disgust. They'd insisted that breeding with humanity would corrupt what was left of the Lathar gene pool and lead to the destruction of their race.

There had been several attacks, the most prominent at Cat and Tarrick's wedding. But there had apparently been more after, leading to Daaynal installing the heavy-duty security to protect the unmated human women since they didn't have mates to ensure their safety.

The chirp from the comms console in the corner grew more agitated as she crossed the room. "Okay, okay, keep your bloody hair on," she grumbled as she slid into the soft seat in front of it.

She hit the answer button and smiled when her mother's face appeared on screen. Almost instantly the expression faltered as she registered the worried expression and the tears in her mother's eyes.

"Mom? Oh my god, what happened?"

Amanda Kallson wasn't normally an emotional woman—

bringing up three children on her own had seen to that—but now her emotions were written all over her face.

"It's Lizzie, Jess," she managed to get out, tears streaming down her face. "She's ill, really ill."

The words stopped Jess in her tracks, the world... hell, the universe freezing around her. Her twin, Lizzie, had been there all her life since they'd shared a womb together, and although she was the homebody to Jess' adventurer, the thought of her twin being ill... or worse... ripped a hole right through her heart.

"Mom, calm down. What's happened?"

Only her military training allowed Jess to sit there calmly, her voice soothing as she tried to calm her tearful mother down. A chill crawled up her spine as her mom took a shaky breath and wiped her eyes. The tears still cascaded down her cheeks.

"She's been sick for a while. We thought at first it was just a cold... you know we had the arborian flu through here a couple of months back? Well, some people had relapses, so we thought it might just be that."

Jess nodded. While not usually lethal, arborian flu was a nasty son of a bitch, liable to come back for a second or third bite after the initial infection. And, unusually, it didn't target the elderly or the weak, but young and healthy people like Lizzie and Jess.

"B-but then she didn't recover. She got weaker... she didn't want us to tell you since you're... well, *there*." Amanda flicked a wide-eyed glance over Jess' shoulder as though she expected a horde of alien warriors to storm in and snatch Jess away right in front of her eyes.

"She wouldn't let us take her to the medical center, said it was just a bug that would pass." Amanda's voice broke, her face creased with pain. "But she went into the shower last night and collapsed in the stall. She's in a coma. The doctors don't know what's wrong with her. Jess... please, come home. I'm scared we're going to lose her."

"I NEED to see the emperor. Please!" Jess begged the stony-faced guard who had blocked access to the Imperial war-room where Daaynal was supposed to be. "It's a matter of life and death."

"The emperor is in a meeting with his advisors and cannot be disturbed." The guard's face was hard, no give at all in his expression. "I will ensure he gets your message. If he deems it worthy of note, he will get back to you."

"You don't *understand!*" She blinked back tears, knowing that a show of emotion here would get her nowhere with the stony-faced guard. "It concerns Earth—" Okay, so maybe that was a stretch but she didn't care. She had to get to Daaynal, and get him to agree to send her home. "I had a communication from home that he needs to know about."

The guard simply looked down his nose at her. "The emperor will contact you if he wishes. Now, please, move along before I have to remove you from the room."

For a split second, Jess stood her ground. Perhaps if she did kick off and cause a scene, the commotion would reach Daaynal in the rooms off the war-room and he'd come to investigate.

"That won't be necessary," a deep male voice announced behind her. She turned with a small gasp to find Saal behind her, his big frame taut with tension and his expression hard as he walked toward her. His attention wasn't on her, though, but on the guard.

"I'll ensure the Lady Jessica gets back to the women's quarters. She won't bother you further." As he spoke, he took hold of her arm and pulled her away to march her across the big room.

"What the hell do you think you're doing, Saal?" she hissed, trying to free herself from his hold.

His grip was firm though, unbreakable, as he slid her a sideways look. "Keep walking," he warned, a new tone in his voice. "Dvarr is a purist. You really don't want to provoke him or end up at his mercy. Trust me."

She gasped, about to turn and look back toward the asshole guard, but Saal swept her out into the corridor before she could.

"A purist? One of those assholes who attacked Cat and Tarrick's wedding? Are you sure?" she demanded, looking up at him as he stopped. Instead of trying to crowd her against the wall as he always had before, he let go of her arm and stepped back. "How do you know?"

He shrugged, his leather jacket pulling across his broad shoulders. "I hear things, rumors and gossip. Not everyone is happy about having humans here, or happy that you're being kept away from most of us. Most of us just want a fair chance at claiming one of you, but Dvarr isn't one of them. He and warriors like him would happily wipe you from existence to avoid 'tainting' our bloodlines."

"But... that's crazy." She shook her head in disbelief. "You guys have no women. No women, no bloodlines. Someone should explain the birds and the bees to him."

"The what and the what?" The big warrior looked confused. "Never mind. What was so important that you decided to go toe to toe with an Imperial guard?"

She couldn't help it. Far from being an asshole, Saal actually seemed concerned about her. The change threw her and brought tears back to her eyes.

"I need to go home. My sister is sick, like *really* sick. I need to go be with her before..."

She couldn't finish the sentence, the unthinkable stealing her ability to form thoughts, let alone shape them into words.

"Oh goddess... I'm sorry," he murmured in a deep voice and made a move to step forward. At the last moment, he stopped, his hands out to the sides to show he wasn't going to touch her although she read the desire too plainly and clearly in his eyes. "Are you close?"

She nodded, pulling a tissue from her sleeve to wipe at her eyes. "She's my twin... my *litaan,*" she corrected.

His expression cleared, his eyes wide at the Latharian word for twin. "Humans have *litaan*-female births?" he asked in surprise.

"Yeah. It's as common as twin males and male-female twins." It was her turn to frown in confusion. "Why?"

He shrugged. "I've never heard of it before. Lathar *litaan* are usually male, or rarely a male and female pair are born. I can understand now, though, why you need to go home."

"But I can't see Daaynal, so I can't!"

She bit her lip in frustration, letting Saal guide her down the corridors back toward the women's quarters. Any ulterior motive she'd felt from him before had disappeared after his unexpected gallantry in saving her from Dvarr's threat.

Saal stopped, the doors to the women's quarters in sight, his hand on her arm. She started at the unexpected contact, but he didn't try to keep a hold on her. He just stopped her and then removed his hand.

"Listen," he said in a low voice, checking up and down the corridor to make sure no one was listening. "If you need to go home, I have a ship..."

She cut him a sideways look of surprise. "We're under the protection of the emperor. Wouldn't that get you into trouble?"

He shrugged. "Probably, but for you I would."

Jess backed off a step, searching his face. "Are you saying..."

His next words confirmed her suspicion. "I have a ship. Accept my claim and I'll take you home."

HAVING Jess in his arms had rocked him to the soul. Her soft curves against him, the silk of her hair over his hands, the sweet sound of her surrender under his lips as he claimed her mouth. Laarn growled, his palms flat against the cool surface of the counter in front of him as his cock gave a savage ache, not at all happy, even days later, that he hadn't claimed her as his own.

He could have. She was warm and willing, soft and open to him. It would have been the work of a moment to tear her dress from her body and impale her on his cock. Then he'd have had her for always, in his life. In his bed...

And, *lady,* did he want that.

Keeping his eyes closed, he fought to get himself under control. Luckily, the lab was empty, as per his instructions. Since the kiss incident he'd given orders he was working alone, researching the disease that was killing their race. It wasn't unusual for him to do so.

He often shut himself away when he was working on a problem—be it a complex new surgery, treatment plans for a large-scale virus, or this, the most important medical issue that the Lathar had ever faced.

The medical staff were used to it. Apart from leaving meals by the door of his lab, they mainly left him alone, paging him if he was needed in the main med-bay. So far, they'd only had to do it once, when a warrior had required extensive spinal surgery after a training accident. The male had been cleaved almost in two, his ribs detached from his spine on one side and the body cavity open.

The fact he'd made it to surgery was testament to the hardiness of their race, but it had meant Laarn had a twelve-hour fight himself as he battled time and nerve damage to put the warrior back together. He'd done it. He wasn't lord healer for nothing. Complex surgery for battle wounds was one of his specialties.

As was genetic manipulation, a requirement for even *thinking* about ascension to the lord healer position. The Lathar as a race had been extensively genetically modified over their history, to better adapt them for combat and various other reasons. The exploration team that had eventually become the human race, for example, had been modified to be smaller and reproduce prolifically. Further evidence they had been intended for eventual colonization. Where along the way their eyes had changed, he didn't know.

A chirp brought his head up sharply. The holographic display over the main desk in front of him was brightly lit, displaying the results of one of the many tests he was running simultaneously and continuously, trying to figure out how to fix the damage to the Latharian genetic code. There was a pulsing light in one of the sectors, indicating that one of the tests had reached its conclusion.

He frowned as he straightened up, tucking his hair behind his ears as he pulled the information from the edge of the screen into the middle of the display. A flick and spread of his fingers opened the data file, and the information rolled out before his eyes.

Which widened. The test was one of the investigatory ones he'd instigated on the DNA of their human guests when they'd arrived—mapping and exploring the new genetic information. The task had become even more important once he'd realized that the similarities between them as species weren't random... that they were related. Even altered Latharian DNA might hold clues to help him in his task.

As he read the results, his eyes narrowed, his agile mind working over the data and fitting it in with what he already knew. From the look of it, the exploration group that had become the Terrans had left the Lathar before other genetic manipulations had been made. Excitement rose in his chest.

If they had, that explained the lack of slitted pupils, a manipulation that had been made eons ago to adapt the Lathar for fighting in planetary systems with high levels of light in the artorian spectrum. But it also meant their core genetic information might contain information long since lost from the Lathar code.

Leaning forward, his hands moved swiftly over the holographic display, flicking and pinching in midair as he worked his way through the results with a fervor that burned in his chest. His breathing shortened and his body was tight with tension as his big heart pounded. The information he sought was here. He just knew it was. All he had to do was find it.

The universe narrowed down to two things. His gaze zeroed in on what he was reading and his hands as he cut through useless data to find what he needed. Then, in one perfect moment, he spotted it. There was a strand of data he'd almost missed, hidden behind another, and he almost scrolled past it. At the last moment though, his brain kicked him in the ass and he rolled back, stabbing the data-stream with a finger and then flicking it wide to expand it onto his screen.

His breathing all but stopped as the code rolled out. Then excitement burst through him with all the force and brilliance of a supernova. There it was—a pure, unaltered snippet of DNA. He'd never seen it before, never once in the altered and hacked about code he'd been seeing all his life, but its purity shone through like the lady goddess herself.

That was it. That was the answer he'd been looking for. His hands moving over the holo-console at near light speed, he isolated the snippet, turning and manipulating it to fit into the Latharian genome.

"Holy shit..." he breathed as it locked into place, creating a bridge and strengthening several areas he hadn't even realized were a problem. The change caused a chain reaction along the strand, fixing problems one by one until the helix glowed, perfectly healthy and rotating in front of his eyes.

The smallest change, the tiniest snippet of code hidden in the background that, at some point, had been removed or corrupted in the code of the Lathar... and it was the key to everything. From a race some no longer considered Lathar. The humans.

More specifically, one of the human women. The self-same women they'd captured to slack their lust on had unwittingly provided the key to saving them as a race.

How fucking ironic.

"Who are you from?" He spoke to the glowing strand as if it were a person, a frown on his face as he dug deeper into the test results. They only had a few human women here, so whoever it belonged to was here, now. He could run further tests and save his people.

Isolating the sample the code had been extracted from, Laarn's heart about stopped as a name flashed across his screen.

Jessica Kallson, it read, followed by, *Human. Female. Captured by the Lathar from sector nine-seven-three-five-alpha.*

He rocked back on his heels.

His little Jessica was the female who would save them all.

Reaching his hand out, he triggered the comms system, opening a direct line to his uncle, the emperor. "Your Majesty, this is Laarn," he began. "I have results you're going to want to see."

4

It took Daaynal less than ten minutes to reach Laarn's lab, and the healer less than two to explain the situation. After studying the results for a long moment, Daaynal turned and Laarn found himself scrutinized by eyes so like his own.

"And you're sure?" the emperor asked, his expression serious.

Laarn nodded. "I've tested the patch myself several times and I have the healer's hall AI on it, testing out every variant I can think of and probably a million I can't."

The emperor nodded, his expression thoughtful. One hip leaning back against the edge of the console, he studied the data scrolling over the screen in front of them. Even though he wasn't a trained healer, Laarn wouldn't have been surprised in the least if he understood most of it.

Daaynal liked to present himself as the big, dumb warrior, complete with leathers and braids, but it was all an act. The male had a mind like a steel trap, could pilot not only one but multiple *drakeen* at the same time, and his *litaan* had been a mathematical genius who had written most of the base programming for the AIs in use across the empire.

"And the human female, Jessica, is the key?" he asked, proving

Laarn's unspoken theory that he understood the information on the screen by stepping forward and pulling up her records.

The display changed to show Jess' picture on one side. It was the one taken when they'd processed her aboard the *Velu-vias* just after she'd been captured. Laarn's heart clenched at the sight. She looked scared, her dark hair mussed and dirt on her cheek. Her biological information flowed over the section of screen below the picture but he ignored it—he knew it by heart—as Daaynal pulled up the section of code Laarn had found hidden in her DNA.

"This is it?" he asked. "And she's the only one of the females who has it?"

"Yes and yes," Laarn confirmed. "It's the tiniest portion of information, but one that was deleted from our own code eons ago. I think, and this is just a theory at the moment, that it was an anchor point. With it gone, our genome gradually degraded and started to come apart, to the point we are now. As such, it's only going to get worse. Soon we'll lose the ability to procreate at all. Then we'll see the sickness extended to adult males as it did with adult females in the last generation."

Silence fell between the men for a long moment. Both remembered the plagues that swept their society, their women dying from stupid small illnesses in swathes, with no cause they could identify until they'd looked deeper.

Daaynal shuddered, but his voice was hard. Determined.

"No. The empire will not fall on my watch."

Turning, he looked directly at Laarn. Gone was the amiable uncle he'd been talking to, and in his place was the emperor of the Lathar.

"Do what you need to do. *Whatever* you need to do," he ordered. "Jessica Kallson does not leave this planet. Find others with this genetic information in the Terran prisoners we have. If you can't, we'll find them on Earth. Their defenses are pitiful. It won't take long to break the planet."

Just like that, the human women went from being honored guests to prisoners again.

"Yes, Your Majesty." Laarn bit back a twinge of guilt that he'd been the one to spark the change, but he straightened his spine with resolve. He was first and foremost Lathar. If humanity offered the key to their salvation, they had to take it, even if it meant subjugating an entire subspecies. "I'll order the remaining females tested and bring Jess back in for more tests."

The emperor nodded, arms folded across his big chest. "I suggest you claim this particular human female," he said abruptly, his focus fixed on Laarn's face. "If I'm reading your research right, she would be the best candidate for a pregnancy, would she not?"

Shit. He hadn't seen that one coming. Suddenly wary, Laarn nodded slowly.

Daaynal smiled, the expression feral and predatory. "Good. Then that child, the savior of our race, *will* be from our bloodline. Claim the woman and get her pregnant. As soon as possible."

Laarn opened his mouth to argue. A myriad of reasons screamed that wasn't a good idea. She was human, and tiny... he'd already scared her half to death and that was before taking into account she would barely look at him because of his scars. He was a monster to her.

But... the little voice in the back of his head murmured seductively, *she surrendered to you, was soft and pliant in your arms. She didn't scream or fight when you nearly claimed her against the wall...*

"Do it." Daaynal's voice was as hard as a whip and colder than the frozen wastes of *Telu-noresh,* his expression harder. "Or I will."

"No? What do you mean, no?"

Jess felt like she'd been pole-axed as she stood in front of Daaynal, looking up into an expression that lacked the normal warmth and smile she was used to seeing on the big emperor's face. Now his expression was closed off and forbidding as he lounged on the throne, green eyes so like Laarn's boring into hers.

"Have a care, little human," he rumbled, an edge of anger in his deep voice. "That you do not overstep your bounds as my *guest.*"

She shivered at the note in the last word, all her illusions about her place at court stripped away in one spine-chilling moment. He'd lauded Jess and her companions as honored guests but the Lathar were ruthless. It seemed as soon as having them as guests was no longer useful, they'd be downgraded back to the prisoners they'd started out as.

Straightening her spine, she nodded. Something had happened to change the status-quo but she wasn't sure what. There was no way she was asking him either. Just one look at his demeanor and she knew he wasn't going to say anything. The emperor did not explain himself. Ever.

"My apologies, Your Majesty," she murmured with a small curtsy. "I meant no offense."

Her words were calm, but inside she screamed with frustration. The need to get home, to see her twin, was all she could think about.

"It's just my sister is very ill. My mother says she's getting worse."

Daaynal didn't move, still leaning back in his chair, chin propped on long fingers. "Be that as it may, the journey back to Terra is long and fraught with dangers. It would be remiss of me as your protector to allow you to undertake such a hazardous journey."

"B..." She took a breath, schooling her response as she tried another avenue. "But surely with the reputation the Lathar enjoy, deservedly so, within the universe as premier warriors... no one would dare attack one of your ships? Unless of course you intend for me to make the journey back alone?"

How she'd do that she had no idea. She and the rest of the women had been taken from the sentinel base aboard Tarrick's ship, any human ships destroyed in the attack. There was nothing here from Earth she could make a return trip in.

"Indeed, however I have nothing free that I can assign to you, not with the problems in the Rivaas sector. I might consider it in a cycle or so when the situation there becomes clearer."

Tears burning the backs of her eyes, Jess nodded, remembering to curtsy again. "Yes, Your Majesty, thank you."

Daaynal inclined his head, his gaze flicking over her shoulder for a moment. The ghost of a smile crossed his features but she didn't think much of it. She'd thought he was an okay guy, but it turned out he was as ruthless as his reputation had suggested. More fool her. She should have known that just because he looked like a human didn't mean he had the same morals and values.

A gentle breeze fluttered the drapes at the windows, bringing the scent of the flowers from the gardens beyond into the room. The light scent would have made her smile before but right now, she couldn't muster it.

"With your permission, Your Majesty?" she murmured with a curtsy, both signaling her intention to leave and requesting permission at the same time. Normally Daaynal just nodded or waved a hand indicating she could, but this time he looked directly at her.

"A moment, Ms. Kallson. I believe my nephew has need of you."

"He does?" Jess turned with a frown, expecting to find Tarrick behind her. Instead, she came face to face with Laarn, his green eyes piercing as he looked down at her. After their kiss, she'd expected to go beet-red when she saw him again, but thanks to the emotions churning in her stomach because of her sister, she gave him a small nod, her ability to process new emotions frozen.

"Lord Healer," she nodded to acknowledge him, using the term of address she'd heard some of the warriors use around him. "How can I help you?"

His expression shifted, the tiniest hint of a frown crossing his brow. "Lord Healer?" he asked. "What happened to using my name? I thought we were friends, Jessica?"

She lifted a shoulder slightly, keeping her expression level and neutral. Friends didn't kiss each other like he'd kissed her the other day, enfolding her in his strong arms and enticing her with kisses full of dominance and passion. But that had been before she'd found out about Lizzie.

"So did I," she said quietly, unable to keep the bitter little note out of her voice no matter how hard she tried. "The same as I bought the line that we were guests rather than prisoners here. Funny how wrong I was."

JESS WAS UPSET. More upset than he'd ever seen her. Admittedly, he hadn't known her that long—it had only been a little over two months since they'd first discovered the existence of the humans in their little backwater systems—but in that time he'd been closely observing the human women, their manners and behaviors as well as their moods and emotions. He'd seen them scared, defiant, angry, amused, happy...

Jess was none of those things. Her shoulders were tight as she walked beside him toward his lab. Her lips were set in a pursed line and, as he cut a sideways glance down at her beautiful face, he swore he saw tears glinting in the corners of her eyes.

The sight made his heart ache, her closed off mood affecting him more than he cared to admit. What was it about one tiny human female that could affect him so much? He was a warrior of the Lathar. *He* controlled his emotions, not the other way around.

As much as he told himself that, it made no difference. As soon as they stepped into his lab and the doors closed behind them, he stopped her with a big hand on her arm.

"Jessica. What's wrong? Did someone hurt you?"

She looked at his hand and instantly he removed it. A warrior didn't seek to touch a female he didn't intend to claim, not without good reason and never for long. To do otherwise was without honor. Now he had her attention, he had no reason to touch her further, even though every cell in his body urged him to step forward and take her into his arms.

The face she turned up to him was calm and composed, but the pain in her eyes almost brought him to his knees.

"My sister is sick," she said softly. "I need to go home, but Daaynal won't let me. She could die and I won't be there." Before the end of the sentence, a lone tear detached itself from the corner of her eye and slid down her cheek.

Before he knew what he was doing, Laarn stepped forward, wrapping his arms around her small form and pulling her against him. She froze, stiff for a moment, but then relaxed against him, the sound of her soft sobs filling the silence of the lab.

"Shhh, shhh..." he whispered, his lips against her hair. "It will be okay. Your sister won't die." He didn't know that for sure, but he didn't care. He'd promise anything just to take that note of pain out of her voice.

Falling silent, she nodded, her face buried against his chest. He tightened his arms, liking the feeling of her resting against him so trustingly. Guilt stabbed through him.

If she knew what he'd been ordered to do, claim her and get her pregnant regardless of any feelings she had on the matter, she wouldn't cling to him quite so readily. Not if she knew she was a hairsbreadth away from being bonded to him for life.

His mood took a nosedive, his jaw tightening until he could feel a muscle at the side jumping. No matter what his uncle said about claiming her, he couldn't. She couldn't even look at him without his jacket on... there was no way she'd want to spend a lifetime with him.

No, better they avoid that. The little plan that had been formulating in the back of his mind took root and began to grow. All he needed was to confirm that Jess could get pregnant, and that the unaltered sequence in her DNA meant what he thought it meant—that she could conceive a female child, the first female Lathar born for decades. She didn't need to actually *get* pregnant... all he needed was to confirm it in the lab.

"It will all be fine." He smoothed a hand down her back, trying hard not to think about how good she felt in his arms and how perfectly she fit there. "I'll talk to my uncle, see if I can get him to see sense."

"Oh, would you?" she gasped, leaning back to look up at him. Her eyes were wet with tears, but the redness there didn't detract from her beauty in any way. The hope in her eyes hit him in the gut, but that was nothing to when she reached up on her toes and kissed his cheek quickly.

"Bless you. Thank you so much. It would mean so much to me. Lizzie and I... well, there's never been a me without her. To hear that she's sick..." She shrugged. "I'm terrified I'll lose her before I see her again."

He frowned, looking down at her as he made sense of what she said. Thanks to the translation implants, he understood Terran. But sometimes *how* they said things completely baffled him and he had to think about it to decode it.

"What do you mean, there's never been a you without your sister?" His expression cleared. "Do you mean you were born at the same time? That's not possible unless you're—"

"Twins, yes." She nodded, smiling at his obvious confusion. "Lizzie is my *litaan*. Apparently, you don't have female twins in the Lathar?"

"No." Lady goddess, that was it. Realization hit him like a ship at light speed. The bridge code in her DNA was because she was a *litaan*. It was the only explanation.

"No, we don't. Lady goddess, that might be useful. Can I..." he gestured toward the big diagnostic bed behind her. "Could I run a few more tests with that in mind? It might help to cross reference your DNA with the records of other *litaan* in our database. We have male-female pairs and male-male pairs but as far as I know we have never had a female-female pair. If humans do, that makes me wonder why."

"Of course, anything that will help," she said, easing from his arms and approaching the bed.

She stopped and, for a moment, his attention hijacked by the delicate curve of her neck revealed by her up-swept hair, he wondered why. Then he realized the bed was too high. Usually he made sure it was set on the lowest level, one that was easy for the much smaller human women to boost themselves up onto, but his last patient had been one of the bigger warriors, so it was still set near the maximum height.

"Here, let me help you," he murmured, reaching her side in a couple of strides. Normally he'd have reached out and adjusted the height on the side with a wave of his hand, but he didn't. Instead, he stepped in, big hands on either side of her tiny waist and simply lifted her onto the bed.

Once he had her there, though, he couldn't make his hands let go. They remained locked around her tiny waist. She looked up at him, a frown on her beautiful face. He couldn't do it, couldn't let her go despite all the reasons saying he should.

"Laarn?"

His name on her lips was little more than a whisper, but he heard it. All sense abandoning him, he stepped forward, using his hip to push her thighs apart so he could step between them. Her breathing caught, a little hitch that did all kinds of things to his body that should be illegal, and her eyes widened.

A big hand on the back of her hips and he pulled her up flush against him. His cock, hard, heavy and almost busting the seams of his leathers, pressed insistently against her pussy. Her eyes darkened, and the tiniest moan sounded in the back of her throat.

He answered it with a low growl, free hand latching at the back of her neck as he tilted her head up to the perfect angle.

"Forgive me," he murmured against her lips a moment before he claimed them.

His kiss was hard and unforgiving, less a kiss and more a punishment to himself for not having better self-control. For losing it the instant he touched her. He punished them both by deepening the kiss immediately, prying her lips apart to taste the sweetness within. His tongue slid against hers, not stroking gently but demanding her response.

It wasn't enough. Would never be enough. His hand in her hair tightened, and she whimpered against him, her own hands digging into the broadness of his shoulders. The sound brought him back to his senses a little, and he gentled his kiss just enough that her hands relaxed against him. No longer claws against pain, but touching him, stroking him. Teasing him in her own way.

Surprise washing through him, he eased up a little more and slid the hand on the back of her hips further up—a softer touch than he thought he was capable of. Than he *should* be capable of. A warrior born and bred, even with his healer's training, he'd never be a gentle man. But for her he wanted to be, for her... He'd be anything she needed.

His tongue stroked against hers, and he growled in need as his cock jerked and pulsed. Just one little push. That's all it would take, and she could be beneath him on the bed, her hair spread out around her head just like in his daydreams.

But then he felt her hands at the fastening to his jacket. Ice washed through his veins and he froze. Without being conscious of the movement, he clamped a hard hand over both of hers, stopping her undoing the garment. He wanted nothing more than to feel her hands on him, to feel her soft fingers exploring his body, but it wouldn't happen. As soon as she felt his skin, she'd recoil and push him away.

It had happened before. He always had to pay extra at any of the pleasure houses for them to touch him, to suffer touching his marked body, and even then none of them had been able to keep the revulsion out of their expressions. He didn't want to see that in Jess' eyes.

"No."

He disengaged himself, ignoring the howl of his male instincts and the savage jerk of his cock as it was denied the pleasure of sinking deeply into the haven of her pussy. The look she shot him, equal parts confusion and longing, almost broke his control but he stepped back, softening the rejection with a small smile.

"We have work to do," he reminded her gently, unable to resist reaching out to tuck a loose strand of hair behind her ear, his fingertips brushing her cheek before he dropped his hand. "The quicker we can do this, the quicker I can get to my uncle and persuade him to let you go home, okay?"

5

It was all Jess could do to nod slowly and not throw herself at Laarn as he pulled away. Again. Sexual frustration and confusion surged through her, the feeling so strong she wanted to scream. He wanted her, the hard length of his cock pressed against her pussy when he'd shoved his way between her legs had proven that... so why did he keep pulling away? What was the problem?

Realizing he was still looking at her for an answer, she took a deep breath and mustered a smile from somewhere. He'd touched her, voluntarily this time, the quick brush of his fingertips against her cheek leaving a trail of fire like a brand.

"If you'd just lie back for me."

His deep voice seemed rougher than normal as he moved around the bed, the holographic display already starting up as she wriggled backward and pulled her legs up. By the time she lay back, it arched over her in a bridge of brightly colored light. She could see Laarn through it, his attention focused on the readouts, and she took the opportunity to study him without him noticing.

He was the most handsome man she'd ever seen, with strong features and long, dark hair. Filled with warrior's braids, it fell past his shoulders, not tied back like it usually was. Although he was identical in looks to his brother, Tarrick, she'd know the two men apart immediately, not only because Laarn's eyes were green, not gold, but because the way they moved was totally different. Laarn was more self-contained and reserved but with an edge of raw power and suppressed danger that hit her on a very primal level.

He frowned, his lips curling back a little in annoyance at something on the screen, and she couldn't help the slight smile. When he didn't know anyone was looking, his face was quite expressive. Right now, he looked frustrated as hell... it was cute, if a man his size could ever be called cute.

Allowing her gaze to wander over him, she studied the width of his shoulders and chest. Like the other warriors she'd seen, the fit of his jacket indicated he was packed with muscle, that impression backed by the solidity and power she'd felt under her hands a moment ago and the memories from the one time she'd seen him remove his shirt weeks ago.

His scars.

She blinked. He'd been all for kissing her, and more if the state of his body pressed against hers was any indication, until she'd tried to undo his jacket to touch him. Then he'd shut her down and stepped away so quickly her head had practically spun.

Oh shit... Could he be sensitive about his appearance?

Armed with this new possibility, she studied his face and hands again. With his jacket on, there was no evidence of the scars beneath, and he rarely took the jacket off around her or the other women, even though she knew his scars were like badges of honor in Latharian culture. Ones that proved just how good a doctor he was.

"It's warm in here, isn't it?" she started tentatively, wriggling a little on the bed. "Don't you get warm all dressed up like that?"

Okay, crude but it was all she could think of to start the conversation she wanted. He flicked a glance at her, the lights of the display highlighting his features and turning his eyes pale. She sucked a breath in, liking that he looked like a dark angel, ready to swoop in and ravish her.

His gaze flicked to the screen for a moment and his lips quirked.

"I'm fine, but yes, your body temperature is slightly raised. I can drop the temperature on the bed to make you more comfortable."

She shivered as cool air washed over her. She hadn't meant that and from the quirk of his lips, he bloody well knew it.

"Okay..." His deep voice was almost back to normal as he stared intently at the screen in front of him. "I see the link to your *litaan*. There's some code here I haven't seen before. May I take some of your eggs to test a theory? Not many, I'll only harvest a few, and you won't feel a thing."

Jess paused, a frown between her brows. "Eggs? As in from my ovaries?"

He looked down at her through the display. A green light blinked on and off, reflected just under one eye. "Yes. From your ovaries, unless humans have a secondary location for them I know nothing about?"

"No." She shook her head. "It's the ovaries. But... you'll only take a few, right? And I'll still be able to have kids? I...I'd like a baby someday. I don't want to lose that ability."

Instantly as she said it, she kicked herself. Crass thing to say to a man whose species struggled to reproduce. A flush on her cheeks, she tried to cover up her gaffe.

"I mean, with the right man... warrior... of course."

"You see yourself settling down with a warrior from my species?" he asked, his expression unreadable as his hands moved over the display in front of him. She had no clue how the medical machines worked, but she trusted him. If he said it wouldn't hurt, then it wouldn't. "Surely we seem a little... barbaric to you?"

She shrugged and then instantly grew still as he frowned and shook his head at her. Any answer she was going to give had to wait as the machine whirled colored lights around her, the intersecting lines speeding up as they focused on the area above her lower body. She tensed as warmth started to spread out from within her, but before she could fully analyze the feeling, it was gone and the lights clicked off.

"Was that it?" she asked in surprise, a small gasp on her lips when he nodded. "I was expecting, I dunno... something more invasive. Like a big needle or something?"

Laarn chuckled, his darkly handsome face splitting into a wide grin. "Please, we may be barbaric in some aspects, but in medicine? I can assure you we are one of the most advanced races in the universe. Cellular translocation," he added, nodding toward her stomach. "I removed a couple of eggs, which I'll use for my tests. They'll be stored here in the lab rather than in medbay proper, so your genetic material isn't available to any of the other researchers. I appreciate your trust in me."

Something about the way he said it made her tilt her head to the side. Sitting up as the holo-arch shut down, she reached out to put her hand on his arm, speaking earnestly.

"I do trust you, Laarn, with my life. And I don't think you're barbaric..." She trailed off, her pointed look at him making it clear she might hold that view about the rest of his people, but that he was a different matter. "In fact, with the right man..." *Him.* "...the caveman act is rather hot."

"I'M TELLING YOU, I *need* access to the sister," Laarn argued, practically toe to toe with Daaynal just off the main training area.

Warriors around them pointedly looked the other way, apart from Karryl. His crossed arms and set expression said clearly he was prepared to back Laarn up, even against the emperor, but he expected they were both going to get a right pasting for it. Laarn made a mental note to thank his childhood friend later. No, they were more than that if he'd risk Daaynal's wrath for him. That made them brothers in arms, blood-brothers at the very least.

Daaynal's eyes, so like Laarn's own, widened.

"Oh, you do, do you?"

His chuckle was unexpected but welcome, a bolt of relief rolling through the healer. As big-built and accomplished among the warriors as Laarn was, Daaynal was both bigger and more experienced, the first warrior's braids in his hair years before Laarn and his brother had even been thought of. If he'd taken exception to Laarn's challenge, neither his relationship to the emperor nor his standing as the best healer in the empire would have saved him from a beating.

"Why... planning on claiming both of them for your own?" Daaynal crossed his arms, amusement washing over his features. Just off the training grounds, he sported a split lip and a freshly blacked eye that had yet to reach its full purple glory. A quick glance behind the warrior emperor revealed Xaandril training with his son, Rynn. No doubt the source of Daaynal's current injuries, he was obviously the recipient of some in return. Although he was covered in blood and held his left arm at an odd angle at his side, he was still more than capable of defending himself against his son... who appeared to be trying to kill him.

"I'm pretty sure there would be complaints if I allowed you to have two of the delightful creatures," Daaynal mused, rubbing at his stubbled chin with a big hand.

"No, no... I don't want two of them," he added hastily and then caught the glimmer of amusement in Daaynal's eyes, realizing he'd been had.

"Not two, but one at the least?" The emperor's grin broadened.

Laarn ignored him, carrying on talking. "I *do* need to check the sister's medical condition. Apparently, she's very ill and if she has the same genetic information as her sister—"

Daaynal frowned, the amusement gone as he pulled Laarn to one side away from the hustle and bustle of the training arenas into the shelter of the alcoves at the side of the palace.

"Why would she have the same genetic information? Is it possible she has the same bridge code as her sister?" Daaynal's expression sharpened at the possibility and Laarn nodded.

"More than possible given that they're *litaan*." He paused to let that one sink in. "Apparently Terrans have female-female pairs, something we never have, not since antiquity. I've checked the other Terrans we have for the same code and none of them have it, not even the other female who reports she is also... a twin as the Terrans call them. Her *litaan* though is male, which leads me to think it's either solely in the female pair code, or... even rarer... it's solely in the DNA of the Kallson family."

"If it is... *Draanth...*" Daaynal breathed, running a hand through his hair and raking the loose strands from his face.

"Yeah... exactly. Can you see why I want to take Jess and secure her sister as well?" Laarn pushed, knowing how much getting back to Earth meant to his little Terran. Quite when she'd become *his* little Terran in his thoughts, he didn't know, and right at the moment it wasn't important.

Checking that the corridor running alongside the alcoves was clear, he dropped his voice so that only his uncle could hear. "I managed to recover some of her eggs and tested my theory. Under lab conditions, pregnancy is possible. Of the eggs I tested, one is already a viable pregnancy."

Daaynal's eyes widened, a flash of something in the green depths. Satisfaction... hope maybe... or, and Laarn blinked at the thought, longing? He wasn't sure, and the quick flash was gone before he could analyze it.

"So you managed to adhere to my orders in your own unique way... *just,*" he chuckled, obviously amused. "A pregnancy without being pregnant. Unique. And possibly a safer alternative than having Miss Kallson actually be with child... especially with the current mood from certain elements of our society."

Laarn easily read the subtext. The purist idiots had been kicking up since the discovery of the Terrans in their little galaxy in the ass-end of beyond. They'd always had a hard-on against interbreeding with any species, even though with genetic manipulation, the females were only incubators for wholly Lathar offspring, but the arrival of the Terrans had kicked them into a frenzy. The clan leaders with purist tendencies had been very vocal about the Terrans and the threat of breeding with sub-Lathar species. If they got wind of an actual pregnancy, both mother and child would be in danger.

"Exactly. And that being said, surely you can see the reason I want a second test subject with that bridging code?" he pressed, feeling like a shit for hanging the threat of something happening to Jess over Daaynal's head.

Even as he said it, a hot surge of emotion and rage surged up from his soul. No one would hurt Jess. *Ever.* Not as long as he had breath left in his body. She was his to protect, and no one, especially not those bastard purists, would ever harm her.

Daaynal rubbed his chin again, eyes narrowed in assessment. "I can, but I can't allow you to take Ms. Kallson off planet. What happens if the ship you're on is attacked and the only female we have with the genetic code we need is killed? It's too great a risk."

Laarn sighed, frustration rolling through him. Daaynal had a point. Despite his feelings for Jess, he had to see the bigger picture. If they lost her before he could replicate the code and disseminate it through the population, they were back where they started, facing annihilation within a generation.

"But... It may be a suitable proving mission for a younger warrior." The big emperor leaned back against the wall, his gaze not on Laarn but looking out over the training arena to where the Imperial champion and his son were still mid-battle. Laarn raised an eyebrow, surprised to see Rynn still on his feet and fighting. He must be as hard to kill as his sire.

"You'd have her brought here?" he asked, his tone carefully level. If he couldn't get Jess to Earth, bringing her ailing sister *here* where he could treat her was the next best thing.

"Yes. It seems the best solution all around." Daaynal pushed off from the wall with a grin. "It's decided then. Rynn will collect your woman's sister while I and his father decide how to deal with those asshole D'Farans on the outer borders who think I haven't noticed them building a small army out there."

"She's not my—" Laarn started automatically but then trailed off with a sigh as Daaynal swept away, issuing orders and stopping the fight between Xaandril and Rynn with a shout. His uncle seemed to have a mental block whenever he told him that Jess wasn't his.

Even though he wanted her to be...

6

_____

"They're really pulling out all the stops, aren't they?" Jane asked with a grin, settling herself into the seat next to Jess in the covered pavilion that had been set up next to the warriors' arena.

It had been carefully cleared, the blood-stained sand removed and new sand carefully raked so the six challenge areas looked pristine. Seating had been placed all around the large rectangle, and long benches were interspersed with large seats for the clan leaders. Pride of place went to the raised and covered dais for the emperor, with the pavilion for the human women to one side as his honored guests.

"It seems that way, yes. Any idea what it's all in aid of?" Jess asked, mustering a smile as she looked around. Guilt and frustration lay heavily on her. She should be going home, but since Daaynal had blown off her request yesterday, she hadn't been able to get an audience with him again. He mostly appeared to be busy between "Imperial duties" and whatever today was about.

"It's a tournament." Cat joined them in a swish of silken skirts. As the wife of an Imperial prince, she'd almost totally adopted Latharian clothing, a jeweled tiara nestled in her dark curls denoting her rank and status. "In our honor apparently. The warriors will compete against each other as a showcase of their abilities. Daaynal is offering a couple of ships to the overall winner."

"Shit, I should have entered myself. Just think what we all could do with a couple of Latharian ships..." Jane whistled softly.

With her marriage to a Lathar warrior, and her subsequent retirement from the Terran military, the former marine had also adopted Latharian dress. Instead of the silken robes and jewels Cat wore, though, Jane had gone for warrior's leathers, teamed with her own combat boots and a tank-top. Her dog tags were gone, replaced with a set of octagonal tags on a chain.

All the women wore them, Jess' own nestled next to her Terran dog tags, and they opened the weapons caches in the palace and on the ships of the K'Vass, as well as any of their allies. The Lathar had quickly realized that the human women they'd captured were not shrinking violets or damsels in distress. They'd all been personnel on a military base, so they knew one end of a rifle from the other, no matter what planet it had been manufactured on.

"Too right."

The last of their party, Kenna, joined them. Like Jane, she was a dyed in the wool marine, so she wore leathers with her combat boots and a leather bustier top that made the most of her ample bust. She caught Jess looking and winked. "Keeps their eyes off my hands, and the blaster at my hip. Surprisingly effective on any man, even a warrior born and bred, especially when they haven't seen proper women for decades..."

Jess chuckled. Trust Kenna. She was definitely the light relief in their party, and sometimes much needed. Before she could ask anything else, though, a fanfare sounded and the arena started to fill up. Warriors and robed and hooded figures, their courtesans, filled the seating around the main area, a sense of excitement filling the air. To their right, another fanfare rang out as Daaynal made his arrival. Instantly, the crowd were on their feet, shouting and cheering.

"The emperor hasn't called a tournament for years." Cat leaned forward so they could hear her. "It's only open to warriors above a certain ability level, so we're going to see the best of the best."

"Karryl's competing," Jane commented, a proud smile on her face as warriors began to enter the arena.

"Fellow warriors and honored guests!" Daaynal's voice rang out, cutting through the cheering of the crowd. "I bid you welcome to the first combat tournament on Lathar prime for decades. In times past, tournaments of this type were a common fixture at the palace, in the cities, right down to our villages... where the best warriors amongst us would compete to show off our skills and perhaps catch the eye of that special female to prove our worth as warrior and male. I do not need to remind you why such tournaments are no longer held." There was a moment's pause as his words sunk in, the enormity of the situation the Lathar as a species were in a sobering one.

Daaynal spoke again, sweeping his arm toward the sheltered pavilion the women sat in. "But... fate has smiled on us. Thanks to the discovery of the Terrans, a long-lost branch of the Lathar, we once again have the chance to show off our skills and abilities to worthy females."

He gestured to the silent warriors on the sand in front of him. "Before you, you see the best of our warriors. They will fight each other both together and solo until only one remains. The winner will become the proud owner of two of the empire's newest battlecruisers and, if he is lucky, may win the appreciation of one of our delightful ladies here today."

Kenna leaned forward, waggling her eyebrows. "I'd sure appreciate the hell out of half this lot. Have you seen the bodies on these guys?"

Jess bit back a small smile, easily seeing through Kenna's joking manner as she realized the other woman was doing exactly what she was—searching through the assembled men to find that one familiar figure. In Kenna's case, she stopped as soon as she found the tall, broad-shouldered figure of the emperor's champion, Xaandril, but Jess' eyes kept searching.

Laarn was a healer, so perhaps he wouldn't be here. She knew he trained, and could fight, but she wasn't sure if he was considered a warrior anymore or if his position as healer took precedence.

"And for the first time, I have a personal interest in the outcome of this tournament!" Daaynal announced, as a gong rang and two warriors walked out onto the sands, between the rows already assembled. "My sister-sons have taken to the sands, one a warrior prince and, for the first time in two generations, a lord healer."

The gasp that went around the crowd was echoed by Cat. "Shit," she whispered. "He's gone and done it."

"What? What did he do?" Jess asked, her eyes drinking in the sight of Laarn. Like his brother next to him, and the rest of the assembled warriors, he was naked to the waist. She heard the whispers of awe and saw the way the warriors he passed looked at him and the scars covering his body. She knew what they meant, knew they marked his standing as the best healer in the empire, but all she wanted to do was kiss each and every one of them to remove the memory of the pain he must have suffered.

Cat's tone was still shocked. "He's officially named Laarn as Lord Healer. There's no way he can wriggle out of it now."

Unable to tear her gaze away from Laarn as he stood next to his brother—Hells, why didn't he strip more often? The guy was *ripped*— Jess leaned toward her a little. "Why would he want to wriggle out of it? From what I've heard everyone already considers him lord healer anyway."

"They do," Cat confirmed. "But now he's been named, it would mean he will be based at the healer's hall here on Lathar Prime rather than being able to head off on one of the K'Vass ships whenever he wants."

"Ahhh, I see." Jess settled back in her seat, her gaze still riveted to the big healer in the middle of the arena as he bowed to the emperor and then turned and took a place at the front of the rest of the warriors next to his brother.

And she did. Laarn didn't strike her as the type of man who liked his movements curtailed, so being restricted to a planet probably wouldn't impress him any. At the same time, though, she couldn't help feeling relieved. The Lathar were a warrior culture, as apt to fight amongst themselves for power and position as within the empire, so being on a ship was far more dangerous than being on their home planet. And, from what she'd heard, the healer's hall was considered neutral ground. No one fought there, which meant Laarn would be safe there. Although she knew he was a warrior, the thought of him being in danger made her chest tighten uncomfortably.

As it was now, seeing him on the sands in front of her was okay, she told herself. This was a tournament of skill, not a battle. They weren't seriously trying to kill each other.

"Before we start, warriors may take a moment to claim a token from their females to aid them in battle," Daaynal offered, his arms spread widely to give the warriors on the sands permission to leave it for a moment.

As expected, both Tarrick and Karryl immediately broke formation to walk across the sands toward the pavilion where the human women were sitting, and Jess suddenly realized the purpose of the silken ribbons they'd all been given to wrap around their wrists by the servants upon sitting down.

"My Moore Cat," Tarrick murmured, a smile on his lips as he came to stand in front of his wife. "If you would be so kind?"

Jess smiled as Cat stood, the elevation of the pavilion meaning she stood equal height with her taller husband, and tied the purple ribbon from her wrist around his upper arm. Swooping in for a kiss, he only stopped when he was jostled aside by Karryl even though there was plenty of room for all the women to stand at the front edge of the pavilion.

"Com'on, we don't have all day and you're not the only male here with a mate to impress."

Tarrick chuckled, ceding his place to the big warrior as he beckoned to Jane. The kiss he bestowed on the tall marine was no surprise, but what did make Jess' eyes widen was the fact that two men stood behind Karryl.

She had a brief glimpse of the emperor's champion, Xaandril, whose gaze was locked onto Kenna as he stood in front of them. It was the first time she'd seen the big warrior look anything other than supremely confident as he held out his arm in silence.

But then her breath was taken away as the fourth warrior stepped out from behind Xaandril. Laarn. Two strides brought him to the edge of the pavilion, right in front of her. With a start she found herself standing at the edge of the platform in front of him.

"My lady," Laarn said quietly, meeting her eyes with an unreadable expression. "I would be honored to wear your colors... if you find me worthy to."

She couldn't help it. Her gaze slid down his body, from the long unbound hair across his broad shoulders, over the heavy muscles of his chest and downward toward the cobblestone abs. Heat hit her broadside, swirling through her blood and settling into a hard knot between her thighs. Hell, he was gorgeous... and dressed in just warrior's leathers, hot as fucking hell.

"I do." Her voice breathy, she tried to untie the ribbons at her wrist but fumbled it. The knots tightened and she swore under her breath, trying to get them loose, but the edges of the ribbons had wound themselves around each other like a couple of mating snakes.

"Fuck it," she hissed, trying harder to undo them. "Sorry about this."

"Here." He snagged a hand around her wrist and pulled her closer. "Let me."

His long, strong fingers made short work of the knots. He pulled the ribbon free all too quickly and handed it to her with a small smile.

"Does it matter where I tie it?" she asked, sliding a glance sideways to see Kenna had tied her light blue ribbon around Xaandril's wrist, just above his leather bracer.

Laarn's lip quirked a little at the side. "No. The lady picks the location... as long as I don't have to undress."

She darted a glance up to meet his eyes, finding warm amusement in the green depths. The heat and arousal in her body hit fever pitch as she imagined peeling the leathers from his body.

"My eyes are up here, beautiful." His soft murmur made her snap her gaze up to meet his again and her cheeks burned in reaction. Shit, she had *so* not been ogling him, right here in front of everyone, had she? The small grin on his face and the chuckle from behind her said that she had. Fucking hell.

"Come here." She stepped in closer and reached up to quickly braid the ribbon through a section of his hair, tying it off in a knot rather than a bow. "There. How's that?"

He inclined his head a little, the dusky pink of her ribbon a bright flash in the dark locks. "You honor me," he said quietly, his fingertips brushing the inside of her wrist. "Later, if I prove myself in battle, I will claim another token. Perhaps one more... physical."

Yes, oh hell yes. She didn't get the chance to reply as he dropped her wrist and turned back toward the sands, dark hair moving like a cape across his broad shoulders as he went.

"Well... wasn't *that* a turn up for the books?" Cat commented, a look of interest in two sets of eyes as she and Jane turned to consider both Kenna and Jess. "Seems you two have been keeping secrets, haven't you?"

"Later," Kenna cut her off, nodding toward the arena. "It's all about to start."

~

LAARN WAS on cloud fucking nine.

Not only had Jess given him her token, but she'd looked at him. Actually looked at *him*, at his body. The heat he'd seen in her eyes said she'd seen him as a *man,* not his scars. That look would remain stored in his memory forever and even now, as he faced off against the third warrior in his group, the memory was enough to send a bolt of lust through his body.

He growled as the male in front of him launched an attack so predictable he could have countered it in his sleep. How the male had gotten this far, onto the sands for a tournament, he had no clue, but one thing was for sure. He was leaving the competition right now.

Moving like a *liras* snake, Laarn sidestepped the clumsy attack and reached out as the warrior rushed past him. Two fingers jammed into the side of the male's neck hit the nerve plexus and made the left side of his body less responsive. It wasn't much, barely noticeable as he turned to face off against Laarn again, a snarl on his face. But against Laarn, it would make *all* the difference.

Everything around them—the noise of the crowds, the other fights going on in the other challenge circles, the fact that behind him and to his left Jess watched him—fell away as Laarn's focus narrowed to this moment in time, to just the two of them and the circle of sand they stood in.

Fighting was like surgery. It required utter focus, dedication and skill. In the operating theater, he fought a one-man war against death or permanent injury, both far more fearsome opponents than the male opposite him. He was big-built, almost as big as Karryl or Daaynal, but heavier-set, the slight layer of fat over the carved muscles indicating a fondness for good food and wines.

Laarn didn't smile. Instead, he lifted his hand and beckoned the warrior.

The bull-like warrior snarled and charged again. Laarn waited until he could practically smell the male's breath before he launched his counterattack. Two running steps launched him right at his opponent, the move so quick the other male barely had time to widen his eyes in surprise before Laarn had planted a booted foot on his thigh. Launching himself upward, he arched back, snapping his leading leg out to slam it up and under his opponent's jaw.

There was the sickening crunch of bone and a strangled sound of pain as the other warrior dropped like a stone. Laarn landed lightly on his feet, bringing his guard up immediately, just in case his opponent was still capable of an attack. But the male wasn't... sprawled out on the sand with a stunned expression on his face.

Healers and tournament officials swarmed over to them. Two healers dropped to their knees next to the fallen man, quickly checking him over as one of the officials grabbed Laarn's wrist to raise it and declare him the winner.

"No," he argued, looking over his shoulder to where his opponent was still being seen to. "Brother, are you okay?"

He got a raised fist from the fallen man, just visible from behind the nearest healer, and then... a thumbs up. Laarn bit back a chuckle and made a mental note to check up on the warrior's treatment after the tournament was over.

"And the winner is... Laarn K'Vass!" the official bellowed, holding Laarn's wrist aloft.

The crowd nearby erupted into cheers but Laarn didn't care about them. His gaze cut immediately to the pavilion where Jess sat with the other women. His heart leapt as he saw her rise to her feet, looking at him with a smile on her face as she clapped with the rest of the crowd. Their gazes locked and the smile dropped from her face as she looked at him. Even with the distance between them, awareness stretched taut and Laarn realized the inevitable...

When the tournament was over, she was his. He would claim her as every cell in his body ached to. He knew it, and now she knew it, a flush rising on her cheeks as she dropped her gaze from his. A smile curved the corner of his lips as he waited and, sure enough, a couple of seconds later she snuck another look at him from under her lashes, something he'd noticed she did often. Usually when she thought he wasn't looking in the lab.

Later, he promised himself and turned to see who his next opponent might be. Before the officials could announce it, though, two leather-clad warriors approached the emperor, bots standing guard behind them. At the sight of the combat bots in the palace, Laarn straightened up. That wasn't normal. One look at the expression on his uncle's face told him it wasn't and the situation was serious.

Daaynal nodded and rose to his feet, holding his hands out for silence.

"My apologies, ladies and gentlemen, but I am afraid I need to pull two fighters from the tournament. Lord Healer Laarn and Xaandril, my champion, would you please attend me?" he asked, indicating they should approach the dais with the throne. Laarn exchanged a look with the big champion as they walked toward the emperor, but the big man's expression indicated he was as in the dark as Laarn was.

"Please... continue with the tournament. Lord K'Vass... you are excused from the tournament to preside in my place, with your delightful lady wife of course."

7

*L*aarn said nothing as he followed the emperor and his champion into the palace after the messengers. He wasn't surprised at being pulled into such a meeting with the two most powerful men in the empire, not after Daaynal had named him as lord healer in front of everyone at the tournament. Sure, he still had to undergo the lord healer's trial, but that was nothing compared to his healer's trial, a mere formality as he claimed the position. All that mattered was that the emperor had named him, and now his path was set. No getting out of it. Once Daaynal had made his mind up, that was it.

The Emperor made his way into the war-room, turning to watch the rest of them file in. The last to enter were the two messengers, their combat bots taking position to guard the door outside. Laarn frowned. Why were bots being used in place of guards?

"Tell them what you told me," Daaynal ordered the messengers, motioning toward Laarn and Xaandril. The big champion had leaned his hips back against the nearby conference table, arms folded over his broad chest. Laarn took a moment to flick a glance over the guy's markings. Drawn in *serranas* blood and burned right into his skin, they marked all the battles he'd been in over the years. It was an old tradition, not often practiced anymore, not to the extent Xaandril did anyway. Occasionally a warrior marked an important battle. Both he and Tarrick had a starburst marking on their upper arm from their first major battle, but they hadn't bothered since.

The messengers turned, and Laarn easily read the exhaustion on their faces as well as the way the one on the left held himself stiffly, favoring his left side as though he had sustained an injury there. The one on the right, obviously the senior warrior, spoke.

"We've been patrolling the outer borders for the last couple of months," he started and coughed. When his hand came away, Laarn caught the telltale flash of scarlet in his palm. He was right. Both men had been in battle, recently. The messenger continued, "There's been increased activity on the borders. Trade, bounty hunters, general unrest and movement. Several colonies and outposts were attacked and at first we thought it was the Krynassis—"

Xaandril hissed at the mentioned of the reptilian race, but Laarn ignored him. The champion's dislike of reptiles was well known.

"But it wasn't? How do you know?" he asked, a frown between his brows. The reptilian warrior race had always caused issues, nibbling at the edges of the empire's territory or even bold enough to raid colony worlds within it, carrying off whatever supplies and slaves they could get their grubby, clawed hands on.

The warrior shook his head. "We were approached by one of their hive queens, the ruling one in the area. She confirmed that their nests are also being targeted... by Lathar. Fortunately for us, she also knew the identity of the clans involved. Apparently, as the queen closest to our borders, she's been keeping an eye on our politics. She knew these particular clans are not currently in favor."

"Really?" Daaynal had his arms folded across his chest, rubbing at his stubbled chin with a massive hand. Even though he was undoubtedly male, when he looked like that, a keen light in his green eyes, Laarn saw echoes of his dead mother in her *litaan*. "Interesting. They've never shown such awareness before."

The warrior shrugged. "It seems there's been a massive upheaval in their society. There was an uprising, their Brood Queen was challenged and killed, which has filtered down through the Hive Queens. Most have been replaced with more... forward-thinking females, it seems. Still deadly though. We nearly lost a warrior after he hit on one of her guards."

Laarn lifted an eyebrow. The reptiles had females, he knew that. He had even seen a few and had to admit they were striking in their own way. He'd never wanted to take one to bed, though. He probably wouldn't survive the damn night, no matter how attractive she was. Besides, his tastes ran to curvy little Terrans called Jess these days. A fond smile curved his lips and heat rolled through him at the memory of her look as she'd tied her favor in his hair. She would be his soon. *Very* soon.

"So, which clans?" he asked, bringing the conversation back to the point at hand.

"Three. D'Faran, F'Naar and R'Zaa."

Xaandril and Daaynal exchanged a look.

"No surprise there," the champion grunted. "Those three have been a pain in the ass for years one way or another." He fixed his gaze on the emperor. "Are you finally going to let me go kick their asses to the afterlife and back?"

Daaynal ran a hand through his hair, scooping the loose strands back off his face and snapping a band from his wrist around it.

"I think we have to. If those two have linked up with D'Faran, this isn't just clan leaders being a little pissy... they could field a war group big enough to cause serious damage if they tried to take Lathar Prime."

Laarn rubbed his chin and then suddenly became aware it was an almost identical gesture to the one his uncle had used. Quickly he dropped his hand in case they thought he was imitating the emperor. "They won't attempt to take the home system," he said.

"Think about it. D'Faran have purist tendencies, and both the others got soundly spanked by the Terran women... Kenna held a pistol to J'aett's head in front of all his men in the main courtyard and Jane blew Ishaan F'Naar's brains out on his own ship for poisoning Karryl. No, they won't come for Lathar Prime... they'll go for Earth itself. Remove the problem at the source."

"Shit," Xaandril breathed. "He's right. They will."

"Not happening." Daaynal's voice was firm as he straightened up. "Not on my watch. Xaan, you take a war group and head out to the borders. Stop the bastards before they can mobilize. Stop them at any cost. Laarn, take a team of combat healers and go with him. I suspect your expertise will be needed—both on the battlefield and in the healer's bay."

"Yes, sire," both men replied automatically, knowing not to argue when the emperor used that tone of voice, and turned to follow the messengers out.

"Laarn, a moment, please."

He turned at the order, waiting as the others filed out. He tilted his head as he looked over at his uncle. "Your Majesty?"

Daaynal waved in irritation. "Cut the crap when it's just us. Daaynal will do just fine." His gaze was firm. "Make sure you see your little human before you go and cement your claim. I do not want to have to fight fires over females while you're gone, understand me? Especially not one so important to us."

Laarn inclined his head, hiding his determined expression. "Don't worry. Before I go she'll know she belongs to me."

"You're leaving? Now?"

Worried, Jess had slipped away while the tournament was still ongoing to find Laarn in his lab again. This time, though, he wasn't working. Instead, he was packing cases with medical equipment.

"Yes," he replied, his expression grim and his long hair dancing over his broad shoulders. He didn't look at her at first, carefully packing some medical gadget into a padded case and then adding it to a bigger one. "The situation on the outer borders has gone into meltdown. The emperor has ordered a war group to head out and check the situation. Apparently, some colonies have been destroyed, so healers will be required."

"Destroyed?" Her eyes widened. "Will you be safe?"

Worry coiled in her gut, her heart clenching at the thought of him in danger. A chuckle rumbling in the back of his throat, he appeared in front of her suddenly. Sliding a big hand into her hair, he used his thumb under her chin to make her look up and meet his eyes.

"Did you not just see me out on the sands, little one?" he asked, his eyes and voice warm. A shiver hit her as he crushed her cheek with his thumb in a soft caress. "I might be a healer, but I'm Lathar... I'm a warrior born and bred. I'll heal, but I can also kill without mercy. Especially to save my people... and the ones I love."

His voice dropped on the last words, his gaze latching onto her lips. Before she knew it, he'd crowded her back against the counter behind her, his big body cutting off her view of the rest of the room. The air between them heated as he looked down at her, intent written over his face as he slowly bent, lowering his lips to hers.

She moaned, bringing her hands up to his broad chest. This time, instead of the jacket he usually wore, she got to touch his skin. Like the rest of him, it was warm and hard, silky to the touch. The kiss was softer than any he'd given her before. He teased her lips, feathering his mouth over hers as though he were learning the shape and texture of them before he nibbled lightly on her lower lip. She parted them with a whimper, needing more of him, his kisses, but he didn't take her up on the offer. Instead, he carried on with the soft nips, his free hand sliding around her waist to pull her up firmly against him.

She registered the thick, full hardness of his cock pressed against her softer belly and gasped. He was huge, she'd known that, but to feel it pressed against her again took her breath away... and sent thick, dark heat swirling through her body. Anticipation and need weakened her limbs as she clung to him, pressing herself to him in invitation and hoping he'd deepen the kiss, claim her lips like he had before.

He chuckled again at her eagerness, and this time, gave in to her silent demands. Releasing her lip from his teeth, the pressure of his fingers at the back of her neck tilted her lips up for him and he claimed them. She whimpered as he invaded her mouth, sliding his tongue against hers and back again in an erotic dance that fired every cell in her body. Where he'd learned to kiss like that, like a sex god, when the Lathar had no women, she didn't know. It didn't matter. All that did was that he was here, with her.

The kiss started off soft and sweet, slow and languorous, but within seconds, any sweetness disappeared. Heat built and exploded as his kiss grew harder and hotter. A growl in the back of his throat, he pulled her tighter into his body, his hands on her just this side of cruel. But she didn't care, the same feral need gripped her as she slid her hands over his shoulders and chest, the satin of his skin highlighted by the smooth scars as she touched him.

With a gasp he broke away, leaning his forehead against hers. His chest heaved as he fought for breath, and, she realized, control.

"Not here," he said in a voice just this side of a growl. "Not now. I need to go..." At her small cry of protest, the corners of his lips quirked. "When I take you, little one, it won't be a quick fuck snatched before I have to leave. It'll be all night, all day... and everyone in the palace will hear my name on your lips as you scream."

She shivered, biting her lip as she looked up at him.

"Don't look at me that way..." He swore, the heavy Latharian words almost unintelligible. His features just this side of feral, he claimed her lips again in a hard kiss before breaking away. "Perhaps something to remember me by..."

Before she realized what he was doing, he'd boosted her up onto the counter, shoving his hips between her parted thighs to drink from her lips again. She whimpered, the soft sound one of submission as she opened up for him. The answering male growl did things to her on a primal level, and a second later she felt his hand on her leg under her skirts as it slid upward. Her breathing caught as he reached her thigh, and she parted wider for him, arching her back. His rumble of approval was lost under their kiss as he thrust his tongue into her mouth again to seek hers.

His questing fingers reached the juncture of her thighs and a thread of amusement rolled through her as he started, realizing that she didn't wear any underwear. Breaking away from their kiss, he looked down at her, the light color of his eyes swallowed up by darkness. "Only ever leave your underthings off for me," he demanded. "No other male... not unless you want him dead."

Unable to speak, she just nodded, her breathing catching when he swept blunt-tipped fingers between her folds. They were slick, wet with the evidence of her arousal, which he gathered, smoothing the slickness up and over her clit. "This is mine, little Jess," he murmured, lips against her jaw and the side of her throat. "I'll have your release before I go, my name on your lips, but when I get back... you're mine. Understand?"

She nodded, breathless with anticipation as his fingers explored her pussy lips, grazing against her swollen clit. Her breath caught at the slight contact and she arched her back, rocking her hips to try and get more sensation. He chuckled, hot mouth on her skin, and nipped her earlobe.

"Eager for me, are you, little one?" he murmured, the tip of his broad finger circling her pussy. She whimpered as he breached her body just a little before withdrawing.

"Not yet, I don't think..." he breathed, kissing a trail of fire down her neck. Every cell in her body was focused on the path of his lips and that of his fingers as they stroked through her swollen pussy lips, slick with her own desire. He found her clit again, and she stiffened for a second. Then she whimpered as pleasure rolled through her, exploding out from her clit to fill her blood.

He murmured soft words in his own language as he kissed her and circled her clit in small strokes. Lifting her hands, she clung to his broad shoulders, her fingers biting in as he drove her nearly insane with his touch. Her clit ached with each stroke and she arched toward him, offering him more of herself. She needed more, needed his touch... needed *him*.

He moved, sliding a thick finger deep inside her. She whimpered, pressing her forehead to his shoulder as he slid it back and in again. Adding a second finger, he used his free hand to tilt her head back.

"No, Jess, I want to see you. I want to see what I do to you. I want to see the expression on your face when I make you come. Your pleasure, the pleasure I give to you, is *mine*. Understand?"

She swallowed, nodding and biting her lip as he added another finger to slide deep. Her needy pussy clenched, gripping him as he fucked her with the long digits, pressing his thumb to her aching clit. His gaze locked to hers, she couldn't look away. Her breath came in short pants and then a groan as he turned his hand and curled his fingers back to press against her g-spot.

"So sensitive," he murmured, his expression tense and focused on her. "So tight... I'm going to enjoy making you mine. Stretching this sweet little pussy around my thick cock. Will you like that, little Jess... being taken and fucked by a warrior?"

Unable to speak, she nodded, a whimper falling from her lips as her hips began to move, rocking with his motions as her body tightened. Ripples of sensation fluttered through her, centering in her pussy. They grew stronger and tighter, her movements more needy until she was riding his hand, desperate to come.

"Laarn..." she begged. "Please. I need..."

His expression hardened, his eyes laser-focused on hers. "Come," he ordered. "Now."

It was as if her body had been waiting for his words, and rapture exploded through her, spiraling out from her core as she came around his fingers in a hot rush. The force of it sapped her strength, forcing her to cling to him more as she rode out the waves. He held her against his broad chest, stroking her through it. His thumb on her clit drew out the sensations until she shivered, lying limply against his chest and shoulder.

"You look wonderful when you come," he murmured by her ear, "a sight I fully intend to enjoy again, soon, as you come all over my cock when I take you as mine."

Pulling his hand from her, he lifted it to his lips and licked her essence from his fingers. The groan was purely masculine and full of hunger, a hunger that blazed in his eyes as he looked down at her.

"You're mine, Jess. Remember that because I'll be back."

8

*L*aarn had been gone for nearly a week. Days without word from the battle group. Jess found herself jumping each time a door swished open, in case it was one of the emperor's men to update them on the situation.

But it wasn't. Apart from a simple message from Daaynal that all was proceeding as normal, they'd received no word from the battlefront.

"This is ridiculous! They must know something!" Kenna exploded into movement, leaping up from the low couches they'd been reclining on in the garden room attached to their suite. A pleasant breeze swept in from outside, but neither woman noticed the lovely summer day outside. Instead, Kenna was too busy pacing, a pissed expression on her face, and Jess herself was too... empty to enjoy the weather.

Instead, all she could think of was Laarn and the way he'd kissed her before he left. His clever fingers under her skirts, sliding into her pussy and against her clit to bring her to the strongest climax she'd ever had in her life. Everything seemed dull and flat without him here.

"I'm sure they'd have told us," she said flatly, not watching as

Kenna paced the exquisitely tiled floor. There was just the two of them in the suite, both Cat and Jane having gone with their husbands to the front.

"They should have," the marine growled. "There's no way they're stupid enough as a warrior race to lose communications, so they *have* to be in contact with Xaan and his ships."

Jess looked up, mustering a small smile despite her misery. "Oh... Xaan, is it?" she teased lightly. "Should we expect wedding bells soon?"

"Bite me, Kallson," Kenna snarled back, flipping her the bird. "We're just friends."

At that Jess did chuckle. "That old chestnut? Spin me another."

"You can talk," Kenna shot back. "Mooning about after the healer... fuck, we're as bad as each other." She paused in front of the door, indecision on her face. "Fuck it. I'm going to get some answers. Daaynal *will* talk to me, even if I have to fucking sleep outside his door. You coming?" she asked, arching an eyebrow in question.

Jess shook her head. "No, I feel a little odd," she said, pressing her hand over her stomach. "I think I'm going to head down to the medbay and get checked out. I think something I ate yesterday disagreed with me."

"Okay, love. I'll come find you if I get answers. Send someone for me if you need me, okay?"

Jess nodded, but the other woman was already gone before she'd finished hauling herself off the low couch. Her movements sluggish, she headed out of the women's suite and made her way toward the medbay.

Once she got there though, she couldn't face the thought of explaining to any of the healers, all tall, imposing Lathar with serious expressions who always seemed to look down their noses at her. They seemed to dislike her intently, possibly because she was here so often for tests. Why they didn't like her for that, though, she didn't know. Surely all efforts toward solving the problem were a good thing, right?

Obviously not. As soon as the doors swished open, they all

studiously ignored her, obviously finding their screens more interesting than helping her. She shrugged to herself and walked through the main lab, heading for Laarn's personal lab at the back. With the ridiculously advanced level of their technology, she was fairly sure she didn't need them to find out if she had a stomach bug or not anyway. All she needed was to boot up one of those fancy diagnostic beds and have the computers scan her. She'd seen Laarn do it so many times, she was sure she could figure it out herself.

As she approached the back of the room, heading toward the double doors that led to Laarn's lab, she resisted the urge to bite her lip in worry. She was going to look a right idiot if, with Laarn away, the lab didn't let her in. But before she was within ten feet of the doors, the lights within flickered on and the doors swished open in front of her. Breathing a sigh of relief, she walked in and just stood in the center of the space for a moment as the doors shut behind her.

It was strange being in here without him, but there were reminders of him everywhere she looked. One of his sashes, teal to mark his role as a healer, hung on a hook on the wall next to a warrior's leather jacket. On the counter to her left, the one he'd boosted her on and brought her to the most earth-shattering climax, was his mug. She couldn't read Latharian, but she was fairly sure it was a humorous one, something along the lines of "Trust me, I'm a doctor."

To her right was his office area, the surface of the desk littered with not paper, but the thin sheets of plastic-like material the Lathar used, all with Laarn's distinctive scrawl across them. She could even smell his scent in the air, a combination of warm, clean man and some kind of citrus. That was one thing she'd noticed from the moment she'd met him... he smelled *so* good.

Closing her eyes for a moment, she drew a deep breath into her lungs and imagined he was here. It eased some of the ache in the center of her chest.

Opening her eyes, she brought herself back to reality and focused on the matter at hand. "I don't feel well," she announced to the air around her, knowing the lab's AI system would be listening.

It was. The diagnostic bed in the middle of the floor lit up, the flashing lights running down the side of the padded mattress a silent invitation to lie down. Crossing the floor on slippered feet, Jess boosted herself up backward and swung her legs up to lie down in the middle. Once she had, the holo-arch lit up and she watched as the lights whirled and raced over it, scanning her.

"Subject scan complete. Patient alpha five seven nine, Jessica Kallson. Human female," the AI announced. *"Several in-progress tests for this subject. One complete and viable. Proceed?"*

She nodded. Laarn always did a lot of tests on her to make sure she was fit and healthy before he moved on to analyzing her DNA. It seemed the bed was still set up in that routine. "Yes, please."

"Compliance."

The lights whirled again, centering on her abdomen. She watched as they got faster and faster, and then the bed hummed like it was about to take off. Heat washed over her stomach for a moment, starting low down, just over her pelvis, and then washing up. A gasp broke from her lips at the intensity, but within a heartbeat it was gone as though it had never been there. Her hands went instantly to her stomach, expecting to find the fabric of her gown hot, but it wasn't. The silk was just skin-warmed from the heat of her body within, nothing more. Huh, odd.

"Computer? Is that it? Am I okay?" she ventured as the holo-arch clicked off.

"Affirmative. Subject is running a slight temperature and scan reports slight gastro-intestinal distress but no viral or bacterial cause found. Recommend rest and light repast until condition resolves."

She was okay. Jess breathed a sigh of relief. She'd been right, it must have been something she ate.

"Thank you, computer. Can I go now?" she asked as politely as if she'd been speaking to a flesh and blood medic. Since Laarn had told her the lab computer was a sentient AI, she'd treated it as a person, albeit an invisible one. It was only right.

"Affirmative. Please return at the same time tomorrow for condition check."

"Err..." Jess paused in the middle of sliding off the bed. "Sure, if you need me to."

The computer didn't reply, but the lights at the back of the lab started to shut down. Obviously the AI was done with her. With a small shrug, Jess headed out of the lab, ignoring the healers in the main medbay as she left.

"*MOVE ON THE LEFT FLANK!*"

"*Hold your fire! Wait for it...NOW!*"

"*Retreat! Retreat!*"

"*Don't let the bastards get away!*"

Laarn kept his head down as he made his way through the battlefield, his team around him. Two *drakeen* battle bots fought not a hundred feet away, arm cannons moving continuously as they swept the area for enemy forces that might have lingered after the battle.

The big healer watched for a moment, noting the idiosyncrasies of the bots' movements. There weren't many *drakeen*-capable pilots in the battle group. From the way the one on the left moved, Kraan was piloting, which meant the other one was Isan. The other pilots would be off duty, sleeping, apart from Jathor, who had been killed in action yesterday.

Laarn's heart ached for a moment. Jath had been in his and Tarrick's training group during their childhood, a quick and capable warrior with a sharp sense of humor who had dreamed of finding his bond-mate. He'd been so excited at the news of the human women, sure his mate would be amongst them. He'd never gotten to meet them all and find out, bleeding out on a battlefield in the arse-end of beyond fighting traitors.

Laarn turned, his split second of reflection over. Combat bots raced to fill the gaps between the combat teams and the bigger *drakeen*. His medical pack over his back and a rifle in his hand, he kept an eye out as his team moved behind him.

Even now, without battle raging around them, they operated like a combat unit, moving further into the battlefield as they checked for wounded. Some were beyond help, their bodies simply tagged with locator beacons as the team moved on... others were more fortunate, able to be treated and walk out themselves. The badly injured were locator-tagged and evac'ed by bots as soon as they could be.

But that wasn't why Laarn was here. Normally in a battle situation, he was far behind the lines, fighting a war of his own in surgery as he battled death and serious injury to bring a warrior from the brink. But not today.

"*Anyone sees the general,*" he bellowed. "*I want to know. Immediately.*"

His team nodded, a chorus of affirmative responses through his earpiece as they spread out to check the ground the battle had swept through. The word had come through early this morning about an attack through the southern lines, which they hadn't been expecting. Xaandril had taken a company to check it out.

Hours later, three men had returned, battered and bloody, to say it had been a trick. Some of the men within the company had been traitors, purist sympathizers, and the battle had turned into a bloodbath. The general had been lost, last seen fighting ten men and a bot as he held a break in the lines all by himself. Then enemy reinforcements had arrived... No one had seen him fall, but he must have. No warrior could face such odds and win.

The senior warrior, Laarn had been forced to assume command of the entire war group, his duties as healer taking a back seat as he gave orders and sent men into battle. He had gone into battle himself, a rifle in his hand and any mercy he had from his healer's calling locked down tight. It had been brutal and bloody, but eventually they had emerged the victors, sending the traitorous combined forces fleeing broken for their lives. Now, they were on cleanup and body recovery detail.

"Come on, Xaandril," Laarn muttered to himself, scanning bodies as he walked.

"Drag the enemy to the edge of the battlefield," he ordered. "We'll set a pyre before we go to make sure the predators don't get to them."

"More than they deserve," Kriis, the warrior walking next to him, muttered. "Should leave them to get their eyes pecked out and eaten."

"Yeah," Laarn sighed. "I know. But that makes us no better than them and besides, this many bodies? It'll stink the place up for the locals and foul their water supply. They might be no better than oonat, but they didn't ask for this war, or what those assholes did to them. We have a responsibility to try and put things right, or at the least, not leave them fucked up."

"Yeah, I see what you mean," Kriis replied, but his expression was distracted. "Errr... Lord Healer, over here." He broke into a run, sliding to his knees to shove a dead R'Zaa warrior to the side, revealing a male covered in blood. Laarn's heart lurched as he recognized the pale, cropped hair.

The general.

His knees hit the dirt next to Xaandril a heartbeat after Kriis', his experienced gaze sweeping the big warrior.

"Okay, we got multiple injuries... that arm is badly broken. Looks like a gut wound. Get some pressure on that," he ordered, sticking his fingers into the guy's throat. It was too slick with blood and mangled flesh for him to feel anything, so Laarn switched to his wrist and sighed with relief. Xaandril's pulse flickered, weak but there.

"Okay, he's still with us. Get some bots in here," he ordered, snapping out a handheld diagnostic unit and sweeping it over the form of his fallen friend. It bleeped, churning out a list of near devastating injuries.

"*Draanth,* my friend," Laarn breathed. "How you're not dead, I do not know."

Putting the diag-unit down by his thigh, he reached into his pack and snapped together some pressure-sprays, using combination medications that would hopefully hold the general's condition as it was until Laarn could get him into surgery. Pulling the wounded man's bracer away from his wrist, Laarn paused as he spotted the flash of a light blue ribbon. For a moment he smiled, flicking a glance up at the big man's face to find Xaandril watching him, his eyes dark with pain.

"Don't worry, my friend, I'll get you back to her," Laarn promised and pressed the spray to Xaandril's wrist. He nodded a little and his eyes closed as the medication took effect.

Laarn stood up as the bots arrived. He carefully lifted the fallen warrior onto a stretcher and turned to the warrior next to him. Before he could speak though, laser fire sliced through the air.

"Take cover!" Laarn bellowed, his rifle off his back in an instant as he took a position in front of the bots loading Xaandril onto the stretcher. His keen gaze easily picked out the aggressors, hidden in a small copse nearby. Just warriors, not bots with them. "In the trees!" he shouted as the warriors with him all took cover and started firing back. The *drakeen* tank-bots lumbered into place, hunkering down on their six crab-like legs and using their bulk to protect the healers and their patient.

"Lord Healer!" One of the healers shouted, waving for him to take cover behind the safety of the bot wall but Laarn shook his head. These assholes had picked the wrong fight.

"Moving!" he shouted, not waiting for a confirmation as he broke cover and ran toward the trees. Laser bolts peppered the air around him, keeping the enemy's head down as he dashed for cover again. His heart thrilled with the joy of battle as he crashed through the tree line, three warriors on his heels. A war cry broke from his lips as he slung the rifle on its strap over his back again and pulled the big blade from the sheath across his shoulders.

The enemy—R'Zaa warriors he realized as soon as he got a look at their faces—were on them in a hot-second. Half their number broke away from the firefight and raced toward Laarn and his group with blades drawn. He bared his teeth as battle was joined, his blade clashing against that of the first warrior to reach them. Blocking the blow, Laarn let the male's blades slide down his to the guard and twisted, trapping his opponent's blade. As he did, he lifted his free arm and slammed his elbow up and into the guy's jaw.

Bone crunched under the blow, and the male staggered back, his blade falling from his hand as he grabbed for his shattered jaw. Lifting his blade, Laarn swung with brutal force, taking the R'Zaa's head off at the shoulders. It bounced away, and he stepped over the falling body to meet the next warrior.

His blade rose and fell as he sliced and parried, cutting a swathe through the enemy. The fight was bloody and brutal, but within minutes he stood, blood dripping from his blade and the bodies of his enemies lying at his feet. His chest heaved as he sucked in air, and he was covered in blood as he turned around and found the small team that had followed him looking at him with a mix of awe and something near fear.

"Never make an enemy of a man who can dissect you in his sleep," he commented in a low voice, leaning down to wipe his bloody blade on one of the men he'd killed.

"Pick up the rest of the wounded and survivors," he ordered as he emerged from the copse and approached the rest of his men. Turning, he strode after the bots carrying Xaandril toward the waiting shuttle. "And get everyone off the planet's surface before the predators come out at nightfall."

"Yes, my lord. Of course." One of the younger warriors peeled away, setting about his task without argument. Laarn didn't spare him a glance, his boots ringing out on the metal ramp as he boarded. Watching the bots lock Xaandril's bio-stretcher down, he patched his comms into the war group through the shuttle's array and opened a channel.

"This is the lord healer. I have the general. He's badly injured but alive. Prep the main surgery bay for our arrival and have healer teams standing by for my orders."

9

---

*E*ven though she'd been checked out and the medical AI had said her condition would ease, a few days later Jess was feeling no better. In fact, she was feeling decidedly worse. The feelings of stomach discomfort had increased to actual nausea and she felt hot all over, the kind of clammy hot all over that didn't bode well.

Groaning, she turned on her side and looked toward the door of her bedroom. She'd returned to lie down after lunch, but the nap hadn't done her any good. Instead, now she was seriously worried. Something was wrong. Very, very wrong. She needed to go to the medbay.

Her entire body ached as she pulled herself to the edge of the bed. The effort made her light-headed, shivers running over her skin as she made her way to the door. The room spun around her, the walls moving as she made her way through the main room of the women's quarters and into the corridor beyond.

"Lady Jessica! I was hoping to see you," a familiar deep voice sounded behind her.

Spinning on her heel, Jess overshot and stumbled... right into

Saal's arms. His eyes widened in surprise and for a second heat flared in his eyes.

"I've wanted to get you in my arms for weeks," he murmured, his voice husky and seductive, but almost instantly he frowned. Lifting a hand, he pressed it to her forehead. "Gods, Jessica... you're burning up."

"Medbay," she pleaded, her fingers curled in the edges of his jacket. "I don't feel well. Please, Saal."

"For you, my love, anything."

She didn't argue over his endearment as he swept her up in his arms, too busy trying not to be sick, and she closed her eyes as he carried her through the corridors. His frame was big, warm and reassuring and she relaxed, knowing that she was safe with him. For the moment anyway. Even though he'd eased off trying to claim her since he'd rescued her from the purist guard, she was under no illusions that he had forgotten about it. It was only a matter of time before he tried his luck again. She couldn't think of that at the moment, though, not when her skin felt like it was burning off and her lunch was likely to make another appearance.

"Almost there," he said in a low voice, his breathing not even labored as he hurried through the palace with long strides. "Open up," he ordered, his voice pitched to carry. "Lady Jessica needs a healer. *Now!*"

She heard rather than saw the bustle of medbay around them, still clinging to Saal to stop the awful spinning in her head. He murmured soothingly as he bent to lay her down on a soft surface. Risking a small peek, she found she was in the main bay, healers bustling around them and a steely-faced Daaynal watching them both. She didn't miss the icy expression in his eyes. Shit, he was Laarn's uncle as well. If he thought she was cheating on his nephew... she'd be pissed as well if she were him.

"I felt ill," she explained as the diagnostic bed started up, the arch forming over her in a swirl of interlacing beams. "He found me in the corridor and brought me here."

Daaynal nodded, transferring his attention to the healers clustered around her. "What's wrong with her? Find out. *Now!*"

Jess relaxed back against the padded mattress with a sigh. Whatever it was, the computers would figure it out, and hopefully give her something. She shuddered violently as a wave of heat, and then cold washed over her, not listening to the voices and bleeps and beeps of the machine anymore. It all merged into one as she slipped into semi-consciousness.

"She's *pregnant?*" Daaynal's stunned voice brought her out of her doze to find the big emperor staring at the healers. Then he turned an accusing glare on Saal. The warrior looked surprised for a moment, and she caught the flash of fury in his eyes before he blinked and covered it, adding a quick, fake smile.

"I'm what?" she asked, but her stomach rebelled and she rolled to her side and puked into the bucket one of the healers held out quickly for her.

"We are blessed," she heard Saal saying, as he patted her calf. *"We weren't sure but had hoped..."*

Nononono. She tried to shake her head as savage heaves racked her frame, her body purging itself of everything she'd eaten in the last couple of hours, but she couldn't do anything until she'd finished throwing up. A healer gave her a damp cloth and helped her rinse her mouth out before she collapsed weakly back on the bed, her head and shoulders now raised comfortably, to find Saal and Daaynal locked in a battle of wills, steely expressions on both men's faces.

"I claim the Terran, Lady Jessica..." Saal was saying through gritted teeth. "She's carrying my child, so she belongs to me."

Carrying his child... she was pregnant.

"I can't be," she said, her words dropping like a ton weight into the charged silence of the room. "I've never slept with him, nor has he claimed me. I mean, he's *tried,* but—"

"I'm claiming her now," the big warrior insisted. "And I have bedded her. How else is she with child?"

"Lady Jessica?" Daaynal turned toward her, his eyebrow raised.

The frosty expression was still on his face but had thawed a little. He wanted to believe her... that much was evident.

She shook her head. "I don't know. I haven't had sex with anyone since I left Earth months ago..."

"Lies!" Saal exclaimed, only to be cut off as the double doors to the medbay swept open.

"He's the one lying," Kenna announced as she swept into the room. "She's been avoiding him because she's worried he'll claim her and she wants Laarn to."

"*Kenna!*" Jess hissed, panic rising along with the bile in her stomach. Quickly she grabbed the fresh bucket a healer held out for her.

"Oh, shut it," the marine ordered in a no-nonsense voice. "You want to be tied to a man you don't want? I got this."

She turned her attention to the two men in the center of the room, her hand not resting on the grip of the pistol at her hip but relaxed beside it. The kind of relaxed that said she could have the thing in hand and firing within a heartbeat. "No one is claiming anyone today. My girl Mary here just got the shock of a lifetime, so let's all back the fuck down and sort out what the hell is going on, shall we?"

Daaynal frowned. "Mary? I thought her name was Jessica."

"It is. It comes from—" Kenna shook her head, her expression bringing an exhausted smile to Jess' lips. "Never mind. It doesn't matter. Jess, how are you feeling?"

"Like I just got out of high-g training after a three-day bender on Tarinat-four," she grumbled, naming one of the rough and ready outpost stations in the Sol Sector. She transferred her attention to Daaynal. "I have not slept with Saal," she declared firmly. "And I am definitely *not* pregnant by him. I shouldn't be pregnant at all. Are you sure?" she demanded of the healer hovering by her.

He nodded, pulling up a display in front of him and tapping through data she couldn't read until he found the one he wanted. Turning it, he showed her the screen. "See these levels here and here?

The scans all indicate a viable pregnancy in the very early stages. I would say no more than two weeks."

"You can tell that early?" She blinked in surprise, looking up at him. While she'd seen him in the main medbay a lot, she didn't recognize what clan he was from. Definitely not a K'Vass that was for sure. He had high cheekbones and an almost exotic look that she'd never seen before.

"Of course," he replied. "Our technology is far more advanced than yours. We can tell from the moment of conception. Even check the child's DNA and extrapolate what it will look like."

Oh my. She just looked at him, unable to take it all in. "So I really *am* pregnant? Can you..." Shit, this was going to sound so bad. "Can you tell who the father is?"

The healer blinked. "You don't know?"

"*Everyone OUT!*" Daaynal ordered, his loud, commanding growl causing healers and warriors alike to scatter, heading for the double doors at the front of the room. "Even you, Saal. *Now!*"

The big warrior grumbled, looking toward Jess, but she ignored him. Her attention was fixed on the healer, who suddenly looked very nervous. Flicking a glance between the two women, and the emperor, he cleared his throat. While Laarn was away, he was obviously the lead healer, as his scars attested to. They weren't as numerous or as vicious as Laarn's, but certainly more plentiful than the other healers she'd seen in here.

"No," she repeated. "Since I've not slept with a man since I left Earth, I don't know who the father is."

Her hands crept down to cover her stomach in wonder as she spoke. Could it be true? Was she really pregnant, and... how?

The healer frowned. "What does sleeping have to do with procreation?"

Daaynal rumbled in the back of his throat, half a growl and half clearing it. "It's a Terran phrase. It means she hasn't had sex with a male."

"But..." Surprise flowed over his face. "She must have, more than that, she must have had sex with a Lathar warrior..."

"Oh?" Daaynal's gaze sharpened as Jess spluttered. "I can assure you I have *not!*"

"Well, she must have. I can see the human genetic information, but the father was definitely Lathar—"

"Who? What family?" Daaynal demanded, his expression sharp. Jess thought the healer would have a heart attack on the spot, the tension in his frame was so complete as he studied the readings on the screen.

"He took some of my eggs for a test," she said quietly. "He must have fertilized them and implanted them without telling me." It was the only explanation that made sense. Her heart broke as she met the emperor's gaze.

"The baby is Laarn's."

THE SHUTTLE RIDE to the *Keran'vuis,* Xaandril's flagship, was less than ten minutes but seemed like hours as Laarn hovered by the stretcher holding the still form of the general. The big warrior was pale, his wounds standing out stark red against his skin. He wasn't that much older than Laarn, but with his scars and the terrible wounds across his body... he seemed eons older.

"Coming into dock now, my lord," one of the pilots leaned out from the cockpit to inform him.

Laarn nodded, feeling the shuttle slow and the slight bump as the docking clamps engaged. The stasis unit was holding Xaandril's condition steady, but he couldn't remain in it forever. Despite the fact it held death at bay, just, the longer he remained in it, the harder it would be for Laarn to bring him back.

The airlock cycled with heavy whirrs and clunks. Then the door behind him slid open. Laarn was ready, pushing the stretcher out first, scattering the warriors waiting on the other side.

"Move!" he barked in a hard voice, looking through the morass of warriors until he found scars under open jackets and teal sashes. "Is the surgical bay prepared?"

"Yes, my lord... and a support team on standby with a backup healer." A healer shoved his way through the group until he reached Laarn's side, taking over pushing the stretcher as they strode through the corridors.

"We won't need them. This is beyond everything they have," he said, rolling his shoulders as they walked. He needed to be loose and limber for the operation ahead.

Warriors in red sashes trailed behind them, obviously waiting for permission to speak. Their expressions said they plainly didn't like the idea of a healer being in charge but none of them had stepped up to challenge him. He didn't expect them to. Unlike what he'd heard of human medics, who swore to do no harm, healers among the Lathar were something different entirely. They were warriors always and fought if they needed to. Some of the most dangerous warriors in Lathar history had also been healers, his own grandfather among them.

"Orders, my lord?" one of them ventured just before they turned into medbay. Laarn cut him a glance, noting it was one of the general's commanders. Xaandril didn't have a second in command as such, but a team of them. Laarn could see the reasoning. Rather than one person who could directly challenge him for his rank and position, there was a group who had to fight among themselves before they could challenge him. The infighting kept the balance until one emerged strong enough to be named second officer properly.

"Yaraan, right?" Laarn asked, pulling the male's name from his memories of coming aboard nearly a week ago. "Split the war group and create a cordon between this part of space and all routes to Lathar Prime," he ordered. "Keep the patrols tight and capture any of the enemy if you can for interrogation. I want to know what these bastards thought they'd achieve by all this. These colony-worlds hold little value, so it doesn't make sense. Establish contact with the local Krynassis queen. See if you can broker a short-term treaty to deal with this threat, but give no assets away. Understood?"

Through it all, Yaraan stood, his face determined as he nodded.

The fact that Laarn spoke directly to him, rather than the other command officers around him meant this was his responsibility.

"Yes, my lord. Loud and clear." He grinned suddenly. "I won't let you down."

"You'd better not." Laarn transferred his attention to the group around Yaraan. "Who commands the general's flagship?"

"That would be me." An older male stepped forward, his manner and bearing screaming experience. "Draxx. Commander of the *Keran'vuis.*"

Laarn nodded to him, conferring the correct respect to the older warrior. To command a flagship was an honor, even more so when it was a general's ship. The only honor higher was commanding the emperor's ship, the *Misaan'vuis,* itself. "Bring us about and set a course for Lathar Prime. The general is in critical condition and I may need the facilities in the healer's hall at the palace to..." he didn't finish his sentence. They all knew the general was in bad shape.

"Aye, sir," the commander nodded and then growled at the warriors clustered around. "Ye heard the lord. Hop to it!"

The warriors scattered, boots thudding on the deck-plating as the corridor cleared. Draxx turned to Laarn, his expression direct. "Save my brother, healer, and I will forever be in your debt."

Laarn blinked in surprise as the big commander turned and walked away. He and Xaandril were brothers? Now he looked at it, he could kind of see the resemblance—in their builds and the way they walked—and it explained why an obviously capable warrior was content to serve under another.

Turning, he walked into the medical bay, putting everything else from his mind as he entered the cleansing unit to prepare for surgery.

10

*X*aandril was a mess.

Laarn whistled to himself, looking down at the still form of his patient on the table in front of him. There was a big knife wound across his throat, his left arm was at the wrong angle and the shoulder looked mangled, the ends of his collarbone were visible in what looked like raw meat... his gaze moved down as his assistants moved around him, prepping the surgical unit... two gut wounds and one across the thigh.

"My lord?"

At the prompt, Laarn held his arms out to the side, letting his assistants slide the gauntlets over his hands and tighten the straps over his wrists. They were like a normal pair of gloves to the wrist, but beyond neural cables sprouted like spines, falling to the floor to snake around the operating table with its protective bubble enclosing the patient.

The patient. That's who Xaandril had become now. Laarn was an experienced healer. He knew he couldn't let emotion or friendship enter into him as he prepared to be uplinked.

"Neural interface ready, surgical unit online," his assistant murmured by his side, a shadowy form in the darkness around the brightly lit bed. "Ready when you are, my lord."

Laarn took a deep breath, the scent of disinfectant and under it, blood, hitting his sensitive nose and nodded. "Link me."

The healer reached out and initiated the link, the wires connecting him to the unit flaring to life. He had a moment to gather himself as he felt the first flutter of sensation along the link. His consciousness expanded, flowing from his body to fill the operating unit. It was a similar interface as the one used for the combat and other avatar-bots, allowing him to control the machine through the link, but there were differences.

First, it wasn't a bot. It was far more complicated and sophisticated, requiring much more of his mental processing power and concentration, and secondly, unlike a bot, the link went *both* ways. He and the patient were connected, so whatever he felt, the patient felt... and whatever his patient felt, so did he. Everything... from the way his leathers itched a little where some blood had dried and stiffened them, right through to the pain his patients were in as he operated.

And that was what it meant to be a healer. He not only had to operate and heal them, put broken bodies back together again, but through the neural links, he shouldered their pain during the procedure as well, *felt* the operation from both sides. And that feeling, as well as the highest pain tolerance ever recorded in the healer's trials, was what made Laarn so good at what he did.

"Bringing the patient online."

Another nod.

He closed his eyes as the link expanded, bracing himself. Between one second and the next, pain exploded through him. The grunt that echoed in his chest was all the sound he'd allow himself to make, even though his entire body screamed with agony. Leaning back against the support in the small of his back, he took a deep breath and focused.

"Patient vitals leveling..." His senior assistant kept up a quiet running commentary in the background. Laarn may have nodded in reply, but he wasn't aware of it. Instead, he went within his own mind, following the link down into Xaandril's body. Using the link and the remote surgical arms of the bed, he focused on the most grievous wounds.

Nano-scalpels and regenerators moved faster than the eye could see as he repaired and rebuilt muscle and blood vessels within Xaandril's throat. Meticulously, he built layer upon layer and at the same time kept Xaan's circulatory system moving, making sure not to flood the area with blood until he'd successfully rebuilt the capillary system. With a sigh he gave the area a once over, noting the massive reduction in pain, and moved on.

The thigh wound was just as bad, if not worse. The healing sprays he'd used on the battlefield had sealed the wounds, Xaan's own physiology helping by slowing the blood flow to the area. That adaptation, one of the first the healers had made many years ago to the Latharian genetic code, had saved his life.

Sweat pouring from him, Laarn lost track of time as he worked through Xaan's wounds in sequence, starting with the thigh wound and ensuring that all the muscle fibers worked correctly and wouldn't adhere to each other before he moved on. It was no good saving a warrior's life if he couldn't fight. It would be more merciful to let him die, a call that Laarn had had to make in the past. But not now. Not today. Even if he took himself to the edge of exhaustion, he would ensure Xaandril would live to fight another day.

Hours later, he'd done just that as he sealed up the last of the minor wounds and left the bruising to heal on its own. As good as the technology was, he'd long ago learned to leave some things to heal in their own time. Otherwise things could go wrong. Almost like, once wounded, the body *needed* something to heal and if it couldn't find it, got confused and the immune system went into overdrive.

Satisfied he'd healed everything that was critical, he swept his focus over his patient once more and then disconnected with a sigh.

"Laarn to Draxx." He lifted his voice to trigger the comms system. "How far are we from Lathar Prime?"

As he waited for the commander's answer, he slumped against the support. Letting the assistants unbuckle him from the interface gauntlets, he flexed his fists as he drew his arms up to his chest. He was so hungry he could... what did Jess say? Ah, yes. He was so hungry, he could eat a horse. Halfway through the movement, he paused, his gaze riveted on his wrists.

There, wrapped around both like vines were dark marks.

Marks he'd only seen twice before in recent years. On his brother Tarrick, and his friend Karryl. Both warriors bonded to human females.

Bond marks.

The comm crackled as Draxx answered. *"Still a couple of hours out, my lord. How is the general?"*

"He'll live," Laarn answered shortly, his eyes wide as he studied his wrists. "But I suggest you take us to top speed and get us to the capital planet yesterday. We have a new problem."

Her world had changed forever.

The next day Jess lay curled up in a bed in one of the private rooms off the main healer's hall. As soon as her pregnancy and the identity of the father had been confirmed, Tovan, the healer in charge of the hall in Laarn's absence, had refused to allow her to be moved due to her sickness. He and Daaynal had almost had a standup fight in the middle of the medbay over it, the smaller healer standing his ground and going toe to toe with the lethal emperor with determination written all over his face.

He wouldn't have won, not against Daaynal, and they all knew it but it was obvious he didn't care. Jess was his patient and what he said went. In the end though, Jess herself had stopped the fight by throwing up on the floor. Tovan had just looked at Daaynal pointedly and within an hour she'd been moved to a private room with a guard detail at the door.

She'd heard them talking when they thought she was asleep. She was the first woman to have become pregnant by a Lathar warrior in years, albeit it by unusual methods, and they weren't taking any chances. The guard detail on her door was just the start. There were more guards at all entrances to the healer's hall and Daaynal had increased the numbers in the palace.

But for the moment, she was alone, and for that she was grateful. It had taken most of the night for Tovan to stabilize her sickness, the tall, lean healer not leaving her side until he was sure she'd managed to keep some food and water down. Only then had he left her to rest and sought his own bed. She couldn't sleep though. Under the covers, her hand slid across her stomach.

Pregnant.

Even now, she couldn't believe it. The words—someone telling her she was pregnant, even seeing the results on screen, were one thing—but believing it, actually knowing deep in her heart, was another.

A baby.

Wonder filled her as her hand felt heavy against her stomach. Did it feel any different...rounder or harder perhaps? She'd never been pregnant before so she had no idea what to expect. She certainly hadn't been prepared for the wave of love and protectiveness that filled her at the thought of the tiny life nestled deep inside her womb. A baby. *Her* baby.

Laarn's baby.

She frowned, her heart clenching. She'd thought things were going well between them, and they had been. His kisses, his promises to make her his as soon as he got back... why would he do this? Impregnate her in secret, artificially... when they could have just done it the normal way? Hell, why hadn't he even *told* her? She rubbed at her forehead with shaking fingers. If he'd told her that he wanted a baby and the only way they could do it was through technology, she'd have understood. Been happy about it even. She'd always wanted a baby, provided she was with the child's father. So if he'd claimed her, or even promised to, before he put a baby in her belly, she'd have been happy.

Now? She was pregnant without nookie, and the father was

nowhere to be seen. Apparently even Daaynal couldn't get hold of him. He was too busy with casualties on the front line. Jess dropped back on the pillows with a sigh and closed her eyes in exhaustion. Surely, he could spare a couple of minutes to answer an urgent message from his uncle, or even a minute to contact her to see how she was and let her know everything was going to be okay.

Perhaps he was lingering on the front line because he didn't want her...

A tear leaked from the corner of her eye and trailed down her cheek before she could stop it. As soon as she felt the wetness, she dashed it away in anger. What the fuck was she, a woman or a freaking mouse? She was pregnant, so fucking what? Her mom had been a single mom, bringing up twin daughters and a son. She had this, no father required. Especially not a handsome as hell, scarred up, healer who kissed like a sex god.

"Oh, my love... it breaks my heart to see you like this."

The male voice made her snap her eyes open to see Saal in the doorway, concern written on his face. Jess struggled to a sitting position, panic threading through her veins.

"Saal? What are you doing in here? The guards..."

"Hey, hey... you're perfectly safe, I assure you," he said, holding his hands out to the side as he approached. When she edged away, ready to swing her legs over the opposite side of the bed, he stopped dead.

"I would never hurt you, Jessica." His voice was low, his expression sincere. "As soon as I saw you, I wanted you. Even though you're carrying another male's child, I still want you."

"You have to leave. Please, Saal, you shouldn't be here. The emperor..." Now Daaynal knew she carried Laarn's child, he'd kill Saal for coming near her. And since all the guy had done was look after her, she couldn't allow that.

"Go, now, please?" she begged. Her voice was too weak, too thready as the adrenaline surging through her veins sapped her strength. "I couldn't bear it if you were hurt because of me."

His expression tightened for a moment, but then he nodded. "For you, my lady, anything. Just know I am never far away and if you need me, you only need mention it to your guard. Tinaas is a friend of mine. He will make sure a message gets to me..."

A sound in the corridor outside the room made him frown. Something about the way he turned and the set of his body sent alarm bells through her.

"What? What's wrong?"

The sound of laser fire outside the room answered her question and she sat bolt upright in bed. It wasn't right outside, but it sounded close. "Shit, what's going on?"

"I don't know," Saal answered. He was across the room and by her side in a heartbeat. "Can you walk?"

She nodded, taking his hand. "I'll damn well walk out of here."

"Good."

He supported her as she slid off the bed, arm ready to wrap around her waist in case she stumbled. She didn't, finding the strength from somewhere to lock her knees against the trembling. The fact that she only wore a sleep robe that bared most of her legs didn't bother her. Getting out of here before whoever was shooting got here very much did.

"Ready?" he asked when they reached the doorway, a heavy pulse pistol in his free hand and a frown on his face as he looked down at her.

She took a deep breath, the movement making her feel queasy again but she fought it down to nod at him. "Yeah. What are you waiting for, a frigging invite?"

His lips quirked and he moved forward like he might kiss her. But she stopped him with an upraised hand. "Just try it, sweetheart, and mortal danger or not, my knee will be making friends with your crown jewels. Understand me?"

He did laugh at that. "Gods, you're gorgeous."

"Gorgeous and pregnant by someone else. Remember that and I won't have to separate you from your cock and balls. Now, I don't suppose you have a spare one of those, do you?"

He shook his head, moving closer to the door. One hand flat on the panel, he listened and then froze. "*Draanth...* they're right outside. Back... go back."

Before she knew what was happening, he hustled her backward, yanking open one of the doors on a cabinet.

"In," he ordered, cramming her into the small space so quickly her head caught on the top of the opening and her knee scraped against the side. She bit back her yelp, hearing the door to the room slide open a second after he'd shut the door on her.

She was trapped, in the dark, with only a thin piece of wood and a warrior she'd turned down between her and certain death.

She just had to hope it was enough.

11

"We're looking for the human breeder bitch," a rough voice announced, muffled slightly by the wood of the cabinet door. Jess held her breath, convinced they'd hear her frightened rasp even through it.

Saal gave a hard laugh, bitter and without mirth. "You're not the only one, brother. You with Dvarr too?"

There was a rumble, which she could only assume meant assent, because then Saal chuckled. "Yeah, I don't know who's with us or not either. He's playing his cards close to his chest. Can't blame him, though, not with what's at stake. The emperor, Terran-loving bastard he is, gets wind of this and we're all done for. I cleared this room... which ones have you done?"

Saal's voice faded along with the heavy footsteps and Jess sagged, leaning her forehead against the inside of the door in relief. He'd straight up saved her life. She dreaded to think what the purist warriors would have done if they'd found her in the room.

"Don't worry, little one," she whispered, her hand over her stomach. "You and me are getting out of this in one piece. I promise."

Holding her breath, she listened for any movement in the room outside the cupboard. Straining her ears for the slightest sound... the scuff of a boot across the floor, the whisper of leather clothing as it moved, even the whisper of air leaving lungs as someone breathed... but there was nothing. Relief had her breath slithering from her lungs in a rush as she pushed opened the door and unfolded herself from the cramped space.

Her stomach and heart fighting for space in her throat, she padded on silent feet to the door and listened out again. Silence met her ears so she risked sliding the door open and peeking out. If she had this wrong...

The corridor was empty. She didn't have time for relief though. At any moment, a warrior could come around the corner and she was trapped with nowhere to go and no weapon to fight back with.

Scooting around the door, she ran lightly down the corridor. First things first, she needed to find a weapons stash and arm up because until she did, she was a sitting duck. Sure, she might not have been a trained marine like Kenna and Jane, but she knew one end of a rifle from the other and her range scores had always been some of the highest on the base.

Three corridors later and the tension was beginning to mount, her shoulders riding higher as she expected at any moment to be shot between them. But each corridor was empty of both purist warriors and the recessed weapons lockers the octagonal ident tags around her neck would open.

"Shit, please tell me they have weapons in here..." she breathed to herself, reaching an intersection and going left. Left for Laarn, no other reason... which was probably as dumb as fuck but she couldn't stay still. With purist warriors searching for her, staying put was as good as a death sentence. She needed to keep on the move and just hope she was behind their sweeps. And that someone had thought to put weapons caches in the healer's hall.

They would, surely? For all this was a place of healing and... well, *not* violence and killing people, the Lathar were a warrior race. They even took their weapons into the damn toilet. She'd seen the stands.

Turning another corner, she spotted a locker on the wall, half hidden behind a support strut.

"*Thank fuck,*" she muttered under her breath and hurried toward it, yanking the ident tags from under her gown. The skin between her shoulder blades itched as the lock cycled and gave a loud ping as the lights on the front went green.

Shit, someone had to have heard that. Holding her breath, she tried to listen for the pounding of booted feet even as she yanked a weapons belt free. It was too large to go around her hips so she slid it over one shoulder, across her body and jammed a pulse-pistol into the holster.

Some of the rifles were too big, needing someone Laarn or Karryl's size to lift, so she grabbed one of the smaller ones, checking the charge as she'd been taught. It was fully loaded.

A grin on her lips, she turned and clicked the safety off. Let those purist bastards try to hurt her or her baby now.

Her footsteps were as loud as the breath in her lungs as she set off down the corridor. She'd not been in the "ward" area of the healer's hall before except for a brief tour from Laarn when they'd arrived. So she operated on the vague memory of a central area containing the labs, with corridors leading off it like spokes of a wheel. A big main corridor had circled the entire hall with smaller corridors running parallel to it.

Guessing that the purists would likely be holding the main corridor, she ducked into one of the smaller ones, working her way through, maze like, until she figured she was somewhere near the main labs and medbay... and, more importantly, the main door out of the place.

"Got to be the only planet in the fucking universe to stick the damn hospital in the fucking basement," she groused under her breath. Running on light feet to the end of the corridor, she risked a quick look around the corner and quickly ducked back into cover.

There were two warriors covering the main lab. She hissed lightly between her teeth as she considered her options. She was alone behind enemy lines and she'd just become purist public enemy number one. She'd managed to avoid running into any of them so far but she wasn't delusional enough to think her luck would hold out much longer.

Casting a glance back the way she'd come, she nibbled her lip. Should she double back and try and find another way out? There had to be service ducts or something, maybe even maintenance shafts, she could use. Hell, she'd even settle for the old movie staple of ventilation shafts right about now.

Decision made, she took three steps away from the corner when she heard it. Boots. Heavy ones. Not from the two men in the lab in front of her, but in the corridors back the way she'd come. Freezing in place, she listened. Her finger slid off the trigger guard and curled around the trigger as she lifted the rifle into her shoulder. That was more than one man, and they were getting louder. The question was, would they come this way or turn off to search one of the subsidiary corridors?

A couple more seconds and her question was answered as the boots got louder. They were past the secondary corridor junction and were headed right for her. Which meant she had only two options left—face however many of them turned the corner in a moment...

Or take on the two men in the lab.

She cursed under her breath and turned on her heel. Fast steps took her to the corner and she barreled around it before she could think how fucking dumb this was.

As soon as she cleared the corner, she started firing, cutting down the first guard in a hail of laser bolts. Rapid fire, close grouping, just as she'd been trained and the man lurched, his body dancing and jerking before dropping like a puppet with its strings cut.

Jess didn't blink, firing at the other warrior as he dived for cover. She might not have been the dyed in the wool, born for war marine Jane and Kenna were, but when her life... her baby's life... was on the line she could and would kill with the best of them.

Shouts sounded behind her, but she ignored them in favor of darting across the lab, keeping her enemy's head down with covering fire as she approached his position, crouched behind one of the big diagnostic beds.

He tried to dart out of cover to fire at her, but each time his head broke cover, the movement was met with a burst of rapid fire. Before she'd made it halfway across the room, she heard the rifle, designed for the Lathar method of accurate with one round at a time shooting, begin to overload. Grinning like a fool, she rattled off a couple more bursts and then threw the thing over-arm.

It tumbled through the air, the whine from the overloading power pack getting louder and louder. Diving to the side, she took cover behind another bed as the rifle clattered into the wall then hit the floor. The warrior crouching there managed a small curse, the slide of leather and the thump of boots sounding as he tried to get clear.

BOOM!

The blast shook the walls as the rifle went critical and exploded. Her ears ringing, Jess was on her feet in an instant, staggering toward the frosted glass double doors at the front of the medbay. Red lights to one side warned her that the assholes had locked it. With her eyes streaming and warriors about to pour into the room behind her, she didn't have time to stop and unlock it. Instead, she grabbed for the pistol in the holster at her side and, holding it in both hands, aimed at the doors.

As she pulled the trigger, she sent a prayer up to anyone who might be listening.

Please don't let the bloody doors be bulletproof...

THE INSTANT the shuttle touched down, Laarn was at the airlock door, waiting for it to cycle so he could get off the damn thing. He'd showered and changed since he'd come out of surgery, but sleep had eluded him. How could he sleep with mating marks around his wrists? Marks he'd dreamed of being called forward in his skin all his life, but that shouldn't... couldn't be there, not yet.

Even he didn't understand the mechanism but marks were only

called to a male's skin after he'd claimed his woman... or something else happened. Since he hadn't claimed Jess' delectable, curvy little body for his own yet, that left something else.

The thought of what else it could possibly be had his heart thudding against his chest in fear as the door finally opened and he bolted through it. He cleared the ramp in one leap, his booted feet hitting the flagstones of the landing pad hard, but he was already running.

One of the reasons that could call marks to a male's skin was the death, or near death of the female he longed to claim. Fear gripped him as he pounded through the corridors of the palace, heading for the healer's hall. If anything had happened to Jess, that's where she'd be... He growled in frustration... in the care of second-rate healers while he, the best of them, had been on the front line, far away from the woman he...

He couldn't complete the thought, a frown on his face as he realized he wasn't the only person running toward the healer's hall. Two full squads of warriors ran down the opposite side of one of the many galleries on the way. Sure enough, as soon as he noticed them, the palace alarms started blaring.

"Hey!" he called out, altering direction to intercept the squad. "What's happening?"

"Lord Healer." Somehow the warrior at the front of the group managed to incline his head and give the impression of a bow while running at full tilt. "Purists in the palace. They've sealed themselves in the sickbay with one of the human females."

"*Draanth!*" Laarn burst out, exhaustion and fear robbing him of his normal poise. "Which one?"

"The little one... Lady Kallson?"

Nononono... Not his Jess.

Laarn managed to keep his horrified moan to himself and upped his pace, his long stride leaving even the fastest of the warriors in his wake as he sped toward the healer's hall. Making it in record time, he all but slid around the last corner and found the corridor in front of the entrance to the healer's hall packed.

Warriors thronged around the double doors, voices raised in frustration as different people tried to make themselves heard. In the middle of it all stood Daaynal, a dark expression on his face as he obviously lost his patience and bellowed.

"SILENCE!"

All the voices fell silent, and every pair of eyes turned toward the warrior emperor. He gestured to the doors. "Get those damn doors open. I don't care how. Blow them out of the wall if you have to, but get them open."

"That won't work," Laarn cut in, jostling through the crowds to reach his uncle's side. "The hall is designed as a last redoubt if the palace is breached. It's built to withstand even a *drakeen* assault."

"Draanth!" Daaynal hissed. "Why the *fuck* wasn't I informed of that?"

Laarn blinked at his adoption of the human word. If the situation weren't so critical, he might even have smiled and teased his uncle at his forward thinking. As it was, he just shrugged.

"The hall has secrets only the lord healer and his men need to know. The ability to guard the Arc is one of them," he said, naming the central computer and storage core buried deep in the earth below both the palace and the healer's hall.

An ancient installation, it housed the entirety of the Lathar knowledge of genetic manipulation and samples going back thousands of years. It was said that somewhere in the archives was their original genetic code, but the modern systems only went so far back and the older archives were perilous and unsafe to venture into.

"The front doors, you see," he continued, "are backed up by force fields and a vibrational-energy molecular shield. Fire on it, even with an energy pistol and it will return the yield tenfold. Which, given the close confines of this corridor, will kill anyone in here. The *only* way to shoot out the doors is from inside."

"NO ONE FIRE ON THOSE DOORS!" Daaynal bellowed, stopping at least three warriors from doing just that. He returned his attention to Laarn, his expression steely. "When this is over, you *are* going to tell me everything I don't know about the hall."

"Maybe. If you tell me what the *draanth* is going on. Purists in the palace? Again?" he demanded, not caring that he'd just snapped at the emperor himself.

"We were watching a cell, preparing to move in to try and get the leaders, but they moved unexpectedly." Daaynal reached out, using a big hand on Laarn's arm to hustle him to one side.

"Is there any other way in?" he asked in a low, urgent voice. "We *need* to get Miss Kallson out. She's..." Pausing, he looked at Laarn curiously. "You're taking this very well for a male in your position. If that were my female in there in that condition..."

"A male in my position? What do you mean?" Sudden wariness rolled through Laarn and his hand stilled where he'd been about to pull his sleeve back and show his uncle the dark marks around his wrists.

"She's pregnant," Daaynal said bluntly.

Shock and then pain lanced through Laarn, and he couldn't stop the quick inward breath. "We haven't..." he started, his words trailing off under the assault of the thoughts tumbling through his head.

Had he missed his chance with her? Had she taken another male as mate while he'd been gone... His expression hardened. He'd *told* her she was his, that as soon as he got back he'd claim her fully... She'd given him her pleasure, writhing on his fingers as he'd made her come.

"*Faithless female,*" he hissed, drawing his lips back from his teeth, but Daaynal held his hand up, shaking his head.

"No, we had the baby's genetics tested. It's either yours or Tarrick's, and I'm fairly sure your *litaan* has his hands too full with his mate to claim another female."

The baby. His baby. *His* child.

For a moment Laarn couldn't breathe, couldn't think as the thoughts tumbled through his mind. He was going to be a father... an honor that he'd never thought he'd achieve.

And she was locked in the hall with purists...

"We need to get in there. Now."

"Way to go, Captain Obvious," Daaynal threw back, making

Laarn's lips quirk. Seemed someone else had been as fascinated with the Terrans as he and his brother-warriors had. "How do you sugg—"

Before he could finish the sentence, the sound of shots rang out. Both Laarn and Daaynal whipped their heads around, the admonishment already on Laarn's lips not to shoot at the damn doors when both realized the shots had come from within the hall itself.

"What the..."

Like the rest of the men in the hall, they turned toward the glass doors. The shots were muffled, but they could all see the muzzle flashes as a rifle fired repeatedly on the other side. Laarn shot a look at Daaynal, who looked puzzled.

"Human soldiers shoot like that," he explained. "Rapid fire in bursts. We saw it when the T'Laat tried to take them. They bottlenecked a corridor and blew the *draanth* out of them. The T'Laat didn't know what hit them, especially when the rifles started to overload."

"And?" Daaynal demanded.

"They used them as explosives." As soon as he said the words, Laarn knew what Jess was going to do. They couldn't open the doors from this side, but if she had weaponry...

"CLEAR THE DOORS," he shouted. "GET READY TO MOVE AS SOON AS THEY'RE DOWN!"

The whine from the other side of the glass was followed by a clatter, then...

BOOM!

The explosion lit the glass up in a flare of green and gold, so bright the warriors in the corridor had to look away. Before the sound had cleared, there were more shots... two dull thuds on the other side of the glass doors as something hit them. Then they cracked, shattering into a million pieces to spill out over the floor of the corridor, leaving a gaping hole filled with smoke.

Bloodied and pale, his little Jess stepped through the gap, a pistol held in a no-nonsense grip. She looked at them and blinked, shaking her head.

"YOU MIGHT WANNA GET IN THERE..." she shouted and then

shook her head, stepping aside as warriors poured through the gap behind her. "Crap, sorry... hearing's shit at the moment. Purists, in the corridors right behind me. Led by a guy called Dvarr apparently."

Daaynal snarled, anger evident on his face, but Laarn was done talking. Moving in, he pulled her into his arms. She nestled against him with a soft sigh, her hands on his chest as he plucked the pistol from her, handing it off to a warrior behind her and holding her tightly as sheer relief rolled through him.

"Gods, little one. I thought I'd lost you," he murmured against her hair.

Fear the like of which he'd never known had run through him at the thought of her dead or dying, the light in her lovely eyes snuffed out forever. He'd never felt such fear or emotion before, and it humbled him. Somehow, she'd gotten under his skin and become his reason for breathing, for being... for everything.

Closing his eyes, he let the feelings wash over and through him. For the first time in his life he felt... complete. Content. She fit into a place in his heart he hadn't realized was empty. Moving his head, he placed a gentle kiss against her temple, not caring that they were in the middle of a crowded corridor and everyone would see him. As a human would say, fuck them, let them look. She was his and he wanted everyone to know it.

Murmuring, she pulled away and he looked down at her, reluctant to let her go from his embrace. Her expression was taut and angry, giving him a moment's warning before she wound her arm back and punched him in the jaw.

Pain radiated through the side of his face and he blinked, rocking back on his heels a little as he absorbed the blow. It was a good one, delivered well and by someone who had obviously been taught to punch.

"My love?" he murmured, confused. She'd been happy to see him. He *knew* she had. Why else would she cling to him the way she had? "Is there a problem?"

"That's for knocking me up without fucking asking," she hissed.

"Or even fucking. Fucking or asking, either would have been a good thing, don't you think?"

12

Fury joined the merry party of adrenaline and relief surging through Jess' system. She couldn't believe she'd made it to safety, against the odds, but that light-headedness flipped to something darker as she looked at Laarn, standing in front of her as bold as brass, saying he'd been scared he would lose her. Her hand stole down to cover her stomach. Asshole hadn't even *had* her yet, so how could he lose her?

Ignoring the small gasps and interested silence from the crowd around them, she held his gaze, refusing to look away. A challenge, something they'd been warned not to do with any of the warriors, but right now she didn't care. This could develop into a full on bitching out fest and she wouldn't care a jot. Let the rest of them see that their fucking holier than thou lord healer was a man just like them. *Him* included.

"Talk," she advised. "And talk fast."

His gaze never left hers. "My love, I can explain. Let's take this somewhere else and we'll talk?"

Her lip curled back. "Don't you fucking *my love* me. How about you explain right here."

His eyes flickered to the side, the implacable mask slipping for a moment. "We're not alone…"

"Oh, I realize that." Jess laughed. If she'd been herself and people hadn't been trying to kill her for the last hour or so, she'd have winced at the harsh sound. She didn't. Instead, she folded her arms in a silent signal that she was going precisely nowhere and he'd be a fool to try and make her.

"Just as I wasn't alone when your healer basically called me a slut when I didn't know who the father of my baby was…."

The memory of the condemning look on Tovan's face was imprinted on her mind forever. The half second of disgust that slid into speculation before he'd covered it all up with the professional doctor's face, but she'd seen it. Known what he was thinking. That if she'd slept with so many Lathar that she didn't know who'd fathered her child, perhaps he had a chance of getting between her thighs.

"…a baby I had *no* idea I was having because I haven't had sex with anyone since I left Earth. And for humans, there has to be some cock in cunt action for conception to take place. You see where I'm going with this?" she demanded, not caring that he winced at her foul language. He'd knocked her up without so much as a by-your-leave… she had a right to be a little pissy about the situation.

"Jess, please understand. I didn't mean for this to happen." He stepped toward her as though to pull her into his arms again.

Tears thickening the back of her throat, she stepped back with a glare, wishing she hadn't given up her pistol so easily. Now the excitement from nearly getting killed by purists was wearing off, her control and emotions were on a knife-edge. One touch from him and she'd crack, burst into tears and ruin her tough-girl image.

"What *did* you mean to happen then?" she demanded, trying for sharp but managing hurt instead. The sound of the pain in her own voice widened the cracks in her shields and just like that, they began to crumble.

"I thought we had an agreement… an understanding? If you'd wanted a baby *that* badly we could've just… yeah. If you'd wanted to make *sure,* that would have been cool too but…" She coughed, trying to cover the lump in the back of her throat, but it was no good. The tears had already begun to leak.

With a muffled curse, he was on her, hauling her back into his embrace with strong hands. Drawing in a shuddering breath, she didn't fight. She couldn't. She couldn't fight him and the tears that threatened to overwhelm her.

"I mean... it's no secret that I had a thing for you. Right from the beginning I'd hoped that if any warrior claimed me, it would be you, even if you did glare all the time and try and scare me off."

He lifted her chin, wiping her tears with gentle fingers.

"Shhh... we did, we *do* have an agreement," he said in a soft rumble, his green eyes locked onto hers, his stare intense. "And I didn't intend for this to happen. Do you think I would have denied myself your body and your pleasure in favor of getting you with child through other means? Yes, I took your eggs and fertilized them to see if my theory was correct. *But,* I didn't implant them. I swear on my oath as a healer, Jess, I would never do that to you."

He leaned down to brush his lips over hers and she shivered, closing her eyes as she fought the need to surrender to him.

"Jess, did you go into my lab for anything while I was gone?" he asked, lifting her chin up so she had to meet his eyes.

She frowned. "Errr... yeah. I didn't feel well and none of the other healers seemed interested in talking to me so I tried your lab. It let me in, though, and I didn't touch anything, I swear. Just used the diagnostic bed, that's all," she assured him earnestly.

Crap. What if there was a penalty for trespassing in the labs or if she'd destroyed a delicate experiment or something? Then she winced as she realized she'd not only destroyed *all* the experiments, but the labs to boot. If there had been anything delicate in there, it was a shattered, twisted mess now.

But, unexpectedly, he smiled. "That explains it, my love. I didn't destroy the eggs. They were stored in my lab. When you initiated treatment, the AI must have thought you wanted to implant them and did."

She looked at him for long moments, replaying what she

remembered of her visit in her head. "It did mention something about viable tests and if I wanted to proceed." Her cheeks burned as she realized how stupid she sounded, adding in a small voice. "I thought it just meant proceed with treatment for my stomach bug. Then my abdomen got hot, but much lower down than for a digestive problem."

The backs of his fingers brushed gently against her cheek. "That was the implantation sequence, my love."

There was a cough behind them and they both turned to find Daaynal looking down at them. "Laarn, I think it may be better if you took the Lady Jessica to the safety of your quarters while we deal with this situation here."

Laarn inclined his head. "Of course, Your Majesty. Immediately."

She bit her lip as he bent to scoop her up, her skirts rustling around her legs in a swish of silk as he held her high against his chest like she was the most delicate thing in the universe. The leather of his jacket was warm beneath her fingers as she wrapped her arm around his shoulders. Not to hold on, he would never have dropped her, but because she wanted to touch him. Reaching out, she wound her fingers through his hair, savoring the feel of the silky locks against her skin.

"Wait!"

Laarn had barely taken two steps when a harsh voice rang out from behind them. He half turned, Jess peeking from around him, to see Saal in the ruins of the lab doorway. A rifle in one hand and a blade in the other, it was obvious from his blood-stained face he'd been in a hard-won fight.

"I challenge Laarn K'Vass," he announced, pointing at the healer with the big knife in his hand. "For the right to claim Lady Jessica of Earth."

"No."

Laarn's snarl was instinctive. Jess was *his*. Even if she weren't carrying his baby, she would have been soon anyway. And she would be again. Soon. As soon as she birthed this one, he planned on putting another in her belly, the traditional way.

"She's mine. She's accepted my claim. She carries my child."

He didn't miss the flash of anger at his words, particularly the last ones. Of course, he knew Saal had been sniffing around Jess for weeks, but she hadn't paid him any mind, avoiding him wherever she could. The fact that the male had kept up his pursuit, despite no signs of interest from the female he wanted, said he was both too stubborn and too stupid for his own good.

"Your Majesty," Saal spoke directly to Daaynal, who was watching the scene with a big shoulder leaned against the corridor wall and his arms folded. His expression was so forbidding Laarn probably wouldn't have addressed him directly, even though he was the guy's sister-son.

"This warrior," Saal indicated Laarn, "left his mate unattended and in danger. *I* protected her. Therefore, by our laws I have the right to challenge his claim on her."

"That's a load of *trall,*" Laarn snapped, irritated beyond measure that this piece of *draanth* was even still speaking. There was no way he was letting a little fucking upstart, a lowly J'Qess, steal his little human from under his nose. "Jess protected herself. We all saw it."

"Not when they attacked she didn't," Saal argued. "They came to her room first and she'd be dead, or worse, if I hadn't hidden her."

Daaynal turned his head. "Lady Jessica, is this true?"

Jess nodded, her face pale, and Laarn growled in anger. "It means nothing. He's just trying to cover his ass. We all know he was friends with Dvarr. I say we execute him, here and now, for purist leanings."

"No! He's not!" Jess burst out, her arm tightening around his neck. She looked at him, her full bottom lip quivering just a little. "He's not Dvarr's friend. He's saved me from him before when he was guarding the emperor's war-room. I wanted to see you..." she said to Daaynal. "About my twin sister, the ill one? But he wouldn't let me in. Threatened me. Saal saved me then as well."

Daaynal sighed, running a hand through his long hair. "Well, that does put us in a bit of a bind, doesn't it? If he's protected your female twice, Laarn, then he *does* have the right to challenge."

"No..." Jess gasped, clinging tightly to him. Her horror at the idea eased something deep in his chest. "But I don't want him, Saal that is. I mean, I'm grateful to him for rescuing me, but I don't want him as my husband... err, mate. Laarn is my mate."

"Not yet," Daaynal growled as he pushed off from the wall. "Laarn, Lord Healer... do you accept the challenge?"

"Gladly." He let go of Jess' knees and stood her on her feet, pushing her gently behind him. "I'll make him wish he'd never been fucking born."

"You can try, *healer*," Saal spat the word like a curse, throwing the rifle to the side as he advanced. Tension in the corridor rose as warriors moved out of the way, lining the walls to watch. It was rare a warrior of Laarn's standing was challenged, and the lord healer to boot? This would be all around the palace before sundown.

Laarn grinned as he pulled the big sword from its sheath between his shoulders and paced around his opponent, stalking him like a *deearin* stalking its prey. Unlike some warriors, he had none of the big feline DNA in his genetic makeup, but he felt like it now, his eyes narrowing as he focused on the fight ahead.

Although Saal was from a lower ranked clan, that didn't mean he wasn't a good fighter. His position as war commander, albeit of a very small group, stood testament to that, as did his steady gaze and firm grip on the weapon in his hand.

Laarn's amusement fell away as they sized each other up. Neither of them made a move, not yet, too concerned with watching how the other moved, the way he gripped his weapon. Neither was inexperienced enough to think this was an idle or easy bout.

Saal was the first to move, using the big, vicious-looking blade in his hand to test Laarn's defenses. Shorter and wider, it wasn't as refined as the blade Laarn wielded but more brutal, designed for messy, close-quarters combat.

The healer blocked instantly, knocking the blade aside, and sneered. "Is that all you got? A child could fight better."

At his taunt, Saal snarled and attacked in a rush. Laarn met him with a bellow of his own, their blades clashing in midair. Saal grinned, twisting his blade and trying to snare Laarn's up, but he'd been in too many battles to be fooled by such a trick, slamming his elbow up into Saal's face.

The other warrior grunted, jerking his head back so only the edge of Laarn's elbow grazed his jaw. They broke apart, circling again. The next time, Laarn attacked first in a flurry of heavy blows designed to drive his opponent back. In a challenge fight, it would be to the edge of the area and out of it, but today? He planned to pin the bastard to the bulkhead with his own weapon.

Saal kept blocking, so Laarn kept moving, kept driving forward. His hair danced over his shoulders, his body in constant movement as he used the powerful muscles in his torso to make the big blade twist and turn in a deadly dance of flashing steel.

Saal blocked, time after time, but Laarn didn't care, his focus absolute. With each clash of blades, the younger warrior got a little sloppier, a little slower... slow enough to start leaving openings in his defense.

Laarn grinned, an evil expression that had nothing to do with humor, and slid a jab into the next opening he saw. Then a solid kick into the next. Each time Saal left himself open, Laarn capitalized on it. But not with his blade. Oh no, that would be too quick and he wanted this asshole to bleed... to *suffer*... to stand as a warning to every other warrior out there that Jessica Kallson was *his*.

Instead, he took Saal apart with his fists, switching his blade from hand to hand to keep the male's dagger at bay as he got a blow through every gap he could. Blood dripped to the floor as they moved, splattering across the bulkhead with each heavy blow. Saal's blocks got weaker and weaker, the male stumbling backward and desperately blocking. Fear showed stark on his face, his arms trembling as he tried to lift his blade one last time.

Laarn growled and slapped the weak block aside, reaching in to wrench the blade from Saal's grip. Throwing both their weapons aside with a clatter, he grabbed the other male by the throat and pinned him against the wall, his feet dangling inches off the floor.

"Jess is *mine*," he hissed right in Saal's face.

Saal's face was bruised and bloody, one eye already swollen shut... he needed a healer but Laarn didn't care. It wasn't going to be him, that was for sure.

"Touch her again, think about touching her... gods, you even *look* at her the wrong way, and I'll fucking gut you... slowly. Over days." He smiled deliberately. "If I can bring a warrior back from the grip of death, how long do you think I can make you dance on its edge? Think about it."

Letting go, he watched as Saal dropped in a pathetic heap on the floor. Without another word, he turned and walked toward Jess. She watched him with wide eyes as he came to a stop in front of her. He was bloody from the fight, but he didn't care. If she wanted him, she had to accept all of him. Lifting his hand, he held it out.

"Lady Jessica, do you accept my claim?"

13

*A*s soon as she'd said yes, Laarn had scooped her up in his arms and carried her in silence through the warriors lining the walls of the corridor. A walk of triumph, he'd made sure to look each warrior in the eye as they passed, the hard, possessive look on his face making Jess shiver.

Silence had reigned on the walk back to his quarters. A feeling of safety filled her as she curled up next to his broad chest, her arms around his neck, but she was tempered with increasing anticipation and nervousness when he didn't speak.

She stole a look at his face, their gazes clashing. His expression was tight, not the pleasant and neutral one she was used to seeing. A shiver rolled down her spine. She'd spent weeks pushing him, trying to get under his guard and now that she had, she had the sudden feeling she'd poked the bear once too often.

Since she'd first met him, she'd wondered what an enraged Laarn would be like, and she'd seen it in the corridor outside the healer's hall as he'd practically taken Saal apart with his bare hands.

She'd seen many fights in her time—growing up in a crowded tower habitat, illegal bareknuckle fights for money and gang clashes over territory had been commonplace—and only an idiot would have thought Laarn had needed the big sword back in place over his shoulders to take Saal down.

Instead, the weapon had been merely window dressing. Seconds in, it had been apparent that Saal was out of his depth—outweighed and outmatched by the tall, rangy healer. Laarn's attacks had been methodical and precise, that of a surgeon as he targeted his blows for maximum effectiveness. Another shiver hit her. She'd always seen the kind and gentle side of Laarn—kind and gentle for a Lathar anyway —but today she'd seen the warrior and he was awe inspiring.

And deadly.

All to claim her.

She bit her lip as they turned another corner. They were in a part of the palace she'd never been to, one of the western wings and she started to take notice. Although she knew Laarn had to have quarters of his own here, she'd only ever seen him at the lab, even when it was obvious he'd just woken up.

Less than a minute later, he stopped before a set of double doors, which slid open silently in front of them. As he carried her inside, her eyes widened at the opulence of the rooms, quickly glimpsed as he carried her through to a huge bedroom. The decor wasn't the clean, white and marble utilitarian sort she had grown used to seeing. Instead, it was all heavy wood and embroidered drapes, an older style, which made her think of a nomad tent or a desert sheikh's harem.

Laarn didn't stop until they were standing next to the canopied bed, still holding her in his arms as he looked directly into her eyes.

"A better man would give you a choice here," he said, his deep voice low. "A chance to change your mind about my claim and leave if you prefer Sa..." He paused on the name, his lip curling slightly. "A chance to leave and find the warrior I bested. But I am not that man," he snarled, his grip tightening. "You're mine now, Jess, and I'll never let you go. I ache to claim you, to finally make you mine, in every sense of the word."

A thrill shot through her body at his words, arousal and anticipation working their seductive spell. He bent down, placing her on her feet carefully. Too carefully, his entire frame solid with tension.

Standing straight, he looked down at her, his expression unreadable.

"Take the gown off, or by all the gods, I'll fucking tear it off."

She hardly recognized his voice, harsh and guttural. The sudden look on his face, hard and feral, sent a wave of fear through her. Instinctively, she backed up a step, nerves setting in.

Instantly, fury flared across his features and within a second he was on her, his big hand capturing the back of her neck in an iron grip. His eyes glittered.

"Oh no, sweetheart. You don't get to run. Not now. Not after this."

A cry escaped her as he yanked her toward him, his free hand catching on the front of her gown. With a savage yank, he tore it clean down the middle, baring her naked body beneath to his gaze. Frozen, she looked up at him as his eyes slid down her, the hard look in them dissolving into heat as they paused on the swell of her breasts.

He stopped dead, his hand still on the back of her neck as he made a slow perusal of her body. She bit her lip, worry filling her. She'd pushed him to claim her, but what did he think now that he saw her body for the first time? Did he like what he saw... she wasn't model thin, nor toned and fit like Jane or Kenna. She was just... average.

He looked down further, over the stomach she tried to suck in, those last few pounds she could never get rid of no matter how long she spent on the treadmill or how many sit-ups she tortured herself with showing there. The hard look on his face dissolved into heat as his gaze swept down her bare legs and then back up to settle at the juncture to her thighs. She resisted the urge... the need... to press her legs together as she remembered his clever fingers on her clit, in her pussy, as she'd ridden him to orgasm. She'd been able to tell he was a surgeon then, his hands dexterous and agile.

He released her and nodded toward the bed.

"On there. On your back... legs spread."

His voice was still unrecognizable—a rough growl. Instinctively, she moved toward him, craving something... anything. Some sort of softness or tenderness to reassure her that she hadn't made a horrible mistake.

"*Do it, Jessica,*" he snapped, his hands tearing at his weapons belt and jacket. "I'm too close to the edge for you to fight me, little one."

His voice broke on the last word and her eyes widened, sudden understanding filling her as she glimpsed past his implacable mask and saw the stark fear and need there. She'd scared him, badly.

Stepping back, she let the remnants of her dress slip from her shoulders. He watched her like a hawk, his hands stilling for a moment on his belt as he undid it, like he couldn't bear to look away. Like she was the only thing in the universe for him as she moved. Heat flared in his gaze again, and his hand shook as he tore at his buckle.

A surge of power filled her as soon as she saw it. Feminine pride and the knowledge that he was *hers,* that the sight of her naked body held him enthralled, rolled through her as she stepped back. Her movements were as seductive as she could make them as she slid backward onto the bed. Lying back, she kept her knees together for a moment, arching her back and body to show it off to best advantage as she slid her hands through her hair.

Settling back, she caught his gaze and then parted her thighs for him.

He was still watching her, his eyes narrowed but at his side, his jaw clenched and unclenched, the knuckles showing white.

"Touch yourself," he ordered, shoving his pants down off his hips. "I want to see how you pleasure yourself. What you like. Make yourself wet for me."

She nodded, unable to speak, and slid her hand down the front of her body to dip between her legs. As her fingers grazed her clit, his cock popped free, arching tall and proud up toward his flat, muscled stomach. A small gasp left her lips. He was huge and thick, far bigger than she'd thought.

Fisting his cock, he stroked. The broad, flushed head slick with precum played peek-a-boo with his hand as he stepped out of his pants and boots, but his eyes never left her, riveted to her fingers between her legs.

She played with her clit, using her other hand to part her pussy lips as she circled and stroked. She teased the small bud into a hard little nubbin and then rolled her fingertip over the beaded pearl. Her breathing shortened, her hips rocking as she remembered how he'd touched her. How much she'd liked it. How he'd made her come, hard and fast.

"Stop," he ordered when she was almost there, her body straining for release. She did, instantly, locking her gaze with his as he moved to kneel on the bed—one knee, then the other, his cock still in his hand. He knelt between her parted thighs, stroking his cock as he looked down on her with a possessive gaze.

"Hands up, above your head." His chest heaved, breathing short, and each word had a little growl on the end. Wordlessly, she obeyed, putting her hands either side of her head and watching him. Waiting for his next move.

With a growl, he braced himself over her, cock in hand and she tensed, anticipating the press of his hot flesh into hers. He moved, and she jumped as his fingers swept through her folds. His lips grazed over hers. Would he take her hard and fast, claiming her in one thrust? Was that why he'd had her pleasure herself, make herself wet for him?

"*Mine.*"

The word was growled against her lips and then he was gone, sliding down her body. She whimpered as he parted her thighs roughly, wedging his broad shoulders between them. His breath washed over her pussy lips and she tensed. His tongue rasped over her, warm and wet. Her hips jerked off the bed, a soft keen falling from her lips. It was met by a deep growl and his hands closing around her thighs, holding her still as he licked her again. Found her clit.

Sucked.

Hard.

Her head thrashed on the bed as he set about driving her out of her mind. Forget clever fingers, the man had a gifted tongue. She writhed, or tried to, as he took her with his mouth. Licking and suckling at her clit like a man starved before thrusting his tongue deep within to collect every drop of her arousal. Moans slipped from her lips as he brought her near the edge quickly and ruthlessly, her hands moving down so she could slide her fingers through his long hair.

He reacted instantly, tearing from her in an explosion of movement. Grabbing her hands, he surged over her, slamming them back into the bed above her head and holding them there.

"I said, *hands up,*" he growled, flicking his hair to one side, over his shoulder as he transferred both her wrists to one hand. She nodded, breath coming in short pants as he kept her thighs apart with a hard knee. She'd do whatever he wanted, if he didn't stop touching her. He wouldn't hurt her, she knew that without thinking, but this rough, near ruthless side of him, a side she hadn't expected, turned her on like nothing else.

Reaching between them, he brought the thick head of his cock to bear against the entrance to her pussy. She bit her lip, sucking in a hard breath as he pushed, breaching her in one hard movement and seating himself to the hilt.

"Oh, shit..." she moaned, her back arched as she was filled suddenly, his thick cock stretching her inner walls to capacity. It burned. But felt *so* good. "Yes, please, yes."

He groaned, his eyes half closed and his lips parted as his cock throbbed within her, but then he pulled back. Thrust again. Hard and fast. Their moans mingled in the air as he did it again, setting up a hard and fast rhythm.

She gave herself up to pleasure and him, arching her back and rocking her hips to match each of his thrusts. There was no finesse about his love-making now, just raw power as he claimed her. Each rock of his hips drove his cock deep inside her, each grind of his pelvis against hers trapping her clit between them and sending waves of pleasure through her.

"Laarn," she gasped, pulling on her wrists in his hold. "Please... I want..."

He nodded, his hair brushing her cheeks as he leaned down to claim her lips in a torrid kiss. His tongue thrust into her mouth in concert with his cock in her cunt, but he let go of her hands. She wrapped her arms around his neck, kissing him back as he took her. He claimed her in hard thrusts, each one a declaration that she belonged to him, and only him.

Then it was all too much. The tension in her body, in her pussy clenched tightly around him, was all too much. Her movements faltered, hips jerking as she came, crying out into his mouth as he claimed her pleasure as well as her body.

Wave after wave of bliss drenched her body like the waves of the ocean. She whimpered and clung to him, her eyes pressed shut as he sped up, the near-frantic pace of his hard strokes driving her higher.

Then he broke from her lips with a groan, slammed into her a last time and stiffened. She moaned as she felt him come, hard and hot, deep inside her. She held him tightly, hand in his hair at the back of his neck. If she hadn't already been pregnant, there was no way she wouldn't have been now.

She was his.

14

*J*ess was incredible. Utterly amazing. Her hot little body clenched tightly around his cock as he'd taken her over and over was everything Laarn had dreamed it would be and more. Much more.

But as hot as the sex was, lying next to her as she slept, feeling her pliant and trusting in his arms... *That* had been the stuff his deepest, darkest, wouldn't admit to anyone on pain of death fantasies had been.

Lying there with her sleeping in his arms, he'd held her close, sliding a hand over her still flat stomach. Wonder still filled him that she carried his child safely within her and that moment, that memory of holding her, would forever be etched in his memory.

The knowledge that he wouldn't be alone as he lived out his life... the fact he had a female by his side as his partner, to bear his children, had finally sunk in and had he been standing, would have brought him to his knees.

She was his, his mate, his life... An *intelligent* female, not a near animal like the oonat some of his brothers had settled for, but a real woman with wit and intelligence who he could have a conversation with.

He re-entered his, no *their* quarters with an excitement rolling through his veins he hadn't felt for years coming through those doors because he knew she waited for him within.

His cock, semi-hard all day, flared to life and pressed uncomfortably against the front of his leathers. He was as stiff as a flagpole, even though he'd had her more times than he could count last night and then again before he'd left this morning. Leaving her all sleepy and sated in his bed, her lips plump from his kisses, had been the hardest thing he'd ever done.

But now he was back, and the hours he'd spent in the lab were too many away from her and the haven of her sweet body.

"Jess?" he called out, not finding her in the cool shade of the main rooms. Like most Latharian summers, the day was hot enough to burn flesh from bones, the heat only just starting to dissipate as the sun neared the horizon.

"Jessica?" He looked into the bedroom, not finding her sleeping either.

A pang of disappointment hit him. One of his favorite parts from last night had been rousing her from sleep so he could take her again. She'd seemed to particularly like his tongue against her clit, her little toes curling as she came back to wakefulness with a feline stretch that quickly turned into a hoarse scream as she came.

Panic replaced the disappointment, though, as he couldn't find her in the facilities either, but then the soft splash of water from outside got his attention. The bathing pool. A groan whispered from his lips at the thought of her naked in the silky water.

"*Draanth...*" he breathed, his cock jerking savagely. He had to have her again.

Striding out onto the veranda, he stopped short at the side before him. In this, one of the older parts of the Imperial palace, the quarters were larger and more ornate, which extended outside as well. His bathing pool ran the length of the veranda, the cool water reflecting the blue tiles beneath invitingly. But no water could be as inviting as the woman floating on her back in the middle, as naked as the day she'd been born. Her eyes closed, she hadn't seen him yet, a look of such serene relaxation on her face she looked like one of the goddesses themselves, come down to grace the mortal realm with her presence.

She must have sensed his presence or his gaze on her because she opened her eyes and looked right at him. "Laarn!"

A beautiful smile spread over her features, stealing his breath away as she swam toward him. Need and lust raised their heads and roared within him, and in the space between one second and the next, he tore at his clothing, stalking toward her.

His jacket hit the tiles behind him, and he walked out of his boots as he wrenched his pants open, his cock leaping free as he bent to shove them off his hips and down his legs. They were off in seconds, his gaze never leaving hers.

Her cheeks flushed, her eyes darkening as she read the intent on his face, but rather than coming to the steps toward him, she swam backward away from him. His lip curled, a warning growl in the back of his throat, but she just smiled as he waded down the steps into the water.

No words were spoken between them. None were needed. He wanted her, and he was going to have her. The water moved around him as he walked, no, *stalked* her across the pool.

She watched him, the light of mischief in her eyes, a light made brighter the more he growled, acting like the savage warrior he knew humans had dubbed his kind. But his little Jess seemed to like him like this, her cries of pleasure loud when he held her firmly and took what he wanted...what they both wanted.

Before he reached her, she darted to the left, trying to slide past him in the water, but he was ready for her tricks. Throwing himself to the side, it was the work of a couple of powerful kicks and he had his arms around her, hauling her up against his broad chest before she could go under.

She wriggled as if trying to escape, but not too hard. Her delighted gasps were punctuated by the splashes of water around them as he carried her toward the shallower end of the pool. Turning, he sat on one of the inbuilt loungers, the curved tiled "seats" allowing a bather to recline in comfort under the cool water.

It was the work of a moment to set her astride him. She gasped in pleasure as his hard cock slid the length of her pussy lips under the surface, the additives in the water to care for their skin making the ride silky.

Reaching up, he fastened his hand around the nape of her neck, a pang of protectiveness warring with the sheer lust surging through him at how delicate the bones there felt. How delicate she felt. Every time he touched her, he felt like a brute... but he couldn't stop. She was his, his mate... and fire for her burned in his veins.

Pulling her down, he claimed her mouth. Their lips locked and then parted before returning in hot, open-mouthed caresses that drove the need in his body higher. Breaking away for a second, he ran his thumb over her cheek, catching sight of the marks around his wrist. Both Karryl and Tarrick had commed to congratulate him and warn him that if he thought his need for her was slacked now he'd had her, to think again... The lust that burned within for her would only get worse, as would hers for him.

This fact was proved as she wriggled to get closer, taking over their kiss by thrusting her tongue into his mouth in demand. He groaned at the feeling as she teased it along his, rocking her hips to grind her pussy against his thick shaft. That was nothing to the feeling when she slid her hand between them, wrapping her small fingers around his cock and stroking.

"That's it, little human," he broke away to rumble against her lips. "Take it, take what you want from me. It's the Lathar way, and you're mine... so you're Lathar now."

Letting go of her neck, he lay back in the water, spreading his arms in silent invitation. Her gaze shot to his, and then she smiled. The hot look in her eyes had him ready to come then and there. She pumped his cock again, firmer this time, and he groaned as her finger slid over the crown. Every instinct he had urged him to rise up, flip her over and bury himself balls deep in her welcoming softness but he held off. This was for her. For her to take her pleasure from him.

She teased him with her hand, pumping in slow strokes as she reached out with the other. Grabbing his wrist, she brought his hand to her breast in unspoken command. He did as he was bade, cupping and caressing the soft weight of the luscious mound in his hand. She was tiny compared to him, but her breasts more than enough to fill his hands.

He held her, stroking his thumb along the underside before sliding it across the swell of her breast, watching her face as he found her nipple and rubbed it. She bit her lip, eyes closed and head thrown back, a look of erotic concentration on her face. Trying to ignore her siren's touch on his cock, he played with her nipples, stroking and circling, rubbing and tweaking them until they stood out proud, all but begging for his lips and tongue.

Sliding his hand up her back, he urged her to lean forward. A soft swipe of his tongue made her gasp and wriggle, the fingers of the hand on his shoulder turning to claws against his flesh as he teased her anew. Her hand on his cock faltered and she released him for a second to guide the hand he had on her hip between her thighs. Against her breast, his lips curled into a smile at the invite. He didn't need to be asked twice, easing combat-callused fingertips between her slick pussy lips to find her clit.

He stroked and suckled, her body arching and writhing in response to the dual assault. Her hand closed around his cock again, but he kept her too off balance to do more than touch him, or stroke occasionally, ruthlessly driving her up toward need and heat.

"Laarn..." The soft plea of his name on her lips was the sweetest sound he'd heard in his life. "Please..."

"What do you need, little one?" he rasped, sitting up suddenly to claim her lips. "Tell me and I'll give it to you."

"Fuck me," she whispered and he groaned, the words turning him on beyond all belief. "Take me and make me yours again."

He nodded, lying back in the water again. Wrapping both hands around her tiny waist, he lifted her. She helped, repositioning and presenting the head of his cock against her slick entrance. They both groaned as she slid down, impaling herself on his thick cock slowly.

"Ride me, Jess," he groaned, lifting to see where their bodies joined, to where her sweet little pussy stretched wide around his thick cock. Before long, he wouldn't be able to take her like this, she would be too big, her belly swollen with their child. "Ride me as I watch you, looking up in worship of the goddess you are."

"You see me that way? As a goddess?" She looked down at him in surprise, already starting to move. He gritted his teeth at the erotic slip slide as she lifted up and then impaled herself on him again.

"You're mine. My bond-mate," he managed in a rough voice. "I will always worship you, kneeling at your feet if I must to be granted the boon of touching your beautiful body. I will always crave you, always need you, always want you."

She groaned, the sweetest sound he'd ever heard, and then there were no more words. With each rock of her hips as she rode him, she took them both closer to bliss. He held out for as long as he could, letting her have her way with him, but then she began to falter, her hips losing the rhythm.

Opening her beautiful eyes, she didn't need to say anything. He read the entreaty, the need in them loud and clear. With a growl, he took over, his hands on her hips as he drove up into her. The water lapped and splashed around them as he fucked her with long strokes. Crying out, she collapsed across his chest and he held her, his strength enough for both of them as he moved. Driving up. Stroke after stroke almost turning him inside out with fire as he held off his climax to make it good for her.

Then she whimpered, and her pussy clamped down hard around him as she came, near silently in his arms. He grunted, the spasming of her pussy milking his cock. Fire raced down his spine and around to his balls, his cock jerking as he surged up into her one last time and stiffened. His cock buried inside her to the hilt, he groaned as he emptied his balls into her, jet after jet of hot, ropey seed bathing her inner walls in an explosion of bliss the like of which he'd never experienced before.

Then it was over, and he sagged in the water, glad of its support as he held her close and brushed his lips over her temple. Closing his eyes, he sighed in contentment and happiness.

She was his. Forever.

THE LAST FEW days with Laarn had been amazing.

Jess sighed to herself, lost in happy memories. He was a wonderful lover and insatiable. She wasn't an innocent by any stretch of the imagination, even verged on the adventurous, but she'd had no idea sex could be so... *everything.* So fulfilling. Earth-shattering in its rawness and beauty.

The healer certainly was a dark horse. So stoic and implacable all the time, she'd have never guessed that under that unreadable facade lay a deeply sensual streak that delighted in torturing her with pleasure until she was hoarse screaming his name and boneless with the ecstasy he took her to.

It was more than just the sex, though. There was something else there. A look in his eyes when he touched her, took her... something in there that rocked her right down to her soul.

She couldn't stay away from him either, wanting him again even though he'd come back at lunch. He'd claimed her again... all uncontrolled passion against the door in their quarters, too desperate to even make it to the bed.

And she'd loved it. Every single hot, sweaty, needy second of it.

Loved it and wanted more. Needed more. *Craved* more.

Was that normal for bonded couples? This all-consuming, carnal desperation.

She bit her lip as she made her way through the corridors to the makeshift healer's hall, careful to keep to the smaller halls and corridors so she didn't get caught.

Security had been massively increased in the palace after the purist attack and given the fact she was carrying what could be the savior of the Lathar race, she wasn't supposed to even leave their quarters without the security detail camped in the corridor outside the front door. So she'd slipped out of the garden entrance when they weren't watching.

After all, surprising her husband in his office for a quickie didn't need an audience. She was kinky, but not *that* kinky.

Her heart sped up a little as she reached the large hall they were using while the upper levels of the healer's hall was rebuilt. The south wing of the palace was high ceilinged and flooded with light. Instead of walls, there were simply dividers and screens to create rooms and a big tent of plastic material for the quarantine areas and operating theaters.

Making her way around the edges of the hall on silent feet, she passed the recovery "rooms." Xaandril, badly injured in battle and brought back to the palace by Laarn, was in one of them, Kenna in constant attendance. Jess' lips quirked.

Try as Kenna might to insist her concern for the big general was simply that of one soldier to another, it was obvious to anyone with eyes in their head that something was going on between the two of them. It also hadn't escaped Jess' notice that Xaandril still wore the blue ribbon Kenna had wrapped around his wrist at the tournament.

"I was going to terminate them."

The sound of Laarn's voice stopped Jess just as she reached the area at the back of the hall that had been sectioned off for his lab and office. Her hand fell away from the drape dividing it from the room next door that she'd slipped into. Instinct made her shrink back, out of sight of the semi-translucent panel across the upper third of the drape. Slowly, she edged forward, just enough to peek around the edge.

Two big figures moved about in the area beyond and she easily recognized the other figure as Karryl, Laarn's friend and Jane's mate. The huge warrior was leaning against something on the other side of the office, his arms folded across his chest. He was also right in her line of sight, and she his, so she had to be careful. Any movement and he'd spot her for sure.

"You were?" Karryl asked.

"Yeah." Laarn moved around the bed in the middle of the room. From the metallic sounds and the sparks lighting up around him, he was mending it. She bit her lip again; intelligent, a surgeon and good with tools... was there no end to his talents? "I would have done it as soon as I'd confirmed conception was viable."

Her attention snapped away from the hot image in her head of Laarn stripped to the waist with a welding torch in his hands and back to the conversation. Conception. He was talking about her pregnancy.

A chill shivered down her spine in warning. She didn't need to be hearing this, shouldn't be listening... but wild horses wouldn't have dragged her away from that spot, her feet rooted to the floor as Laarn continued to speak.

"I never wanted to implant them at all."

"What do you mean? How the *draanth* did she get pregnant then?"

Laarn's chuckle was dry and a little bitter. "Because I'm a fucking idiot and left everything set up in my lab rather than saving the data and terminating the things."

Her heart stuttered in her chest. Things. He was referring to babies, *their babies,* as things.

"But Jess was ill while I was away, and those *draanthing* idiots in the hall made her feel unwelcome, so she used my lab..."

Karryl took up where he left off, realization in his deep tones. "And she used your equipment... the AI completed the implantation sequence."

"You got it in one." Laarn paused and sighed, the outline of his figure moving as he dropped his head, his hand coming up to scoop his hair out of his face. Tears welled in the corners of her eyes as she watched. How many times had she seen that gesture?

"Honestly? I never intended to implant them at all, or claim her. I never wanted that—"

The tears fell, a sob rising in her throat as she backed up, her ears ringing. He didn't want her. He'd never wanted to claim her. Pain lanced through her chest and she stumbled unseen from the hall. Her vision blinded by tears, she somehow made it through the hall and out into the corridors without anyone seeing her.

15

*S*he was in the Imperial gardens. Jess blinked, her eyelashes wet with tears as she looked around. Curled up on one of the benches, she was well out of sight of the main pathways. How long had she been here? It couldn't have been too long. Once her guards had discovered she was gone, all hell would have broken loose. She'd have heard the alarms.

She was glad they hadn't found her though. Not in this state.

A shuddering breath left her as she realized tears still ran down her face silently. She was a fucking idiot. Laarn didn't want her, never had, and he hadn't claimed her until his hand had been forced.

Until *she'd* forced his hand, pushing and pushing him into a relationship with her. Her cheeks burned with embarrassment. She'd hung around so he couldn't help but notice her, mooned after him like some fucking love-sick teen over her first crush. Then, she let out a bitter laugh, she'd pulled the age-old underhanded female trick and gotten herself pregnant by accident.

Never mind that they hadn't even had sex at that point. Oh no, she'd managed to find a sci-fi equivalent of the immaculate conception. Someone slap her ass and call her fucking Mary. Her hand shook as she shoved it through her hair, the elegant braid she'd put it into this morning long gone under Laarn's hands at lunch.

The memory of their tryst earlier brought fresh tears to her eyes. He fucked her, sure, and he was good at it... so very good... and she'd even thought she'd seen something in his eyes, some sort of emotion. Her snort was bitter. Love. She'd thought it was love, hidden way back there. A love he couldn't admit to yet, hampered by his warrior's training or something. But now she realized differently.

He hadn't wanted to bond with her, so what man wouldn't make the best of a bad job, particularly a man who hadn't had access to a woman for years? No wonder he fucked her with desperation. He was frustrated. Probably had the worst case of blue balls for a fucking century, so when he'd been forced into what amounted to a shotgun wedding...

She closed her eyes and groaned. Oh my god, how fucking stupid was she? No wonder he'd been putting off a bonding ceremony. "After the baby," her ass. He didn't want to be bonded to her at all, and with his knowledge of genetic manipulation... shit, he was probably already looking for a way to remove the bonding marks from his skin.

A wave of exhaustion and nausea washed over her. She'd made a complete and utter fool of herself. Chasing a man who wasn't interested. Had *never* been interested. She'd convinced herself that he was shy or something. He was dedicated to his duty to save the Lathar, but he wasn't shy at all. He never had been.

Casting her mind back, she tried to think of any point when he'd shown interest in her at all. And came up blank. Sure, of all the human women, he'd requested her the most often... she groaned again and let her head rest against the cool marble.

Stockholm Syndrome. She had a classic fucking case of it.

Steps sounded behind her and she jerked upright, grabbing the hem of her skirts to wipe the tears from her eyes. The last thing she wanted to do was admit why she was crying to anyone, to admit her failures and that she'd been a fucking idiot. A small measure of relief filled her as she realized the tread was heavy and male. A Lathar, thank god. She could fool a warrior... fooling one of her friends would have been entirely more difficult. Impossible. After all they'd been through, they could read each other like a book.

Her eyes widened as Saal came into view. A few days had taken care of most of his injuries but he still looked like a man who had been beaten, and badly.

"Shit, Saal..." She looked around in panic. "You have to go. If the guard sees you near me, he'll kill you."

"What I have to say is worth the risk." He managed a small smile as he came nearer and sat on the other end of the bench. His movements were slower than normal and obviously painful. At her little look he shrugged. "None of the healers will touch me past ensuring my life is not in danger, so I have to heal the old-fashioned way. Slowly. To teach me a lesson."

Her heart clenched for him as she took in the bruises on his face, one eye still nearly shut, and across his chest and body. He had to be in agony with the wounds Laarn had inflicted, but to then deny healing as well... a shiver hit her at her mate's ruthlessness.

"I'm sorry," she said softly. "I didn't know accepting help from you would make him do this..."

"No," he interrupted her. "*You* didn't do this. I did. I didn't need to challenge him for you. I didn't need to use you accepting my help as a route to issue that challenge, especially when you did not know our laws. It was a dishonorable move... a, how do you humans say it, a dick move?"

Her lips quirked a little, even through her sadness. "You've been talking to Kenna or Jane," she said, recognizing the comment.

He nodded. "I was reassigned to Lady Jane's protection detail. She's... not you, but is pleasant to be around. I'm hoping that my compliance will stand me in good stead and I might eventually be granted permission to travel to your system. See Earth for myself."

"Yeah?" She smiled, grateful for his understanding and the fact that he hadn't queried the tears on her face or her red, puffy eyes. She shuffled more upright, smoothing her hair down. She must look a right sight. "Are you sure that's because you want to see my planet, or because there are human women—a lot of human women—there?"

He grinned, ducking his head a little and looking up at her through his bangs. "It's the women. You can't blame me, not when I see you and the other ladies here... You're all beautiful and any male would be proud to call you his own."

She shook her head. "Word of warning when you meet more Terran women? Don't go around declaring you own them... we don't like that. It smacks too close to slavery, and we abolished the right to own another human centuries ago."

He blinked, surprise on his face. "You think that's what we mean? That by claiming you, we make you our slaves? *Gods!*"

Shoving a hand into his long hair, he looked at her again. The depth of the shock in his pale eyes would have been amusing if it wasn't so profound.

"You really don't understand our males at all, do you?" he asked. "The dream of all of us is to find a female to claim and call our own. A worthy female who will call the mating marks out of our skin for all to see... but it's not the male who makes a *slave,*" he all but spat the word, "of the female, but the other way around. And willingly. Once those marks are on a male's wrist, *he* belongs to *her.* Body, mind and soul. There will never be another female for him as long as he lives. His body, his cock, will never work for another."

Her mouth opened but no words came out, the depth of her surprise was so great. Finally, she cleared her throat and managed, "What. Ever?"

Saal shook his head and then paused and frowned. "Maybe if she died? After years have passed? Usually bonded males whose mates die... well, they're never the same, if you get what I mean? They often go berserk in battle, just keep attacking the enemy until they're exhausted and get killed."

"Oh my..." She really didn't know what to say to that, but was saved from answering as large figures closed in on them suddenly.

Hard hands yanked her off the bench and she screamed, the sound cut off as a hard hand was slapped over her mouth. She carried on screaming, struggling like a wildcat while next to her, Saal bellowed with rage and fought back. But the dark-clad figures around them were too numerous and she watched in horror as they surrounded him. In his injured state, it was obvious any resistance wasn't going to last long.

Her captors lifted her but she twisted and turned, trying to keep him in sight. She managed it just long enough to see him hit over the back of the head, collapsing to the ground in a heap. Lifeless. She didn't stop screaming and struggling as they carried her away until something sharp was pressed against her neck.

Every cell in her body froze as she stilled, her heart pounding in her chest as a voice rasped in her ear.

"The price for you is dead or alive, Terran bitch. Your call."

"I CAN BLOODY well feed myself, female. Give it here!"

Laarn chuckled at the growl from the general's room as he and Karryl passed, pausing for a moment to get a glimpse into the "room" Xaandril was recovering in and biting back a small smile.

The big warrior was bed-bound, his shoulder and arm bandaged right the way up to the neck with movement suppressors in place, their bright blue lights winking in concert. He couldn't have moved the limb to save his life, just the way Laarn wanted it while his body healed. Sitting next to him on the covers was Kenna, one eyebrow arched as she held out a spoonful of soup.

"And just how are you going to balance the bowl and the spoon without wearing it and burning yourself in the process?" she demanded. "Stop being a big baby and just let me feed you."

Karryl whistled softly, murmuring, "Did she just call the Hero of the Nine Wastes a big baby?"

Laarn chuckled as they passed. "Yes, I do believe she did."

"He's a goner." Karryl fell into step with him as they walked into the main area of the hall. "He just doesn't realize it yet."

"When we took the humans, we assumed they would be docile and biddable like the oonat. Seems the gods played a hell of a joke on us, didn't they? The human women go after what they want, and they don't stop until they get it."

Laarn nodded with a wry smile, stopping by the main station to call up a list of the injuries logged in for treatment. They were the usual assortment of training injuries and one serious burn from engine fuel. Looked like the idiot stuck his arm against a running vent. The healer shook his head at such stupidity. Really, some males should be stopped from breeding.

Karryl's smile was broad as he leaned his hips back against the console next to Laarn, his arms folded over his chest. "Finally realized you were hunted, brother? How do you feel about that? Of all of us, you were the one I never thought would fall..."

"Why not?" Laarn selected one of the open cases for treatment. "I'm a man like any other. A red-blooded male with all the usual drives and needs..." He slid a sideways glance at his friend. "And what makes you think I wasn't the hunter? I had my eye on Jess as soon as I saw her on that base."

And he had. One of the first warriors onto their command deck, he'd noticed her immediately. Kneeling with her hands on the back of her head in the middle of the mass of humans, his gaze had gone directly to her. It didn't matter that there were other females in the room. His attention had been solely for her. She'd been clad in that gods-awful uniform the humans wore, the one that concealed the lines of a woman rather than celebrating them like clothes should.

Then she'd lifted her head, their eyes had met and he'd been sunk.

"*Trallshit,*" Karryl snorted. "You were running scared and everyone knew it."

Caught. Karryl had always been able to see right through him.

"Yeah. But I came to my senses. Thank the gods she managed to get herself with child in my lab before that *draanthic* Saal could make a move on her.

"Speaking of..." Karryl nodded to the other side of the hall. Saal was in the doorway, one hand propping him up. He was covered in blood and unsteady on his feet.

"Huh." Laarn raised an eyebrow. "Wonder who else he pissed off to get another beating?"

Saal staggered forward, his gaze latching onto the two warriors. "The gardens... they took the Lady Jessica," he gasped and then keeled over unconscious on the floor.

BUNDLED into an *oonat* robe with a veil over her face, Jess was taken from the palace and hurried through the streets of the city below. She'd been into the city a couple of times before, but those journeys, in a comfortable carriage surrounded by guards and warriors, bore no relation to being frog-marched through the back streets, only able to get snatched glimpses of where she was through the thick material covering her face.

She tried to remember the twists and turns they took, and how many paces, but before long she was hopelessly lost. Through it all, the hard hand on her arm gripped cruelly, painfully, but thankfully there was no longer a blade at her throat.

But she could hear, and when they hit a crowded area she tried to struggle, opening her mouth to cry out.

Before she could, though, a hard voice said at her ear, "Don't bother. All they see is a handmaiden, a slave. Scream all you like. They wouldn't raise a finger to help you even if we beat you to death right in front of them."

Tears filled her eyes as she realized that he was right. The robes rendered her invisible. The veil was something else, used for handmaidens whose features were presumably too non-Lathar to be palatable. Disgust rose. It was the Lathar equivalent of the human joke about putting a bag on an ugly woman's head so a man could fuck her.

But it meant that he was right. No one would help her, even if she struggled or screamed. She'd seen the scenes themselves. Seen the harsh way some of the Lathar treated their slaves, like they were little more than animals. Not the K'Vass though. She'd never once seen one of their number raise his hand to the robed handmaids. Sure, there was no kindness but there also wasn't cruelty.

They turned a corner and she stumbled on the dusty, hard-packed dirt between two tall buildings. The shadows were chill here and she shuddered in reaction.

"For *draanth's* sake, keep ahold of her," a voice in front of her growled. "She needs to be in good enough shape for the ceremony."

She had to press her lips together hard to suppress her cry of pain as she was hauled upright again and half-carried, half-dragged along. What ceremony? What were they talking about? A bonding ceremony? Fuck that, they'd never get her to agree to bond to anyone, not even if they tortured her.

"Fucking waste if you ask me," the guy holding her growled. "Prime bit of cunt. Why can't they use a beamer to get the brat out, rather than cutting her open? That way we can all have a fuck before we kill her."

Her heart stuttered. Holy shit... They planned to cut her baby out of her? Why? Her question was answered as the man in front of her spoke again.

"Because Dvarr says it's a sacrifice to appease the old gods. They speak to him, have said the bitch's spawn is the goddess made flesh again, and she'll use the Terran women to enslave us."

They were all fucking nuts. Fuck this. Jess started to struggle and scream.

"HELP! I'M TERRAN. THEY'VE KID—"

Pain flared over the back of her head and she staggered, falling to the ground as her vision darkened. Her body went sluggish, no fight in her as she was picked up. There was the sound of booted feet running and then a door crashing open.

"Bitch started yelling but I don't think they followed us."

Dumped unceremoniously on the floor, her veil was yanked off over her head. She was in a house, but not one like the palace.

Instead of smooth marble, this one had sand-colored walls surrounding an interior courtyard. Looking up, she saw the central part of the ceiling was missing, allowing her to see the blue of the sky above, but nothing that would help her.

A fountain gurgled in the middle of the courtyard, water cascading down to the small pool at its base. Sheer panels of floaty fabric fluttered gently in the breeze, their tails brushing the tiled floor gently. All in all, it looked like illustrations of the Roman villas in her automated teaching lessons as a child. She'd always thought they looked so pretty and peaceful—the exact opposite of what she was feeling now as those panels were pushed aside by a warrior as he strode through.

Swallowing her nerves, she scrambled to her feet, stopped from backing up by the two big men behind her. Looking up, her gaze slid over the familiar leathers and parted jacket of a Lathar warrior, and then into the hard, familiar face of the purist leader, Dvarr.

He smiled.

"Welcome to my home, Lady Jessica."

16

"Get me a fucking location *now!*" Laarn growled over the commlink as he stormed through the lower city streets, a blade in one hand and a pulse pistol in the other. He knew he presented a formidable sight in full battle armor, his hair flying around his shoulders as he kicked doors down and stormed through houses.

Maids scattered as he entered the next house, the high-pitched shriek of terrified *oonat* getting on his nerves as he ripped through rooms but found them empty of his prey.

"*FUCK!*" He turned in a circle in the shady interior courtyard, fists white-knuckled around his weapons.

They'd stolen Jess right out from under his nose. From the palace gardens no less. He still couldn't understand why she'd even been there on her own, and he'd raged at her guards. Demanding to know how the *fuck* they'd let her out of their sight when they knew what was at stake. When they knew the entire fate of their race rested on the shoulders of one delicate little Terran female and the child she carried.

No.

He stopped dead, a frown creasing his brow. The drapes

whispered around him in the breeze that lifted strands of his hair across his face. The rage inside him, the panic... it had nothing to do with losing the last piece of the puzzle to save his species. Even if Jess had been just a normal woman, nothing remarkable about her DNA or the child she carried, he would *still* be incensed... furious... terrified and desperate to find her.

Because she was his, the baby was his and he loved them both.

He blinked, every cell in his body motionless as the knowledge resounded through him.

He loved her.

He loved Jessica with every fiber of his being.

Closing his eyes, he let his head drop back as he let out a groan of despair.

He loved her and he might have lost her forever.

Fear gripped his heart as he pushed himself into motion again, storming from the house. New purpose filled him. If he had to search every fucking dwelling in the city to find her, he would. Someone, somewhere, knew where she'd been taken and by whom. When he found out, he was going to tear their spines from their bodies with his bare hands.

And *when* he found her—when, not if—he growled under his breath, "I am *so* chaining you to that fucking bed."

"Somehow, I don't think that was for me." Karryl grinned as he appeared at Laarn's side, fully armed and armored the same as the slender figure behind him. Laarn lifted an eyebrow, recognizing Karryl's mate, the human soldier, Jane.

"Don't ask." Karryl growled as he spotted the direction of Laarn's gaze. "You know human women. They do what they want, when they want. At least if she fights with me, I can keep an eye on her."

"True." Laarn's gaze flicked down to the blood across Karryl's neck and the eyebrow went up again. "Yours?"

"No." The warrior shook his head, his braids dancing and the valor beads catching the light. Soon it was likely both he and Laarn would have to cut their hair: Laarn to take up the role of lord healer and, if the rumors he'd heard were true, Karryl to become a war commander with his own group of ships.

"We ran into a mouthy one. Sympathizer. He's had an attitude readjustment."

"Readjustment?"

Karryl chuckled. "He made a crude comment about human women where Jane could hear him. She educated him on the error of his ways." Suddenly the warrior frowned, touching the comm in his ear. "Someone two blocks over saw a couple of warriors dragging a veiled female through the back alleys a while back. Want to bet that's our girl?"

"*My* girl," Laarn growled possessively. Even though he knew Karryl was mated and equally possessive over the woman at his side, he didn't like any other male laying claim to Jess, even verbally.

"*Your* girl, got it." Karryl held his hands up in surrender as he and Jane turned to go. Laarn couldn't help noticing that already they moved as a unit, Karryl watching the rear as his slender mate took point. The big warrior cast him a glance. "You coming or not?"

By the time they got two blocks over, the emperor and reinforcements had arrived, warriors crowding into a back alley that had been cleared of merchants and furniture from the street cafes. Laundry from the neighboring houses fluttered in the breeze overhead, shielding them from the baking sun.

Daaynal was grim-faced as he flung a bruised and battered warrior into the dirt at Laarn's feet. Blood streaked one side of his face and his left arm hung limply, the upper arm at a funny angle. The healer in Laarn, though, was well and truly dormant as he looked down at the male. It was one of the guards from Jess' security detail.

"This fucking *draanthic* sold us out. He's one of Dvarr's. We caught him trying to steal out of the palace on the sly."

"Shit," Jane breathed, pulling off her helmet to look down on the fallen male with disgust. She looked up and met Laarn's gaze, looking between him and Daaynal. "It all makes sense now. I couldn't figure out how she'd slipped past a group of battle-hardened warriors like that. I mean, me or Kenna?" She shrugged. "Yeah, you boys haven't a hope in hell of stopping us if we want out…"

A warrior behind Daaynal snorted. "Really? A woman? Our warriors would easily catch you and restrain you."

A chill descended as Jane looked the young warrior right in the eye. Laarn almost felt sorry for him as her voice, cold as space, sliced through the silence.

"Really? Perhaps you should have been on hand to offer your wisdom to Ishaan F'Naar or maybe the T'Laat then. I'm sure Ishaan in particular would have benefited," she said, naming the clan leader she'd shot point-blank between the eyes and the clan who thought it would be a good idea to try and kidnap the human women from the K'Vass.

The warrior wisely shut up, backing up a step under Jane's steely gaze. She returned her attention to Laarn and Daaynal. "Jess was Ops, so the idea that she could slip past your detail didn't sit right with me."

"Ops?" Laarn asked with a frown.

"Base operations… traffic I think. Basic military training but not combat personnel," she explained. "We wouldn't put her on a battlefield. She's too valuable doing her primary role."

Karryl advanced on the bloodied warrior, a snarl of anger on his face. "So this asshole let her go…"

"…And told his buddies where to find her," Daaynal finished the sentence for him, reaching the male before Karryl and hauling him to his feet with a hard hand on the back of his neck. Trapped between the two bigger warriors, he went pale, and started to talk… words falling from his lips in a panicked stream.

"It was Dvarr… he threatened us all," he stammered. "Threatened to wipe out our entire clan if we didn't find some way to get the girl to him. When she wandered off by herself—" He squawked as Daaynal's hand tightened. "He's in there. They were going to perform the ceremony at sunset."

Laarn's eyes narrowed. "What fucking ceremony?"

Silence fell in the small group as they waited for the answer, all eyes trained on the pale, panicked male.

"A...a sacrifice to appease the gods. If the Terran and her spawn die, the gods will favor us."

Fear that he might be too late tried to take hold but a glance at the skyline assured him that sunset was still a way off. It was traditional to offer sacrifices as the sun went down and Dvarr was a traditionalist... so surely he wouldn't do anything before sunset in case that displeased the gods. But... He was also a fucking lunatic. Who knew *what* he was thinking?

Laarn roared, rage and panic filling him, but before he could land a blow on the sniveling creature, Daaynal wrapped a big arm around his neck and wrenched. The loud crack of bone snapping filled the alleyway before the warrior dropped, lifeless, to the ground, his neck snapped and his eyes wide and unseeing.

"To live without honor is no life at all," Daaynal snarled. "So he will not live. Apparently Dvarr is holed up in there—" He nodded to the bigger house at the end of the street opposite them. "What say we go and crash this fucking ceremony they have planned?"

Laarn was already moving, intent on marching down the street and kicking the door in to rescue his mate. Rage surged through him, white hot and volatile, ready to explode at any moment. They had his woman, and his child, and they planned to kill them.

Daaynal stopped him with a large hand in the middle of his chest and nodded toward the roofline. In his rage Laarn had missed the squat outline of automated defenses half hidden in the tiles.

"Don't be a hero, son," the big emperor murmured. "At least until your female can see and coo appropriately."

Laarn snarled, about to knock his uncle's hand away when a new sound registered. The *thump-thump-thump* of bot feet. *Heavy* bot feet. As he watched, a troop of *drakeen* combat bots rounded the corner and took up position in front of them, slowly moving forward toward their target.

"Nice to see the big guns here," Karryl whistled, falling into place beside Laarn and Daaynal as they followed the bots, using the cover they afforded.

True to form, before they'd gotten halfway up the street, the automated defenses on the roof of Dvarr's villa activated. The cover plates lifted, twin snub-nosed canons edging into view. Instantly they locked onto the group and the next moment the air was filled with laser blasts.

The bots moved, their mechanical arms a dance of metal and energy fields as they caught the incoming fire, protecting the men, and one woman, behind them. Laarn shot his uncle a sideways look. The destroyer-bots of the Lathar armory, *drakeen* were rarely deployed in groups of more than two, yet there were five in front of them and at least three bore the personal insignia of the emperor. Which begged the question, where the hell had Daaynal found so many pilots. *Drakeen* were hellishly difficult to pilot, and not many had the aptitude for it...

Then he spotted the uplink band around the back of Daaynal's head, half hidden under his hair and snug to the scalp, and blinked in surprise, looking at the three bots with the emperor's mark again. Sure enough, all three moved easily, but with a strange synchronicity that the other two didn't.

"All three are yours?" he asked, catching his uncle's eye as he rechecked his primary assault weapon automatically.

The corner of Daaynal's lips quirked up as he did the same, sliding the weapon back into the sheath at his thigh. Two more pistols were in bandoliers across his wide chest. None of his movements betrayed the fact he was also piloting three heavy bots when most couldn't pilot one without lying down in a dark room.

"Your mother rewrote the code for them when we were kids," he murmured with a wink. "Don't tell anyone... it'll be our little secret."

Shit... Laarn blinked again, rolling his shoulders as they neared the villa. No wonder no one had ever challenged Daaynal for the throne, not when he had tricks like that up his sleeve.

Then there was no more time to think about anything other than getting his female and baby out of Dvarr's clutches.

"The plan?" he demanded as the bots formed into a line, bringing their guns to bear on the front doors of the villa.

Daaynal grinned, unsheathing both his sword and rifle. "Kick the doors down, kill the bastards inside and rescue your woman. What else?"

Laarn grinned, weapons in his hands as the canons on the bots whined when they powered up.

"My kind of plan."

THEY WERE GOING to kill her.

Jess bit back her whimper, not wanting to give the men who held her, her arms twisted painfully behind her back, the satisfaction. Dropping her head, she let her hair cover her face and squeezed her eyes shut tightly.

She'd been dragged into the main hall of the villa a few minutes ago to find it packed with warriors. The furniture had been cleared to the side to make room for them all to stand in lines, like they were in church. Forced to her knees on the hard stone floor in front of them, Dvarr stood a few feet away, chanting.

She winced as she moved, trying to clear the rubble and dirt digging into her knees. Lifting her head, she looked around. The floor hadn't been swept, and the cobwebs gathering in the corners of the room said the villa had been unlived in for a while. Which meant no owners to come home and find a bunch of fanatics had taken it over.

Dust motes danced in the air as Dvarr spoke, twirling in the shafts of sunlight from the vents above them. For a moment she allowed herself to get lost in their simple dance, stretching out the moment of just being alive as long as she could and pushing back thoughts of the horrors she knew were to come.

His voice rose and fell hypnotically. It was a language she vaguely recognized as Latharian, but couldn't make out properly. Like it was an older version of something similar. Perhaps there were other languages on their planet—like French, English and others on Earth... It was beautiful, even if it did fill her with dread.

Whatever he was saying, his audience were rapt, their eyes trained on him fanatically. She shivered at the looks on their faces as panic and fear welled up.

Dvarr was going to kill her. Worse, he was going to cut the baby right out of her body. Her gaze focused on the knife in his hands. Curved and serrated on the back, its wickedly sharp inner blade glinted in the dim light.

A whimper broke from her lips and she struggled again, but it was no good. The two men at her side held her easily, their hands biting cruelly into her arms and shoulders. They were so close she could smell their sweat and the sickly-sweet odor of whatever they'd used to draw a red line down one side of their faces. The same red line as all the Lathar in the room had... a sign of their cult or whatever they called their group.

Tears formed at the backs of her eyes, welling up to stream down her cheeks in scalding rivers. There was no way out. It wasn't fair. Always in books or films there was something clever the heroine could do to extricate herself from a tricky situation, or the hero charged in at the last moment to save the day.

This was real life, though, not a story. No one knew where she was and it was becoming painfully apparent that real life didn't give a shit about her expectations and what was fair. The universe was a cruel and unforgiving thing... there would be no happily ever after for her and her baby. No crib in the beautiful room next to their bedroom in the palace. No seeing Laarn hold their daughter for the first time. More tears ran down her face as her heart twisted savagely in her chest... she'd never see if she had her father's eyes.

Dvarr turned to her guards. "Get her up here."

She was yanked to her feet, kicking and screaming as she was hauled in front of the fanatic leader. One of the guards growled, quelling her fight by pulling an arm back and punching her in the jaw. Her head snapped around, agony and blackness welling up as blood filled her mouth. She managed to spit it out, woozy as Dvarr made her stand in front of him, tsking under his breath as he had to support her with an arm around her ribs just under her bust.

He continued chanting, the sound making her head swim. She watched in horrified fascination as he lifted the blade. It hung in the air above her, the edge caught in one of the shards of sunlight piercing the shadows of the room.

It plunged downward. Tore into her stomach.

She gasped, looking down. Blood welled around the blade, turning her skirts scarlet. Eyes wide, she watched helpless as Dvarr's hand tightened around the hilt, seesawing the blade through her flesh, and she realized the terrible screaming in her ear was coming from her own throat.

The sound of pain and suffering was only drowned out when the doors exploded inward, killing three warriors instantly, and the gap was filled with warriors.

It was too late.

She smiled as her gaze met Laarn's horrified one, the angle shifting as Dvarr dropped her to the ground and raced forward to face the intruders, willing him to understand it was okay.

Then her eyes fluttered shut and she couldn't open them again.

17

"*No!*" Laarn saw Jess fall and his heart felt like it had been torn clean from his chest to tumble to the floor next to her. A feral, wounded bellow escaped him, ripping its way up from the depths of his soul to give voice to his pain. Launching himself into movement, he tore into the warriors in front of him, carving a path with blade and assault pistol.

No one who stood before him survived. Red-striped faces fell and were instantly forgotten as he fought his way toward the crumpled figure on the other side of the room. The war cries of his fellow warriors sounded behind him but he paid them no mind, his entire focus on reaching Jess. Everything passed in a blur, so fast, yet it felt like an eternity until he reached her, falling to his knees by her fallen form. His weapons clattered discarded to the dusty floor, no use to him now.

"Gods, Jess... can you hear me?"

For a moment, he was frozen, paralyzed into place as his hands, usually so sure, hovered above her crumpled body. She lay on her back, her hair spread around her head like a dark halo, the horrific wound in her abdomen staining her dress and the floor around her bright scarlet. She was so pale and still that his heart stuttered, all his senses telling him that he'd lost her.

Then her eyes fluttered open and his healer's instincts kicked him in the ass. Shoving his hand down over her stomach to apply pressure, he bellowed over his shoulder for his healer's pack and a stretcher.

"You're going to be okay, Jess. I promise," he told her, groveling in the dirt next to her to smooth the hair back from her face. "Just stay with me, love, please." He was begging where everyone could see him, the proud lord healer brought low, but he didn't care. He'd give anything to save her, including his rank, title... even his life.

She blinked at him, her eyes unfocused and he thought she was slipping again, his heart giving a savage lurch. Then her small hand crept over his.

"Save her..." she whispered, her voice weak. "You didn't... want me... or her. But save her, please..."

Her eyelids fluttered down and he panicked, grabbing with one hand at the pack someone dropped down next to him.

"What? No... Jess, stay with me." Tearing the pack open, he reached for pressure-sprays one-handed, snapping them open and pressing them into her flesh around the tear in her stomach.

His keen eyes studied the site of the wound, watching as the pressure sprays took effect and slowed the bleeding down, but it was only a patch. It wouldn't hold long. *Shit.* Where was the damn stasis stretcher? It was taking too long. Before he could open his mouth to yell, though, he heard Daaynal's deep voice shouting at people to move out of the way.

"Stay awake, love," he urged Jess. "Tell me what you mean. I've always wanted you."

Her eyes took longer to open this time, and her voice was so weak that he had to lean forward to hear her. "Heard you... Karryl... You were going... terminate. Didn't want to be bond—" Her words cut off as her head fell to the side, her delicate frame too weak to keep her conscious, but he heard her and her words sliced him right down to the soul.

She thought he didn't want her. Had used her last strength to beg him to save their baby, no thought for her own life. In that moment Laarn was truly humbled, his little mate displaying a strength that had nothing to do with speed or muscle or combat ability. Standing back, he kept a sharp eye on the stasis team as they loaded her gently into the stretcher and activated it. He only let himself breathe a small sigh of relief when the unit was active and he could see her vitals level out.

The fight was done, but he didn't even spare a glance for Dvarr and his men, either those that had been captured or those who lay dead on the floor around them. Walking by the stretcher, he paused for a moment when Daaynal caught his attention.

"How bad?" The emperor didn't mince words, his hand on Laarn's arm and his expression concerned.

"Bad." Laarn didn't bother to hide the distraught note in his voice. "I need to operate. Now."

Daaynal dropped his hand, nodding. "Go. We'll sort this."

Laarn paused for a moment, his gaze sliding to the prisoners. Dvarr was on his knees, force restraints around his ankles, wrists and neck. Hatred surged, hard and fast, almost cutting off Laarn's breathing.

"Him. Make sure he's still alive when I'm done," he snarled. "I want to fucking gut him myself."

With that he turned and followed the stasis stretcher out of the ruined building. Before he could exact revenge, he had to save his woman.

They were rushed back to the palace with a *drakeen* bot escort. The big machines surrounded them, making sure people on the streets moved out of the way. Laarn had the impression of curious faces, then sorrow and anger as those in the crowd realized that one of the human women had been badly hurt.

"Gods guide you, Lord Healer."

"Gods bless the Terran lady."

"May the gods save her."

Voices called out blessings and well-wishes as they passed, and

Laarn managed a smile or two in thanks. It was reassuring that most of the Lathar weren't of the same mind as Dvarr and his asshole followers. Most of them seemed genuinely upset and worried about Jess' health. He made a mental note to pass that onto Daaynal later but then realized he didn't have to. Two of the bots surrounding them had Imperial marks, so what they saw, the emperor saw.

Tovan waited for them at the entrance to the healer's hall, his arms folded and his expression forbidding. As soon as he saw them, he hurried forward, peering into the stasis stretcher. At the sight of Jess lying there, motionless and covered in blood, he paled, visibly shaken as he looked up at Laarn. "We heard on the comms but I didn't think... he tried to..."

Laarn's voice was hard as he motioned the stretcher in ahead of them, all his emotions locked down. "Dvarr tried to cut the baby from her womb. I've applied pressure patches but we need to work fast or we'll lose them both."

"That *animal*," Tovan hissed, his expression furious. "Never in my life have I been ashamed to call myself Lathar, but I am now. How could any male worthy of the name hurt such a lovely creature as Lady Jessica?"

Laarn looked at him, noting his expression and the faces of the healers behind him. They were furious and he knew in that moment that no purist out there would ever receive treatment from an Imperial healer ever again. Tovan took a shuddering breath and looked at him directly. "The main theater has been prepared for you, my lord. Please, come this way..."

When they walked into the main area, sweeping through the drapes in a rustle of plastic, Laarn was surprised to find not the usual one, but three operating units set up.

"We won't let you take this one alone, my lord," Tovan said quietly. "You've been in battle and the lady is badly injured. We'll be standing by in case you need us to take over. Between us all, we can save her."

Laarn inclined his head. Tovan had been one of the most outspoken of the healers against the possibility the Terran women could be the saviors of their race, so to go from that to being willing to take on Jess' pain and save her... it would have warmed him through had he been thinking right.

"Support only, monitor her vitals and inform me if any other issues crop up. Do not initiate the link unless the worst happens," he ordered, knowing damn well the only way he'd hand over responsibility for Jess' healing was if he no longer drew breath. "She is my woman and my responsibility."

The other healers nodded, stepping out of the way as he stripped off his armor and leather jacket, letting them drop unheeded to the floor. Stepping through the decontamination unit, he kept his eyes locked on Jess as he approached the uplink unit. Arms out, he just nodded as Tovan and his assistant slid the gauntlets over his hands and wrists, locking them into place.

"Neural interface ready, surgical unit online," Tovan said, looking over. "Ready when you are, my lord."

"Do it." Laarn's voice was clipped and firm. "Take me in now."

"Aye, my lord. I'll ease you in—"

"*No!*" Laarn barked. "She's in pain, a *lot* of pain. Give it to me, all of it."

He heard the hiss as Tovan prepared to argue but then silence. Protocol was to ease into the uplink, giving the healer time to prepare to take the pain load, but they didn't have time for that. Just one look at Jess' vitals said she was in trouble and he needed to work fast.

"Transferring."

Laarn grunted as pain exploded through him, all centered in his lower stomach. It was a cutting, biting agony that stole his breath and nearly his reason. The wound was... would have been mortal. He could feel the very wrongness of it. It should have killed her but somehow hadn't.

Straightening, he activated the unit, his keen eyes already spotting where he would need to be working. The blade had dug deep, curling around her womb and nicking it, but not cutting into the amniotic sac. The baby was okay... would be okay... *if* he could save her mother.

"Heart rate increasing..."

Tovan's voice sounded in the background, a constant update on the readouts Laarn wasn't paying attention to at the moment as he started to work on the terrible wound in Jess' stomach. He worked fast, sweat pouring from him as he fought his own fear and feelings to maintain the link with her. To take her pain away even as he worked to repair the damage to her body. He created new molecular strings, binding them together to mend the rent flesh. He stitched cells, mended veins and arteries but try as he might, as soon as he mended one area, another failed.

"Shitshitshit..." He began to panic. He couldn't do this. Couldn't maintain the neutral focus he needed to operate when it was the woman he loved on the table. His grandfather had been right. He couldn't be lord healer and love as well.

"Blood pressure dropping. We're losing her!"

Tovan's voice was sharp and almost at the same moment, Laarn felt a new presence alongside him, brushing his mind with reassurance.

"Who's uplinked?" he demanded, his voice sharp with anger. He'd told them all to stay out. His grip on this was tenuous enough. He couldn't have someone else in here fucking it all up further.

"No one! There's no one else in there with you, I swear," Tovan replied, confusion in his tone.

Laarn blinked, his hands still as he analyzed the new presence. He'd uplinked with others before, usually for training, but he'd never felt a healer this strong. Never. He blinked as the new healer added their strength to his, allowing him to take the lead in a quiet, understated way. He breathed a sigh of relief as some of the pain load reduced and he could focus.

Starting work again, he kept his focus on repairing the terrible wounds but also studied the new presence alongside him. As his hands moved, part of his mind was detached from what he was doing, working through the puzzle. Whoever it was, they were easily as strong as he was. Tovan swore no one had uplinked through the other units, and a quick query proved that was true. And he'd never heard of anyone being able to remote uplink to a surgical unit. Ever. Yes, it was possible for the bots, but not surgery. So that meant whoever it was, was in the room and not uplinked. Which narrowed down the candidates to just the two people in... the... link.

It couldn't be Jess, the healer read as Lathar... Laarn blinked, his hands stilling for a moment as he focused on the other presence. A healer he'd never met, one as powerful as he was himself, maybe even more so... He sent an incredulous query and was met with a burst of pleasure, love, and a greeting.

His daughter.

Tears rolled down his face. Somehow, impossibly, his daughter was already aware and just as determined to save her mother as he was. With the added strength, his hands moved faster, faster than he'd ever thought possible. Where before he'd been mending at the molecular level, he went deeper, at the nano-molecular and beyond, checking the atomic layer. He'd never been this deep before, and curiosity spurred him forward until a small chide from his daughter's presence wrapped around his and pulled him back.

Full of wonder, he returned to his task, the sense of urgency gone now. He could *see* at a glance what he needed to do to save Jess' life... the life of the woman he loved. She was everything, his life, his love... his very reason for being, and he loved her. He'd thought he couldn't have both, love and be lord healer... his grandfather's words that love weakened a healer had always haunted him, but as he worked he realized something.

His grandfather had been wrong.

Love, his love for Jessica, the love he had and felt returned from his daughter, it was *everything*. Denying his feelings had only hampered him as a healer. Denied him his true power. So he let go of his mental blocks, the fetters he'd trained to put on his emotions. Instantly, a jolt of power flowed through him, surprised voices from the healers in the room heard but not listened to as he surged into motion. Repairing. Rebuilding. Healing.

Finally, he was done, removing the last traces of the scar across his little Terran's abdomen with a smile. His body ached with remembered pain and tension racked his broad shoulders but he didn't care. He'd done it. He'd saved his mate's life.

They'd saved her.

With a burst of gratitude and love directed at his daughter, he wrapped his mental presence around hers for a long moment in the nearest he could get to a hug. Warmth filled him in return and for a moment, he saw her in his mind's eye—tall and slender, with his eyes and Jess' dark curls, she was stunningly beautiful. And... he realized, his gaze dropping to her scarred arms... a healer like him. With a curve of her lips, the image disappeared and he dropped out of the link, convinced he'd just had a glimpse of the future.

He opened his eyes as Tovan unclipped the gauntlets, wonder in his eyes and a smile on his face. "Your mate is resting peacefully, and her prognosis is good. My lord... you did it. Well done."

Laarn smiled, his gaze flitting over the sleeping woman. Her color was good, and all she needed now was rest. As did he.

"Thank you, my friend. Wake me in a couple of hours."

With that, he made his way to organize a cot so he could sleep next to her.

18

*H*e looked worn out.

Jess lay on her side, watching Laarn sleep on the cot next to her bed. She'd woken a while back, warm and comfortable, surprised to find herself in the healer's hall and, it appeared when she investigated her stomach, healed. There was no wound, or even any dressing, to mark where Dvarr had plunged a knife into her stomach. Panic had assaulted her, her first thought for the baby she carried, but within a few seconds a sense of warmth and calm had washed over her and the worry had receded. Try as she might, she couldn't bring it back. Everything would be okay. The baby was fine... Laarn would have seen to it.

He really was handsome. Her gaze wandered over him. He lay on his back on the cot, his wide shoulders filling the narrow space. He'd left off his jacket, so all his scars were on display, but they didn't bother her. Instead, she traced each and every one with her gaze. They were proof her man was amazingly strong.

"I always worried that they'd bother you."

His deep voice was low and rough. She blinked and looked up. He hadn't moved at all, but his eyes were open, watching her intently without a hint of sleepiness in his gaze.

"Why would you think that?" She kept her voice low to match his. Intimate. Secrets shared just between the two of them.

He shrugged one big shoulder slightly. "I read your medical texts. Humans remove scars whenever possible. Jane corroborated that as well, said it's common and your species also alters their appearance with cosmetic surgery. These..." he paused, and indicated his body. "I'll never get rid of them. I will always have them."

She frowned, shook her head as he levered himself up to a sitting position. His hair, unbound, fell around his shoulders as he rested his elbows on his knees to look at her. There were lines of strain around his eyes and he still looked tired.

"I don't want you to get rid of them. They're who you are. And, despite the fact that some of my species are all-consumed by appearance, I'm not one of them."

She moved to sit up and he was there instantly, strong arms wrapped around her to help her.

"Easy there, you just had major surgery. You might be a little sore," he warned, settling her back against the pillows. She refused to let him go, wrapping her hands around his heavily-muscled upper arms and looking up into his face.

"The baby?"

A smile curved his lips. "Our daughter is fine. Healthy."

"Oh, thank god." Relief made her feel weak and she leaned her forehead against his shoulder, savoring the embrace. "I was so scared, Laarn. I couldn't do anything to stop him killing her... me... We would have been dead if you hadn't rescued us."

He'd come to her rescue... and she had to let him go. Her relief faded away, replaced by misery. She loved him but she had to let him go, had to let him live the life he would have had before she'd forced decisions upon him.

Gathering herself, she looked up, into the green eyes she loved so much.

"Thank you for saving me too... I didn't expect you to. I just wanted you to save her." Drawing a shaking breath, she let him go. Every cell in her body cried out at the loss but she steeled herself against it. Her baby was alive. That's all she needed to know. All she could... *would*... ask. "But I'd like you to leave now, please."

"What?" Sharpness entered his voice as he stood in front of her. "Leave? You're my mate... *and* in case it escaped your notice, I'm also your healer. I'm not going anywhere. Jess? Jess... look at me. Has this got something to do with what you said before? That I didn't want you?"

"I heard you talking." She managed to get the words out but refused to look up, mangling the sheets over her lap in her hands. "Heard you tell Karryl that you'd never intended to implant... to get me pregnant. That you never wanted to claim me."

Taking a shuddering breath, she looked up, knowing tears welled in her eyes but not able to do a damn thing about it. "So I release you from the claim. I'll divorce you, or whatever the hell the Lathar call it... I'll let you go to live your life."

He looked down at her, his face unreadable, apart from the small muscle in the corner of his jaw that pulsed. "We have no divorce." His voice was hard, pulsing with anger. "You can't release me from the claim."

"But why?" It was a plea, pure and simple. "I thought you'd be happy about it."

He moved, faster than she'd expected, and gathered her into his arms, drawing her into his lap on the bed. She gasped as his lips claimed hers, determined that she wouldn't respond. That lasted all of three seconds before she whimpered and kissed him back, her emotions overwhelmed. She hadn't thought she'd get the chance to kiss him again, either through her own death, or letting him go. Whatever, being in his arms again hadn't seemed at all likely so she had no defenses against him.

When he lifted his head, she was breathless... looking up at him silently.

"You're not releasing me. *I'm* not releasing you," he growled, strong fingers under her chin. "For the simple fact I love you, and I'm fairly sure you love me too."

She blinked, eyes wide. "You... what?"

"I love you. And I'll keep kissing you until you believe it." He leaned down to kiss her again, this time his lips lingering for long moments.

"You only heard *half* the conversation with Karryl. If you'd stayed to listen to the rest, you'd have heard me tell him that no, I didn't want to claim you... but I'm so fucking glad you did the claiming. You'd have heard me tell him that I didn't want to implant those pregnancies, because I wanted to get you pregnant the old-fashioned way... but that I'm not sorry that you are."

He tucked the loose strands of her hair behind her ear gently. "Jessica Kallson, I've loved you since I saw you kneeling on the floor when we captured your base. Why do you think I kept pulling you in for tests? I didn't need them. I just wanted to see you, and I was too much of an idiot to realize it. I thought..."

He dropped his head back for a moment and closed his eyes.

"This is going to sound so fucking stupid. As healers we're always told that we can't have emotions, that we can't feel because it interferes with our ability to heal. I didn't think I could take a mate and still be a healer. Still be the lord healer the empire needs."

Her hopeful mood, the seed that had been growing in the center of her chest, stalled. "I-I wouldn't want to stop you doing your job..."

"You won't." He dropped his head and speared her with his gaze. "When Dvarr took you, I was terrified I'd lost you... when I saw you fall..." His expression became haunted.

"Nothing mattered anymore. All my life it's been about duty, about becoming strong enough, skilled enough, to become lord healer... about saving the Lathar. But when you fell, when I thought I'd lost you—" He broke off and shuddered. "I didn't care about any of it. Without you, there is nothing. No meaning. No reason for any of it."

The raw emotion in his eyes, in his voice, brought tears to her eyes. She couldn't look away, reaching up to touch his face, smooth her fingertips over his jaw. Opening her mouth to speak, she didn't manage a word before he cut her off.

"No, please... let me get this out." He settled her more

comfortably against him. "I had always been told emotions were anathema to a healer. That we should remain dispassionate and neutral. But when *you* were there on the table, someone taught me that emotions are the most powerful weapon I have as a healer. Taught me to *use* them. I wouldn't have been able to save you without her or that lesson."

He slid his hand into her hair and tilted her head up for another kiss. "I love you, Jess. Now, please, put me out of my misery and tell me I haven't lost any chance of you loving me back."

He loved her. He really loved her. Tears in her eyes, she shook her head. "I've always loved you, from the moment I saw you, I think. I just couldn't bear to think that I'd forced you into a shotgun wedding, or that you were only with me because of the baby."

"A shotgun wedding?" He frowned, a puzzled smile on his lips. "Does that mean I have to kidnap you from your family armed to the teeth to make you mine? I'll do it, if you need me to. Whatever you need, whenever you need... I'm yours, Jess. I love you. Be mine?"

"Yes... *yes!*" Throwing her arms around his neck, she hugged him tightly, burying her face against his neck. She never wanted to let him go.

"I love you," she mumbled into his hair, her eyes closed in sheer and utter relief. "Please, don't ever leave me again."

"Love," he rumbled by her ear. "I don't intend to let you out of my sight ever again. The last time I went off planet you managed to get yourself pregnant. The next time, I plan on getting you with child myself."

She laughed, pulling back to look at him. His green eyes were alight with love and amusement. Reaching up, she kissed him again. It was a long, slow kiss, delicate and sensual but full of promise and love. Finally, she broke away to look at him and frowned.

"She?"

He blinked, confusion on his face. "What?"

"You said she... that she taught you to use your emotions? Who was she?"

She ran through the names of the human women on the planet in her mind, wondering who it was that had that level of wisdom and awareness so she could thank them. But Laarn just smiled and moved to place a big hand on her stomach.

"Our daughter."

Deep within, almost as though she could feel her father's hand, there was the tiniest flutter. Jess gasped and looked into his eyes for confirmation. He nodded, spreading his fingers wide as if to protect them both.

"She's aware of us both, and powerful. A more powerful healer than I am for sure. She helped me see that I needed to use my love for you to save you, and she helped me do it. You're mine, Jessica Kallson, both of you. And I'll love you both as long as I live. On that, you have my word as lord healer, a warrior..."

He dipped his head again and brushed his lips over hers.

"...And the man who loves you."

***

ALIEN HEALER'S BABY

WARRIORS OF THE LATHAR: BOOK 4

MINA CARTER

1

"*L*aarn, if you ever fucking touch me again, I swear to god I'll gut you with a blunt fucking spoon!" Jessica hissed to her absent mate as she waddled at a slow pace along the corridors between their quarters and the palace's temporary healer's hall. She'd been grumbling under her breath at the distance before she'd recalled the healer's hall, the Lathar equivalent of a hospital, had been relocated for a very good reason.

She'd blown it to hell.

"Well, technically, little one," she murmured, rubbing her bump as she walked, "I only blew up the lab. How was I to know it would cause a chain reaction in the power cores and take out the entire hall? And it was for a good cause... those asshole purists had it coming."

She skirted off that subject, a flash of pain warning her the memories weren't good ones. Because of the purists, she'd almost lost the daughter she carried and her life. The second she could live with, but the first had almost broken her heart and reduced her to begging Laarn, her mate, to save the baby even if it killed her.

"But you didn't let that happen, did you, sweetie?" she asked with a smile down at her bump, pausing for a moment at an intersection on the way to the hall. "You helped your daddy save mommy... you were so brave and I'm so proud of you."

The burst of warmth through her heart and mind was like an all-over hug, and love for the baby filled her. She'd thought the way she felt about Laarn, her mate, was overwhelming, but this... the love of a parent for a child, was something else.

"Do human females always talk to their unborn offspring?" A deep male voice broke into her musings and she turned to find Xaandril, the emperor's Champion, standing behind her with a perplexed look on his face.

Jess couldn't help the pleased smile that broke over her lips at the sight of the tall warrior. Along with Daaynal, the emperor of the Lathar, Xaandril had been one of the first faces she'd seen at court. Although the big warrior was gruff and sometimes less than talkative, the last couple of months they'd both spent in and out of the healer's hall had proven he was all bark and no bite... with Jess and the other human women anyway.

"How's it doing?" she asked, her gaze dropping to the arm in a sling over Xaandril's chest. Severely injured in battle months ago, just before the purist attack on the palace, he should have been dead several times over.

Xaan's expression flickered a little, but he kept the mask in place. "It's healing. Slowly."

Those three words and the control behind them told Jess everything she needed to know. Latharian warriors were not patient creatures—warriors of Xaandril's level even less so.

"But..." he carried on, looking at the bump that made her feel the size of a small whale. "You didn't answer my question. Is it normal for human females to have conversations with their young before the birth?"

He took two steps closer, offering his good arm so they could continue on to the healer's hall. Her energy all but depleted by the short walk so far, she took it with a small murmur of thanks. She wouldn't have for just any warrior. Latharian males were highly possessive, especially when mated, but Xaandril was one of the few males Laarn trusted without question. There would be no issue with Xaandril helping her. Which was Latharian shorthand for her mate wouldn't try to kill him.

No, there would be no try. Her mate was lord healer, only *the* highest ranking and most qualified doctor in the empire, and a warrior. And Jess couldn't think of anything more dangerous than a man who knew how the human—or Latharian—body worked trying to kill you.

"We do it a lot," she answered his query with a small smile, noting how he'd shortened his stride to match hers. For all their bluster about being the biggest and baddest warriors in the universe, most Lathar treated women like they were the finest porcelain. "Normally the baby doesn't answer back, though. At least, human babies don't. A human-Lathar hybrid…"

She let the sentence trail off and shrugged. Everyone in creation had to know how unique her pregnancy was. The first Latharian child to be born in decades, and the first ever human-Lathar hybrid, her daughter was unique.

"The child speaks to you already?" Xaandril asked, shooting an interested glance down to Jess' bump. "My mate… when she was carrying… reported no telepathic communication."

Jess shrugged. "Perhaps it's something to do with the mixed genetics? Or because… well, Laarn says she'll be a healer. And more powerful than he is."

Awe filtered over Xaandril's craggy features. "It is in the bloodline. There were more than a few K'Vass Lord Healers. But a K'Vass Lady Healer would be something to behold."

Jess rubbed her bump again. After months on Lathar Prime, it was easy to decode the different terms and signifiers on the family names. She was now no longer Jessica Kallson, but the Lady Jessica K'Vass, mate to Lord Healer Laarn K'Vass, sister-son to the emperor himself. Her daughter would be a Princess of the Blood.

She'd joined up to travel the stars and ended up married to an alien prince, her daughter fourth in line to a dynasty that spanned more years than human history.

Holy and *shit* didn't quite cover it.

"Your mate... was she Xaandrynn's mother?" Jess asked as the healer's hall came into view. She kept her voice light, hoping that she wasn't venturing where angels feared to tread. Laarn had hinted that there was tragedy in Xaandril's past, and the big champion wasn't a talker.

"No." His reply was tight-lipped and for a moment silence reigned. Jess winced, convinced she'd blown it, and then he sighed. "Xaandrynn was oonat born. I needed an heir."

She nodded. The oonat were a sentient, if dull-witted, race the Lathar often used as servants. Bovine-like, they were like hooded shadows, often ignored as the Lathar went about their business. With no females of their own, many Lathar used them as concubines and gestational carriers. Jess had been outraged when Laarn had explained it to her. That they'd altered the species genetics so that any child fathered by a Lathar would be pure Lathar.

"Not far now," Xaandril murmured, taking her silence and scowl as discomfort. His hand clenched as he looked at her with concern. "Do human females struggle with childbirth?"

She laughed at that. "I wouldn't know. This is my first baby. I'm told it's no walk in the park though."

He looked confused. "Why would you want to walk in the park when you are so close to birthing your young?"

She grinned, once again surprised by the literal way some Lathar took things. "No walking. It means that childbirth is difficult and painful for us. Sometimes it can be fatal for mother and child."

Xaandril's expression changed to something near to panic. "We should get you to the healer's hall. Laarn can call in all the healers to see to you in your confinement."

"One... humans have been giving birth for thousands and thousands of years and two, I'm not about to give birth right now." Chuckling, she patted his arm. "So... why the sudden interest in human childbirth?"

He went pink, his mouth opening and closing for a second before he said, "If the Lathar are to build alliances with humanity, then as champion I need to know your physical capabilities."

She arched an eyebrow as they reached the entrance to the temporary healer's hall.

"And to do so, you need to know how human women give birth? Xaan, pull the other one, it's got bells on. Are you sure it doesn't have more to do with a certain lady marine..."

At that, the pink tinge that covered Xaandril's cheeks deepened. "No... no, not at all. Why would you think that?"

"Oh, no reason," she said lightly, her gaze sweeping the main hall. Large and circular with twenty beds arranged in a circle, it doubled as the triage area. Warriors occupied some of the beds, healers as big and heavily muscled moving between them. That had been the thing she'd struggled to reconcile in her head the first few weeks here.

Latharian healers... doctors... were all trained warriors and didn't wear white coats. Instead, they dressed the same as the men they treated—in leather and armor. All were armed. The only marks of their profession were the teal sashes a few wore and the scars that covered their bodies. Marks from their healer's trials.

The Latharian empire was the only place she knew of that you wanted your doctor to look like he'd survived a multi-vehicle pileup and an encounter with a slasher-movie level serial killer. The more scars, the higher the training of the healer.

Her gaze caught on a familiar, broad-shouldered figure, and a burst of warmth spread through her as she recognized her mate. Laarn was busy treating a warrior on the other side of the room, his jacket slung over the hook at the end of the bed as he bent over to attend to what looked like a busted leg.

Walking toward him, she looked away as she spotted the white of bone in the warrior's thigh, bile rising as Laarn made a sharp movement. There was a crunch and a soft sound that could have been a muffled scream from the warrior on the bed. Then Laarn straightened, his lips set in a grim line as he looked at the healer with him. Younger, his impressive selection of scars looked barely healed.

"Take over from here, Renza. Check the bone has fused correctly and close. Make sure you check the nervous feedback to ensure there's no damage we need to attend to," Laarn ordered.

"Yes, Lord Healer." The younger healer slid into place, and Laarn turned away, his face breaking into a broad smile the instant he spotted Jessica.

"My love... what are you doing here?"

IT HAD BEEN A LONG MORNING, so the sight of his mate in front of him was a welcome distraction. Laarn smiled for her as he stepped forward, instantly at her side to take her arm. She was heavy with child, *his* child, and he couldn't help the surge of pride as his gaze swept her swollen belly in assessment. He'd done that, he'd given her that child. His daughter.

"I wanted to see you," she said, a small pout curving her lower lip as she caught the slight chide in his voice. She should be resting... he'd told her she should be resting. The other human women had told her she should be resting. Was she resting? No. Instead, she was making the trek from their very comfortable quarters to the healer's hall.

His gaze flicked to Xaandril for a moment, noting the light touch of Jess' hand on the big warrior's arm. Jealousy surged for a moment but he fought it back. Xaandril was an honorable male, one Laarn trusted with his life. With Jessica and the baby's life. He would never act dishonorably toward Laarn's mate.

"Thank you, General," he said with a small inclination of his head, knowing full well that Xaandril would have ensured Jessica took the walk at a sedate pace and didn't overexert herself. "Itaal will conduct your checkup, if you would like to proceed to his station. I will check with you in a few moments."

"Of course. Lord Healer. Lady Jessica."

Xaandril took his leave with a small nod of his head, striding across the middle of the hall toward the indicated healer's station. Itaal stood waiting, his hands behind his back in the classic at-ease posture. Laarn had been amused to find out it was something the human military also used. A common mannerism provided further evidence they were linked.

"So, my love..." He turned to Jess and pulled her into his arms. That they were in the middle of the healer's hall didn't bother him one iota. Jess was the woman he loved, the woman who had called mating marks to life around his wrists, and if he wanted to show everyone how he felt about her, he would.

"What was so important that it couldn't wait for me to come to you?" He leaned down to graze a kiss over her lips. Even heavy with child, she fit against him perfectly. But he had noticed that, as her pregnancy developed, she leaned into him more, as if seeking his strength to bolster her own. Sudden worry spiked through him, and he spread a hand over her stomach. "Are you okay? Do you have any pain?"

"There you go, right into healer mode!" she chuckled, reaching up to stroke his cheek and pull his head back down to hers for another kiss. "I'm fine, my love. I just needed to move. I feel like a marshmallow whale lying about in bed all day. And you'd think I was in danger of starving to death with the amount of food the servants keep bringing. There's just so much of it..."

"Well..." he said, picking his words with care. "You need the nutrition now. For you and the baby..."

Since she'd started to show, Jess had become obsessed with her size and how much weight she was putting on with the pregnancy. He didn't understand why. In his eyes she was perfect, and the changes in her body only increased his desire and need for her.

"*And...* you ladies said it yourself. Our chocolate cake isn't fattening," he reminded her, pulling out his... what did humans call it... his ace in the hole.

"Well, this is true," she admitted, and the small frown between her brows faded under a brilliant smile as he leaned down to kiss her again. This one was deeper, hotter, and he couldn't help driving his hand into her loose hair to hold her still as he plundered her lips.

When he lifted his head, she was breathing raggedly, her eyes dark and her lips full from his kiss.

"Laarn!" she complained, still clinging to him. "We're in public... everyone can see!"

"Let them look," he growled. "And if you keep looking at me like that, they'll have a lot to see."

"Laarn!"

This time her gasp was near-scandalized and he couldn't help his broad grin. "What? I am a mated man... It is my business when and where I show my appreciation of the gift the lady goddess has granted me."

He pulled her closer to plant a lingering kiss on her lips. She leaned into him, her body soft and her lips pliant as she surrendered to him. He didn't get a chance to savor the kiss, though, because at that moment the double doors at the end of the hall opened, the sound of heavily booted feet and the shouts of warriors announcing yet more patients. He broke away with a sigh.

"Hold that thought for later, mate of mine. I have work to attend to."

"REMIND me I need to find an alien hottie and get knocked up. *Soon.*"

Kenna Reynolds sighed as she looked at the dining table in Jess' suite. The servants had just finished laying out the light afternoon repast Jess had requested, which meant there wasn't an inch of the wooden surface visible under mountains of food. She wouldn't have been surprised to hear the legs groaning under the weight.

"Another alien hottie? The general not cutting it for you these days?" Jess cut a glance sideways at her friend as she held out a fork, noticing that Kenna's eyes had slid to the chocolate cake at the side. As they always did.

Kenna took it, grabbing a plate and selecting a huge slice of the decadent-looking treat. But, despite its looks, the cake was a dressed up version of Latharian field rations. It was designed to kick a warrior's metabolism into high gear to deal with the extra energy load.

In other words, as Laarn had reminded her earlier, it was a treat that didn't make you fat.

Jess' mouth watered at the gooey, moussey consistency but before she could cut herself a slice, the baby gave her a swift kick. She sighed, turning toward the platter of vegetables and piling her plate.

"Awkward little parasite," she grumbled as she rubbed her stomach. "I'll be glad when you're out and I can eat what I want."

She flopped down into the sofa opposite Kenna with all the grace of an upturned hippo. Crunching on the alien equivalent of a carrot stick, she watched Kenna shovel the cake in with pure and utter envy. One upside of being pregnant, and the size of a house, *should* be the fact she could eat what she liked. *Should*. Instead, she'd been lumbered with a kid who knew exactly what was healthy for her and Mom to eat as well as a kick like a pit pony. One she wasn't afraid to use when Mom, aka her gestational lackey, didn't do what she was told.

Kenna raised an eyebrow. "Kid still giving you jip?" she asked, between one mouthful and the next.

"Always. She's as bossy as her damn father." Jess rubbed at a sore spot on her stomach again with a fond smile. She must have gotten a stitch or something when she was walking to the healer's hall earlier. "I can't wait for her to be born so they can butt heads. It'll be epic. I should sell popcorn. But..." she said, "you didn't answer my question about Xaan."

Kenna wrinkled her nose, the now empty plate held in her lap as she sat cross-legged on the opposite couch to Jess.

"I dunno what's going on there. Half the time he seems interested... the rest of the time he's like a damn statue. The stone-cold general his men call him you know? I can see what they mean." She blew out a breath, running her hand through her hair. Her expression was pained as she looked back at Jess. "Am I making a fool of myself over a guy who's not interested in me? You would tell me if I was, right?"

Jess snorted. "You're asking me? I didn't think Laarn knew what his dick was *for* other than pissing out of at first. I'm sure Xaan is interested. They just have a strange way of showing it."

Kenna huffed. "You mean, like, not at all? Why aren't they more like Tarrick and Karryl? Cat and Jane knew right off the bat they were interested."

Jess rubbed at her side again, careful to keep her grimace off her face. Even a hint of discomfort was enough to have her friends, the traitors, scurrying to summon Laarn. She was fed up with being wrapped in cotton wool. She was pregnant for heaven's sake, not at death's freaking door.

"Well... Jane isn't a good example, is she?" Jess winked. "She scares the shit out of half the warriors she and Karryl train, and she led him a right dance before she agreed to mate him. Not to mention, she blew F'Naar's brains out. I think that's why half of them are scared of claiming a human female now. They might get a Jane."

"Too fucking right. They should be scared. I'd eat half of them for breakfast." Kenna grinned.

"Yeah, but you'd rather eat a certain handsome general, wouldn't you? Perhaps you should challenge and claim *him* rather than wait for him to do it."

Kenna blinked at her, her expression surprised for a moment, but within a heartbeat Jess could see the cogs working behind her eyes.

"Now that's an idea, isn't it?" She smiled, leaning forward to put her empty plate down on the table between them. "So... when are you going to tell me you're in labor?"

2

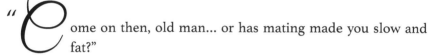"Come on then, old man... or has mating made you slow and fat?"

Laarn hissed between his teeth at the taunt from his brother and blocked the obvious blow to his side.

"No more than you, *insolent pup*," he snarled and fired off two quick jabs at his *litaan's* face. Tarrick laughed as he danced out of reach, wheeling around for another attack. Like any set of twins, the argument about age was as old as they were and often mentioned.

Laarn kept his guard tight as he watched his brother. They were identical in height, build and combat ability, so he had to keep his wits about him when sparring with Tarrick. Even though he wasn't a warrior in the traditional sense of the word, his healer's oaths taking precedence, having his younger—by a few minutes—brother wipe the floor with him would do nothing for his male pride or standing in the clan.

So he kept his guard close and his attention on his opponent even though the edge of the circle they fought in was ringed with warriors. It was always the same when the senior K'Vass warriors stepped into the ring. Other warriors thronged the hall to watch... some to marvel at the sheer speed and strength he and Tarrick traded blows, hits that would have incapacitated or even killed lesser warriors... but some came purely to watch the emperor's nephews fight.

Laarn, though, sparred to clear his mind.

Fighting, pure combat, was a form of meditation. There was only the here and now. No worrying about the future, or the past. No second guessing, or hindsight. There was action and reaction, reaction to the reaction—a chain of events that were purely in the present. Each second was lived only to reach the next.

Right now, promoted to the lord healer's position, mated to his beautiful Jessica, and about to become the first father of a female Lathar in a generation... Laarn *really* needed the distraction.

"Besides," he threw back, nodding at the marks around Tarrick's own wrists. "I'm not the only mated male here, am I?" He twisted and launched a series of lightning fast punches, most of which landed in his brother's rib cage, and raised an eyebrow. "Perhaps we should look at *your* training schedule, or Karryl will have to take over as war commander."

Tarrick grunted and blocked the last blow in the series by dropping to the floor and sweeping a hard leg at both of Laarn's. Used to that tactic, Laarn just laughed and jumped backward out of the way. Tarrick flipped back to his feet, an impressive display of strength and agility in such a large warrior.

"Ah, now that's where the *lord healer* is behind the times," he teased. "Karryl does not need to challenge for my command. Daaynal has given him one of his own."

"Really? That's excellent news!" Pleasure on behalf of his friend filled Laarn, until he almost missed the hard right hook coming at his face. He stopped talking for a second to pay attention to the fight. It wouldn't do for the lord healer to turn up for his shift black and blue... and even worse for him to return home to Jess that way. Since she'd become pregnant, she'd become so protective of him. He suspected it had far more to do with the purist attack that had almost ended her life, that she was scared of something... anything... taking him away from her, or vice versa. Time though, was a great healer, and *nothing* would ever separate them again.

"It is. One less cocky warrior with an eye on my sash. Just a thousand more in the clan to deal with." Tarrick chuckled, the conversation between them flowing as they moved between combat combinations, landing blows that would have felled lesser males. He frowned midway through a side step and nodded to something behind Laarn. "Heads up. Incoming..."

In a fight, Laarn normally wouldn't have believed a word his *litaan* said, but the human phrase caught his attention and he turned to catch sight of Kenna in his peripheral vision. He dropped his guard instantly and turned toward her. Normally he'd have never turned his back on a warrior, not even his own brother, but the expression on her face almost stopped his heart in his chest.

"Kenna? Is everything okay? Is Jessica okay?"

She nodded once, briskly. "All good, but you're gonna need to scrub up, doc. Oh, and bring your battle armor. She's about to drop and she's cussing up a fucking storm, threatening to remove certain parts of your anatomy... with a blunt spoon."

GIVING BIRTH WAS, as Jess was quickly discovering, *definitely* not a walk in the park. Nowhere near it. All through her pregnancy, she hadn't worried about the part between being pregnant and not being pregnant anymore. Yeah, sure, she'd been aware that there would be pain involved and pushing, but...

"I'm telling you," she yelled at the surrounding healers. "I can't push something the size of a freaking watermelon out a hole the size of a fucking lemon, comprende?"

At the mere mention of her hoo-ha, several healers went white and backed off. Another hard band of pain wrapped around her stomach and she grunted, clinging to the side of the bed. Kenna had gotten her into the healer's hall but had then abandoned her at a run to the tender mercies of a bunch of doctors who had never seen a pregnant woman of their own race, never mind a human one.

"Oh, for heaven's sake," she snapped when the contraction had passed, hauling herself up onto the bed. "What do you do when the oonat are pregnant?"

"The cattle?" A frown crossed one of the healers' brows as he ventured forward and activated the diagnostic bed. She searched her memory for his name. Itaal. One of Laarn's protégés.

He shrugged, his attention focused on the readouts in a holographic arc over her barn-sized bump.

"We have birthing pens set up at the back of the hall for them. Generally, they huddle and birth the young themselves. If there are any problems, we then intervene surgically."

"Ah," she nodded. "We have C-sections on Earth as well. They're quite common."

Itaal paled at her words, his hands still on the console in front of him. "On fertile females of your own kind? The death rates must be astronomical."

"Death rate?" She didn't get what he meant for a moment but then her eyes widened. "You mean the female doesn't survive surgical intervention to remove the baby?"

Itaal's long hair danced over his shoulders as he shook his head. "No. We wouldn't put a Latharian child at risk to preserve the carrier's life. There are plenty more oonat."

"*Riiiight.*" Jess' mood took a nosedive as another contraction gripped her. She grasped the sides of the bed in a white-knuckled grip and tried to remember her breathing. Pretty fucking hard when it felt like she was being cut in two.

"Birthing seems well established now," Itaal added in a low voice.

She nodded, lying back on the bed. She was like a damn upturned turtle like this. "How many centimeters am I dilated?"

Itaal's face turned gray, then green, and then white. "I don't know..."

"You don't check..." she hissed as he backed up to join the other healers, all of whom looked at her as though she were their worst nightmare and impending horrific death combined. "No, you *won't* check. Will you?"

All the men shook their heads, several nudging Itaal, who seemed to have been nominated, unwillingly, as their spokesperson. "No. Lord Healer Laarn warned us all that no one was to look at or touch you... *there.*"

"I'm gonna fucking kill him. How am I supposed to give birth if none of the doctors will fucking touch me?" she grunted, tensing as another wave of pain washed over her.

The contractions were closer together and faster now, which meant she wasn't far off from giving birth. Fuck... why hadn't she insisted that Laarn go grab a midwife or seventeen from Earth? Hell, even an orderly would do if they'd seen the inside of a labor suite. Anything would be better than a handful of healers terrified of even looking her way because she was the lord healer's mate.

"Simple," a deep voice answered from the doorway. "Because I will always be by your side to help you."

"Laarn!" she cried out in relief as the tall form of her handsome mate swept into the room, scattering the assembled healers like leaves on the wind. "Itaal, stay," he ordered. "The rest of you... Don't you have other patients to attend to?"

The hard look he swept over the little crowd suggested that if they hadn't, they'd better damn well find some, or he'd create patients from amongst their number. Jess chuckled as they stampeded for the door.

"Hey girl, how you doing?" She opened her eyes to find Kenna at her side. She accepted the other woman's help to sit up, smiling at the care the other woman took plumping the pillows behind her.

"Not bad, apart from the fact I'm being ripped in two."

Kenna wrinkled her nose. "It feels like shit, but it'll pass, and then you'll have your baby and you'll forget all about it. I promise."

"You've attended births before?" Laarn asked, moving around them and doing something to the bed. The screens over Jess changed to show enlarged views of her womb and... other areas.

"Crap," she breathed. "Is my ass that big?"

"You're pregnant." Kenna chuckled. "So it's allowed. And yes," she directed at Laarn. "Four older sisters dropping brats with alarming regularity. I'd seen more births than the colony doctor before I was ten. Why do you think I went fleet?"

"You're drafted then." Laarn nodded, shucking his jacket and stepping up to the bed. The feel of her mate's large hands on her swollen stomach sent a wave of relief through her. He was here. Everything would be okay.

"Yes, sir," Kenna answered, military to the core even though Laarn wasn't an officer, and they weren't in Terran space anymore.

Laarn shot her a small smile of thanks as he examined Jess. Itaal kept his distance and stayed at the control consoles at the head of the bed throughout the procedure. She grinned to herself. If he could have done his job with his eyes shut, he would have, but even so... she could sense the curiosity rolling from him in waves.

"Laarn," she said softly, getting her mate's attention between contractions. They were getting harder and stronger each time, so she wasn't sure how much time she had left to talk. "If your warriors will be bonding humans, more of us will be pregnant. Wouldn't it make sense for your healers to be trained in childbirth?"

Laarn's expression set. She didn't need to be a genius to guess at the internal battle between the healer who sought knowledge for the good of his race and a possessive mate who didn't want any other male even seeing his mate in such a manner.

"Yes... no!" he growled.

Another contraction hit and Jess growled back through gritted teeth. "Then you're a fucking idiot and babies will die! Is that what you want?"

She grabbed for Kenna's hand, gripping it with white knuckles as she pushed down the instinctive need to fight the pain and breathed through it.

"*In-in-oooout... in-in-oouuut.* That's it, girl. You got it. Easier than a route march, but these pussy men couldn't do it, eh?" Kenna coached her through the crest of the wave, holding her hand and smoothing her wet hair back from her brow. Fuck, she was sweating buckets. When had that happened?

She dropped her head back onto the pillows and closed her eyes. "How much longer?"

"You're not yet fully dilated," Laarn said from the bottom of the bed. "It'll be awhile yet, my love."

Kenna hissed between her teeth, shooting the tall healer a "look." "Men," she hissed under her breath. "Dumb whatever the species." Raising her voice, she got his attention. "Doc... you might wanna give her something for the pain?"

"I cannot advise it," Itaal piped up from his station. "While humans and Lathar are genetically the same species, we are much more enhanced. Our pain responses are much altered, and therefore our medi--"

"Save me the details, doc," Jess hissed as another wave hit. "And get me some fucking drugs before I reach through that fucking screen and *you're* the one who needs drugs."

LAARN, lord healer of the entire Latharian Empire, knew all there was to know about battle, about combat injuries and about every disease and ailment his people had ever come across. His knowledge was as expansive as the scars that marked his rank on his body were deep.

But he knew absolutely *nothing* about childbirth.

He'd read all the historical texts. He'd studied the words of previous lord healers and watched all the historical records. He'd even used the healing hall's jury-rigged AIs to run simulations of childbirth scenarios. Which meant, he'd *thought* he was prepared, that Latharian medicine, being so much more advanced than humanity's, meant that he didn't need to pull in any human specialists.

But faced with the reality of his mate being in labor, being in pain, he realized that was a load of *draanth*. While he'd been studying up on Latharian childbirth, *human* labor and childbirth was an entirely different thing.

The pelvis is a lot smaller in humans, he subvocalized to Itaal, who was manning the monitoring station. *If the baby was breech, we'd have to turn it before it entered the birth canal.*

Indeed, Itaal sent back over the link, nothing in his manner or expression to indicate he and Laarn were communicating silently. Laarn was grateful. Call it professional pride, but he didn't want either woman knowing just how much he was... what was the human phrase... crapping himself that he didn't know what the hell he was doing.

Not breech though, fortunately. But the records said nothing about this level of pain, he sent, unable to keep the note of concern out of his mental voice. Everything he'd read indicated that childbirth was a calm and serene experience, the baby brought forth into a tranquil environment.

Jess, her expression twisted with concentration and pain, looked anything *but* tranquil and serene.

"Breathe through it, girl," Kenna, still by Jess' side, urged while clutching the mother-to-be's hand in a tight grip. "You got this."

The sharp look she shot Laarn clearly stated that someone had to because he hadn't. Shame filled him and when the next contraction had died down, he motioned to Itaal to take Kenna's place and summoned the marine to join him outside with a jerk of his head.

They'd barely gotten outside when the human woman rounded on him, her eyes alight with anger.

"What the *fuck* are you doing in there?" she demanded. "Give her something for the fucking pain already. She's tired and the longer she spends trying to fight the pain, the more exhausted she will get. And exhaustion? Let me tell you... that's not good. Tired mothers struggle, and struggling in labor? That kills mothers and babies. You reading me?"

"Loud and clear." Laarn sighed, running a hand through his hair. "I'm out of my depth. Latharian labor is nothing like this. There's no pain, no struggle, not as far back as I can go in the records. This... this is barbaric. She's in so much pain and I don't know what to do..."

"I'll tell you what you're gonna do." Kenna's expression was firm. "You're gonna stop finny-fannying around. You're gonna get back in there and do whatever you can to ease her pain. Use your fancy machines, hook her up and get that fucking baby out. Because if you don't, she's gonna be in trouble real fast. And let me tell you," she stepped forward and jabbed him hard in the chest, "if you let *either* my friend or her baby die, I'll show you what humans mean when they say the female of our species is *way* deadlier than the male."

Laarn nodded, a frown crossing his brow. "There might be a way..."

He didn't explain, simply strode back in the room to find Itaal comforting his laboring mate. For a moment, possessiveness wanted to rear its head, but then he noticed the pained look on the younger healer's face.

I think she might have crushed the bones in my hand, Itaal said mentally. *How did the humans ever survive as a race if their women go through this to bear young?*

That I have no idea. Their females must be much stronger than even we thought.

"Bring the units online," he ordered aloud, striding over to the gauntlet station. He didn't understand human childbirth, but he had to trust that Jess would do what she needed to do. That her instincts would kick in. But what he could do was ease some of her pain.

"Right away, my lord." Itaal relinquished his position by the bed, leaving Jess panting. Another ripple of pain crossed her face and Laarn knew another contraction was on the rise. "Do you want me in on the link, just in case?"

Laarn shook his head but then stopped the movement and nodded instead. "Yes, but remain in the background unless you see something I have missed that requires immediate attention. Observe, learn... the more of our healers who understand the process of human childbirth the better."

"Understood, my lord."

"Just a little longer, my love," Laarn leaned over Jess, brushing her sweat-soaked hair back from her brow to lay a gentle kiss there. "And the pain will be gone. I promise."

She nodded, managing a quick smile between her pants. "Still doesn't mean you are ever getting laid again, handsome. Ever."

He wasn't stupid enough to reply to that, not with her in her current state. He smiled as he slipped the uplink gauntlets on.

"Neural interface ready, surgical unit online... Initializing uplink," Itaal said in the background. "Bringing patient online... merging feeds... Your patient, my lord."

Laarn hissed as pain slammed through him, concentrating in his lower abdomen. For a moment, the sheer scale of it took his breath away and his amazement at humans increased exponentially. He'd only experienced such levels of pain with severe combat injuries. For a moment, the natural arrogance that had been instilled in him from birth that the Lathar were superior at everything tried to reassert itself, but he fought it down and concentrated on his patient.

Slowly, he picked up the pain signals and slid himself between them and Jess' brain, stopping her from registering the agony that coursed through her body.

"Little less," she opened her eyes and spoke directly to him. "I need to feel something so I know when to push."

He nodded, every instinct in him as a healer and her mate arguing as he allowed her nerves to register more pain.

"There," she nodded. "That's good. I got it."

For the next few hours, Laarn held back the tide of the pain, allowing his body to be abused and battered in a way no healer of his race had ever experienced before. His features tightened, the need to hold Jess torturing him as she labored to bring their child into the world.

"*PUSH*... that's it, girl," Kenna encouraged, checking between Jess' sheet-covered thighs. "I can see the baby's head. One more push and she's here. I promise."

I got this, my lord, Itaal's mental voice broke through Laarn's fugue state. *Let me take the load so you can help your daughter be born.*

Thank you. Laarn nodded as the younger healer slid into the link behind him and took up the load.

"I'm here, Jess," he murmured, joining Kenna and intending to help her with the birth of the baby. But just at that moment Jess screamed, the sound full of pain and triumph. Kenna gasped and then grinned as she lifted aloft a tiny bundle. The thin, thready cry was music to Laarn's ears.

Their daughter was born safely.

The first female of his race... the first Princess of the Blood... for a generation.

The first hope for a generation.

3

"*You're* still not getting laid... for a very long time. Understand me?"

Jess smiled up at her mate as she lay with her daughter in her arms. He sat next to them, his arm around Jess' shoulders and the other around the baby swaddled carefully against her chest. He was as close to them as it was possible to get without actually being in the bed.

He grinned. "An hour ago, it was ever again. Now it's just a very long time. I think, my beautiful little mate, I'll wait to see what you say tomorrow before commenting."

"Asshole healer," she muttered, but she couldn't help the small smile as she looked down at her daughter.

"Hello sweetpea," she whispered, stroking the delicate little cheek with a reverent finger. "It's nice to finally meet you."

As though she knew she was being spoken to, the baby opened her eyes and Jess gasped. Laarn's green eyes looked right back at her, filled with knowledge and wisdom.

"She has an old soul," Laarn murmured, seeing what Jess was seeing as the baby blinked at them both. "And she will be very powerful, beautiful like her mother."

"She has my hair," Jess gasped in delight, stroking the fine down on the top of the baby's head. "The Kallson hair. It's a curse."

"A curse?" Laarn frowned, looking down at her and then at the baby. "It looks normal to me. How can hair be a curse?"

She chuckled. "You wait until she can't do a thing with her hair. It's a woman thing."

"She had wild, beautiful hair in my vision. Like yours but... bigger?"

"Yeah, that's the Kallson hair all right. She's gonna hate me."

Jess watched as their daughter's eyes drifted closed. She kept jerking them open as though she didn't want to stop looking at her parents. The fascination was mutual. Jess didn't think she'd ever need to sleep again, not if she could peer at the vision of perfection in her arms.

"Did she tell you her name at all?" she asked, fascinated by the connection between Laarn and their daughter. Though Jess carried her under her heart, Laarn had connected with her in a way Jess never could. "When you spoke to her... before."

She didn't need to say anything else. Their baby had reached out to Laarn when Jess was dying, a deep abdominal wound putting both her life and the baby's life in danger.

Laarn shook his head. "It was just a glimpse of the future. Of the woman she will become. We didn't really chat."

"Daaynalina," A voice announced from the doorway. They both looked up to find the emperor filling the frame. "As the first princess of the blood born for a generation, she should of course be named after me."

"Absolutely not," Laarn and Jess said in unison. Then they had the unique experience of seeing the Latharian emperor, possibly the most powerful and dangerous man in the entire universe, speechless. His mouth opened and closed, but no sound emerged from his lips. Itaal found somewhere else to be. Fast.

"No?" Daaynal blinked. "Now that's a word people don't say to me often."

"Better get used to it," Laarn advised, his voice firm. "Because there is no way I'm calling my daughter Daaynalina. It's a *draanthic* mouthful. And not a true female name at all."

"Miisan," Jess said quietly. At the sound of the name, that of Laarn's mother and Daaynal's twin, the baby opened her eyes and made a pleased gurgling.

"Miisan... " Laarn and Daaynal's whispers echoed each other. Then the emperor bowed, an odd expression on his face. If Jess were to guess, she'd say he was touched. "You do the royal house, and me, a great honor."

"Thank you," Laarn brushed a kiss against Jess' temple. "I'd thought you would want to name her in the human tradition. I didn't expect that you would pick a Latharian name."

"Well." She reached out to brush the delicate soft down on the top of the newly named baby's head. "It seems humans *are* Lathar anyway, and its women are making this all possible. So how about Miisan Amanda K'Vass? To celebrate both cultures, and both our mothers..."

"*LAARN! She's gone! The baby's gone!*"

His mate's panicked cry brought Laarn out of sleep in an instant. He jerked upright on the cot set up next to her bed in the healer's hall. In an instant he was on his feet and by her side. Sure enough, the cot they'd put their daughter down in after her feeding a few hours ago was empty.

Jess turned fear-filled eyes on him, clutching at his arm with panic. "They've got her, the purists! Somehow they've gotten into the palace again."

"Ssshhh, shh. They can't have," he reassured her, dropping a kiss against her forehead even as he disengaged himself from her clutches. Fear lanced through him, making his heart race and turning his blood to ice.

The purists were a plague. Lathar who believed that to crossbreed, even to save their race, was a sin against the obscure goddess they served. One the rest of the Lathar had left firmly in the past. They'd almost managed to kill Jess before, so the thought that they might have Miisan... so tiny and defenseless... nearly stopped him in his tracks with panic.

"I'll find her. Stay here," he promised, grabbing his weapons belt from the hook by the door as he strode from the room.

"*Healers!*" he bellowed as he went, not caring that he would wake recovering warriors. If they had a purist attack on their hands, those warriors would want to be awake to defend themselves. If a purist attack kidnapped his daughter, *he* wanted them awake to hunt the *draanth* down. And not just the patients. He wanted every warrior on their feet and armed. Ready to fight to protect—

He blinked as Itaal appeared in the doorway of one of the rooms, his finger against his lips as he pointed down the hall. Frowning, he followed the corridor Itaal pointed to. It was one of the outer pathways, with high stone arches that looked out over the city and onto the mountains beyond.

They looked unprotected, but the occasional shimmer confirmed that the energy barriers were active. Should they fail, heavy shutters of Terralon steel would drop into place and secure the palace. It would take orbital weapons powerful enough to destroy the planet to get through them, and even then, the shutters would probably still be there, floating in the debris unharmed.

"And down there is where my sister, your grandma, and I used to play. Can you see? Just there by the Herris trees. In a few months, you'll be running around down there as well."

Laarn followed the deep voice, his anxiety beginning to reduce as he spotted a tall, familiar figure at the end of the pathway. Daaynal stood by the stone wall, fully armed, with the tiny form of Laarn's baby daughter held tenderly in his arms. For a split second, Laarn got a glimpse of the emperor's face completely unguarded. Saw the delight and fascination with his grand-niece as he cradled her head and cooed back when she gurgled at him.

"What the fuck do you think you're doing?"

The fact that Daaynal could order his, or any warrior in the empire's, execution on a whim didn't even occur to Laarn as he strode forward, the righteous fury of a father fueling his movements as he stormed toward his uncle.

Daaynal blinked as he turned around, surprise evident on his face. "I was showing the new princess the palace."

"You can't just take her like that! Jess is beside herself with panic." Laarn's heartrate began to return to normal as he swept an assessing glance over his daughter. A lock of Daaynal's black hair was wrapped around her fist, her fingers opening and closing as though investigating the strands' texture. Abruptly, she yanked on the lock, making Daaynal turn. The look she gave him was far more advanced than it should have been for an infant mere hours old.

"Hmmm, yes. She said you'd both be worried," Daaynal nodded, giving a sheepish little smile. "But she was crying and I didn't want to wake either of you. So, I told her she'd be perfectly safe with me and her mother would understand."

This time it was Laarn's turn to blink. "You can converse with her?"

The emperor inclined his head. "Of course. There are some benefits to the K'Saan bloodline. Although, as the last of my line, I never expected to feel the touch of another's mind against mine ever again. Miisan here is a double blessing in that regard."

His uncle was lonely. The realization stunned Laarn, and the rest of his anger leached away. How could he be angry now? Daaynal had held the throne far longer than any emperor before him, surviving goddess alone knew how many assassination attempts and coups. And through the years, he'd never managed to beget an heir, even though Laarn knew he'd tried. And... when it came down to it... with a history like that, the baby princess couldn't be in safer hands.

He offered a small smile. "Just tell us next time, okay?"

∾

"She's happily asleep."

Jess smiled as her mate walked through the arch that separated the nursery area from their sleeping chambers. After many hours and more checkups than she wanted to think about, she and Miisan were released from the Healer's Hall. She was sure Itaal and the other healers would have done anything to keep the baby there, for observation "just in case," but a glare from Laarn put paid to that. It was hard for a doctor to argue, though, when the Latharian equivalent of the Surgeon General was the one signing them out.

She wasn't sure it was all about the tests, though. All afternoon, warriors found reasons to be in her room. The excuses ranged from checking errant readings on the diagnostic equipment to ensuring the ventilation systems were working correctly. One warrior, complete with toolbelt, even arrived expressing concern that the lighting system was in the wrong spectrum for infant eyes.

If she'd been on her own, she might have been worried. Even though she'd successfully thwarted a purist attack by herself, that had been with the element of surprise and by being... well, human. They were still rare enough in the empire that most Lathar had absolutely no idea how they'd react and what they'd do next. She simply used that to her advantage. But one on one, even the least-trained Lathar warrior could easily beat her.

She wasn't on her own, though. Not only had Laarn been with her most of the time, but many of his clan found reasons to drop in. She hadn't realized quite how scary the K'Vass could be until now.

But they didn't need to be. Every warrior entering the room gravitated to the crib. It was kind of sweet to see such big, hard men reduced to complete softies, admiring courtiers as her baby daughter held court. And hold court she did, giggling and cooing at the men bent over the crib like they were her own personal entertainment.

One thing was for sure, Miisan would have no shortage of "uncles" prepared to lay down their lives for her.

"I'm not surprised. She's had a full day," Jess replied sleepily, watching Laarn cross the room. He was dressed for bed in loose silken pants that rode low on his hips. She appreciated the view, even if she couldn't do anything about it at the moment. Latharian medicine was amazing, but even it couldn't heal the female body and mind from childbirth within hours. Both Itaal and Laarn had told her she needed to take it easy for the next couple of days. But when her husband looked like that...

The bed dipped as he climbed in next to her, and an instant later she was wrapped in his strong embrace.

"She's not the only one who's been busy today," he murmured, his lips against her hair. "You were so brave, my love. I had no idea that human women suffered so much during labor."

A smile curved her lips as all the old jokes about a woman in labor could almost imagine what a man felt like when he had the flu hovered in the back of her mind. But Laarn actually *felt* what it was like to be in labor. Possibly the first man ever to do so.

"It's the circle of life," she said softly. "Did you know that on Earth, like way back in history... the only Spartan women who got gravestones were the ones who died in childbirth? And the only men who got them died in battle? They equated labor with combat."

"Obviously an enlightened people."

He rumbled deep in his chest as she stroked her fingertips over the scars on his chest. Once they'd horrified her. The thought of the pain he'd gone through to get them seemed barbaric. Now, though, she just saw them as a part of him. A part of the man she loved more than life itself. The alien warrior she'd fallen for who'd given her a perfect little daughter.

Reaching up, she brushed her lips against his. The brush turned into a long, sweet kiss.

"What was that for?" he asked, a smile on his lips when he lifted his head.

"Nothing. Just because." She shook her head, knowing she should really get some sleep but unable to. She was still wired from the events of the day and she was more than comfortable leaning against Laarn's broad chest.

"We did it. She's finally here. We're parents." She twisted to peer up at him. "In case you missed it, Mr. Kallson, I love you."

"Oh... it's *Mr. Kallson* now, is it?" He chuckled, bending his head to rub his nose against hers. "What happened to my lord?"

"Pfft. That's only for when I want something. And there's no reason why you can't have a human name as well as a Latharian one, is there?"

"None whatsoever. But none of them matter." He gathered her up closer, his touch gentle as he cradled her. He moved her hand to place it over his heart. He smiled as he placed his own hand over hers, trapping it under his larger palm.

"Because the only names or titles I care about are Jessica's mate and Miisan's father. And I will love you both until my heart beats its last in this mortal realm."

I hope you enjoyed this little peak into Jess and Laarn's life :)

***

Ready for the next Warriors of the Lathar story?

Thank you for taking a chance on **Alien Healer's Baby**. I hope you enjoyed it!

If you did, it would be great if you could leave a **review** - even if it's just a little one. Every review makes a huge difference to an author and helps other readers find and enjoy the book as well!

I'm happy to say that the next book in the Lathar series, **Adored by the Alien Assassin,** is ready and waiting for you! (Turn the page for a preview of the cover if it doesn't show!)

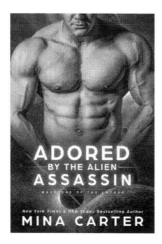

P.S. Sign up to my VIP mailing list and I'll shoot you a quick notification when my new books releases: **https://minacarter.com/index.php/newsletter/**

ABOUT MINA

Mina Carter is a *New York Times & USA Today* bestselling author of romance in many genres. She lives in the UK with her husband, daughter and a bossy cat.

SIGN UP TO MINA'S NEWSLETTER!
https://minacarter.com/index.php/newsletter/

Connect with Mina online at:
minacarter.com

facebook.com/minacarterauthor

twitter.com/minacarter

instagram.com/minacarter77

bookbub.com/authors/mina-carter

Manufactured by Amazon.ca
Bolton, ON

33614595R00260